In praise o

DEACON'S WINTER

"An intriguing tale by a native Chicagoan who knows his way around the neighborhoods and the people working in the Catholic Church. A gripping read."

Paul Johnson OP

"Caught between heaven and earth as Deacon is, he may be less noir than Lee Child's Jack Reacher, but he's just as tough. The city of Chicago, Political corruption, sadism, and a church whose movers and shakers aren't always saints need him to be. I haven't enjoyed a series character this much in a long time, and I can't wait for the next Deacon installment."

Bruce McAllister, author of DREAM BABY

"You've gotta love Deacon. He's a smart tough guy with a heart of gold and a soul in torment. Pair him with a gorgeous woman, who's got the guts to keep up with him. Then pit them against the cruelest of villains and you've got an irresistible story. Bring on the sequel."

Donna Kennedy, writer, editor and teacher

"This was a fascinating mystery full of twists and turns. Fun reading and at times it was difficult for me to put the book down. It was filled with intrigue, fighting, danger, scary moments, humor, good morals, sex and romance. I could see this being made into an exciting series or movie into the future."

"Women will be drawn to Deacon's character. He's no James Bond but a man trying to be honest, see justice done and at the same time be true to his faith and himself. There are moments when you'll want to check your own thoughts and deeds and do a bit of soul searching."

Colleen Forsyth

"This book was filled with intrigue, action and guesswork. Always wondering if the victims would be found alive. It has a moral foundation; will he continue in the Catholic Church or go on to be involved with the lady that captivated him? I could hardly put the book down. I highly recommend it. I'm waiting for his next book."

Elizabeth J. Parker

"Deacon's Winter is a very satisfying read. Burgraff's ability to layer and weave plot lines draws the reader from page one and doesn't let go. I enjoyed Deacon's Winter and look forward to Deacon's next adventure."

D. Larson. Editor and author

"I enjoyed reading 'Deacon's Winter' as much as any of the current thriller writers such as Lee Child, Harlan Coben and John Connolly. My wife and I really liked the Deacon and how he relates to other characters in the story. It was a compelling read. I hope to see more of the Deacon."

Roger Schneider

"Deacon's Winter. One learns the meaning of cold and generally crumby Chicago winter weather. You can't help wanting the Deacon to mete out justice to the villains while rooting for his various friends to be successful in their roles in the book. It draws you in, a good page-turner. Well done. A good read."

Tom Wallace

"This book is the best page-turner I've read in years. It's almost impossible to put down and it's chock full of action, suspense, mystery and romance. Deacon is a well-drawn character (as are most others in this saga) who is torn between his fidelity to a flawed church, his retributive sense of justice, his loyalty to his street chums and his passionate love of a woman. The setting – Chicago is well known to the author ands he propels the reader through its frigid streets, exposing its grandness and grit."

Stephen Griffin

"This book keeps the reader in suspense and then leaves the end for the follow-up to be guessed what happens with the main characters."

Sally Padilla

"I loved this book. A mystery that kept me fascinated, a down to earth but sophisticated writing style, and characters that I could really get involved with."

Martha Bryan

DEACON'S WINTER

ROGER BURGRAFF

abbott press®
A DIVISION OF WRITER'S DIGEST

Abbott Press books may be ordered through booksellers or by contacting:

Abbott Press
1663 Liberty Drive
Bloomington, IN 47403
www.abbottpress.com
Phone: 1-866-697-5310

Because of the dynamic nature of the Internet, any web addresses or links contained
in this book may have changed since publication and may no longer be valid. The views
expressed in this work are solely those of the author and do not necessarily reflect the
views of the publisher, and the publisher hereby disclaims any responsibility for them.

Any people depicted in stock imagery provided by Thinkstock are models,
and such images are being used for illustrative purposes only.
Certain stock imagery © Thinkstock.

ISBN: 978-1-4582-1491-1 (sc)
ISBN: 978-1-4582-1492-8 (e)

Library of Congress Control Number: 2014904648

Printed in the United States of America.

Abbott Press rev. date: 04/24/2014

CHAPTER ONE

I'd just ushered a dozen homeless people out of Saint Sebastian's Catholic Church. I hated doing it. Chicago in January is brutal for anyone on it's streets. The homeless came to the church for some warmth and to snooze in the pews. Our pastor, Father Posjena, wouldn't allow the church to be open all night. So, I had to send them away in the late evening. "The church isn't a hostel for these people," as Father Posjena put it.

He didn't like it, but I told him I thought the church was for everyone—even in the middle of the night.

"You're not even a priest yet, Deacon," he said. "Pity doesn't make us holy." It was only one of our ongoing disagreements. What a putz, as my friend Rabbi Mel Cohen would say. I was fed up with our pastor and I'm sure the feeling was mutual.

Still, Saint Sebastian's had been hit by its share of theft and vandalism, so the pastor had a point. When the wind chill plummeted to zero, the men's club and the Knights of Columbus, at my prodding, managed to persuade Pastor Posjena to keep the place open all night-- with supervision. I took turns keeping watch with the more dedicated parishioners on Chicago's coldest nights. I told them their sacrifice was a way of getting closer to Christ. I wasn't sure if it was them I was trying to convince or myself.

After locking up I headed down the center aisle to my rooms just behind the church when I spotted a small green light above a confessional chamber.

One of the street people was in there hiding from me, I told myself. But when I opened the door ready to say, "I'm sorry, but you can't stay … " I saw, instead, a badly beaten woman slumped in the priest's armchair.

It wasn't my first rodeo. I'd been an MP in Iraq, and I knew that when drunk, soldiers—the mean ones—beat on anyone they could. But this woman was the most terrified I'd seen.

She jerked back and whimpered, crossing her arms in front of her bloody face.

I knelt down on one knee. "It's okay, I'm Deacon Adelius. I can help you."

She didn't answer. All of her energy was being spent on shaking.

I took her arm slowly, raising her to a sanding position, and we limped down the center aisle. She was clutching a large handbag. Her face was swollen, the way a face gets when it's hit more than once. Her clothes were unsuited for the weather. Short leather skirt and jacket, high heels. Her blouse was torn to the waist, and bloody. Parts of her face were bleeding, but you don't die from that. The old statues on the walls of the church seemed to look down on us with pity.

Finally she made a sound. A sob.

When she collapsed at last, unable to walk even with my help, I carried her out the side door and locked it. We went into my sitting room and I set her down gently on my couch.

"You're safe now."

She sighed like a body giving up the ghost, dropped her head back ready to go to sleep. I couldn't let her. I had no idea what damage they'd done to her brain.

"You need to sit up, Ma'am."

She fought it, but I got her upright. I could see her eyes wandering as they surveyed my humble digs. I got a blanket and put it around her. She let me. I left her for a moment, wet a towel and wrapped it around some ice cubes.

Before I could ask permission to place the cold towel on her face, she spoke abruptly. "They were going to kill me!" Her voice was ragged as her blouse.

I asked the obvious, "Who?" I kept it gentle as I placed the ice pack on her swollen left cheek. She didn't need an interrogation.

She shook her head but didn't answer. Instead, her eyes glazed over and she began to breathe more steadily. Shock was loosening its grip.

"Why were they after you?"

"My 'tell'." She drifted off.

"Tell?" My guess was that she had information someone wanted very badly.

Her arm hung off the couch near the purse she'd dropped. I opened it to find a wad of cash, a .22 Beretta—loaded—and a small Bible, but no ID. I dug deeper and pulled out a handful of business cards. Circular, purple, edged in gold. "Amber" was embossed in gold on one side, a phone number on the other. Creative. Expensive.

I tucked a few in my pocket-I don't know why-and opened the Bible. It was the New Testament only with mother-of-pearl cover. Still no ID. The first pages had been torn out. But a makeshift pocket had been glued on the inside front cover. Wedged in the pocket was a long flat key—the kind that opens metal boxes. Two arrows had been painted in red—probably nail polish—on one side. Letters and numbers were painted on the other. *Interesting.*

I returned the key to its pocket and put the Bible on my battered coffee table.

Amber was still out of it—unresponsive as a rag doll. I stripped off the remnants of her blouse and pulled one of my sweatshirts over her head. I was clinical—businesslike—until I saw the three cigarette burn marks on her breasts. "Jesus, have pity." What kind of low life bastard could do that? Expensive flashy clothes, cash and the Beretta. It wasn't a stretch to figure she was probably a prostitute. No judgment. Just a woman in trouble. "What's your full name, Amber, and how did you get into this fix?"

At the sound of my voice, she twitched into consciousness.

"What the hell ... where ...?" Her eyes bored into mine. "Oh, yeah, the church. Thank God."

I sat back. "I'll thank God with you. How're you feeling?"

"Are you kidding?" She slumped back and closed her eyes. "Like a friggin' train wreck."

"Let's get you to an emergency room and call the police. You're pretty banged up... "

She stiffened and raised her palm. "No.... No doctors. No cops. Need to get away. Give me a mirror... please."

Bad idea. "Here, keep holding this towel against your face. It'll keep the swelling down."

She closed her eyes. "Got any aspirin?"

"Sure do. And something to warm you up."

I made a mug of hot tea laced with lemon, honey and a splash of Southern Comfort. Amber smiled weakly as a thank you and gulped the hot drink with four aspirin. "I was so cold. God, that's good. Thanks." She took a few more long sips, then tugged the blanket to her chin and curled into a fetal position. "I'll just close my eyes for a second. Then I gotta get away."

Her voice faded as if she were talking to herself, but I caught some words: "I can bring 'em down. Bastards...Tamara ... murderers ... Andy. Got to get... " Her breathing slowed, and she was out again.

Her words replayed in my head. What the hell had she gotten into? What had I gotten into? Maybe I did attract trouble. Father Posjena accused me of it often enough. Never mind her profession—she needed help. To me, the choice was simple. I'd help.

Not like the choices facing me about the rest of my life. I lay back in my Lazy Boy, opening my eyes now and then to check on Amber. She slept on, murmuring intermittently. As I dozed and looked at the woman, my mind drifted to the decisions that faced me. Rejoin the seminary and make a life- long commitment to the priesthood? Turn to a totally secular life? Or maybe remain a deacon and work for the church in ... special ways.

I couldn't deny the tug of the religious life. I loved ...the peace, the rituals, the power of the faith. I'd been conflicted about those choices even as a youngster. My ideas about justice still sometimes clashed with the church… and the law. I'd ended up joining the Army as an eighteen year old. I had a good reason: Join up, and avoid prison. Several other juvenile delinquents had been given that option. Irony of ironies, I ended up an MP. Honorable discharge nine years ago.

I was drawn to the seminary—three years of it. Then I left. I had my reasons. Might have separated from the church altogether, but I'd promised Archbishop Laine I'd work here at the parish five more months. I am a man of my word. Other reasons compelled me to stay in this limbo …

I drifted in and out of a restless sleep. So I was helping a woman in trouble, what harm could come of that?

CHAPTER TWO

Nothing like a door crashing in to wake you up. Two men rushed in. Two others—one with a cane—stayed at the door. Amber screamed as one of the men went for her. The other guy raised a sap and swung at me, but I side-stepped the blow, grabbed his arm and jabbed a solid left hook to his ribs. When the first man dropped Amber and came for me, I backed up and reached for the weapon I'd dubbed Bat. I'd used a steel baton in Iraq, but my youth baseball bat works just fine in Chicago. And it's legal, I sized up the big guy coming at me, his fists cocked. I lunged Bat forward breaking his nose. He stumbled backwards and sat hard, blood gushing. Bat—twenty-five inches long, eight ounces of aluminum—had done its job. The first man charged me with a stiletto. I parried, spun, threw my elbow into the man's left ear and backhanded Bat into the side of his right knee.

"Jesus Christ!" He flopped to the floor, clutching his knee and rocking back and forth.

"Don't take the Lord's name in vain." I said as I kicked him in the chest.

The guy with a bloody nose pulled a gun, and I hurled Bat sideways like a helicopter blade. It hit just as Amber shot him with her Beretta, the blast deafening in the small room. He spun around in a macabre dance and went down for good.

The man with the cane in the doorway shot Amber and turned the gun on me. I dived downwards, but not in time. Pain seared my left shoulder. Then a blow to the back of my head brought blackness. When I came to, Amber... the men... everybody was gone. Only blood remained. *Shit... laid low by a guy with a cane.*

I punched 911 into my cell phone and passed out again.

CHAPTER THREE

I woke up in a hospital, mouth parched, vision blurred.

My head and shoulder were bulky with bandages, and I smelled like something that belonged in a medicine cabinet. I opened my eyes wide, trying to focus. The room was bright from the sun streaming through the window. A person came into view.

"Good morning, Mr. Adelius," said the very white uniform. "I'm Wanda, how are you feeling?"

I blinked until I could read *Dixon* on the nametag. Her sweater was a blinding pink and she had strange blue-gray dyed hair, but I liked her smile. "Actually, I don't feel too bad." I croaked.

"It's the medication. Some nasty sensations may return."

Thanks a bunch, I thought. *Didn't need to hear that.*

Nurse Wanda smiled again, professionally. "Press the buzzer if you're in any discomfort and we'll give you something. We want to manage your pain."

"Where am I?"

"Saint Mary's Hospital. According to your chart, paramedics brought you in at 3:30 a.m. I wasn't on duty yet."

"Water, please." My mouth was the Sahara.

"Certainly." She pressed a button somewhere and raised the bed to a 45-degree angle. She reached for a Styrofoam cup and slipped a straw between my lips. Her fingernail polish matched the color of her sweater.

I sipped. It helped. "So, how bad am I?"

"The doctor will have details. In short, you sustained a gunshot wound to the shoulder. Superficial graze, no bones broken.

Sustained a gunshot wound? Who talks like that?

"The blow to your head is of more concern," she continued.

Oh, yeah. Hit from behind. I remember.

"You've had a brief neurological workup and so far everything looks fine."

Visitors were next on the agenda. Two men. First in was good old Father Casmir Posjena, known to one and all as "Father Casey."

For once, I had to look up at him. He probably liked that. I towered over him at six-foot-four Even my thick mop of hair was probably an irritant, since he had a wispy gray comb-over. We tolerated one another. Civility was required, so he wished me a good morning. "You feeling better?"

"Yeah, I guess. What's the time?"

"Just after eight-thirty."

Behind the good father was a bull of a man in a topcoat. He had a broad pock-marked face, close-set eyes and a scar across his mouth. "Detective Rick Ditmar," he said, tapping his badge. He didn't look happy. "Excuse me, Father. I need a few words with Deacon Adelius… privately."

"Certainly," said Father Casey, "but I need to stay."

I wasn't surprised.

Ditmar nodded and turned back to me. "It may be a long shot, but we were hoping you can help us out. We fished a dead woman out of the river this morning. No ID."

A knot tightened in my gut.

"God have mercy on her soul," Father Casey said, "but what does this… this violence have to do with Deacon?"

"He may have been the last person to see her alive, Father. She was wearing a Saint Sebastian's sweatshirt about five sizes too big. She'd been shot dead. Beaten and tortured, prior." The detective lifted an eyebrow and waited for my response.

"The shirt's mine," I said quickly, "and the woman's name was Amber." Just saying her name brought her face to my mind. I'd probably be haunted by it for some time. I promised to keep her safe. Now she was dead. *Those bastards.* My skull throbbed, and I pressed the buzzer. Would a painkiller deaden my guilt? I doubted it.

I described the sequence of events and told the cop everything I'd seen, heard or guessed about the woman called Amber who carried a gun and purse full of money.

Ditmar took furious notes as I repeated her words: "Bring 'em down ... Tamara ... murderers ... Andy ... "

"Bring who down?" he asked,

"Don't know. She was out of it."

"Would you recognize the man who shot you and her?"

Probably not. "Tall, dark hair, slicked back, had a cane. That's it."

When I'd finished my story, he narrowed his eyes. "So, you had this prostitute named Amber in your apartment late last night."

"I told you, I found her in the church confessional, beaten and bloody. Check out the confessional in the church."

"And you didn't call the police."

"No, she didn't want me to."

"So you went along with it."

He kept up the barrage of questions, and I cooperated. The guy had a job to do. I told him she was the reason for the break-in, that she probably had information they wanted.

Then he got personal. "She was wearing your sweatshirt—"

"Yeah, she was shivering with cold. I helped her out of her bloody rags and into my sweatshirt."

"Uh, huh. The shirt off your back, so to speak? And how well did you know this woman?"

My face went hot. "Aren't you listening? I didn't know her at all."

He kept hammering. "Any money exchanged between you and this Amber?"

"What? Hell no." My fists clenched on their own.

"Doesn't look good." Ditmar switched his attention to Father Casey. "You're his boss, right?"

"That's one way to put it." Father Casey's face turned dark red. "He works for the parish."

The detective angled a thumb in my direction. "He ever have woman problems before?"

"Certainly not."

"You priests do stick together." He scribbled something in his notebook.

"He's not a priest. He's a deacon. Deacon is also his first name."

"How 'bout that? We've got a Sergeant Sargeant at the station. Funny thing about names and jobs sometimes.... well, that's all for now. I'll be around."

"You've got this all wrong," I said.

"Yeah, right. Think of anything else, call me." He threw me some parting shots. "No last name for the woman, huh?"

"No."

"She leave anything behind?"

"Just the blouse."

"The one you helped her out of, right?"

I didn't dignify that one with an answer.

Ditmar's face went broad and blank. "One of the forensic boys will come around and pick it up. Later."

After he left, Father Casey raised his arms toward heaven. "Well, you've done it again!"

"Done what again?"

"He clasped his hands together as though ready to pray for me. "Got yourself mixed up with street people—criminals. A murdered prostitute no less. And your mother wanted you to be a priest. Even Archbishop Laine thought you were God's Golden Boy. Now we're dealing with police inquiries and dead prostitutes. Jesus, Mary and Joseph."

I tried once more. "She was hurt and came to the church for sanctuary. Was I supposed to throw an injured woman out in the snow?"

"Dial 911 next time. That's simple isn't it? What a parish!" Father Casey marched out the door.

The pastor was all about control—of others, not himself--and living the good life. Father Casey performed all the weddings, then ate and drank himself through all the grand Chicago receptions that followed. The food would've fed the parish poor for days.

He'd carry on about the important people he'd dined with, all the old money people and politicians. The pastor was a good sermonizer, had a gift for fund-raising and was politically astute. Most of the parishioners viewed him as a favorite uncle. He was bucking for monsignor. *God forbid.*

Me? I was the parish workhorse. Maintenance, funerals, baptisms, youth programs and visiting the sick, you name it. Local citizens saw me as intimidating. I was big. I'd seen action in Iraq, and I was seen as someone connected to the church. All of which made for high currency in the neighborhood.

I'd made a commitment to some important people. Even though I'd left the seminary, I'd finish this practical part of my training. Truth to tell, I had nowhere to go. Sometimes not deciding is a decision in itself. I still felt a strong connection to my Lord.

The pastor had told me I was too independent and too much of a smartass to make a good priest anyhow. *Yeah, that's me.* I looked skyward for guidance... or maybe deliverance. With church servants like Father Casey, how can we be strong? Instead of sustaining me, my faith distanced me from the body of believers. *God, show me the way.*

My thoughts crashed to earth, smoldering at the cop's insinuations, regretting that I couldn't protect a woman who came to us for help. She wound up saving me. I had this uncomfortable habit of righting wrongs and feeling responsible. The pain in my shoulder and head reminded me I had a score to settle. This was not over.

Pain was returning. Where the hell was nurse Wanda?

CHAPTER FOUR

The man with a cane had taken his name from the Bible. From a fire-and-brimstone preacher espousing the power of Malachi. He'd been a kid when he heard the sermon, but he liked the name—the power—so he took it. Took it like everything else he wanted.

Stupid. Stupid, he thought. His men had been stupid to let her get away, and she'd been stupid to try it. He gripped his cane so hard his fingernails left crescent dents in his skin.

Malachi remembered what Bernie had said, "Stabbed Jack and broke free. She musta ducked in somewheres down the street. Couldn't get far, not in the shape was in." He'd spit out a harsh laugh but went silent at the look on Malachi's face. "We'll get her, boss."

There'd been only one light on the street. It was coming from the huge stone monstrosity called Saint Sebastian's Catholic Church. "That's gotta be where she went."

Bernie had eased the black Caddy a half block and parked in an alley. The four of them headed for the lighted window. Bernie looked into the small space between the window shade and the sill. It was dim inside but he could make out a woman's body on a couch. "This is it boss." They kicked down the door to get the girl back.

Then all hell broke loose.

She shot one of his men, and the man with her fought like two tigers. He wielded a cudgel of some sort. They had to shoot him… and her. Too bad but it couldn't be helped. She had a gun and was aiming it at Malachi.

Her secrets had died with her. A major problem. And who knew what she might have told the man with her. He'd been unconscious but alive.

Loose ends.

This contract would have been easy enough if his employers hadn't been so careless. Politicians were stupid. Had to be, to let themselves be vulnerable to blackmail. Malachi was being paid to take care of it and quickly. He was left to his own methods.

Now his reputation was on the line. He was known as "The Finisher" for his ability to put together a team to get a job done.

And this job was *not* done.

Malachi sat on the edge of his chair and swung his cane back and forth like a pendulum. He and Bernie were in a back booth of Vinny's bar and grill on Division Street, trying to figure a way to discover what information she had been using to blackmail his client.

"Get somebody to keep an eye on the back of the damned church. I want to know who goes in and who goes out. And get a name for the tall guy… the one who thinks he's so tough. Tail him … Let's see where he leads us."

CHAPTER FIVE

Two nights and five diagnostic tests were enough. I left the hospital AMA.

After visiting me, my mother would be at morning Mass to pray for my speedy recovery. Fine with me.

Back in my mini-apartment, it was my turn to pray... for Amber. She left this world in pain and fear. God, I wish I could have done more for her. I replayed the fight in my apartment trying to see where I went wrong. Maybe I should have called the paramedics or the cops right away despite her protestations. Or I could have driven her to an ER nearby. Maybe ... maybe ... Amber could still be alive. I tried to distract myself, tackling the parish bills. I wasn't successful. Father Casey had accused me of ruminating too much. Maybe he was right, for once.

My gaze wandered toward my coffee table and there it was—the pearly little Bible. Why the hell would a prostitute be carrying this?

I took the key secreted inside the front cover and stuck one of Amber's business cards in the little pocket. Turning the key over, I examined each side. Arrows pointing in opposite directions. Meaning what? North and South? Up and down? On the other side, "BG" and "415?" I didn't have a clue to the meaning.

I thought about calling Detective Ditmar, but I was still pissed. He had no right to assume I was intimate with a prostitute. He *did* ask if Amber had left anything behind, though. Had he expected to find something?

I flipped through the book, trying to make out the notations on the inside margins on some pages. They looked like Biblical references. Each followed by a series of numbers and letters.

A code.

Amber had died for this. For what? Then an idea hit me. I picked up the phone and dialed the best code-breaker I knew.

"Saint Catherine's. How can I help you?"

"Sister Mary Margaret, please."

"May I ask who's calling?"

"Deacon Adelius from Saint Sebastian's." My name usually got me past the gatekeepers. *Thanks, Mom.* She'd named me "Deacon." She thought a *holy* name would lead me to the religious life like my father, a missionary who had died in the Middle East. My mind drifted a bit like it always did when I thought of my father. I'd never known him. Didn't know what I'd missed really, except when I watched dads hug their sons or cheer for them on the ball field. Yeah, I'd missed that. Felt a little sorry for myself from time to time. I liked to think I would have made a good son, one who would've made his father proud.

The phone clucked its own technical language, shaking me out of my ruminations. Soon I heard a musical voice I'd know anywhere. "Hi Deac."

"Hi Meg. Could you spare an old friend some time today?"

"Sure, big guy, what's up?"

"Tell you when you get here."

"Now you've got my curiosity up. How's about an hour or so?"

"Great."

"See you then. Tah-tah."

Two hours later, Meg was there with a hug and the wholesome scent of Ivory soap and incense.

"So what's been happening, big dude? How's the shoulder?"

"Sore. Thanks for coming over."

Sister Meg and I grew up a few blocks from each other in Chicago's Water Tower District and went to Saint Ferdinand's Grammar School.

Tough neighborhood, but we survived. We even dated a few times, with more interest on my part than hers. I was eager to know her in the biblical sense, but she wasn't having it. Of course, back then I wanted to know all girls and some of their mothers in the biblical sense.

She had chosen the religious life, and we remained close friends,

As I prepared her favorite—ginger tea—I told her the whole story of Amber, the thugs and the detective.

"God help us, what a cruel world… The poor woman."

"Yeah, for sure." I picked up the little Bible. "The thing is … she left this. It's got a code or something inside. I know how you love the crosswords. I thought you might be able to deciph—"

"Well now, Watson, let Sister Sherlock have a look." She took the Bible from my hands, bent over the pages and then looked up at me. "Don't just stand there with your face hanging out. Give me a cigarette, will you?"

I'd quit a few years ago, but kept some cigarettes around for Meg. Her little secret vice. She bummed one or two a week from me. I pulled a small ashtray from the bottom drawer of my desk and set it down next to her.

While she enjoyed her smoke, she was trying to decipher the markings in the bible. I looked her over. Same beautiful Irish face, cobalt blue eyes, white clear pale skin, rosy cheeks and dark curly hair—cut short. She'd put on ten pounds since her teens, but it suited her. She looked good,

Meg hadn't worn a habit in years. Jeans and sweatshirts were more her style. She ran a soup kitchen, taught and counseled troubled girls at Saint Catherine's convent and school. But she always wore her silver crucifix.

"I think the first number is a biblical reference," she said.

"I thought so, too."

"You know, Deac," she said without looking up, "I'd like to run these through a computer decoding program. Play around a bit. Can I use your computer? Our old PC is sooo slow."

"Great." I paused then, not sure whether I should say anything more. What was I thinking? This was Meg. She could handle the truth. "It would mean a lot to me… and to her … if you find something. Maybe then she won't have died in vain, Amber, I mean. God, I wish I could have done more. She probably saved my life."

"Deac, don't do that to yourself. You did everything you could. For God's sake, you were conked on the head *and* took a bullet trying to help that woman."

"Yeah… maybe." I thought for a moment. "Hey, finish your tea—and your smoke. Take all the time you want. When you're done, just leave the Bible on my desk. I've got to get over to the gym. Set up equipment for the kids. Thanks again. You *are* special, you know."

She stood, raised up on her tiptoes and kissed me on the cheek. I smiled to myself. It was good to know this woman loved me. Even if it wasn't in the biblical sense.

I threw on my overcoat and hurried toward the gym. It was bitter cold. I pulled down my fedora and leaned into the stinging wind as I crossed the schoolyard. Then I looked back, suddenly uneasy. The feeling passed.

CHAPTER SIX

Darkness fell early in winter. Meg was gone by the time I got back. As I sat in my room, my thoughts turned to Amber... again. I had to find out more about her. After scarfing down a bowl of chili and some garlic bread, I walked two long blocks north and then turned east toward the Gold Coast, leaving a trail of footprints in the white powder of freshly fallen snow. I wasn't worried. I had Bat tucked into a belt loop, just in case. A little paranoid after being shot? Sure.

Through the flitter of light snowflakes, I saw and smelled smoke rising from a stoop where four teenagers were sitting. The aroma was sweet and irrefutable. They nodded once in my direction without smiling. A gesture of respect.

Good enough for me.

I nodded in return. I'd tried to reach some of these young toughs, for all the good it did. Still, I managed to turn a few.

That's how I looked not so long ago. Maybe the books saved me from going of the rails completely. Mom guided me toward the classics—*Tale of Two Cities, Robin Hood, Knights of the Round Table*—stories of good guys who fought hard and turned out to be heroes. My mom said my Dad was a hero. I believed her. Maybe that's where I picked up my habit of trying to right wrongs.

At the corner, three young girls scuffed through the snow toward me. I recognized them from the parish.

"Hi Deacon," one of them chirruped.

"Evenin' ladies," I touched the brim of my fedora in salute. It was my dad's, and I'd worn it for years—long before the hat made a fashion comeback. I suspect the hat made me feel close to him in a way.

The girls giggled, their coats open to the wind and snow. I guess a zipped coat was just too nerdy. One of them waved a pink-mittened hand. They smiled and chatted as they passed, flirty and shy at the same time. Made me smile too.

In the middle of the block, next to the XXX Adult Shoppe, I spotted her. "Glitter" was her street name. Her fluffy white jacket was open, too, hers showing the merchandise.

She was a blonde concoction in a low-cut red top, tiny silver skirt and her trademark, glitter. She shimmered as she stood there— eyelids, fingernails and skirt sparkling. She didn't have a client at the moment.

"Evenin' Glitter."

"Hey Deac, how they hangin'?" She beamed. We'd been buddies ever since I'd put in a good word for her with the police. Then I'd straightened out a john who'd gotten rough.

"I'm okay."

Up close, she smelled like roses watered with gin,

"So, you finally getting horny enough to spend some time with Glitter?" She shook her breasts east and west, teasing.

It would be an insult not to look, so I did. "Great offer. Not tonight."

She pouted. "I'm disappointed. A big guy like you. I'll give you a discount for the braggin' rights."

I laughed. Hard not to like her. "I need to talk. Buy you a coffee?"

"Nah, Leo'll be pissed." She lost her smile and shook her head. "Not much action tonight, yah know."

"I'll square it with Leo. He and I go way back. Besides, the law says you get a break every couple of hours."

She laughed at that. There was no such law and we both knew it.

I was stamping my feet to keep from freezing. "Let's go inside and get warm."

Glitter cocked her head to one side for a moment, deciding. "Okay." She slipped her arm in mine and snuggled to my side. "Lead on, my hero."

Her body felt good against mine. She'd said the magic word, "hero."

"I'd like one of them hot Irish coffees," she said, "with whipped cream. You know, the ones they got at O'Neills."

"One Irish coffee comin' up."

We'd walked in that direction, her chatting about this and that. She was quiet for a minute. Then she looked up at me, a question in her eyes. "Ain't you, like afraid someone'll see us together? You know, late night and you being a priest-like guy and all. What'll people think?"

I hugged her a little tighter. "I don't give a rat's ass. After all, my boss hung out with ladies of the night, street people and even dreaded tax collectors."

It took Glitter a full five seconds to respond. Then she smiled, "Oh yeah, huh, I get it. You're a hoot."

I could see the inviting green neon blinking a block away. We'd be snug inside soon. Just then a couple of men staggered out of a bar and stood in our way.

"Well, look what we got here," said the man in the leather jacket with greasy-looking hair. His speech was slightly slurred and his square head looked too big for his body.

I stared at him. I could see what was coming, so I unbuttoned my coat and put my hand on Bat.

The man stepped in front of us so we couldn't pass. He looked Glitter up and down. "Hey, chickie, how 'bout you come along with me and my friend here? Dump this asshole. You look like you know how to give a couple of guys a good time." He looked at his big friend in the Navy stocking cap. "Whatdaya think, Larry, you in the mood for a chickie sandwich?"

Struggling to contain myself, I said as calmly as I could, "You don't want to dance with us tonight. Get out of the way."

He laughed. "No, faggot. I don't want to dance. I want to fuck."

"Right on," his buddy grunted, and stepped closer.

My hand was on Bat, ready for action. "Last chance to move." I was irritated with the interruption. I had more important business this night.

The man in the leather jacket grabbed Glitter by the arm, nearly yanking her off her feet. He'd hit my trigger, and there was no going back. I thrust "Bat" forward and smashed the end into his right eyebrow. He stumbled backwards, slipped and fell on to the snowy sidewalk.

His muscular partner charged, his fists flying wildly. I parried the first punch, but the second landed a glancing blow to my cheek. I spun around, threw a roundhouse punch into his solar plexus and drove BAT down onto his foot.

"Jesus Christ," he yelled, flopping down next to his buddy. He clutched his foot while struggling to breathe.

The words were Catholic school, but the tone was street tough. Now he'd really pissed me off. "Don't take the Lord's name in vain," I snarled.

Glitter stepped forward, eyes flashing. She'd pulled a thin, very sharp stiletto, seemingly out of thin air. "Turn over the one who grabbed me, while I shove my pig sticker up his ass."

The two men looked like wide-eyed rats in a trap.

I turned away from the men and winked at Glitter. "Another time, maybe." I bent over the two men, holding BAT in a ready position. My voice softer this time. "Remember, God loves you, so don't act like asshole bullies."

Glitter and I resumed our walk, and she grabbed my arm again. "I think they learned their lesson. Never fuck with a man of God and a good-lookin' hooker." She threw her head back and let out a throaty laugh. She rose on tiptoes and kissed me hard on the cheek, then rubbed off the lipstick print with her thumb.

Finally, we walked under the green lights at O'Neill's. I held the door for her, and we walked into the warmth of an Irish pub swathed in emerald drapery. There was even a carved leprechaun by the old-fashioned cash register. It had a faint smell of beer and cigarette smoke.

We sat at the far end of the bar and ordered the Irish coffees. I had to admit, the steaming drink hit the spot. I reached into my pocket and pulled out one of Amber's business cards. "What can you tell me about this?" I said, sliding the purple and gold disk toward her.

"Oh, I know that bitch all right." Glitter sneered and took another sip of her drink.

"Why 'bitch?'"

"I tried to work for her and she turned me down... the bitch. Said I was a little 'long in the tooth' for her *clientele*." Glitter made a prissy face and pursed her lips, "clientele my ass."

"So Amber's... uh... like Leo?"

"Like, but not. She has a stable of great young lookers. I'll give her that, but she's not street. Her business is strictly upper class. Her johns pay through the nose for 'escorts.'"

"Escorts?"

"Yeah, they go with a guy on a cruise or to a fancy political dinner or some special event. You know... all dressed up fancy, eager to please, hanging on the guy's arm."

"Can you describe her?"

Glitter licked at the Irish cream above her upper lip, looking like a little girl with a milk mustache dressed up in her mother's clothes. In a way, she *was* playing dress-up, but she was no kid.

"Skinny bitch, no ass at all, on the tall side. Reddish hair, cut short."

Sounded like the woman I'd found hiding in the church.

"What do you care?" she asked.

I thought about my reply and decided less was best. "Our paths crossed recently... Then the police found her body floating in the Chicago River."

"Holy shit. She piss off the wrong guy?"

"Don't know... maybe. Know her last name?"

"No friggin' clue. We're not big on last names around here, y'know?"

I pushed a little. "Anything else?"

"Nah." She took a long pull of her coffee. "Aaaahhh, that is good." She tilted her head back and looked at me through long heavy mascaraed eyelashes. "There's rumors."

"Rumors?"

"That her clients are... were pretty high up the food chain. Powerful men you don't want to screw with. 'Screw with.' Hey, that's funny." She threw back that corona of blonde hair and laughed. She caught the eye of several of the patrons.

I smiled to acknowledge her joke and finished my coffee. "Hate to run, but I have to get back to the parish." It was true. I got a kick out of Glitter. She was a good sort, despite her line of work. "Thanks for talking to me. I'll square the time with Leo." I knew he wouldn't care. We'd been buddies since we were kids. Plus, after his last run-in with the cops, and the beating they dispensed, he'd closed most of his gambling joints and let most of his girls go. "He's got his mind on pizza these days."

Glitter nodded. "You got that right. Thanks. Good coffee." She slid off her stool and planted another one on my cheek.

Things were looking up. That was my third kiss of the day,

I slipped in a commercial message—"God be with you. Don't be a stranger at Mass"—and threw a twenty on the bar.

"Bye, sweet cheeks. Take care."

When I looked back, Glitter was back at work, making eyes at the guy next to her at the bar. *God help her.*

A man barged through the narrow doorway just as I was leaving. He looked me in the eye, sneered and intentionally threw his shoulder into mine—my injured shoulder—as he passed. It hurt like a son-of-a-bitch.

Not again ... a hat trick of bullies in one night.

Some other time I might have let it go. Not tonight. I grabbed the back of his red-and-black Bulls jacket and yanked him out on the sidewalk. Then I kicked his feet out from under him, and he went down.

He bounced up, looking thoroughly pissed. Return of Bat. I thrust the business end into the guy's chest, and he went down again.

He looked up at me more surprised than enraged.

"Apologize."

He looked at me blankly.

"You rammed me in the doorway ... remember?"

"Oh, yeah. Sorry," said the former tough guy. Bat had knocked the cockiness out of him.

"Accepted."

He stood up mumbling and went into the bar, probably hoping no one had witnessed his disgrace.

I replaced Bat in my belt, the cold night air feeling good after all my *exercise*. After a couple of blocks, my mind turned in on me. Two scuffles in the space of an hour. *I wasn't the bully ... was I?* Nah, those guys had deserved a lesson from Bat. I'd done nothing wrong, no confession necessary.

I hustled back to Saint Sebastian's, thinking about the upside of my little apartment behind the church. I could walk to the Gold Coast, the church, the gym and the even the construction sites where I carried lath and wallboard to supplement my so-called income.

I was also accessible to anyone from the street that needed a buck, a favor or a quick fix to their problems. I hadn't decided whether that was an up or a downside. It suited the pastor. I was handy for any chore he threw my way.

Back home, my attention zipped back to the mystery of Amber. I plucked the Bible from my desk drawer. She'd been clever to hide information in a child's Bible, especially given her profession. But what was she hiding? Had to be connected with her business. A list of clients could be dynamite information in the wrong hands. I flipped through the Bible, pondering the cryptic inscriptions. I hoped Meg would figure it out.

As I paced the room, thinking about Amber, I noticed two envelopes in my mail slot—obviously hand delivered since all postal mail went directly to the rectory. I picked up the top one, a glossy flyer inviting honored *friends* to a social gathering with *special guest* State Senator Frank Clayton.

Humph. Worthless pretty boy politician. What's he up to now? More fund raising, no doubt. I tossed the flyer in the trash.

The second was a familiar gray envelope.

No postage, of course. It bore the crest of the Gabrians: a shield with a lily in the center, backed by a cross with a gold trumpet and spear forming an "X."

My heart jumped. Another "announcement," a hard-ass assignment. They always were.

Inside the envelope was a date and time: tomorrow—late.

CHAPTER SEVEN

I went about my normal duties the next day and steeled myself against what I'd be called to do this frigid Chicago night. I'd done it before. It was necessary. I could see that. But it didn't mean I had to like it. There'd be no time—or appetite—for eating later, so I nuked half a sausage pizza I had in the frig for a few days. Rubbery but not half bad. I washed it down with a Pabst. I held up the bottle, looking at the familiar blue ribbon. *I really should start eating healthy.*

I'd had taken some side-trips on my way to becoming a Gabrian. Fifteen month tour of duty in Iraq. Four years at DePaul University on the G.I. Bill for a degree in religious studies. *Nothing else seems to catch my interest.* I kicked around Chicago for a while, taught PE and worked in construction. Couldn't settle down to a job I liked. Then with the archbishop's urging, I joined the seminary. Why not? Was the priesthood really my vocation? Though I'd always felt the pull of the church, I wasn't sure. Several priests confided in me that they were never competely sure. Archbishop Laine had planted the seed. "Anyone with the first name of 'Deacon,' should try." He also said, "Your father would be so proud." That was the clincher. My mother was overjoyed.

Archbishop Laine pops up in my life from time to time. He seems to have faith in me for whatever reason. He got me a financial grant, and four years later I was ordained to a transitory Deaconate. It was a final step toward the priesthood.

Soon after, I was invited to be a Gabrian.

So here I was again, answering the Gabrien call. I bundled up and jogged to the parish station wagon. The cold tightened my face. Unfortunately, it took a while for the old buggy to warm up.

After parking near an apartment complex off North Avenue, I pulled on my fedora and took a circuitous route down a basement gangway, through the back gate, a vacant lot and two alleys.

Paranoid? Just a little.

I circled back and dashed up the steps to a venerable old flat. I used my key then pushed through the double doors that led to Monsignor Vito Salvatore's offices.

I knocked twice on the inner door.

"Enter." The elderly Monsignor rose slowly behind his desk and waited for me to come to him. He took my hand in both of his. "Good to see you my son. God bless you for coming out."

He was a head shorter than I was, but impressive, dressed in black with scarlet piping on his short cape. His hair was still black, but there was silver in his perpetual five o'clock shadow. Dark Sicilian eyebrows bristled over his deep brown eyes.

"Monsignor."

The room was foreboding. Too dark for my taste, even with light from the fireplace. A picture of an agonized Christ on the cross, hung on oak paneling behind his desk.

The monsignor motioned me to a comfortable armchair facing him. "How's your shoulder?"

"Healing. Thanks for asking."

"How are you and Father Casey getting along?"

"Pretty well."

His eyes closed to slits and his mouth hinted at a smile. "You *do* know that lying is a sin, my son."

"Yes, well, we do the best we can."

He looked at the ceiling or was it the heavens beyond? "I understand. And have you considered resuming your studies at the seminary?"

"Not at the moment."

"I pray you give the Church another chance." He sighed, and pierced me with his stare. "You'd make a grand priest."

Despite my indecision about my future, I was glad so many people had faith in me.

"It's a cold night. Have a nip with me, and then you can be on your way." He poured a full measure of Christian Brother's brandy into a pair of delicate cordial glasses.

"Polish crystal." he said, seeing my admiring glance.

The golden liquor glided down smoothly, warming my belly.

"Ahh," said the monsignor, "another of God's wonderful gifts." Then his face darkened with seriousness. "Here it is." He handed me the usual Manila envelope, an address on the front.

"The evidence is, as always, indisputable. You can pick up the *prie-dieu* downstairs." The Monsignor put his hand on my shoulder. "Give him a chance to see the light. It's *tough love*, as they say, but necessary for his sake, that of our Holy Mother Church and that of the innocents."

"I'll do my best."

"You're a good man. We need soldiers like you."

I knelt to receive his blessing, and then stood to say goodbye. He hugged me and said, "peace be with you."

I left with the responsibility weighing heavily on my shoulders. I loaded the prayer kneeler to the car. Was I doing the right thing? Monsignor Salvatore had assured me it was the will of God. The monsignor answered directly to Archbishop Laine. Besides his personal attention to me, he was regional head of the Gabrians. He'd given me my final briefing six months before.

I'd been awed by the solemn secret ceremony held in the sub-basement of Holy Name cathedral. Only other members of the Gabrian brotherhood were allowed to attend. At the time—and even still-- I'm honored by their trust in me.

I like to set wrongs right, but sometimes Salvatore's passion for what he calls "the eternal battle of good versus evil" seems to go beyond what I would consider *the will of God*. The monsignor had been brief this time, but sometimes his eyes glistened and his voice grew shrill when he talked about cleansing the Church of the evil within. He might border on the fanatic, but he was right about the legal system. The perps and pedophiles *would* get light sentences if they were turned over to the law. Three to six years and then they—at least 80 percent of them—would be out of prison, preying on more innocents.

The Gabrian way *did* work. It ended their transgressions for life. As Salvatore said more than once, "Someone has to take out the garbage and scour evil from the Church."

Father George Baksian was next.

CHAPTER EIGHT

I stopped for coffee and a scone and brought them back to the car. Outside the door a teenager was shoveling snow. I gave him a thumbs-up. I sat behind he wheel reviewing the folder on my lap.

The priest's transgressions—his depravity—made the lousy coffee worse. I'd have to work at controlling myself with this bastard. God knows my temper and a quick hand with Bat has gotten me into a lot of trouble.

I'd lost it during the "incident," my word for the pivotal experience that derailed my straight-and-narrow spiritual track at the seminary. For the first time in my life I'd wished two men would go straight to hell. And I'd come close to sending them there myself.

The memory flattened me once again.

I was in my last year of seminary and stopped by Saint Stephen's on the South Side for an impromptu visit with my spiritual advisor.

Big mistake … for him.

I walked in on the bastard and another church leader sprawled butt-naked on cushions, a couple of bewildered young girls under them. The girls were barely fourteen, I found out later. Freshmen at the church high school.

I knew how to inflict pain. And I punished those ungodly men. Left them in two bloody heaps on the floor. Could have killed them. Could have gone to jail. Didn't care. Still don't.

Forgiveness? I'm sure God has forgiven me. The trusted men of the church deserved punishment and I couldn't wait for society to administer it. I prayed that someday I'd want to forgive them. I knew that was better for me.

I packed up and left the seminary. Didn't have the stomach or the heart for the priesthood after that. Maybe later. Being a Gabrian was different. I was under orders to clean the church gutters of scum like that.

Father Baksian's parish was in the western suburb of Elmhurst, an hour's drive in the snow. A white fog restricted my vision. It seemed appropriate that I couldn't see any further than twenty feet ahead of me. I could almost see amber's face in ghostly white.

The Gabrians knew Father Baksian would be alone in his rectory tonight. I don't know how. Their tentacles are far reaching.

The utilitarian *prie-dieu* under one arm and Bat under my long topcoat, I rang the bell.

A priest answered.

"Father Baksian?"

"Yes?"

He was tall and slender with a prominent nose, receding chin and styled light brown hair. His brown eyes looked shifty to me... nervous.

"I have a gift for you." I pointed at the single kneeler to be used for individual prayer.

"Really?" The priest brightened. "A gift from whom?"

"From people who care. They sent you a red lily earlier."

"Yes, yes. This *is* mysterious. Come in, please."

He was so slick. Black trousers, a gray cardigan over his soft white shirt.

Good, that will make my job easier.

"Let's go to my office, Mr.—"

"Deacon Adelius." Few people remembered my name after hearing it only once. This was a good thing in Gabrian business.

I picked up the *prie-dieu* and entered.

"A primitive piece," he said. "Let me help."

I needed no assistance but allowed him to take one end. Once inside, I could see the wooden kneeler was out of place in the room filled with antiques and expensive knick-knacks.

"Anyone else here tonight?" I asked.

"No. My associate is visiting the nursing home over in Rosemont."

The priest sat down behind his large mahogany desk and motioned to the upholstered chair in front of him.

"I recited from the script I'd memorized. "I'm here at the direction of higher church authorities to deliver this gift and to make an important announcement,"

Father Baksian leaned toward me, weak chin thrust forward as best he could. "Go ahead, please."

"The girl's name is Teresa Aguilar. She's fifteen. One of the young girls in your parish youth group,"

The priest's left eyelid twitched, but he said nothing...waiting.

"Evidence just came to light. You forced yourself on this girl. Sinned against an innocent... and against God.

The priest's face went from pale and quizzical to purpled outrage. "How dare you!"

He rose, and so did I.

"Sit!" I growled.

He sat.

"I'm here to announce that you will be leaving tonight."

"What the hell... I'm not leaving."

I pushed aside my coat, pulled out Bat and slammed it on his shiny desk. A fancy reading lamp toppled. Pencils and papers bounced.

"Sit and listen. Your life... the life you knew... is over."

"Who *are* you?"

"I am a Gabrian. Think of me as the announcer.... I bring you *choices*."

He went pale, his fingers bouncing on the arms of his chair. "I've heard... rumors... not real—"

"Oh, we are *very* real." I produced a sheet of legal-sized yellow paper from the Manila envelope. "Your choices: You can turn yourself in. We have a mountain of evidence and witnesses against you. So arrest, conviction and prison is one of your choices. Understand?"

His mouth moved, but no words emerged.

"Or you can choose to relocate for a life of contemplation, self-mortification, work and prayer in one of three places: St. Alphonse's Monastery in the upper peninsula of Michigan, Saint Cyprian's Hospice off the coast of Newfoundland, or the retreat house on the Isle of Skye in the Inner Hebrides off the coast of Scotland. In one of these isolated locales, you can repent and still be useful to the church."

His outrage had faded and his voice trembled. "If I walk away?"

"Third choice. Got a DVD player?"

He pointed toward a closed cabinet.

"If you run, pray that the cops find you before we do." I slid the DVD into the player. "If not, *this* is your future."

I inserted the disc and pressed *play*.

Father Baksian looked a little green, like I'd put a knife to his throat, as he watched a surgical castration—close-up view—on the screen.

His voice was so low, I had to lean forward to hear. "You c-c-can't do that."

"Afterwards you will be turned over to civil authorities."

The priest made a mad dash for the door. I used Bat cut him down. A tap behind the left knee was all it took.

"Get back in your chair, you deviant hypocrite. Pray and accept your fate. Be thankful you have a choice." My voice shook. "If I had my way I'd hand the girl's father a baseball bat like this and leave you alone with him.

"But the Gabrians have mercy and offer you a chance to repent and to avoid prison. You *do know* what happens to inmates who are child molesters... particularly clergy."

Father Baksian stared blankly into space, rubbing the back of his leg.

"The church will provide the girl counseling. Perhaps she can one day recover from your *abuse*. She will receive scholarships to Catholic high schools and colleges... everything that can be done to try to blot you out of her life."

The priest's eyes were glazed and unfocused. I slammed Bat against the desk again to get his attention. "I have your tickets, should you choose the path of repentance."

I tapped Bat against the *prie-dieu*. "Kneel, ask God's forgiveness and make your choice."

Father Baksian knelt, still trembling. "Oh, no. No. I can't.... Please."

"Someone will arrive later tonight to start you on your new path, whichever it is to be. Pack light."

The pastor bowed his head, his voice a whine. "How long do I have to stay... at one of these... um... places?"

"Until you grow old and die. There, you will be removed from temptation. You will have no opportunity to repeat your heinous crimes. This *prie-dieu* will follow you. Use it to beg for forgiveness."

As the pastor knelt, I studied the Gabrian crest that was burned into the front armrest of the wooden kneeler, the details painted in lacquered color: white for the shield, red for the lily, gold for the trumpet and spear. A gold cross loomed in the background.

The Gabrians had been created, in secret, by a passionate few in high places to address the scandals and misconduct of some of its clergy. Their lofty four-fold purpose: to hold the clergy accountable, protect the innocent, help and compensate victims and to give perpetrators a chance at redemption. The public and the rest of the church could never know.

Father Baksian stood abruptly. "I'll go, but this isn't the end. You think you're tough with your club. You think I'm helpless, but I'll make calls all the way up the hierarchy."

"Call the devil for all I care." Fury built behind my eyes. *The scumbag thought he could escape... use his connections.*

I was literally seeing red, my teeth grinding, as the nightmarish memory returned: Two adolescent girls pinned to the floor that night in South Chicago, tears of pain and humiliation welling in their eyes.... This is what I saw whenever I felt any pity for one of these holy hypocrites.

Announcing always intensified my emotions. I was already primed by Amber's death, my wounds, the detective's insinuations, Father Casey's tyranny... and now this creep.

It had been a helluva four days.

CHAPTER NINE

The hot hazy soup kitchen smelled of cabbage, Clorox and humans. Forty street people stood along the dingy green walls wordlessly waiting for a bowl of stew, a hunk of day-old bread and a cup of hot tea. For many, this would be their only meal for the day.

Upbeat religious music was the only sound besides the clank of spoons and the murmur of the servers. The food was donated by several restaurants, bakeries and cafes in the neighborhood, thanks to a healthy dose of induced guilt and some arm-twisting from the sisters of Saint Catherine's. The nuns were creative in making the food stretch.

"That her?" Malachi whispered. He nodded toward a young woman serving stew, her long silver crucifix gleaming against her black T-shirt.

"Yeah," said Bernie. "The one on the left. She don't look it, but she's a nun, Sister Mary Margaret O'Sullivan. Two days ago, our guy saw her go in the apartment behind the church."

Malachi's mouth pulled to the left. "First a hooker, then a nun. The guy's a stud."

"No, no. It ain't like that. He left right after she got there. He's a deacon besides."

"You're the Catholic. What's a deacon, exactly?"

"Sort of priest light, like Bud Lite." Bernie snickered at his own joke. "Anyways, he ain't a priest, but almost. Name's Deacon Adelius.

Does things around the church—funerals, weddings, baptisms, sports for kids."

Malachi nodded. "And he takes in prostitutes. Did you see that nun carry anything out of his apartment?"

""Not that our man could tell. What are we looking for?"

Malachi tapped his cane on the floor in quick little bursts. "That's the fuckin' trouble. We don't know. One of Amber's bitches said her boss had rock-solid evidence against our employers. Could be a book, micro tape, computer disc, maybe one of those thumb drives."

"So whatta you want us to do?"

"For starters, give the deacon's place a thorough toss. Look for something small... something suspicious. If you don't find anything... " He licked his lips. "The good sister will be a big help."

Just then, Sister Mary Margaret looked up from her ladling and saw two men standing at the back of the soup kitchen. They were out of place. They were well dressed, and they didn't look hungry. A shiver of fear went down her spine.

When she looked again, they were gone.

CHAPTER TEN

When I got back to my digs after morning Mass, it looked like a hurricane had blown through. "What the bloody hell?" I muttered out loud. Papers, books, cushions and all the detritus from my desk drawers was strewn everywhere.

I knew the code was the object of the search. But the mother-of-pearl Bible was on the floor with the rest of my stuff. The assholes didn't think to look for a prostitute's Bible. I had to figure this out. Maybe Sister Mary Margaret had decoded the cryptic notations by now.

I stood in the middle of the room. *Shit!* The cleanup would take hours, maybe days. I might be casual about paperwork, but I liked order in my life. A place for everything and everything in its place, as my mother always said. And this was chaos.

I got to it and had the top layer clean by nightfall. I was efficient. I'd learned my housekeeping skills in boot camp. But I wasn't in good spirits. Well after dark, my phone rang.

"Hello, Deacon Adelius here."

After a pause, a strained familiar voice said, "Deac, come get me. They want the little Bible. Hurry—"

"Mr. Deacon ... don't talk, just listen. Bring the ... Goddamned Bible with the code, and come alone. Hurry, so the good ... sister won't suffer any more."

My stomach knotted. *"Suffer?"*

The strange voice continued, haltingly. "So... get to it."

"How?" I strained to listen. I had to get this right.

"ASAP. Let's keep it simple. We get the book. You get the woman." He gave an address in the warehouse district. "Come alone. Go up the stairs and put on the hood. It'll be on a chair at the top landing. Got it?"

"Yeah."

The phone went dead.

Call the detective?

Can't risk it.

What have they done to Meg?

Can't think about that. Got to get to her.

All my fault. I brought her into this.

My heart was anvil heavy as I stuffed the Bible in my coat pocket, grabbed Bat and got in the station wagon. I felt like an observer, watching myself move in impossibly slow motion.

Oh God. Meg.

Damned bastards had been watching my place. Must've seen her come and go.

The snow had stopped, but it was cold as hell... and silent except for the crunch of tires on the dry packed snow. My headlights illuminated streets that looked lonelier and dirtier than ever. Chicago is a somber city in the dead of winter.

The warehouse was shabby, looked deserted. I pushed through the outer metal door and raced up the stairs two at a time. Found the hood and put it on. It stunk. I wasn't the first to wear it.

I rapped, and the door creaked open. The next instant, I took a blow to my stomach. Fell to my knees, gasping. Another blow in the back knocked me to the concrete floor. I hit my chin hard.

"Don't move, asshole."

Not the same voice I'd heard on the phone. This man had an accent, and I registered every nuance of his voice. *I'll deal with him... later.*

"Deac, is that you?" Meg whispered.

I heard a slap, followed by a faint moan.

"Stop… I have what you want," I said. *Son-of-a-bitchin' bullies.* I couldn't do anything and I wasn't used to that. I reached back to my military training: Breathe, focus, think, be patient, survive.

"Where is it? You'd better not be shittin' us."

"Left coat pocket."

The bastards hadn't bothered to search me. Still had BAT and my cell. I was lying on them.

I felt a hand dig into my pocket. "What the fuck is this?"

"Bible… with a code."

"If you ain't right, your little nun friend's gonna pay."

"Open the book… Check the inner margins."

"Yeah, okay."

Someone a distance away spoke in measured tones. It was the voice I'd heard earlier on the phone. "Bring it to me."

Footsteps, silence, whispers.

The air electric… smelled old and musty. No heat. I couldn't see.

I picked out three separate voices: the first—gruff, accent, threatening; the second—careful, sinister, the boss; the third—an underling, nervous.

The *boss* aimed a question my way. "What does the code mean?"

"Don't know. We were trying to figure it out."

"This had better be the genuine article."

"It's all I have." That was a lie. I had the key. But they didn't ask. They didn't know about it.

A door opened and I heard boots tramp down the stairs.

Unbelievably, they were gone. For now. But they knew where we lived.

I whipped off my hood and caught a flash of Gothic lettering—*Chicago White Sox*—on the back of a jacket before the last man disappeared.

Then I looked at Meg and nearly wept.

CHAPTER ELEVEN

Oh my God. The horror in Iraq had been bad. But this was personal. Meg had been bound to a chair. Shivering, blindfolded. Jeans gone. T-shirt in rags... bloody. I untied the heavy cords, wrapped her in my top coat and dialed 911. I held her gently.

Her eyes were at half-mast, her voice a whisper. "Thank you, Deac."

"The paramedics are on the way. Hang in there."

She strained to speak. "I told them about the Bible... right away. The one man ... so evil ... he cut me. Ex... exposed... me." Tears rolled down her swollen face.

She was covered with shallow gashes oozing blood.... *My God, the bastards had tortured her... for nothing.*

"Hang on, Meg. Help will be here soon.... God have mercy."

She breathed harshly, painfully. "Please, before they get here... a favor. Don't look. I'm so ashamed."

"Anything you want."

She moved slightly. Cried out. And I heard a faint clank as something fell to the floor. It was her silver crucifix, coated in blood.

"Keep it for me."

"Anything," I said again. "This is all my fault. I'm so sorry." God, why hadn't they taken me instead? I slipped the crucifix into my coat pocket.

"Not your... fault. They're just... evil."

The paramedics rushed in. They tried to mask it, but I saw their horrified looks. They tried to gentle me away from Mary Margaret. "Let us do our job now," said the older man with a gray crew cut.

"Wait," she said, her voice fainter still. "Deac, two more things." She pulled me closer. "In case I pass out."

"Yes?"

"I made copies... incomplete. The code is... a list. I stuck it in my large Bible."

"Sister Sherlock... " I tried for a smile. "And the other thing?"

"Get those bastards for me."

"Yes, sister."

She lost consciousness. A blessing.

They took vitals, started an IV, applied pressure dressings and wrapped her in a heavy blanket. The younger, ruddy-cheeked EMT peered at me. "Hey, your chin could use some stitches."

"Later, maybe."

"Some first aid, at least."

I nodded, and he came at me with antiseptic cream and a large square bandage. He stuck it onto my chin. "That'll hold you."

"Thanks."

We carried Meg down the steep old stairs on a stretcher.

"Grant Hospital," the older EMT told me, before I could ask. "It's closest. We'll have to notify the police."

"Yeah, sure. Might try for Detective Rick Ditmar. He's on a related case."

"Will do."

Keep some pressure on that chin," said the younger guy. "It'll stop the bleeding. Don't worry. We'll take good care of her." He handed me my topcoat.

I watched the ambulance disappear down the deserted, wind-blown street. I wished I could stay with her.

I picked up a handful of snow and held it against my bleeding chin. Felt no pain. Never did when I was wired.

I had an idea. It'd be a long shot... but long shots paid off once in a while.

I prowled nearby bars, the low-end kind with neon beer signs in the windows. I was hunting, and I intended to go at it 'til closing time.

Consequences? I shrugged. "Get those bastards," she'd asked me. And I would.

She knew the worst about me—the incident that drove me from the seminary—and I loved her.

God. She'd been tortured because of me.

I cruised the bars, gave patrons the once-over and moved on. If the joint was dark or narrow, I'd push through the aisles, scrutinize everyone and leave.

No one held my gaze and no one spoke. The look in my eyes, the battered chin, the blood on my coat… they could see I was a powder keg. And no one wanted to be the fuse,

At Clyde's Tap, I spotted a black-and-white Sox jacket over a broad back. The guy was hunched over a stein of beer, his thick neck ending in a flat top.

Lots of people in Chicago wore jackets like that. I didn't want to make a mistake. The guy hadn't seen me, so I waited outside.

Not a long wait. The big man lumbered out, farted and pigeon-toed down the street.

I approached fast. "Hey, buddy, got a light?"

The man turned. "Yeah, I guess." The voice was unmistakable. It was the man from the warehouse… the one who'd hit me.

He flicked the lighter. "You!"

The word barely left his lips when I threw my right fist into his gut.

He folded forward and I pushed him into an alley between two buildings. When I tapped him on the back of his head, he went to his hands and knees and puked.

I side-armed Bat and heard bones break as I connected.

Sox cried out as his left arm went limp. I whipped Bat around and forehanded it into the man's right shoulder. The right arm sagged, useless.

"*No más!*" the man shrieked. Stress and pain brought out his native language. I'd guess he was Puerto Rican.

"*No más,*" I repeated. "Did you grant the woman mercy. Or did you just keep cutting her?"

"I didn't touch her. *¡Honrado!* Honest. You can ask her. I was there, yeah, but I didn't do nothin' to her. *¡Dios Mio!* She's a nun."

"You were there. You let it happen. That's enough for me. Did you enjoy watching, you piece of shit?"

"No man, it make me sick, honest, the other big guy too."

"Stay on your knees, lean your head against the wall and listen." As if he could've done anything else with two broken arms.

I bent down and growled, "What's your name, asshole?"

"Guilherme."

"Guilherme, God will always love a sinner. You know that, Guilherme? You are a sinner, aren't you?" I was breathing hard.

"*Si*, yeah, I'm a sinner... anything you want."

"Now pray."

"Pray what?"

"Pray for forgiveness.... Pray that I won't lose control and beat you to death. How about, 'The Lord's Prayer'.., the 'Our Father'."

"*No recuerdo.*"...The man was sobbing. "*Nuestro Padre*...I forget."

"You'd better remember or I'll hit a ground rules double off the center field wall with your head." Bat zinged as I swung it in the still night air.

"Okay, okay, *Nuestro Padre* ... " he began. "Our father ... " He stumbled through the prayer, mixing in a little Spanish.

Close enough.

I leaned close to the man's left ear. "If you didn't hurt her, then who did?"

"*No sé.* Not the big guy–Bernie. The other one did the hurting."

I stood up, holding my weapon like a mad batter. "Here comes the three and two pitch."

"Hold on. *Dios*, I hurt."

"God knows you hurt. And He felt the pain of an innocent woman tonight... a bride of Christ. So, who did this evil?"

"Calls himself Malachi. He's *loco... malo.*"

"Yeah, I'd say so. Where do I find the sick bastard?"

"*No sé.* I have no idea. He picks me up in bars, coffee shops. He pays me later and I leave. *Eso es todo.* That's all."

"What else are they planning?"

"What? *Nada.* I don't know nothin'." Guilherme was sobbing.

I stepped back and drew in a deep breath. "You know God forgives you. He forgives all of us. Unfortunately for you, my personal account is empty right now. I will call the paramedics. After you heal, you will leave Chicago… for good… forever. *Comprende?*"

"I do. I understand. I leave."

"Swear to God?"

"I swear to God."

I couldn't ratchet down. Once home, I paced. My skin crawled as I washed the blood off Meg's silver crucifix. I knew only one way to get through this.

Lacing up gym shoes and grabbing a towel, I went into the church basement. My Everlast body bag—old and stained—hung from an overhead pipe near the furnace. I turned up the volume on a 24-hour rock 'n' roll station and started punching the bag. Lightly at first, then harder.

I was hitting the bastard who had brutalized my friend…every bad-ass cowardly bully… every sexual predator in the world. And I was praying.

Dear God. Please help my friend to heal in body and spirit. Help me to avenge her. Help me bring these bastards to justice….

It was too soon to ask for forgiveness for my own actions.

I punched and prayed. Punched and prayed. I was about done when Bill Haley came on… the oldest of old: "We're gonna rock, rock, rock, 'till broad daylight… "

It wasn't yet daybreak when I quit, gasping for air, sweat pouring off my body. I could feel physical pain now. Sweat stung the cut on my chin. My shoulder and head ached. I'd take some of nurse Wanda's pain-killers. "We want to manage your pain," she'd said. I grimaced to myself. As if she… as if anyone could do that.

But maybe, finally, I could sleep.

CHAPTER TWELVE

The snow was glaring the brightest of whites outside, so I squinted when I walked into the fluorescence of Grant Hospital. It was six-thirty am. Visiting hours hadn't begun but my name and church credentials worked again. The floor nurse reluctantly led me to Meg's room.

She was asleep—probably medicated, looking vulnerable in blue cotton flannel pajamas with little white stars. *Funny, the details one notices.* A strong scent of Betadine and alcohol permeated the room. Her hands and face were bandaged, the exposed skin red and swollen.

I knew enough about post-traumatic stress to worry about her emotional well-being as well as the physical damage she'd suffered. I sat by her bedside, smothered by a sodden blanket of guilt. This was my fault.

About forty minutes passed before she stirred. "Deac... dreamed about you."

Oh God, had she dreamed that I let her down? That I'd failed to protect her? I couldn't speak... not yet.

She struggled against sedatives to be coherent.

"You were running in the dream looking wild." She began to cry.

"Shhh. I got to one of 'em," I said.

She cried harder.

"No, I'm sorry. We don't have to talk about it."

"It's okay." She wiped her eyes. "Everything came flooding back on me." She took a deep breath and couldn't stop coughing. It looked painful. "Whoa... screw that." She said.

I handed her a plastic cup of water and she sipped. "You... " She cleared her throat, her voice a hoarse whisper. "You found one of them?"

"Yes."

"And... "

"He won't be hurting anyone for a while."

She closed her eyes. "Shouldn't have asked you... but, God forgive me, I'm glad, too. Did you... did you find out anything else?"

"A couple of names."

I'd meant to bring her some comfort, but I'd made it worse, said all the wrong things.

We were both silent for a while, thinking our own thoughts, I guess.

"Bible to Bible," Meg murmured.

I leaned forward to catch her next words. "Enlarged some coded words 150 percent—made copies—so we both can study them. Look in the big Bible next to my desk." She smiled a little and then winced, like her face hurt. "Appropriate, Bible to Bible."

Some code. One woman died for it and another was badly beaten. "We'll look at it together, later." I touched her hair so lightly she probably couldn't feel it. She smiled though, before she drifted off again.

When I stepped into the hospital corridor, Sister Claire Conselleta was bearing down on me like an oncoming locomotive. She was built like one, too, large and square in a gray business suit and short head veil—her badge of nunhood.

"Deacon Adelius. How could you get Mary Margaret involved in this? Did you see what they did to her? Poor child." She'd built up a full head of steam, white bushy eyebrows bristling as she rattled on. Meg's mother superior never had liked me nor the easy-going relationship Meg and I had.

Others in the corridor stopped what they were doing to listen to her tirade. "I'll be talking to Father Casey, make no mistake about that," she fumed.

I bowed my head, accepted responsibility and apologized all over myself. I knew it was my fault. I didn't need to hear it from Sister Conselleta.

Walking away, I saw someone waiting for me.

CHAPTER THIRTEEN

Detective Rick Ditmar was leaning on the counter at the nurse's station, shaking his head at Sister Conselleta's outburst. When the nun disappeared into Meg's room, Ditmar turned his attention to me. "Just the guy I wanted to see."

He tilted his head toward the cafeteria, and I nodded.

Once there, we bought coffee and headed for a table far from the other diners. The detective shed his topcoat, displaying a pair of suspenders over a muscular torso. "Well now, one woman murdered and another tortured and beaten half to death. So, what do they have in common?"

He stared at me for a long moment and answered his own question: "You. Care to tell me what's going on?"

I gave him the abbreviated version: how I found Amber's Bible in my desk, saw the code and asked Sister Mary Margaret to help decipher the coded pages.

"You involved a nun in a criminal case." It was an accusation, not a question. He arranged his broad face into a look of disgust. "It never occurred to you to turn the book over to *the authorities?* You didn't consider reporting the kidnap?"

Guilty as charged. I had no defense.

He gulped his coffee. "Did you come up with *anything?*"

"Not much. She… Sister Mary Margaret said it looked like a list of some sort."

"That's it?"

"No time. They took her hostage in exchange for the book."

"So, they have the Bible and the code? Good work." Ditmar wasn't quick witted enough for anything but the broadest of sarcasm. "Where'd they nab her? Where'd they take her?"

"Soup kitchen... warehouse." I gave him the addresses and asked what he'd learned about the case.

The detective stared at me for several long seconds. I could practically see the wheels in his head turn as he pondered whether giving me infomation would buy him anything. "Okay," he said. "I'll tell you this much. Amber was really Allison De La Croix, a high-end madam."

He tapped his coffee cup with his pen. "Last night, paramedics found a guy with two broken arms near that warehouse address. He's at White Memorial. He was vague about the details. You wouldn't know anything about that, would you?"

"I'll pray for him."

The detective gave me a crooked smile. "You were in law enforcement once, an Army MP. Right?"

I nodded."

"Overseas?"

"Yeah, Iraq."

"I did my time in Indian Country," said Ditmar. "You know, jinglies and towel heads."

I said nothing, but he probably could read the disgust on my face. Only lowlifes used that racist slang. His credibility was flat lining. He didn't know shit about bonding with a brother-in-arms. First, he was too obvious about trying to get me to open up. Second, he was insulting.

I didn't like Ditmar, and I was losing respect for his boss. I'd heard talk on the street about the police commissioner. Nothing you could put your finger on. Still, he was a tough ex-cop from good Chicago stock.

Yeah, I had an impulse to help with the investigation, but it had nothing to do with either one of them.

Ditmar narrowed his eyes, trying to look tougher, I guess. "This ain't Iraq and it ain't Afghanistan. Now tell me what you know and quit playing a *Rambo* vigilante. This is not your fuckin' investigation."

Bad approach. *It was my investigation. I was going to find the perps.* "Look, this Amber... this Allison woman came to the church scared to death. I told you that. Somebody wanted her 'tell' and she hid it in the Bible. The scum didn't know that. I tried to help, but I was too late."

"Who's 'the scum'?"

I shrugged. "Does the name Malachi ring a bell?"

Ditmar wrote the name in his notebook.

"The name Bernie also came up. Anyhow, the scumbags took the Bible, but Sister Mary Margaret made a copy of some pages with codes on them."

"I'll need those as evidence. One of our computer geeks can crack the code."

"I'll pick them up. Who knows what it is: maybe the girls, the clients and details about Amber's operation."

Detective Ditmar read over his notes silently and looked up again. "Anything else?"

"Amber mentioned Andy and Tamara. I told you that. Did you check those names?"

Ditmar returned question for question as he slurped his coffee. "Last names? Addresses?"

"No." I still wasn't telling him about the key. I'd keep that ace in the hole. Sure, he appeared competent, but he was an arrogant, racist SOB who had jumped to conclusions about me and Amber.

He repeated his warning to stay out of his investigation, and I glared at him as I took a last swig of my coffee.

Fat chance, I'd give up, not after what they did to Meg and Amber. I stopped in at the ER to get my chin sewed up. The male nurse took one look and put me in a separate screened off area. He'd been a Navy corpsman and, despite his meaty hands, he put in four delicate stitches.

CHAPTER FOURTEEN

I couldn't believe it. A gray envelope with the Gabrian crest was waiting for me. The "announcements" usually came weeks, even months, apart. And this appointment was for tonight.

I picked up a message from Leo on my cell. "Urgent. Come by the pizzeria." Everything was urgent with Leo. I'd been meaning to stop by anyhow to clear Glitter. Then the parish secretary called about a funeral to be arranged … for Allison De La Croix. Between funeral plans and the Gabrian summons, Leo would have to wait.

I sighed and buried my head in my hands. Appropriate. Allison had come to the church for help and died. The least we could do was bury her. I hoped the ceremony would bring some peace to me.

The parish secretary began the paperwork and made an appointment for me to see Allison's contact—her sister—the next day at 11 a.m. The diocese would soon rescind my duties, since I was no longer in priesthood formation, but administrative wheels turn slowly.

A wave of sadness rolled through me. I'd miss these privileges… bringing the sacred rituals of life and death to my brothers and sisters. Until they formally took away my privileges, I'd continue to perform these duties I'd come to love.

I put in a mandatory call to Father Posjena, telling him about the upcoming funeral service. "Was she Catholic?" he asked with an edge to his voice.

"Yes, she was raised Catholic." I didn't know, really, but he'd never check. To make it sound more realistic, I added, "but like so many, she'd not been practicing for a while."

"Obviously." If the man had any compassion, his tone would have softened, but it didn't. "Keep the service short and simple. No photography, no media. Understand?"

"I understand." At least he wasn't going to meddle in the funeral.

Next, I went to Saint Catherine's to pick up the copies Meg had made. I tossed up a special prayer that I wouldn't have to encounter Mother Superior again. Seeing her made me feel like a small boy back in Catholic school.

My prayers were answered. Mrs. Zalenski, the assistant administrator, greeted me warmly. She took off thick glasses and tucked a stray hair into her tight bun. "Ah, Mr. Adelius. How is Sister Mary Margaret... really?"

"She's strong" Meg had called from the hospital to authorize my entry. If she hadn't discussed her health with Mrs. Zalenski, I certainly wasn't going to.

The friendly woman smiled and smoothed non-existent wrinkles from her close-fitting dress. Then she laughed self-consciously and made small talk about the weather as she escorted me to Sister Mary Margaret's room. Could she be flirting?

I tried not to be rude, but my mind was on Meg and the code, not this conversation. I rushed in fully aware that only Meg's call and my title enabled me to enter a nun's room.

The room was simple and bare, except for the corner occupied by Meg's desk, filing cabinet and bookshelves. The messiness of her workspace was a stark contrast to the rest of her room. The keyboard of her computer was nearly obscured by papers and files. Still, the corner seemed blessed. Light from her double window illuminated a statue of the Holy Virgin on a corner of her desk. Meg had a great view of the Chicago skyline.

I took the copies of the code from her big Bible and left.

Seeing the code numbers blown up several times their normal size didn't help me any. One page listed a few names she had deciphered, but there was no context. And they weren't any city bigwigs I'd ever heard of. These were followed by *S & M, bndg* and *XYY*. Sexual notations?

Two Chicago police officers sent by Detective Ditmar picked them up later that afternoon. I wished forensics luck in deciphering it. I knew what the list *probably* was, but the code itself was a mystery to me.

Night dropped like a funeral veil over the frosty city. It mirrored my unease about the Gabrian meeting tonight.

Vito Salvatore was his usual somber self. He put on his topcoat and the biretta with scarlet piping. "Walk with me, Deacon."

"Where are we going?"

"To see the boss." He took my arm. Monsignor Salvatore's home was about one long city block from his church, Sacred Heart. At his age, walking on the frozen snow and ice could be treacherous.

He was curiously taciturn. We walked in silence through the cold night.

When we got to the church, the elderly monsignor unlocked a creaky side door, entered and bolted it behind us. "Let us pray."

We knelt in the first pew.

As we prayed a voice from the sanctuary interrupted us. "Thank you both for coming out on this cold night. Come and join me." It was a command, no doubt about that. Archbishop Xavier Laine's voice and stature—even his face—added to the impression of strength and authority.

The archbishop was nearly as tall as I was with dark hair and eyes like mine. Instead of the costume of a high-ranking church official, he was dressed all in black: suit, turtleneck and topcoat accented by a white silk scarf. A gray sable Russian hat sat on a side table. He looked dramatic, like a film director or a foreign spy rather than a church official.

I suppose his vitae held its own drama: He was regional sponsor of the Gabrians, skilled in administration and devoted to social causes. Beyond that, he was an astute politician. Not only within the church but also in secular Chicago.

The archbishop had always treated me with great warmth and pride, perhaps because of my deceased father. He appeared at auspicious times in my life, presiding over my confirmation and later my initiation into the Gabrians. I was curious, but never found a subtle or polite way to ask the reason why.

As always, he seemed concerned with my well-being. "How are you feeling?"

"A little sore but I'm fine."

"A shame about the murdered girl and Sister O'Sullivan. So much violence." He looked down, slowly shaking his head. After he had dispensed with the proprieties, he got to the point: "Recently it has come to my attention that a woman named Amber, a madam, came to Saint Sebastian's and left coded information with you in a little Bible and was later found murdered."

"Yes, Your Grace, all of that's true."

"Then Sister Mary Margaret O'Sullivan was kidnapped, beaten, and tortured in order to obtain the coded Bible. Is that right, my son?" the customary "my son" always sounded more personal coming from him.

"Yes, she suffered terribly and without cause," I said, pausing. "I blame myself." My thoughts flashed back to the horror in the warehouse and I said in a rush, "They didn't need to hurt her. I would have given them the codebook. The man who tortured her did it for no reason—"

"Evil, truly evil. God preserve us." He sighed. Here was a man who carried heavy burdens. "Please don't be too hard on yourself. How *is* Sister O'Sullivan?"

"Okay, I guess."

Archbishop Laine looked thoughtful, his lower lip forward. "We will, of course, get her the best counseling and whatever support or therapy or medications she may require."

We sat in silent meditation until the archbishop continued: "This unholy business happens to fall under the Gabrian purview. So, we need the code."

I shook my head. "I don't have it. I gave Sister Mary Margaret's copies to Detective Ditmar."

The archbishop leaned forward. "We need that information. The list may be detrimental to the church… if it includes clergy. We Gabrians must root them out before we have another public scandal."

Although he struggled to remain impassive, the archbishop's breathing came in uneven bursts. He looked at Monsignor Salvatore and then at me. "Deacon, *we need copies.* We must study them independently of the police."

"I'll do my best. The detective and I don't get along—"

"Make every effort. Please. Once you have, you are to step away from the investigation."

"Step away?" the monsignor burst in. "But Deacon is close to every aspect of this matter. Should the clergy be involved, as a Gabrian announcer, he could visit the perpetrators."

"Under other circumstances I might agree, old friend, but in this case Deacon is to leave it alone. Understood? The police are quite capable and my people… ahem… the department will keep me informed."

Monsignor Salvatore nodded, but his face reddened and he spoke through clenched teeth. "The cardinal has ordered this. I know it."

"Vito," the Archbishop said, his voice slicing the night air. "The cardinal has information we are not privy to. We must obey. You will continue to act as a conduit between the upper echelon and Deacon. And you will support him in other Gabrian business." He took a deep breath and gave us his blessing.

"I don't understand," I said, musing over the meeting as we walked to the monsignor's home.

"Weak," he retorted. "The archbishop may have a sophisticated intelligence network, but he cows to authority. He is not the ideal general to lead us in this battle."

Battle? We'd reached that level? And the archbishop and monsignor have separate intelligence networks? Interesting.

The monsignor continued, "The archbishop has an intelligence network to rival the CIA. He integrates the information to guide the diocese and, of course, the Gabrians. He keeps this intelligence close to the vest so I don't know all that he knows. I do know the cardinal has never been in our corner."

Sweet Jesus. I couldn't believe what I was hearing.

"The cardinal isn't supportive of the Gabrians? Why?"

"I don't know his reasons. But from what I hear, he accepts no Gabrian correspondence and acts as though we don't exist. In this one matter, he defers to Archbishop Laine."

"But if the cardinal doesn't support the Gabrians... and the archbishop is the regional sponsor... "

The monsignor bypassed my words and continued to speak his thoughts aloud. "Our cardinal has political enemies. He's outspoken about corruption, and he's irritated some powerful people. I respect his principles, but he needs to be more circumspect, less public about his opinions. More undercover—more Gabrian—in his approach. He knows how I feel, but he pays no heed."

I waited to see where the monsignor was headed.

"I want you to continue working on this case. Can you do it quietly?"

"Against the wishes of the archbishop... and the cardinal?"

Salvatore's eyes bore into me.

"Should I still get a copy of the code... for them?"

"If you can, certainly."

I knew Salvatore was passionate. I knew he wanted to lead the local Gabrians, not merely serve as a messenger from the upper echelon. But to go against his... our... superiors? Against the archbishop?

My thoughts flashed back to Army days, the times I'd done what I thought was best, against orders. This was just a different Army, after all, and I had personal scores to settle. The monsignor was actually giving me permission to do what I wanted to do.

"I'll do my best," I said, my usual noncommittal response.

"I thank you. Our Mother Church thanks you. I'll tell your pastor you are on assignment for the archbishop. Nothing must stand in the way of our mission."

Holy Mother of God. My feelings of unease had been on target before the visit. Now I felt like I *was* a target. I had just agreed to join the monsignor in going against orders from the archbishop and the cardinal. I had to deal with Detective Ditmar. I was hunting those who had murdered Amber and tortured Meg. And I would continue "announcing" for the Gabrians.

Not that I disagreed with any of it. Evil must be brought to justice, God's justice. Every time I felt the pain in my head, chin and shoulder, I knew it was personal. I kept seeing Amber's face and sister Mary Margaret in that dumpy warehouse.

It all came down to a bastard named Malachi.

CHAPTER FIFTEEN

After morning Mass, I gathered up a few papers and walked to the rectory to meet Pastor Posjena regarding the funeral of Allison De La Croix. She was still *Amber* to me, and my mind flashed to the night she was killed, how she looked, how I'd failed her.

Father Posjena's whining interrupted my dark thoughts. He wasn't happy with the call from Monsignor Salvatore. Of course he wasn't. He'd have to give up control over his personal servant and let me go whenever I pleased. I paid little attention to his complaints. He knew he had to follow orders... and stay sober occasionally... if he wanted to make monsignor.

A splash of pink on his robe told me he'd jumpstarted his day with communion wine. But that was none of my business. At least he wasn't slurring his words yet.

"The monsignor tells me you're working on a special project for him and the archbishop. All hush-hush."

"That's about it," I answered.

"Well, keep Saint Sebastian's out of it. I've run this parish for twenty years, and I don't want you interfering with my success here."

Success. I had to choke back a laugh. He did practically nothing but cater to the wealthy in our congregation. "I'll do my best."

He nodded and squinted. "You do that."

I sat behind the desk in my sparse office in the rectory. The two other chairs filled the tiny room. Light from a small window illuminated a stylized crucifix on the wall. I closed my eyes and began to pray.

He died for our sins, I repeated to myself. If I were forgiven, why did I feel so hollow inside? For the thousandth time, I saw the young rape victims' eyes fill with tears... the cuts on Meg's body... Amber's battered face. My Lord challenges my faith. Yet I must trust in Him.

A loud buzzer announced my visitor. The pastor had declined to join us, clearly wanting nothing to do with the funeral of a murdered prostitute. When I opened the door, I blinked in shock—and pure masculine appreciation. The woman was tall, stunning... and she looked like a more elegant version of Amber.

She extended her arm, cocked her head sideways, a question in those blue-green eyes. "Deacon Adelius? I'm Ann Drew... Allison's sister... um, Drew is my married name."

I took her hand, finally. "Yes, I'm Deacon Adelius. I'm sorry, but I was taken aback by the resemblance." This was only partly true. "I'm so sorry about your sister. May God be with her ... and you."

Ann closed her eyes for a moment and swallowed hard. "Thank you."

I pointed to a chair and she sat, trying to smile and failing. "Before we discuss the funeral, I need to know... " She paused, took a deep breath and began again. "I understand you were with her that... night."

Ann Drew didn't know what she was asking. "Maybe we should talk about that at another time. It could be upsetting... so soon after her death."

"No, please. I need to know," Her gaze was direct and determined. "Did she say anything?"

"Your sister was badly injured, and rambling. She said she had to get away, that someone was trying to kill her." I paused, hoping that was enough information.

"And... "

I wondered how much should I reveal to her about her sister and how much should I withhold? I saw no reason to talk about the little Bible or its contents. "Well," I said finally, "she mentioned the names Tamara and Andy."

Neither of us spoke for a long while. I tried not to look at the long legs peeking out from under her long camel coat or even the auburn hair with a hint of curl. There was no denying it. I wanted to take her in my arms and console her, a feeling I had almost forgotten. She was grieving... and married. I should feel guilty.

But I didn't.

She looked away, avoiding my eyes. "I don't know a Tamara."

Her body language made me suspect it was a lie.

"But I can clear up one thing. I'm Andy. It's been Allison's pet name for me since we were children."

One small mystery solved.

"I understand you were injured as well," she said.

"Minor injuries. Your sister shot the man who was about to kill me. She saved my life and then he... the other man... well, that was the end."

Ann stared into the middle space between us. "She was practically fearless. Even as a kid."

"You've spoken to the police... "

"Of course. I identified her body."

"Must have been tough."

Ann nodded. "We were pretty close. I knew all about... her lifestyle. I loved my sister, but I knew she was in... the game."

She shrugged out of her coat but kept it on her shoulders, revealing a ribbed, brown sweater and tan tweed-looking skirt. I noticed and appreciated fashion more than other men... maybe because I'd been surrounded by institutional uniforms much of my life—Catholic school, the Army, the seminary.

"Well," she said. "Allison was going to ... get out of that line of work." Ann drifted then, her eyes glassy with tears. "We were going into business together." She looked down, struggling to regain composure.

I focused on her short brown boots. I was struggling, too. The woman had me mesmerized. *Get a grip.* I cleared my throat. "What kind of work do you do?"

She took a couple of deep breaths. "I have a spa on Michigan Avenue—women only. We have facials, massages, exercise classes, hot mineral baths, the works. You probably think it's frivolous."

"I try not to judge." I sounded as stuffy as a musty old priest. I tried to recover, to sound more like myself. "That's nice. Sounds … um …. rejuvenating for women."

"We were going to be partners, run the spa and open another." She covered her face with her hands. "Now she'll never have a chance to change." Ann was full-out weeping now. "We were always close… except for her business. Now she's gone."

Eventually Ann and I did manage to make the arrangements: flowers, music, the eulogy, and cavalcade to St. Adelbert's Cemetery. The sisters had plots already reserved.

"We were raised Catholic—baptism, communion, confirmation— the whole bit. We fell away, as they say, but I do want her service in the church." That opened a floodgate of tears. I hated to see women cry. They seemed so vulnerable, and I always wanted to help. Sometimes I overdid it. I'd performed this service with grieving women before, though none as lovely as this one.

Thankfully, my training and experience clicked in. I slid a box of tissues toward my visitor and looked out the window while she regained her composure.

Ann coughed slightly to get my attention, but she needn't have. My senses were so tuned to her that I could hear and feel every movement. "Thank you for making this bearable," she said. "I'd like to talk to you again… about Allison and myself. It would be a relief to me. Would that be all right?"

Her words were an unexpected gift. "Certainly. Do you want to include your husband?" God, I thought, that was as subtle as a stick in the eye.

"I'm a widow—the Gulf." She rose to slip into her coat, preparing to leave.

"I'm so sorry. A lot of good men didn't come home." Images of Iraq flooded my consciousness. I drove them away, but Ann must have seen the shadow cross my face.

"You were there."

I nodded.

As I opened the door to let her out, her hair brushed my cheek. It smelled of cloves.

If she saw Iraq in my face, what else had she seen? I think I blushed then, when her back was turned. Outside my office, we said our goodbyes again, and I watched her walk to her car. Gracefully.

I looked forward to seeing her again … and soon.

But a steamroller of bad memories ran over me the instant she drove away. Iraq mentioned twice in two days was too much for me. Why didn't the good memories come back—the camaraderie, the laughs, the bravery? Somehow, the good had faded. What remained burned in my memory was the heat and filth, the violence and the bestiality of the men.

Worst were the crimes against the children, especially when the perpetrators were other soldiers. The troops were young, frightened and filled with testosterone. For a few bucks, they could forget their fears in all the perverse delights imaginable.

As an MP, I'd arrested them. I had my own ideas on justice. I'd "re-educated" some of them. And I'd been formally chastised a few times. A moral standard of behavior existed in the military, but there were lots of gray areas.

As the flashbacks pounded me, my anxiety grew. I'd have to spend some time with the bag in the basement again tonight. That was the only way I knew to fight the demons that bombarded me from the hot days, cold nights, stinking bars and back alleys of the desert.

CHAPTER SIXTEEN

Finally I found time to see Leo. I climbed the back stairs above Giovanni's Pizza Palace and knocked on his office door, Leo let me in himself. "Hey Deac, how you doin'?" We exchanged a quick hug. "Come in. I just opened some *primo vino*. Have a glass with crackers and clams. *Salud!*"

"*Salud!*" I said and got down to business. "So, Leo, you wanted to see me. First, let me confess that I took Glitter out for a coffee the other night. Don't hold it against her. I needed some information on another woman in the... um... business."

Leo's mood—always volatile—went into overdrive. "You think that's why I called? Like my Ma used to say, you don't know bad cheese." His mouth turned up on the side like a gangster. "I don't give a shit if you talk to one of my girls or take 'em out for tea or fuck their brains out in the choir loft. Something serious is goin down."

Serious business? I had no idea what he was talking about. He had my full irritable attention. "Okay wise-ass, what's going down?"

"That's what I was goin' to ask you." Leo was near shouting. "Here's the thing... " He started pacing and waving his arms, not taking his eyes off me. "The night after you talked to Glitter, she picks up a well-heeled john. He takes her to a fancy hotel on Lake Shore Drive. She gets there and there's another guy waitin' in this suite on the top floor with a fuckin' Halloween mask on. Now, mind you, I got all of this from her roommate, Heather. What do you supposed these creeps do?"

Leo took a long sip of his wine. "Those cocksuckers make her undress and kneel out on the fuckin' balcony, bare-ass naked. Shit, it's got to be ten below zero outside. Then they ask her what she and you talked about. She told 'em right off. I mean I don't blame her. She's freezin' her tits off out there. But they act like they don't believe her and keep askin' her over and over.

Anyway, one of the johns, an asshole with a cane, hurts her in some real bad way. I don't know what. She wouldn't even tell Heather. Anyway, Heather says Glitter was scared shitless—I mean she was outa her fuckin' mind, scared. She packs, empties her bank accounts and takes off. Later, Heather finds blood all over the bathroom floor."

Leo stopped pacing. "Glitter didn't tell Heather where she's goin', nothin. Just tells her to say goodbye to me, and just like that, she's outa here. I would have found that prick and taken care of him good. You know what I mean? I thought Glitter knew that. So... " Leo was red in the face and spilling wine all over the floor, he was so mad. Nobody messed with his girls. "So, I ask you again, what the fuck's goin' on?"

I shook my head. "I don't know exactly. I wouldn't have talked to Glitter if I'd known it was going to get her into trouble. Shit." I felt like somebody had squeezed the breath out of me. I fell into a chair. The suffering was multiplying... and it was all connected to me. "So sorry." The words came out in a gasp. An apology was worthless. I had to find these bastards. Three women brutalized on my doorstep.

"You're sorry? I'm out real income here." Leo had turned all tough guy. Glitter had been with him the longest of all his girls and I knew he cared what happened to her. But even though I suspected he was faking the money angle, I wasn't backing down on *that* subject.

"I'm not apologizing for *that*, my friend. You know I don't approve of your flesh peddling. We don't do slavery in this country any more."

He rose up to his full five feet six inches. "Listen, you long drink of holy water, I take care of my girls. Ask anyone. I'm *glad* you helped Glitter get off crack. I'm *glad* she was going to beauty school. She had to leave the street soon anyhow or really go downhill. She wasn't cuttin' it anymore, y'know? Younger snatch out there."

I took a couple of deep breaths, trying to ratchet down my temper. Leo and I went way back… middle school even. "All I did was show her a *business* card from a woman who crashed into Saint Sebastian's all beat up and scared. I wanted to find out who the hell she was." I flashed him the card from my pocket.

Leo grabbed the card from my hand and looked at it closely. "Amber, huh? You shoulda asked me. I know Amber. Runs high-class pussy. I heard she was settin' herself up to retire soon."

"Well in case you didn't catch the *Tribune* a few days ago, Amber was fished out of the Chicago River, wearing my sweatshirt."

"Holy shit. Murdered, huh?"

I looked down at the wine swirling in my glass. "Someone must've seen Glitter and me talking. God, I just pulled her right into this." We drank in silence. "One of Amber's murderers had a cane. He's a sick son of a bitch. Glitter could've been killed, too." We both backed off letting our emotions settle. Leo had gone off the boil quickly. "Have some more *vino*," he said by way of apology. "We're *pisanos*. I don't blame you. She does need to get out of the business, but not that way. I hope she's got money. Tell you what, if she calls, I'll send her some dough, as a going-away present. How's that?"

"That would be fine. And if *you* hear from her, tell her I'm sorry. Better yet, have her call me so I'll tell her myself."

Leo clenched a fist. "If I find out who scared her and hurt her so bad, I *will* pay him a visit."

"Call me, if you hear anything. There's a cop sniffin' around, too. Says he's on the case."

"Who?"

"Detective Rick Ditmar."

Leo shook his head. "Don't know him. Don't want to know him. I'll nose around on my own."

We clinked our glasses again and finished the wine. Leo insisted that I take a bottle with me.

I raised the bottle in thanks. "Listen. Don't be a stranger at Mass. And I expect a little something extra in the basket, *capisci?*"

"Yeah, yeah, okay," said Leo. "But don't blame me if Saint Sebastian's goes tumblin' down when I come in. *Ciao, compagno.*"

CHAPTER SEVENTEEN

"Well, Mitch, are we clear or what?" The skin around Frank's eyes twitched with nervousness.

"Soon." Mitch Halloran wasn't prone to anxiety. Muscular and impressive in either a police uniform or business suit, his deep voice boomed confidence. The former Marine was a shoo-in for mayor, given his backing by practically everyone in Chicago politics.

State Senator Frank Clayton had a good chance at the governorship, thanks to support from minorities and scandals in the current administration. Single, he had a boyish charm that attracted women to the voting booth.., and his bed. But he was always worried. Maybe it was the strain of being a light-skinned black man walking the line between black and white worlds.

The two men's paths crossed naturally several times. Clayton had introduced Halloran to the use of "professional" women to put opponents in compromising positions. Such positions were useful in manipulating their opponents' behavior and obtaining their financial support. As Clayton always said, "It's a matter of *allocating resources*."

Halloran had been a decent cop in the beginning, but his corruption had spread like an infection from small bribes to piles of drug money. His wife, Helen, had her own dalliances, but she was careful. Mitch had a definite cruel streak.

The two politicians kept an uneasy alliance. The duo enjoyed full war chests from various special interest groups, bribes and "assessments." If both were elected in eight months, they would exert considerable control in Chicago and Illinois—possibly a swing state in the next presidential election.

It was Clayton's idea to escape the daily grind by taking private booze cruises on Lake Michigan, the yachts provided by their supporters. Appropriate playmates were selected carefully by Clayton through Amber, his favorite madam. In the winter months they could use one of the suites at the yacht club.

The last such outing had ended in disaster.

To these men it was unthinkable that a dependable whore-madam like Amber would try to shake them down. They'd been her best clients for years. Now Amber was safely gone, her death untraceable to them, and they were relieved. The only remaining concern was any evidence that she could have left behind. She'd claimed irrefutable proof of their most serious crimes and their cover-ups. She had demanded hush money—big money.

"Can you trust this Malachi?" Clayton asked.

"You can't trust anyone, but Malachi's done sensitive work for me before. He's in my pocket. Besides, it's just business. He performs, and he gets paid. He'll find Amber's so-called proof." Halloran threw back a shot of single malt. "Relax, Frank. You'll drive me nuts." Clayton sipped his chardonnay and continued to pace.

Amber had been a major wake-up call for both of them.

Halloran held up Amber's bible/codebook. As police commissioner, Halloran had all the resources of the Chicago Police Department at his disposal. Selecting a code-breaker was critical. He did not want to trade one blackmailer for another.

CHAPTER EIGHTEEN

Norman Balthazar, computer wizard from the INTEL Division of the Chicago Police Department, was running for his life. He'd always been at a desk, never seen street action. Now he was dodging bullets in a dingy underground parking garage.

Oil slicks looked like car droppings in the half-deserted garage. Overhead lights cast eerie shadows among the support columns and vehicles. It was a dismal place to die.

Norman had been assigned a simple decoding project by Commissioner Halloran, who told him to keep it confidential. The secret job was child's play for Norman. He cracked the code and double-checked it in three hours.

What he found was not child's play, and Norman was scared. But he also saw the project as the hand up he needed. All he wanted was some recognition and a promotion. That was hard to come by for a tech expert in INTEL. After this project he thought he had it made.

When he'd decoded the little Bible, he asked to see Halloran, as he had been instructed. Norman was instantly admitted to a private office suite. Wall-to-wall windows, sleek modern furniture and objects d'art in subtle earth tones. The office reeked of power.

Norman was careful. He knew that what he had to report was a bombshell. *Hell, it was a nuclear bomb.*

He presented his findings concisely, accurately and without comment or interpretation. The biblical references used the initial letters of the first two words as the initials of Amber's clients. The letters were reversed and a person had to go backward through the alphabet according to the number *preceding* the letters to determine the correct letters. The numbers and letters following the biblical references indicated heterosexual, homosexual, bi-sexual, gender, S & M preferences, number of partners, pedophiles, special trips, fantasies, sex toys used, etc.

The first part read like a Who's Who of Chicago: business leaders, clergymen, bankers, attorneys, police and politicians. High on this list were State Senator Frank Clayton and Mitch Halloran. When Norman read Halloran's name from the list, the commissioner showed no emotion. He stared out at the Merchandise Mart and a section of the bleak Chicago River. His hands were clasped behind his back at parade rest, a term Norman remembered from a semester of ROTC.

"Anything else?"

"One critical item, sir. There is mention of a DVD."

Halloran remained impassive, but he turned to face the tech. "I see. How many and where are they?"

"The material refers to one original. No data exists on a location."

"How many people know of your findings?"

"None, sir."

"And your work product?"

"All here, sir. There are no copies, nothing on the computer or anywhere else. Here is the Bible, the decoded translation and the copies you gave me." Halloran took the materials.

"You've done extremely well." Halloran managed a smile. "Great work kept confidential is deserving of reward and recognition. You are currently a D-2 with the pay-grade of five, is that correct?"

"Yes, sir."

"Let's move you to a D-4 supervisor's position, pay-grade twelve."

Norman had tried to remain calm, but inside, he'd turned somersaults. This was far more than he'd hoped for. "Thank you, sir."

"I also see a special cash bonus showing up very soon in your future."

Norman could only nod and smile.

"Absolute secrecy, you understand."

"Of course, sir."

"We'll talk from time to time about your career advancement. Again, great work."

They shook hands.

The man who held the list had power in his hands, a source list for future campaign contributions and beyond.

After a grateful Balthazar left, Halloran made a call.

That was only four hours ago. Norman was acutely aware that he'd been a fool. A fool to trust Halloran. A fool without a backup plan to cover his ass, And he prided himself on his brains. *This was stupid, really dumb,*

Except for the one gunshot, the man who hunted him was silent. The bullet meant for Norman had ricocheted off the doorframe of his car, narrowly missing his head. He'd feel like a sitting duck trying to start the balky car in freezing temperatures, so he took off running, his dress shoes clomping like wooden clogs. *Shit.* Too easy to track.

Fuck the cold. He removed his shoes and threw them in a trash barrel. Norman had two things going for him. He was a long distance runner, and he knew this garage. He'd parked there daily for three years.

As he ran down from the upper levels to the lower, there were fewer and fewer cars. He was out in the open. When he hit the bottom floor, his pursuer would think he was trapped. But Norman had passed over the threshold of fear and was focused on survival. He had a plan.

Another shot rang out – way off target. Either the shooter was trying to scare him or he was a bad shot.

Norman was terrified, but his brain was working. Think and live, he thought. If … no, when I get out of this, I'm going to the district attorney. He's not on the list. I'll have Halloran's ass in a sling.

Norman wanted to live. Halloran underestimated me, he thought. The boss fucked with the wrong guy. Funny thing was, I wouldn't have talked. I don't give a shit about the sex lives of those people.

When he hit the lowest level, Norman was in the open. He ran hard, faster than he'd ever run a road race. The square columns stretched before him like concrete soldiers on parade. He headed for the northeast corner... to the one-person elevator used by the parking attendants. It was on a continuous loop. No doors. You just stepped onto the moving platform and ascended.

If he could make it, he'd be whisked to ground level. His pursuer would be left at the bottom. Once there, he'd step out onto Dearborn Street and safety.

Another shot rang out. Closer this time. Norman ran in a zigzag pattern. He dodged behind a pillar, slid on an oil slick and went down. A big man was bearing down on him, gun drawn, but the guy was breathing hard... slowing down.

Norman's adrenalin rush spurred him forward. He wove between the square supporting columns, heading for the elevator. Reflections off the oily cables showed the platform was moving. *Hurry. Hurry,* he muttered to himself. He couldn't miss his only chance.

A yellow *down* arrow signaled the arrival of the next platform. Norman refused to die in this stinking underground garage. He had one chance and took it—dashed into the open, jumped two feet up and made it onto the open platform.

"Oh, shit," shouted a voice behind him.

Shots rang out. A searing pain cut through Norman's right calf muscle, and then he was safe, rising in a closed tube like a rocket emerging from a silo. The big guy was too slow to reach the next level before he did. Even if he did, Norman would be out of the garage and onto the street before the man reached the surface.

He'd made it.

Norman took in a deep breath of satisfaction. He glanced at his leg. Not bad. The wound burned, but the bullet hadn't hit bone. Probably a flesh wound.

Up and up he went--fourth, third, second ... ground floor. The little elevator didn't stop, so he prepared to jump. As he did, his leg buckled and he fell. A security guard rushed toward him. "Harold," the metal nametag on his uniform jacket read.

"Help me, please... Harold," Norman cried.

"Certainly, sir."

Norman thought it was odd to see a security guard with a cane,

The "security guard" helped him up with one hand, raised the cane with the other and brought it down on Norman's head.

Sixty seconds later Bernie stepped off the one-man elevator.

"Drag him out of sight," Malachi said. "Take his wallet and watch. The cops will call it a mugging."

Two hours later, perplexed investigators found a body with a cracked skull and flesh wound to the lower leg. The dead man wore an ID lanyard that read *Norman Balthazar, INTEL Chicago Police Department*. He had no wallet, no watch and—oddly in this weather—no shoes.

CHAPTER NINETEEN

Allison De La Croix's funeral service was a surreal snapshot of another subculture. Next to Ann in the first pew was a transvestite introduced to me as "Micky." He was six feet tall in high-heeled black and silver boots with a matching skin-tight suit and fur jacket.

Ann was dressed in basic black with no discernable make-up, in contrast to the *working girls* scattered throughout the church. They were stylishly dressed, wearing dark colors. Most wore boots. Several had fur coats. No doubt they were women who had worked for Amber.

Three sprays of flowers—one in questionable taste featuring pink so-called little boy flowers—were arranged on tripods next to the closed casket. One tripod displayed seven photos of Allison from infancy to womanhood. The battered woman I met that night in the church bore scant resemblance to the flawless face in the pictures.

Detective Rick Ditmar stood next to the ancient baptismal font at the rear of the church, obviously scrutinizing those in attendance. Also in the back was the usual assortment homeless people—those smart enough to slip into the warm church for open services of any kind. They were as unobtrusive as shadows. When I was in charge, I let them stay until after the service was over.

One of the church cantors sang "Amazing Grace" a cappella to open the service. I greeted as many mourners as I could. As part of my consolation commentary—I included all present in the hope of eternal life. I mentioned that Allison had come to the church at the end of her life, and that we had talked. I gave no details.

By strict liturgical law, eulogies were not permitted, but I always allowed those close to the deceased to say a few words if they wanted. I was known to screw with the rules. *What the hell.*

Ann approached the ambo with dignity and grace. Her short eulogy was about her sister's generosity and their closeness when they were younger. "She gave me part of herself that I might live," said Ann, "and never considered the consequences." Ann wept softly and then explained that when they were in their early twenties, her sister had given her one of her kidneys.

I thought of the parallel of Christ giving himself to humankind so that we might live. As Ann spoke, I began to understand more about the terrified woman I'd met as Amber. She'd been courageous even before she shot at our assailants.

Ann continued, "Our plans for our future together were cut short by evil. I hope she's in a more peaceful place now." She stepped down from the raised platform and touched the coffin. "I love you, Alli," she said quietly, though most could hear.

I incensed the casket and slowly recited the "Twenty-Third Psalm," concluding with "*Donna Nobis Pacem.*" The cantor concluded the service singing "How Great Thou Art," which always sends chills up and down my spine.

I'd managed to remain professional, not too distracted by Ann. But when she embraced me briefly after the service, as she had several others, it was electrifying.

"Thank you for everything," she said.

I think I managed a "You're welcome. God be with you," but I'm not sure.

For a while, Ann remained alone with the casket. I asked the homeless people to leave and waited for Ann to leave, so I could lock up. Walking out, I noticed a tall, white-haired man standing to the side of the main doors. He looked distinguished in his long Chesterfield coat.

I couldn't see his eyes behind tinted glasses, but he smiled sadly, as he held out his arms to Ann.

She walked to him, but instead of accepting his embrace, slapped his face. "Bastard," she said, through clenched teeth. Then she rushed down the church steps.

He didn't follow.

I approached the man. "My name is Deacon Adelius. I'm sorry. Ann is very upset."

"I know," he said, extending a gloved hand. "I'm William De La Croix. Her... their father."

CHAPTER TWENTY

"Thank you for the beautiful service. As you've probably guessed by Ann's display, we are estranged."

I nodded, trying to read the man. Estranged? *That was an understatement. What could he have done to deserve this?* De La Croix's slumped shoulders and tremulous voice showed a man in anguish.

De La Croix's dark eyebrows were knit tight. "I want to change that. It's too late for Allison, but I'd like to be there for Ann." He pulled a black snakeskin wallet out of his pocket and handed me a business card. "You've met both my daughters…" His voice broke. "Ann seems to trust you. If you see her, could you tell her, please … tell her I love her."

I promised, and he hurried to his silver BMW. I could only guess at his pain at losing a child… to murder. *God help you, William De La Croix.* I looked around at the people still gathered outside the church. A heavy-set man in a dark topcoat was watching from across the street. He turned away abruptly when I glanced in his direction.

Once again, I drove to Grant Hospital. The winter-bare trees looked like skeletons hovering over the streets and sidewalks. People walked hurriedly, hunched over to protect themselves from the icy wind whipping off the lake. This visit with Mary Margaret had to go better than the previous one.

Ann Drew kept intruding on my thoughts… beautiful in grief… beautiful in anger. I could still feel her embrace. Where the hell was this going? I tried to put her out of my mind. Couldn't do it.

As I entered the hospital, I spotted a hefty man leaning against a late model Cadillac. Was it the same man I'd noticed outside the church? Coincidence? I couldn't be sure. Why the hell would someone follow me?

The man held a cell phone to his ear briefly and drove away, but not before I got a good look at him: Six feet tall, maybe 250 pounds, blondish, military haircut, clean shaven, thick neck. Hell, he looked like thousands of other middle-aged Chicago men.

Meg looked one hundred percent better than the last time I'd seen her. Her hair was washed and combed. The facial swellings had gone down. She was even sitting up in bed watching TV. Commissioner Mitch Halloran was on screen giving his usual spiel on fighting Chicago crime. Applause nearly drowned out his booming voice. The guy was charismatic, I'd give him that.

"Morning, Meg," I chimed with my best smile. "I see you're well enough to stomach the commissioner."

"Hey, good morning yourself." She dismissed Halloran with a wave of her hand and clicked off the TV. "Enough of that. Whatcha got behind your back?"

I handed her a two-pound box of chocolates.

"Oh, Fannie Mae, yummy." She tore open the cellophane, popped a candy in her mouth and held out the box. "Take one, quick. Otherwise I'll eat them all."

I was glad she liked the chocolates. It's my fault she's here.

I sat on the edge of her bed and took her hand. "So, how's the patient?"

"Better. I still hurt when I move, and I'm bored. But I'm energized now that we're in bed together." She giggled.

What a glorious sound. "You wicked lady... off to confession for those impure thoughts."

"As if you were immune."

She seemed her old self, but I knew how real PTSD was. I watched for any delayed reaction to the horror she had experienced.

"So, don't just sit there with your bare face hanging out," she said. "Tell me the news."

"Fox News Halloran isn't enough for you?"

She scoffed, and I gave her a rundown of the funeral with its odd attendees and the incident between Ann and her father. Meg made the appropriate noises and asked about the code.

"I gave it to the detective. I'll ask him for a copy."

"You don't have to. It's on my computer, file name: "holycode." She paused and smirked at me. "*If* you can get to it."

"Are you calling me a tech idiot?"

"Well—"

"Yeah, you're right, but I can do basics. Give me your user name and I.D. I'll get it." We didn't talk about the incident that had put her in the hospital.

She told me her daily routine, the other patients and her visitors, making the hospital stay sound like an adventure. Street characters from her soup kitchen had brought strange gifts—stolen flowers, a battered Romance novel, and a baggie of marijuana. "For medicinal purposes, Harry told me. He was *so* serious."

We laughed over that one and chatted some more. I mentioned something vague about Allison's sister being, "quite a woman."

Meg didn't let that slide. "Quite a woman," she repeated. "What's going on here?"

"Nothing. It's just... um... people deal so differently with the death of a loved one."

"Oh, I see. Just an observation." She smirked again and rolled her eyes at the ceiling,

After more banter and more chocolates, I kissed Sister Mary Margaret goodbye.

On the way out, I was hyperaware of all the people milling about. Staff, family, visitors and delivery people, and no visible security. Damn, Meg was way too vulnerable here.

CHAPTER TWENTY-ONE

Malachi waited in the tiny rehearsal room he'd rented by the hour at Chicago's music conservatory. Private, sound proof, rear entrance. Perfect for *business* meetings. He tried to pick out "My Way," on the well-used Steinway.

"Time for next steps," Halloran said as he entered and took the other straight-back chair. "Get the nun's computer. I have the coded Bible and printouts she made, but she'll probably have a copy on the computer."

"No problem."

"No problem, huh? Assuming we get to the computer first. And there's a DVD out there we've got to find. Any ideas?" He leaned back in his chair and cracked his knuckles.

"DVD, huh… " Malachi rested his chin on the talon head of his cane and thought out loud. "As I see it, we let the deacon do our searchin'. He's a sucker for the 'hero-savior' role. We'll use the nun or the whore's sister as incentive." Malachi switched gears. "The DVD isn't in our original agreement."

"I thought you might go there," Halloran said.

"Hey, business is business."

"Get it done and soon. First the computer, then the video." He slapped a manila envelope on the piano keys, making a discordant sound. "Here's a packet to inspire you. You'll get another just like it when we have them. There's one other piece of business." Halloran paused. "I need you to take a contract."

"Who's the target?"

The commissioner gave him a steely glare. "A Prince."

"What?"

"A prince, complete with scarlet robes and a mitre. Head of the largest organization in Chicago. And it's got to look like an accident."

"Malachi whistled when he heard the name. I'll get on it." He smiled and reached for the envelope, but Halloran grabbed his hand.

"This is for all three. Got it? The computer, the video *and* the hit."

Malachi yanked his hand back from Halloran's grip. One eye strayed as he fixed Halloran in a malevolent stare.

The men glowered at each other like two cobras, who'd met unexpectedly.

No more was said.

Halloran left, and Malachi counted the packs of bills. A hefty payment, for sure. And another half to come. Now he had to get the damned computer out of the convent. Once that was done, he'd get to this deacon character and track down the DVD. Then he'd worry about the assassination.

To get the computer, he'd need a woman.

CHAPTER TWENTY-TWO

The payoff was good. Rosa could play the simple dramatic role, but first she'd had to satisfy *him*. An involuntary shudder ran through her body. Disgust, humiliation and a touch of terror. That was sex with Malachi. She thought she'd hardened herself to those things, but not quite.

He wore a mask throughout, running his cane along her naked body, prodding her with its silver tip, gently at first. She followed his detailed sexual instructions while he remained nearly motionless, except for the hellish cane. "You're particularly plain, perfectly suited to my purpose," he'd told her. Rosa ignored the insult, grateful that she hadn't been hurt. Just a scratch on her left breast.

She took an extra long shower, scrubbing off his touch. Malachi was squeaky clean, physically, but she still felt dirty. Like some unseen filth lay beneath his skin. She tried to throw off the feeling. Some johns were worse than others. Justine had taken over from Amber, and Rosa felt she couldn't say no. Besides, the worst was over. And the money was good.

She'd played many unpleasant fantasy games as one of Amber's girls, and she could always make her johns believe she was having a good time. But Malachi hired her to play a different sort of role, a relatively easy one. It made no sense to her, but she knew better than to ask questions.

Rosa spent a couple of hours on a frigid blustery day observing the nuns of Saint Catherine's. Then she purchased her costume at a thrift store: non-descript gray skirted suit, sensible black shoes a woman like her wouldn't be caught dead in, baggy brown sweater and olive green car coat. She added a short head veil, wire rimmed reading glasses and a cheap crucifix on a chain.

She stripped off her makeup, pulled her thick black hair into a tight bun, sprayed on touches of gray and looked in the mirror. A satisfied smile gazed back at her, Rosa set off for the convent with a manly gait.

She pushed open the large oak door. Approaching the reception desk, she said, "Good day. I'm Sister Roseanna here to see Sister Conselleta." Rosa had called earlier to determine exactly when the mother superior would be out.

"Hi," said the young receptionist. "Sister is not in. Can I help you?"

"No, my dear. It's Sister Conselleta I need to see. Will she be long?"

"I'm not sure, probably not too long."

"Could I sit and wait for a while? I'm quite tired from the bus ride."

"Sure." The teen pointed to a small waiting room.

"And where might I freshen up?"

The girl waved her to the right, "Down the hall."

"Thank you, dear. Oh, and may I ask, how is Sister Mary Margaret O'Sullivan? Is she better?"

"Yes." The receptionist showed some interest in this question. "I heard she was. Ain't it awful what happened to her?"

"Yes, awful. Will she be able to get to her room all right?" Rosa smiled slightly, smugly. She was so very good at fishing for information,

"I should think so. She's only one flight up."

This was going to be too easy. "Thank you, dear. Sister Mary Margaret spoke of having a good view from her room. Which way does she face?"

The girl's face brightened as she provided the insider answers she was privy to. "For sure her view is great. I've been in her room. It's in front and faces The Loop."

"Well, that's nice for her." When the young girl turned away to answer the phone, Rosa hurried down the hall toward the restroom. Before she got there, she glanced back quickly, ascended the stairs and turned to the right on the second floor.

She found Sister Mary Margaret's room in less than two minutes. The nameplate on the door made it easy. That was it. She was home free.

Rosa descended quietly and adopted her slow clumsy walk as she passed the young clerk. "I'm going to step out for a few moments; I'll be right back." *No way in hell,* she thought.

Outside, she pulled out her cell phone and punched in a number. "Room 228 on the second floor, front of the building." She broke the phone contact and said aloud, "Asshole!" A middle-aged couple stopped dead in their tracks to hear a nun cuss out loud. Rosa laughed. They'd enjoy telling their friends about the nun who swore in public. Another Catholic gone nuts.

Two thousand bucks for a half-day's work. This was a change from screwing overweight businessmen. She hurried home to discard her ugly costume.

She wondered, briefly, why anyone would want the precise location of a nun's room in a convent? But she quickly forgot the question as she counted the hundred dollar bills to make sure it was all there.

CHAPTER TWENTY-THREE

At one-thirty a.m., a man wearing black with surgical gloves and a ski mask inserted a pick into the rear door lock of Saint Catherine's.

Bernie found Mary Margaret's room quickly from Rosa's description and swept the beam of his skinny flashlight around the room, illuminating a statue of the Holy Virgin. Bernie hesitated. Bad karma.

What the hell? Averting his eyes, he concentrated on the computer, disconnecting the cables. He opened a few drawers, looking for a DVD. No time for more. He stuck the flashlight in his mouth and carried out the computer.

He almost made it.

Outside, a young man was returning one of the girls who had snuck out for the night.

"Hey, whatcha doin?" the boy blurted. The girl screamed when she saw the ski mask.

"Shut the fuck up, both of you," said Bernie. He looked to see if anyone else was around.

The street tough came closer, ready for action.

Bernie kicked him in the shins. As the boy bent over, he slammed his head with the edge of the computer. Blood gushed from the kid's temple, and he collapsed without another sound.

The girl stood wide-eyed, knuckles to her mouth. Petrified.

"Look sweet thing. Stay quiet until I leave, and you won't get hurt. Got it?"

She nodded vigorously. But Bernie wasn't convinced. He set down the computer, dumped out her purse and smashed her cell phone. "Gimme his phone." Trembling, she followed his instructions, and Bernie smashed that one on the pavement.

"Now, you gonna be good?" Bernie snickered. "I'm outa here—for now-- but I still know my way around this place. I *could* come back for you. So, you be still and quiet for a few minutes."

Sobbing, the girl knelt on the cold pavement beside her unconscious boyfriend.

Bernie returned with the computer.

"Any problems?" Malachi asked.

"Not much. As I was leaving, some punk was bringing his little fuckfriend back to the convent. I shut him up. They didn't see nuthin'. I was still wearing the mask."

Malachi frowned but didn't comment. "Next, we pay Amber's sister a visit and look for that DVD. If it isn't in her apartment, we'll find out what she knows." His eyelids drooped and his mouth turned up at the edges. "Yes, we'll *extract* that information. Soon." He licked his lips.

CHAPTER TWENTY-FOUR

After Mass, I received a summons from Detective Ditmar. He had a lot of nerve. I was pissed by his attitude, but I'd been a cop, so I didn't hate the police with the same passion our parishioners did. They saw all cops as insensitive, intimidating and even brutal. I could be more discerning and pick out the specific few bad apples. Sure, they were less than perfect, but I knew they had a challenging and thankless job. As for intimidation, I used it myself on abusers and pedophiles within the Church. It was efficient and it felt right to scare the crap out of those hypocritical bastards.

The station was swarming with cops, and desks were littered with half empty coffees and Cokes. It was a bustling place and smelled of stale cigarette smoke, body odor and the fear, the latter oozing from the pores of anxious people hoping for mercy... or justice ... or escape. The grayish walls reeked of institutional dullness and a heavy wash of disinfectant.

Ditmar's summons and the station itself had put me in a foul mood. But the detective's third-floor office was surprisingly neat. His polished mahogany desk was stacked with folders on one side of an emerald green blotter and a computer monitor and keyboard on the other. He wasn't smiling, and he didn't rise to greet me.

"Deacon Adelius, please take a seat. I asked you to come here to discuss recent events surrounding Allison De La Croix's murder."

His little speech was unnaturally formal. Not a good sign. "You're holding out on me, and I'm pissed," he continued.

He was right, but I don't know what made me do it. Maybe pride, maybe mistrust. The little key with the arrows was burning a hole in my left trouser pocket, but I wasn't giving it up. I played innocent. "What are you talking about?"

"First, why did you go to Sister Mary Margaret's room? What did you take? Don't deny it. I was at the convent this morning and heard all about it."

The man must be under pressure from somewhere. Was he losing his memory or playing a power game? "What the hell are you getting at? You asked me to get the code, remember? I got it. I gave the copies to your men."

"Next time tell me and I'll get the copies myself," he muttered. "Do you know a Ronnie Sheridan... a young tough?"

Where was he going with all this? "I know a lot of kids... might know him if I saw him. Why?"

"He was assaulted behind Saint Catherine's late last night. Apparently he and one of the girls interrupted a burglary.... Sister Mary Margaret O'Sullivan's computer was taken. Now why do you suppose some yahoo would do that?"

"To get the codes?"

"Right."

Damn. I hadn't acted quickly enough. Now they were gone.

"There's more. What do you know of Ann Drew?" With every question, I was more on guard.

"She's the sister of Allison De La Croix."

"Did you know Ann Drew aka Ann De La Croix has a rap sheet?"

The words punched me in the gut. I sank back in my chair, trying not to show my shock as Ditmar read me her history: prostitution and possession of a controlled substance.

"Looks like she's been clean for over six years. No arrests anyway."

My mind whirled. Was this the same woman? Something was very wrong. Something was missing. *Or maybe not. We all have a history. People screw up. People change. Look at me.*

I tried not to show my shock. "What does a grieving sister have to do with the case?"

Ditmar went on as though he hadn't heard me. "How about that—two sisters in the world's oldest profession. You know, Ann has a swanky spa on Michigan Avenue for women only. What do you suppose all those bitches do together in those massage rooms and hot tubs?" He wore lascivious smile. "Sounds kinky to me."

I wanted to punch the detective in the mouth, but I held my temper. "He thrust an index finger at me, shouting his next question. "What else are you holding back? You hold anything out on me and I'll throw your Roman Catholic ass into a cell for impeding a murder investigation."

Damn, the man was showboating. "Holding back?" I clenched my jaw, hard. "Ann Drew arranged her sister's funeral. I officiated. You know that, of course. I saw you there."

Ditmar wasn't finished. "What about their father?"

"What about him? He attended the funeral."

"What do you know about him?"

The detective's ridiculous line of questioning was tiresome. "Nothing." I gritted my teeth. "He said he was estranged from his daughters."

"We're looking into his background now." The detective switched gears again. "This Guilherme punk we found with the broken arms, he helped carve up the nun, right?"

"I don't know."

"An eye for an eye?" He gave me a knowing look that nearly sent me into a rage. I looked away, trying to blank out my memory of Meg sitting tortured and bloody in that freezing warehouse. I felt no remorse for what I'd done to Guilherme. Was that a Christ-like response? Hardly. Maybe Ditmar was right. Maybe I was stuck in the Old Testament—an eye for an eye.

When it came to the New Testament, I gravitated toward Christ as a man of action, like the picture of him driving moneychangers from the temple. He was pissed and doing something about it. That I could relate to.

"I'll let that go," Ditmar said. "The guy probably couldn't I.D. you anyhow."

Silence. I recognized the technique.

"If he does I.D. you, I'll have to arrest you."

"You gotta do what you gotta do," I said, resorting to cliché. "Anything come up on the name Malachi? Did you bring him in for questioning?"

"Don't go telling me how to do my job."

"Zip, huh?"

"Don't get smart. I got ears on the street. That other name you gave me—Tamara?"

"Yes."

"She worked for Allison a.k.a. Amber. She's missing. Curious, no?"

He paused again, waiting for applause I guess, like he'd done anything beyond the obvious. "What about the kid at the convent? Ronnie, was it?"

"He'll be okay. And stay away from him. Got that?"

"If he belongs to my parish, he's my responsibility. I'll see him if I want to."

Stony silence this time.

"The kids give you any info on the perp?"

He'd changed approaches again. Now he was belligerent and blustering. "Not that you need to know, but the guy was big, white, wore a mask, drove a black Caddy."

Big and a black Caddy. Hell, that sounded like the guy I'd seen at the church and the hospital.

Ditmar stood up, probably so he could look down at me. "I'm finished, but let's get one thing straight. Anything else you stumble into, you tell me... right away." He pierced the air with his index finger. "You fuckin' understand me?"

This guy blew hot and cold. "Understood," I told him. "Am I free to go?"

"Yeah, but remember what I said."

Back at Saint Sebastian's, I went into the church to talk to God, plain and simple. That was how I saw prayer ... a private discussion. The violence to Amber, Meg, Glitter and now this kid, Ronnie, was getting to me. Those things, my sore shoulder and the lump on my head motivated me to nail down these bastards. I prayed for guidance.

CHAPTER TWENTY-FIVE

Six calls awaited me at the parish. Four were parish business; Father Casey could deal with those. The other two were from Ann Drew and William De La Croix. After what Ditmar had divulged. I wanted to call Ann but decided to start slow… with her father.

So, here we were, in the same interview room where I'd first met Ann. "Thank you for seeing me on such short notice," Mr. De La Croix said. "I haven't been able to get Ann out of my mind since the funeral."

That made two of us.

He apologized in avance. "I thought if you heard our story, you'd understand and help me to get through to Ann. It's a long story,"

"Go on, please."

"Well, I have to confess first of all, that I was an 'absent father,' as they call them now—always at the office, always working. When the girls were old enough to go to school, my wife returned to her job as a loan officer at the bank. She had chronic back pain. The problems started when she increased her use of painkillers. In a nutshell, she discovered stronger prescription drugs and became addicted."

"I was away so much… for a long time I didn't even notice her problem." He choked out these last words.

"Can I get you something to drink?"

"Coffee if you have it."

I left the man to compose himself and went to the snack room. When I returned with our coffees, De La Croix told me the rest: how his wife had gone through their savings, lost her job and even sold household items to support her habit. How she tried rehab—years of it—and how their daughters were lost in the shuffle.

He paced as he told of his wife's slip into prostitution to pay for her habit. She was also selling dope. They divorced and somehow she won custody of their teen-age daughters. "After that, the girls would have nothing to do with me."

"They were out of control and finally left home. When they couldn't make it on their own, they went into their mother's… um… line of work. First Allison, then Ann."

I struggled to keep my own emotions out of the mix. Ann's father had avoided the actual word, but he confirmed the police report. Ann had been a prostitute. I felt my heart heavy in my chest.

I forced my attention back to De Croix. For a second, I thought he was going to cry like he had at the funeral, but he straightened his back and continued in a stronger voice. "You *could* say my daughters inherited my business sense. "You *could* say they both were successful… in their own ways. I mean, Allison saw the wisdom of going into 'management,' and Ann went back to school and eventually started a day spa for women. Of course she doesn't know I arranged for the start-up money for the project."

"The girls blamed me for their mother's addiction and her death from an overdose eight years ago," he said. "It's true in a way. I could have been more sensitive, more supportive. I should have worked less and stayed home more."

"I want to make amends. I'll do anything." He collapsed into the chair opposite me. "Will you help me?"

I didn't know much about fatherhood, but I could see how much the man loved his daughters, how much he wanted to be proud of them. I had to separate De Croix's relationship with Ann from my attraction to her. I had to act like a deacon.

"God knows how you feel," I told him, hoping I didn't sound too pompous. "I hope you will talk to Him and have faith that the situation will improve. I don't know what I can do, but I *will* talk with Ann. Love is a powerful force… "

My words felt woefully inadequate.

CHAPTER TWENTY-SIX

Ann's butterscotch voice was a siren's call. When I'd phoned her, she'd asked me to dinner—tonight—8 o'clock.

All afternoon, I caught myself nervously checking the time like a teenager. I hadn't felt like this for a very long time.

What to wear? Enough of the black. Navy slacks and a light blue shirt would do it.

What to bring? Two bottles of wine: one white and one red, since I didn't know what she was serving.

This was not a date, I told myself. Ann wants to know more about her sister's final hours. Okay, so I was attracted to her. Attraction between male and female. Propagation of the species and all that. We were made this way.

I almost convinced myself.

I arrived too early. That wouldn't do. I'd park and wait. I read the street anyhow, a leftover from my MP days. The neighborhood was upscale vintage: multi-story brick buildings, solid dark wooden doors, tall oak trees and high curbs. Out of place was a dark sedan with two men in the front seat. Just sitting there.

A stake-out? Someone watching the building... waiting for someone? Waiting for me?

I didn't like it.

I drove around the block. No other occupied parked cars. When I turned the corner, a black Caddy with two more men slowly passed the front entrance of Ann's apartment building and parked down the block. The two got out and walked to the other parked car. The driver's side window rolled down, and the men in the street leaned in to speak to those inside. I couldn't see their faces. I liked this less and less. I could almost feel the hairs on the back of my neck stand up.

The street was deserted, the cold blackness broken only by circles of hazy illumination from the old streetlights. After a couple of minutes, the two new arrivals looked up at Ann's building and crossed the street to the entrance. *Damn*, not good.

Ann picked up my call on the second ring.

"Ann, it's Deacon. Get out of your apartment now!"

"What do you mean?"

"No time to explain. Two guys are coming for you. Trust me, get out of there."

"Okay, I'll just get my coat and turn off the oven."

"No—just get out!"

No answer.

"Ann!"

"I'm here."

"There's no time—leave now!"

"Okay, Okay. I'm coming. Wait... I hear something. Someone's at my door."

"Can you get out another way?"

No answer.

"Ann, listen to me. Focus on my voice. How else can you get out?"

"Fire escape?"

"Good. Go for it. I'll be in the alley below."

Long seconds passed. I could hear her breathing... hard. "I can't get the window open—it's stuck. My door—they're doing something to my door."

"Is there another window?"

"My bedroom."

"Try that one. If it won't open, throw a chair through it."

Silence.

I wheeled the car into the alley and leaped out, motor running. I parked directly below the fire escape.

"It's open," she said. "It's so dark. I hate heights. It's four stories down."

"Can you see me?"

"Yes." Her voice was breathy and faint.

"Listen to my voice. Get out on the fire escape and close the window behind you."

Slowly, she emerged from the window onto the top platform of the fire escape. "I can hear them. They're inside."

"Start down.., one step at a time."

"Oh Jesus, I'm going to fall."

"You're not going to fall. Don't talk."

"My shoe's caught," she whispered.

"Step out of them. Throw them down."

I heard two light thumps as the shoes fell onto the pavement next to me.

"You're doing great." Three more stories to go.

Her window opened directly above her. "Stay back," I whispered.

I caught the metal glint of a handgun as a man leaned out and called down. "Hey you." Ann flattened herself against the building.

He pointed his pistol down at me, but I knew he wouldn't fire through the metal grating and risk a ricochet. Shit, if he came out on the fire escape, he'd see Ann.

"Whaddaya want?" I shouted up at him, slurring my words like a drunk.

"See anyone out there?"

"Yeah, my guardian angel screwin' your Mama." I began a dirty version of, "My Bonnie Lies over the Ocean." The role of foul-mouthed drunk was easy for me. I'd seen plenty of them.

Ann hugged the building. I willed her to stay still and quiet.

I tried for another distraction, banging the dumpster open and climbing inside. I rummaged around and held up a half-pint bottle with a little whiskey at the bottom. "See what I tol' you. The angel left me something to drink.., or was it your Mama?"

"Asshole."

Then I heard something like, "It's only a drunken bum in the alley," as he backed away from the window and slammed it shut.

"Ann, are you all right?" I whispered.

"No."

She looked back at her window.

"Don't look back. Don't stop. Come on, Ann. You're doing fine."

"I'm *not*." Her voice was tight with fear and anger. She gripped the handrail and looked down. Then she lost her balance and slid down five or six steps on her backside. She stifled a scream.

Her cell phone came clattering down and hit the lid of the dumpster. *Damn*, now I couldn't talk to her. I beckoned to her and she shook her head, wildly, but she kept backing down.

At the landing above the alley, the ladder was stuck, so I stuck her cell phone in my pocket, pushed the dumpster underneath the fire escape and climbed on top. "Can you hear me?" I said in a loud whisper.

"Yes." She sat slumped on the bottom step.

"I can't reach the ladder. Here's what you have to do." I told her.

"Oh, God."

"Hey, it's okay to pray, but we don't have much time. Now, do what I say."

I watched the window above. God, I hoped no one opened it again and looked down.

She rolled onto her stomach like I'd instructed her and edged her legs over the side. Slowly, gasping and half-crying, she backed off the platform, the lower half of her body dangling four feet above me.

"Oh no, oh no."

She was frozen.., stuck.

"Please, Ann, let go. I'm here to catch you."

Silence.

I tried a different tact: "Dammit, let go now. We can't stay here all night. I'm right here. Now do it!"

She let out a muffled cry and let go. I caught her, but a sudden pain shot through my back. As I set her down on top of the dumpster, she spun around hugged me fiercely, shaking and crying.

My back hurt, but it felt good having her in my arms, no matter the circumstances. "It's over. Well done, brave-hearted woman."

"Brave? I was scared out of my mind."

"That's what made it brave." I jumped off the dumpster, groaning involuntarily as my back went into spasm. I blinked back the pain and helped her down. I had to smile when I saw her purse safely on her arm. After all that. What was it about women and their purses?

She was shivering as I picked up her shoes and got into my warm car. I got in, too, gripping the steering wheel, tight. I had to think.

"Bastards," I muttered. "We're not finished yet. God only knows what they would have done… " I stopped myself as Ann started shaking again, frowning in my direction.

"What do you mean, 'what they would have done'? That doesn't make sense."

"They want something, and they'll do anything to get it. I saw what they did to your… " I stopped again. I was an insensitive boor, but I had to warn her… had to protect her.

"Let's get the hell out of here," she said.

"In a minute. I've got a plan." I handed her my small utility knife. "Use the corkscrew to open these bottles of wine. A couple of swallows might help you relax. Then empty the bottles outside the car."

As I opened the door, she grabbed my coat sleeve. "Don't leave me alone. Let's just go!"

"Wine bottles." I squeezed her hand, as reassurance. "I'll be right back." To think I'd agonized over what wine to buy for tonight.

I rummaged around the dumpster again, keeping an eye on Ann's apartment above.

Nothing useful in the dumpster.

Down the alley, I could see junk behind a chain-link fence. I ran for it and scaled the fence, fast. Slipped and gashed my palm. When I landed on the other side, my back screamed at me again.

There it was ... an old washer with hoses. I whacked at the rusted clamp with an angle iron and threw the hose over the fence. My palm was sticky with blood. As I reached the car, a man approached.

CHAPTER TWENTY-SEVEN

I continued the drunk act. "Hey, whadddaya want, man?"

He was wary. "You're dressed better than any alley drunk I've ever seen."

I grinned stupidly. "I got this here good coat, that's why... It was just hanging there at Macy's, waitin' for me."

"Don't tell me this is your car with a woman inside?"

Ann stared at us through the window, wide-eyed as a scared fawn.

"No, it ain't my car. It ain't my bitch neither. We just met at this bar. She told me she just left her old man. It's his car. I'm helpin her, you know?" I tried a leer.

"Hey, you," the guy said, peering through the glass. "Me and my friend wanna talk to you."

I staggered over to him. "Hey, wait a minute."

The man pulled a knife with a ten-inch curved blade... serrated edge. "Get the fuck out of here or I'll cut you bad."

Ann started screaming, a high, piercing sound. The man looked away from me, just long enough. I threw a right hook to his face. With my left, I grabbed and twisted his arm until he dropped the knife. He swung wild—glancing blows—while I pounded his ribs like he was my punching bag. Looping the hose around his neck, I yanked him head first into the brick wall. He crumpled like a pile of dirty laundry.

"You killed him," Ann said, her face frozen. "What kind of a man are you?"

"A pissed-off one." I stooped over to catch my breath. Absentmindedly, I picked up the wicked-looking knife and slipped it into my coat pocket. "He's not dead," I muttered, "just out cold."

"But he's bleeding."

"So am I." Now she felt sorry for the bastard?

She backed away, hugging her arms to her chest. Probably in shock.

"Don't be scared." I wanted to say it was over, but I knew that was a lie. We had minutes—maybe seconds—before the other thug turned up.

"Are you okay?" Her voice was faint.

"Ach, just cut myself on the fence. Hand me the bottles."

I knelt gingerly on the ground, put one end of the hose into the gas tank, bent low and sucked on the open end of the hose, creating a siphon. As the acrid gas touched my lips, I spat, spilled some on myself and placed my end of the hose into the first wine bottle. When it was half-full, I switched to the other bottle. I lifted the hose and broke the siphon.

Now I needed rags. I scanned the dumpster. Not so much as a shred of cloth. I leaned over the man on the ground. Oh well. This will do. I unzipped his coat and ripped the front of his shirt.

Ann said, "Are you out of your mind?"

"No time to explain." Steam jetted out of my mouth as I worked to tear the fabric into smaller strips. I stuffed the strips into the wine bottles and turned them upside down to soak the material with gasoline.

"Got a lighter?"

"No," Ann said, looking away.

I searched the unconscious knife-wielder. No luck. I drove without lights to the end of the alley.

Ann tugged frantically on my sleeve when the car rolled to a stop. "Wait! Aren't we going?"

I put the keys in my pocket. Not that I didn't trust her... "You'll see."

The street was empty except for a bulging shopping cart and a figure in a blue stocking cap and three overcoats and galoshes. He was bending over a trashcan. I approached slowly, not wanting to startle the man.

"Excuse me, do you have a light?"

"Fuck off…. Shit, you smell like gasoline. What you goin' to do, light yourself on fire? Because if you are, I'd sure like to see that, yes I would."

"Wonderful, I'll give you five dollars for a book of matches or a lighter."

"Five bucks, heh? You a desperate prick, ain't yah? If it's worth five, it's worth ten."

"You drive a hard bargain." I nodded to honor the transaction. "Done."

"Let's see yer money."

I held out two fives. The old man tried to snatch them, but I pulled them back. "Let's see the matches."

"Ain't gots no matches."

"What?"

The old man smiled, showing a handful of crooked yellow teeth. "I gots me one of them BIC lighters." He dug through the overburdened shopping cart and pulled out a shocking pink lighter. "Ain't she a beaut?"

"Yeah, very nice. Let's see if she works."

The old man clicked the little plastic lighter with his thumb. A small flame shot up and we made the exchange. Chicago commerce at its best. The old man cackled as we separated. "Dumb asshole."

Ann had stopped shaking and was watching us with interest. I returned to the car. "I have no idea what you're doing."

I handed her the keys. "You okay to drive?"

"Yes. I think so."

"Do *exactly* as I say."

She nodded.

"Turn right at the corner. Drive by the front of your building, very slowly. Now this is important. When I give the word, stop the car."

"What for?"

"Payback and a little insurance… I don't want them following us.

As she drove around the corner, a single car approached. "Pull over for a second."

We waited, and watched. "Okay, it's clear. Drive on…. Now stop!"

I got out of the car, stayed low and lit the wine bottle wicks. I threw one bottle at the dark car where two men still sat in the front seat. I threw the other at the unoccupied Caddy.

The broken bottles burst into flames, and the double explosion engulfed both cars. Two men scrambled out of their flaming car screaming obscenities. Ann screamed, too.

I got back in the car. "Drive ahead—quickly, if you please."

She peeled away, giving me a sidelong glance. "You didn't *really* do that because we'd be followed, did you?"

"Well, sort of."

"Then why?"

"For the satisfaction."

I called Detective Ditmar on the cell. When he picked up, I said, "Break-in at Ann Drew's apartment. Two cars on her street experienced some sort of spontaneous combustion."

"Wha—"

I hung up.

CHAPTER TWENTY-EIGHT

"**S**orry about dinner," I said.

She made a sound that was almost a laugh. "My place is out." Her mood appeared to be softening a few degrees. "We—you— aren't exactly ready for restaurant row. You're dirty, bleeding, and you stink."

"You sure know how to flatter a guy."

"What we need is a place to crash and clean up. I know the perfect spot."

It was a short drive to Michigan Avenue. We parked in the underground garage and took the elevator to the fifth floor.

Ann's spa was beautiful, art deco with a few modern touches. Indirect lighting filtered through green glass. Exotic aromas permeated the rooms.

Now that we were away from thugs, knives and fire escapes, Ann's good humor had returned. "First, a shower for you, my dumpster-digging friend. I'll make us some coffee." She led me to the showers, where a clean robe hung next to each enclosure. "There you go. Thirsty? Sparkling mineral water is above the sinks."

"Great, thanks. How are *you* feeling?"

"Better. Still shaky."

I drank a bottle of mineral water in one gulp. The hot shower was marvelous, but the gash on my palm stung like crazy and started bleeding. I held it away from the water and luxuriated under the hot jets for a long time. The largest terrycloth robe I could find didn't even cover my knees. Ladies spa, I reminded myself. I soaked a washcloth in cold water and applied pressure to my hand.

"Over here," I heard.

I followed the sound of her voice. A fresh pot of coffee squatted on the low marble inlaid table in front of a white leather couch. More mineral water and a feast of bagels, fruit, yogurt, granola and nuts were laid out before us. Ann had also lit several aromatic candles.

"Let me see to your hand." She applied antiseptic ointment that made my eyes water and nearly curled my toenails. A subtle smile broke at the corners of her mouth,

"Enjoying this?" I asked.

"Just a little. You scared me to death tonight." She plastered a bandage on my palm and replaced the one on my chin. "Like new."

When we sat down, I twitched inadvertently as my back muscles complained.

"One more thing," she said. "Nice catch in the alley, but I know you pulled a back muscle doing it." She fetched a soft gel ice pack. "The massage comes next."

I hoped I wasn't blushing. I'd never had a real massage. "You've thought of everything."

She opened the drapes to a spectacular view of the South Chicago skyline along Michigan Avenue and Lakeshore Drive. The dazzling lights and moving headlights and tail lights spread out in bright contrast to the blackness of Lake Michigan to the east.

God, she's beautiful. Her auburn hair was still damp from a shower. She wore no earrings or makeup. Her eyes seemed blue at the outer edge fading to green near the center.

I'd never seen her without a coat. She'd changed into form-fitting chocolate brown slacks and a deep green sweater. And—I couldn't help noticing—no bra.

I tried to focus on the food and instantly discovered I was very hungry. We *had* missed dinner, after all.

We ate eagerly, and quietly, from the spread in front of us.

"What did those men want tonight?"

"Incriminating evidence is my guess. They may think you have information from your sister or that you know where to get it."

She frowned at that. "I have no idea what they're looking for."

"*They* don't know that."

She changed the subject. "Could you tell me about Allison... about her last moments?"

"If you're sure—"

"Yes, really. I want to know."

I thought for a moment, wondering how best to describe Allison's condition to her loving sister. I heaved a sigh. Ann wanted the truth, so I had to give it to her. I lowered my voice, choosing my words carefully and telling her just the facts. "She'd obviously been beaten, and she faded in and out of consciousness. She said *they* were murderers, that they were after her 'tell.'"

"What tell?"

"I think it's a code written in her little Bible."

Ann's eyes welled. "She carried a Bible?"

I nodded. "And a pistol. She saved my life with that."

"Why did she come to you?"

"She didn't come to me, exactly. She needed an immediate refuge, and the church was open and the lights were on." I stopped to let my words sink in and continued. "I found her hiding in the confessional. I gave her some tea and she fell asleep. I relaxed in my recliner and drifted off, too." Then I told Ann about the four men who attacked us, and that a man who stayed in the doorway shot us both and someone knocked me out. When I came to, she was gone."

Ann nodded and wiped her eyes, but she didn't cry.

We sat in silence at opposite ends of the couch, sipping her rich Colombian coffee. She kicked off her shoes and tucked her feet beneath her.

"I thought Allison might be doing something dangerous. She talked about 'making a killing'... that it would bankroll our business. She knew a lot about important people. That came with the business."

"Are you suggesting blackmail?"

"I didn't say that, but it's possible."

I told her my suspicions about the code and, as gently as I could, about Sister Mary Margaret being held hostage for the Bible. "They released her when I brought it to them. She'd been deciphering the code. The police have the copies she made."

"Is the sister all right?"

I'm sure Ann could see the pain on my face as I talked of Meg. "She's strong, but they were brutal… tortured her for no reason. That's why I was so worried when the men came after you."

Ann blew out a relieved breath. "Well that's over."

"For now. I found one other clue in your sister's Bible." I handed her Allison's key. "What do you make of this?"

Ann looked at both sides. "I have no idea what it's for but it must be important."

"I think so, too. The key was hidden in a little pocket in front of Allison's Bible. You and I may be the only ones who know about it."

I put the key back into my wallet. I didn't want to push her, but I had to. "Have you ever heard of anyone named Tamara? I may have asked you before."

Ann jumped up and started pacing. "Yes," she said, almost angrily. I knew her." She paced some more. "I lied before. I knew a lot of Allison's girls." She turned away from me and looked out over the city, her voice drifting back to me.

"I didn't know how to tell you before… I was hoping I wouldn't have to, but for a brief time I used to be… involved in the business."

I was glad she trusted me enough to reveal her past, but I didn't want to say the wrong thing. So I skipped over her revelation and told her what the cops had told me—that Tamara was missing. "I'm sure she's connected to all of this somehow."

She sat and her shoulders heaved.

"Shhh, now." I reached out and held her hand. She began to cry softly. Ann tucked her head into my shoulder. It felt like the most natural thing in the world. God, she felt so good. I didn't dare move or speak for fear I'd break the spell.

"I've felt so alone and scared."

"It's going to be all right," I whispered. *I had no idea if anything would be all right.*

"I should feel more shame now that you know about me."

"You don't have to beat yourself up. The past is gone. You are a vibrant, beautiful, courageous woman." My words tumbled out of some deep secret place. I listened to myself, almost as if someone else were talking. I'd never talked to a woman this way.

"I feel safe with you. You don't know how good that feels."

She slowly separated from me, stood and declared an order, "To the massage tables."

"No, thanks. It's all right. A few aspirin and a good night's sleep, and I'll be as good as new."

She looked at me, suspiciously, one eyebrow raised. "Are you *afraid?*" she teased. "You talked me down a four-story fire escape. Now *I* know best. You need a therapeutic massage. Right now."

"Okay, I guess." I got up and followed her.

Maybe a more sophisticated guy might feel at home naked on a padded table with a towel over his butt. For me, it was a little weird.

Looking at my feet hanging over the edge of the table, she said, "You don't fit." She dragged over another table and shoved it under my legs. "There."

With the aid of soothing oils, her hands worked the muscles up and down my back. "Have you ever had a massage before?"

"Not from a trained professional."

"Hmmm. When I hit a spot that hurts, tell me."

She did, and when I told her, she focused on that area using a different oil that got very warm.

After ten minutes, I was a believer. "I've gone to heaven and I'm still alive," I told her.

"Shhh, no talking, just relax. These muscles need massage after what they've been through. I haven't said so yet, but thank you for helping me get out of there." She hummed softly as her hands soothed my aching muscles. I relaxed so deeply that I nearly fell asleep.

"I made a bed out of mats in the exercise room," she said, when she was finished. "When you feel like it, go there and have a good night's sleep. I'm exhausted. I'll see you in the morning."

It sounded good to me. And what would the morning bring?

CHAPTER TWENTY-NINE

My cell phone woke me. I padded into the next room to shut it off. I checked the number, disgusted. At 5:15 a.m. and still dark, who else would call but Father Casey. He could wait.

I slipped back onto the mat for a few more winks and drifted off again, dreaming of boats and fog and people chasing me with bats and serrated knives.

An hour later, I heard Ann moving around. While I was asleep, she had washed some of my shirt and set it out. As I finished dressing, she showed up wearing a pink terrycloth robe and carrying two steamy cups of coffee. "Good morning, you man in my woman's spa. Coffee?"

"Thank you, kind lady." I said. It felt strange, but good, being alone with her in the morning in this place. As she bent over to sit beside me on the mat, the open "V" of her robe fell forward, slightly. The sight warmed me more than the coffee.

"How's the back?"

I twisted and stretched a bit. "Like new, thank you." I picked up one of her hands, pretending to examine it. "I think they're magic." Then I remembered what her father had said. I didn't want to tell her something else she didn't want to hear, but I took promises seriously. And it seemed like a deacon's duty to bring a father and daughter together. "I'd planned on telling you last night, but, well, things got complicated."

"That's an understatement."

"I had a long talk with your father."

Ann pulled her hand from mine and turned away. "I won't listen."

I knelt to face her. "He told me he loves you and wants to be in your life."

"When hell freezes over."

I went into serious deacon mode, quoting something a wise priest had said: "A friend told me that holding hate and resentment is like taking poison and hoping the other person will die."

"Keep your platitudes to yourself." Ann went silent, sulking like a child. Then she blurted, "Did you know my dad made my mother get an abortion when she started taking drugs? You're the big deal Catholic. What do you think of that?"

I wasn't going to be drawn into either side of the family feud. "I've kept my promise to your dad," I told her. "I believe he's sincere. All the crap from the past needs to stay in the past."

"There you go, quoting homilies again."

I considered telling her about the loan her father had facilitated for her Michigan Avenue spa, but decided against it. He'd have to tell her himself. She was dealing with enough for now. Still, I couldn't help comparing our experiences with fathers: I'd never had one, and she was rejecting hers. I wouldn't hold it against her. She didn't know.

Ann changed the subject, which was fine with me. "Did I hear your cell phone go off, this morning?"

"Yeah, I'd better check my messages."

"I'll rustle up some breakfast."

I picked up my cell. *If Father Casey could see me now.* "Hello Casey, you called?"

"Damn right. Where the hell are you? Don't answer. I'm not sure my heart could take it. If it weren't for Monsignor Salvatore, I'd... Just get over to Grant Hospital. It's Sister Mary Margaret."

"What happened?"

"She had a bad incident last night. Disgusting ... I don't want to talk about it. Holy Jesus, much more of this and Sister Conselleta is going to take another bite out of my hide and have you publicly flogged." His voice turned even more sarcastic. "If you weren't doing such *important work* for the Archbishop, you'd be sorting mail right now. Apparently, I'm not to *interfere.*"

Thank you, Monsignor.

I dressed and made my apologies to Ann. "I'm so sorry, but I've got to leave—right now."

"What happened?"

"It's Sister Mary Margaret, she had some kind of bad incident last night. I don't know much else, but I have to go to her."

She gave me a parting hug. "Of course you do. *C'est la vie.* Call me?"

"I promise. You have security for this building, right?"

"Excellent security."

"Please don't leave until I *do* contact you."

"All right."

I took coffee and a bagel with me and left.

CHAPTER THIRTY

A s I drove to the hospital, the winter fog felt like it had seeped into my brain. *What the hell am I doing?* One day I'm a deacon, assisting at Mass, the next I'm a thug for the church, and now I'm mixed up with murderers. To further thicken the haze in my head, I seemed to be falling in love. Or should I call it *thrall?* What's the difference anyway?

"Ann Drew," I said aloud, savoring the sound. "You're one dynamite lady."

Ann's extraordinary blue-green eyes swept into my mind, the silkiness of her hair… her braving the fire escape. How did this relate to my faith journey?

What a ride.

I blinked myself back to the present and the Grant Hospital parking lot. *What the hell.* I pulled into a doctor's-only space and shot up to Mary Margaret's room.

"Deac, I'm so glad you're here." She grabbed my hands and pulled me down beside her.

"Meg, what happened?"

She winced, as though the memory were a physical pain. "Terrible. I woke up in the middle of the night and saw *it* hanging from my bed light, dripping…. " She pointed to an opaque plastic bag—the kind hospitals use for patient belongings.

Inside, were the bloody feet and talons of a large bird. "My God, Meg, it's a calling card."

She grimaced. "From that man?"

"Malachi," I said, confirming her fears. "That's my guess."

She cried, and I held her. I couldn't think of anything comforting to say. The message was clear. Malachi could get to Sister Mary Margaret anywhere...

"They... he was right here in my room." She gulped back her sobs.

"Did you see anyone?"

She shook her head. "They've got the Bible and the code. What else could they want?" She looked past me, speaking as though to herself. "They can hurt me... anytime they want."

"No, we won't let that happen. You can walk, right?"

"I'm mobile, but no high hurdles yet."

Good, her sense of humor was a saving grace. I used my best gangster voice, "I'm going to spring you out of this joint."

She smiled, just a little, and I touched her shoulders, gently. "Be ready. I'll be back with a plan. We'll get you out of here—my way—in case someone is watching."

CHAPTER THIRTY-ONE

Malachi was fuming. The fight in the alley, the fire bombs, Ann's escape—all perpetrated by the deacon. "He's interfered too many times." Malachi stretched the syllables, his voice a nasal whine. "The bastard should've died with the hooker after I shot them."

He drummed his fingers on the head of his cane and turned to Bernie. "If I know … our tough guy, he'll be at the hospital next, saving the nun. He's got to protect the women. Can't resist. He's got a real savior complex."

Bernie showed no impatience. He'd learned that as an altar boy. But Malachi's cane had taken that forbearance a step further: You don't interrupt, and you pretend the boss talks normal—or else.

"As for the other one—Ann—I've got a tracker. It's small, high tech. We'll plant it in her purse." He fixed Bernie with his malevolent stare. "Can you handle that?"

"No problem."

"Do it. Another thing, find out where the hooker actually lived. That apartment in the city? Just for …business."

Bernie nodded.

"Our employer *needs* that DVD. Once the deacon and his little girlfriend find it, we'll take him down." Remembering the photos of Ann in her apartment, Malachi raised his eyebrows and grinned. He'd taken a definite fancy to that girl. He'd take his time and enjoy her.

"After we deal with the deacon, I got another job to do and then I'm out of here." He was quiet for a moment. "I'm so sick of the cold," he muttered, half to himself.

In his mind, Malachi was already sitting on the veranda of a Caribbean beach house as scantily clad girls cavorted on the white powdery sand. Of course, he'd have an aviary, too. Birds—especially birds of prey—had been a passion since childhood. He'd watch them through a small window at ground level—loving them, hating them for flying free, while he was locked in a miserable cold basement.

He pulled his mind out of that punishing cellar. "Who knows, maybe the deacon will get the DVD to us soon." Even as he said those words, he doubted them.

CHAPTER THIRTY-TWO

Traffic was light, so I took the call on my cell. At first I couldn't understand the voice. It was strangely nasal and high-pitched, and the words were stretched out. I'd heard it before on the phone when Meg was kidnapped...

"Hello... Deacon. We need to talk about a...very important matter."

I pulled over to better concentrate on the voice. "Who *are* you?"

"Never... mind that. Names aren't important." He laughed.

It was a strange sound—like an evil laugh in an old flick—and it gave me a chill. I bit back my feelings. "What do you want? I gave you the Bible and code."

"Yes, and it's... been most helpful. Thank you, sincerely. And you're right, we do... want somethin' more. Amber made a... DVD. I'm afraid we need that also. Then, truly, our business is done. No one else need... suffer."

"I have no idea about any DVD."

"That is your problem, not... mine." He paused. "If you don't find it, we will fetch the little nun and Amber's pretty sister, Ann. And then— until we get that DVD—we will, shall we say, *enjoy* their company." He snorted a laugh.

"This is business to us," the voice continued. "You can't avoid us or escape us. We have the resources... to get what we want. You get the picture? Do not tell your friends in blue about this." He paused again, but I said nothing. "Tell me you... understand."

"I understand you are a living shit."

"Tsk tsk, and you a deacon of the church. Your opinions, however, are of no importance. It was delicious to spend intimate… time with the little nun. Perhaps Ann would enjoy my… ministrations as well. Oh yes, especially Ann."

Bile rose in my throat at his sarcasm, but the harsh coldness that followed was no better. "Get us the… DVD, and all this can be avoided. And don't take long; we have limited patience." He paused again.

"Get us the fuckin'… DVD."

The phone went dead.

Once home, I paced and planned, swinging Bat in furious loops.

Malachi's mocking threats echoed in my head. He had resources. But I have resources, too.

First on my list of resources was William De La Croix. I called him. "Yes," I told him, "I've spoken to Ann on your behalf, and I'll continue to do so. But right now she's in danger." I laid out the predicament and my plans. De La Croix was eager to help. He agreed to send cash by courier to sustain Ann and me—and to grease some palms—while we searched for the DVD.

"Anything I can do to protect Ann… and anyone else." My respect rose for the man. He gave generously even though his help could not assure reconciliation with his daughter.

Finally, I mentioned the need for having to find a safe house for Sister Mary Margaret.

He immediately offered his suite of offices on the twenty-eighth floor of the Prudential Building. "There are two apartments there—fully stocked. I use them when I work late or when an associate or overseas visitor needs lodging. They're at your disposal if you need them."

"Great. No one knows your connection to Sister. The fewer of us who know her whereabouts the better." I thought for a moment. Maybe the man already knew, but I'd better lay out the risks. "We're dealing with very dangerous men. Besides, killing Allison, they've tortured Sister Mary Margaret and a friend of mine. They almost got to Ann last night."

"I've let down my daughters in the past. I'll do anything I can for them… for Ann. Do you need help getting the nun here?"

"I can handle that. I'll be back in touch."

By the time I'd taken a quick shower and packed my duffle, De La Croix's courier arrived with a substantial amount of cash. I'd take the parish station wagon. Father Casey wouldn't be seen in the old wagon. He drove a silver Continental, bequeathed by a wealthy parishioner.

I threw the duffle and Bat in the back seat. I'd be on the road for a while.

CHAPTER THIRTY-THREE

I called the spa. "Hi Ann. You okay?"

"Sure, how's your friend?"

"Better. Can you meet me in the Palmer House lunchroom? We've got to talk. I'm downstairs I'll follow you there."

"I'll be right down."

As Ann emerged from the building, I was on high alert to watch for people who might be watching her. Tough job. Several men's heads turned as she walked by. Suddenly a well-dressed elderly man slipped and fell on the icy sidewalk in front of her, knocking down another couple of pedestrians. My adrenalin kicked in as a small crowd gathered to help. I scanned the group around Ann carefully—nothing. Obviously an accident; no one had bothered Ann.

The posh lunchroom was almost empty after the noontime rush. The décor was subtle but spoke of opulence in subdued tones of gold and crimson. We sat in the corner and ordered sandwiches and coffee.

"Ann, they want a DVD your sister made."

"But I don't know anything about that."

"Any idea where she might have hidden it?"

"Her apartment?"

"We'll check it out. Can the spa get along without you for a few days?"

"I've got good people. They can handle it."

I told Ann I wanted to sneak Meg out of the hospital. "She's not safe there. If they find her, they'll use her to get to me. Your father offered the use of his apartments at the Prudential Building."

"I see." She sighed and turned away. "All right." Her voice faint. "If you think it's best."

"I do think so." We ate in silence for a while and then I blurted out my plan for us. "I hate to ask you this. It could put you in danger, but *together* we have the best chance of finding the DVD. I'll understand if you don't want to come with me. But, if we find that DVD, we can bring them down, whoever the hell *they* are. And, we've got the key. It could unlock where the DVD has been kept."

I tried to give her a choice, to state the facts without emotion. "If you decide it's too dangerous, I can put you in a protected place like Sister Meg. Make no mistake; these people are determined and ruthless. It's up to you." I waited while she sipped her coffee and considered the proposition.

She looked at me, and I could see by the steadiness of her gaze that she'd reached a decision. "I'm scared, but I'd feel safest with you. Let's find that DVD and get Allison's murderer."

I closed my eyes and sighed in relief. I was grateful for her help... and for her presence. "I'll pick you up at your spa later tonight. I know you know this, but I've got to say it: Be careful, stay around people and keep your security close."

"I will, and I'll be waiting."

I felt a swell of emotion. "Ann ... we can do this." It felt good to say aloud what I'd felt ever since I'd formulated the plan.

I walked her back to the spa, wondering if she really understood the danger.... She hadn't seen Sister Mary Margaret tied to that chair at the warehouse... and I was very glad she hadn't. With God's help, I would protect these precious women and hunt down the killers.

CHAPTER THIRTY-FOUR

I was running out of time. I knew Malachi wouldn't wait much longer.

I called Meg with De La Croix's offer and my plan.

"I'm in," she said. "Bless him... and you."

"I'll be there ASAP. Be ready."

Next call, Monsignor Salvatore. I told him the basics—that Meg wasn't safe in the hospital—but I held back on De La Croix and the Prudential Building. The fewer who knew, the better.

The Monsignor agreed. I could almost see him nodding sagely as he spoke.

"Will you make excuses to Sister Conselleta? She'll wonder about Sister Mary Margaret's absence."

"I'll pass the task onto the archbishop. He has more clout."

I had to smile. No one crosses swords with Sister Conselleta if they can help it.

All was in place. I picked up Ann at the spa and gave her instructions and a small bag.

I let Ann out of the car at the rear entrance to the downtown Hilton. A doorman in top hat escorted her into the lobby. Our bait-and-switch had begun.

Ten minutes later, I picked up "a blonde" at the front entrance who wore tinted glasses, a plaid scarf, black velvet beret and a matching coat. No one could recognize Ann in that disguise.

I'd parked the parish wagon underground and switched to a rental PT Cruiser—silver with dark tinted windows. It was a little tight for me. Then I pulled down the brim of my fedora, slumped in the seat and drove onto the street. I made some quick turns and lane changes to elude possible followers... just in case.

Bernie called Malachi from the underground garage. "Can't figure it," he said. "They've disappeared. Maybe they're in the lobby. What's the tracker show?"

"They're on the move; they've switched cars." Malachi hung up and called his men in the van. "Don't lose him." Then he called Bernie again. "It looks like they're headed to the hospital. Get over there and follow my plan."

"Okay, boss."

"The tracker's only good within a two-mile radius."

CHAPTER THIRTY-FIVE

I had one more stop: Pazadelli's Pizza Palace on bustling Damen Street. I'd called in advance.

"We have time for pizza?" Ann asked.

"Business. Leo and I grew up together," I told Ann. "He's a good guy, but he's got one foot on the dark side. We need a favor, and he owes me." I didn't tell her any details.

We parked in back and entered through the alley. The moonlight cast blue shadows everywhere. And the savory aroma was overwhelming. "He'll feed us. That's the Pazadelli creed. When I was a kid, I hung out in Mama Pazadelli's kitchen."

Sure enough, after hugs and introductions, Leo grabbed a couple of slices of pizza from the serving counter and poured three glasses of *primo vino*. "Welcome, my favorite deacon. And you, Miss. *Mama mia*." He bent to kiss her hand and led us to a back booth.

"I shall return... with a gift."

We bit into the pizza, and soon Leo was back with a jacket and a baseball cap, each adorned with the Pazadelli's Pizza Palace logo.

Ann looked puzzled until I motioned her to put them on. "They're your cover," I whispered.

"Ohhh." She turned around, slipped them on and pivoted back to face us. "How do I look?" The jacket was at least two sizes too large for her, but she looked charming in it.

"*Excellente, bravo*," exclaimed Leo.

"Perfect. You were born for the role," I said.

"The pizzas will be out in a few minutes." Leo squeezed into the booth next to me. "Something heavy going down, huh, Deac?"

"Can't get anything by you, Leo." Better you don't know much about it."

"*Capicsi.*" He scanned the room, his eyes narrowed. "Here," he said, pulling a revolver from under his apron, "in case you need it—not traceable."

"God, Leo. Put that thing away before you hurt yourself."

"If you say so." He tucked the gun back in his belt. "But it's here if you need it. Like it says in the second amendment in this great country, you got a right to bear arms." He headed back to the kitchen. What a patriot.

We'd finished the Chianti by the time he returned with an insulated carton of pizzas. "Here you are, four of my best with extra pepperoni."

"Thanks. What do I owe you?"

"Call it a contribution to the church. Tell you what—bring Ann back here sometime. I like her. She makes the place look beautiful." He gave her his most lascivious wink and pulled her close for a big hug.

Then he hit me in the shoulder. Thank God, it was my *good* shoulder.

"Hey. Don't be a stranger at Mass. And bring your Mama." I gave him the commercial message every time I saw him, and he always gave the same reply.

"Yeah, yeah, but Saint Sebastian's walls might go tumblin' down. *Ciao, compagno.*"

I chuckled to myself. Leo at Mass would be a some kind of a miracle, at least to his mother. Ever since Leo and I were kids, she looked to me to lead him in a righteous direction. I tried.

Ann glanced at me with a quizzical look on her face, "What are you smiling at?"

"Just thinking of old times with Leo."

"Like what?"

"Oh we tagged a boxcar or two, smoked a little weed and did some drag racing out in Schiller Woods. We even double dated a few times."

"So you have a past?"

"Don't we all." I regretted saying that as the words came out of my mouth.

The emergency room was busy at Grant Hospital, so we could enter separately without notice. My Roman collar and Ann's pizza regalia were our free tickets to anywhere.

"I'm scared again."

"That's natural."

We took the elevator up and separated on Sister Mary Margaret's floor. It was after visiting hours and very quiet. I watched from around the corner as Ann carried the pizzas toward the nurse's station, the aroma of pepperoni wafting down the hall,

"These are for the night shift," Ann announced, as she swung the carton onto the counter. Heads turned toward the savory smell.

The nurse in charge looked up from her computer, puzzled. "We didn't order any pizzas."

"Yeah, I know, Ms. … Chen," Ann said, glancing at the nurse's nametag. "They're from a former patient. He said the night shift deserved a snack. You know… as a thank you."

"What was the patient's name?"

"First name John. That's all I know."

"Well now, wasn't that nice of him." She passed the good news onto the rest of the night shift. Ann retrieved the insulated bags. Before long, a congregation of chatty nurses, orderlies and housekeepers clustered around the nurse's station devouring the hot pizzas.

A perfect distraction. I slipped into Meg's room, finger to my lips. "Hey Meg, time to get you out of here."

I wrapped her in blankets, pulled a knit cap over her head and whipped off my woolen scarf for her neck. "It's freezin' outside but a warm car is waiting. Here we go."

I wheeled her down to the elevator at warp speed. So far, so good. We got off on the ground floor and headed for the front door.

"Hey! Where do you think you're going?" The overweight rent-a-cop looked serious, but he wasn't packing.

"Hello, officer."

"It's after hours." His voice was low, but he spoke with authority. "There are no 'after hours' in church matters, officer. I was called to hear this woman's confession. She's going in for surgery tomorrow morning. Do I need to clear this with the hospital administrator?"

"No, no. But why take her outside at this time of night?"

"Pardon me, I should have explained. Missus O'Grady begged for a bit of fresh air, just to clear her mind, don't you know."

Meg looked up at the security guard. "I have some serious ...private things to tell Father." She motioned to him, and he bent closer. She whispered to him.

He nodded and straightened abruptly. "Oh, yeah. Sure, I get it. A few minutes outside. Good idea." He pointed down the hall. "Then you can use our little chapel."

Meg managed to look misty-eyed. "Thank you for understanding."

"You're welcome." He turned to me. "She's ready now."

"You're good," I whispered to Meg as we exited. "What did you tell him?"

"Never you mind." Sister Mary Margaret looked as mischievous as she had back in grade school. "It was just a little white lie."

CHAPTER THIRTY-SIX

Ann had pulled the PT Cruiser close to the entrance. I helped Sister in, then put the wheelchair in the trunk—just a loan. Ann got in back to help Sister.

As I pulled out, between rows of parked cars, I could see a large SUV up ahead, motor running, headlights off. Not good. I backed up—fast—until I saw lights in the rearview mirror. *Shit*, we were blocked fore and aft.

"Hang on." I took a hard right through to the next aisle.

I bumped over a curb onto the grassy embankment, praying we wouldn't turn over.

That's when I heard the first shots. I careened into the multi-level parking garage, mentally taking stock: No snow or ice inside, and the tires had good traction. I raced up the levels, watching for the alternate route down. Sparks flew as the speeding Cruiser scraped the wall. As I neared the bottom level, I saw the black SUV again, nearly blocking the exit.

"Brace yourselves!" I aimed for the narrow opening, intending to clip the front of the SUV and damage its tires or steering.

Shots rang out. "Stay down!" I ducked my head. There was a jolt and scraping sound, but I kept going. No one followed. Maybe I did incapacitate them.

"Everyone okay?" I glanced over my shoulder and saw Ann's arms around Sister. Both were pale and trembling.

"Thank you, God," murmured Meg.

I felt my left eyebrow go up. We were a big target, yet only a few bullets had hit our car. Was this a miracle from God, were they aiming at the tires and missed or was this a charade intended to scare us?

CHAPTER THIRTY-SEVEN

"You stopped them! They're not following us." Ann's voice hit some high decibels and then faded to calm. "God, I've never been so scared."

I glanced at the women in the rearview mirror. There was already more color in their cheeks, but I could see questions in their eyes.

"Those men were in my apartment, weren't they?"

I'm not sure, could be."

"And the ones... " Meg's voice quavered, and she started over again. "Who *are* these people?"

"One may be named Bernie and the other, Malachi."

"What do they want *now*?" Meg asked.

I made a guess." To scare the crap out of us so we'll find a DVD that Ann's sister made."

Ann and I told Meg what we knew about the DVD, which wasn't much. "Some kind of incriminating information, I'd guess."

Ann nodded furiously. "She... um... knew some important people, rich ones."

"After tonight I guess we all know to be very careful. Meg, no phone calls, no e-mails—nothing. You must stay in Mr. De La Croix's apartment and out of the loop."

"But I don't know anything."

"I hate to bring it up, but... well, they used you as a bargaining chip once. They *could* do it again."

"What about us?" asked Ann.

"We're in the loop whether we like it or not. We have a DVD to find."

By now, we had reached the Prudential Building, back entrance. I honked three times and the door opened. De La Croix waved us in, and seconds later, the large roll-down doors shut behind us.

We helped Sister into the wheelchair, and I made the introductions. Meg was effusive in her thanks, but Ann merely nodded. I watched them safely enter the elevator and drove the Cruiser to the Water Tower Plaza parking garage nearby, just in case we were tailed. I walked back to the Prudential Building.

Sister had already discovered a box of chocolates by the time I got to the apartment. She gazed at the Chicago skyline and the well-appointed suite, lush with thick carpeting and sofas highlighted by plants and artwork. "Just like my room at Saint Catherine's."

Her joke broke the tension, and we all laughed… a little.

"This means a lot to us all," I told De La Croix. "Meg has suffered enough. It's a relief to know she's safe."

"I'm happy to do it." He pointed out the fine amenities. "The Prudential Building is like a little city. If you need anything, it's probably here: bank, pharmacy, boutiques, post office and about twenty-five other businesses. You have my cell number."

Ann suddenly looked panicked. "Oh dear. Where's my purse?" She looked around hurriedly, frowned and then relaxed a little. "Oh, In all the excitement I probably left it in the car. I *never* do that. I've got to check. We're ready to go, right?" We said our brief goodbyes.

When we got to the parking garage, Ann rummaged under the backseat of the Cruiser and found her purse. "Phew! At least it was out of sight."

We drove toward Evanston, a trendy address near Northwestern University. No one appeared to be following us, but I figured the scumbags would have Allison's address, too. I asked Ann to call the local police. "Tell them a few unsavory men are lurking around the building. If our *friends* are there, they won't stick around to be questioned."

"Sounds like a plan. You're good at this."

I hope I'm good enough not to get us killed.

CHAPTER THIRTY-EIGHT

Our timing was lucky. A squad car drove up and two officers emerged just as we arrived, immediately, a man scurried from between the buildings. He got into a gray SUV... a big one, maybe an Escalade... and took off.

"Let's remember that gray SUV." We waited while the officers looked around the building. Once they left we proceeded to Allison's apartment.

Ann picked up the newspaper and unlocked the door. I gave the place a quick walk-through with Bat poised for action.

We were alone.

The spacious modern apartment had a "decorator" rather than a "lived-in" look. Chrome and black with splashes of red. Ann wandered around slowly running her fingers across some of the framed photos. She sat down at the kitchen table absentmindedly and picked up the newspaper. Her face suddenly changed. "Oh my God, listen to this: Two plain clothes policeman were targets of a fire-bombing two nights ago... and another vehicle was damaged as well. That was us."

"Sure was. Those cops *are* working with the dirt bags who were coming for you. They must be the resources Malachi was bragging about."

"So, who do we trust?"

"God, each other, and a very select group of friends."

We set to our task, meticulously searching every drawer, every corner. Every conceivable place a DVD could be hidden. No DVD, no clues and no indication as to what the numbers and letters on the key meant. Ann tried hard to be detached. She was suspiciously silent, her hands trembling as she touched her sister's belongings.

We finally abandoned our search and took a break. Over Italian beef sandwiches and fries, beer for me and sparkling water for Ann, I broached a delicate question. "Did Allison routinely shoot DVDs of... you know?" I averted my eyes from hers.

"I never heard of it. Bad for business. Clients would go crazy. There'd be hell to pay if they found out."

"Then maybe she *didn't* shoot the video. Maybe someone else did."

"Possibly, unless this was an exception... part of her final blackmail scheme."

Ann searched Allison's computer but nothing turned up. It was after midnight when she stood and stretched. She was comfortable in my presence. I liked that. A lot.

We separated with a quick hug and took separate bedrooms. My mind raced, most of my thoughts fixed on Ann. She's so very close, and we're in this together.

CHAPTER THIRTY-NINE

A storm was brewing in Police Commissioner Mitch Halloran's wood-paneled office. It was late. State Senator Frank Clayton was skittish as a colt. Halloran was irritable.

In contrast, Detective Rick Ditmar sat quietly smoking one of Halloran's hand-wrapped Cuban cigars. If he was nervous, he didn't show it. Thanks to Ditmar and Malachi, Halloran had the coded Bible, all the copies the nun had made and the computer she'd used to make them. Everything except the DVD.

Clayton kept talking about Tiko, Tamara's partner on the last party *cruise*. "If that little Jap whore talks, we're screwed."

"Relax, Frank. Talks to whom? About what? All she knows is that Tamara was with us at the club and left early."

"That'll connect us to Tamara."

"Tiko knows not to talk about clients. Even if she did, I'd be the first to know. And where *is* Tamara?" He let that last question hang in the air. The commissioner appeared calm, but there was sharpness to his voice. "We have more pressing concerns right now. The deacon's making fools of us. Malachi says he can get the DVD without his help, but I'm not so sure." Halloran leaned back in his chair and put his feet up on the edge of his desk, a studied move.

"Once we have the DVD, we're in the clear. We'll 'leak' an altered version of the code and implicate our beloved DA with the prostitute ring. The accusation alone will boot him out of the running for office. I will, of course, be publicly *appalled* by his immoral behavior. The press will eat it up."

Clayton continued to pace, giving both men furtive glances... like the guilty man he was. He hadn't slept well in days. "How do we bring the deacon to us?"

"Let me ask you this. Besides his little lady friends, what, or rather, who, is dearest to the deacon?"

Ditmar said, "His parish."

"Right on. I'll call Malachi. I know how we can bring the deacon to us."

CHAPTER FORTY

Ann and I were about to leave Allison's apartment when my cell rang. It was Monsignor Salvatore. "Deacon, the police are after you. They've been instructed to arrest you on sight."

"What now?"

"Numerous charges. Let me see." I heard a shuffle of paper. "Starting at the top, there's assault, setting fire to government property, obstructing justice and impeding an official murder investigation. You have been extremely busy. I hope this means you are closing in on the DVD."

"Regretfully, no."

The monsignor sighed. "Disappointing. Other bad news. I'm sure you remember Father Baksian, your last assignment."

"Yeah."

"He's doing office work at the diocese. The archbishop rescinded his exile orders—Cardinal Schneider's personal request. The archbishop and I are appalled. How dare the cardinal interfere?"

"Did he give a reason?"

"The same gibberish about individual rights and forgiveness. We suspect a connection between Baksian and the cardinal. What if Baksian violates another innocent? The cardinal should stay out of Gabrian business." The monsignor choked out a bitter laugh. "And the cardinal has received more death threats. The police are looking into it. What a joke."

"Thanks for the warning. I'll stay in touch."

But the monsignor wasn't finished. "Oh ... my secretary left a note saying that you're wanted at the parish."

"Any reason given?"

"Nothing more on the note, and I can't ask her. She's gone to lunch."

I tried the school, but I got the usual recorded message. I had a bad feeling about this. "Ann I need to get to the school. I got a message but it was vague. I'd better check. We can't be too careful. Do you mind if I drop you off somewhere safe? I've got to find out what this is about. It could be a trap."

"But maybe I can help."

"Maybe, but it's too risky. You need to be secure for a while. I know a place near the school."

In the middle of our drive, Ann looked at me like I was crazy when I dashed into City Do-nuts for a box of two-dozen—assorted—and headed for a high-rise construction site on Elston Avenue.

"What in heaven's name... " she began. I kept driving through the mud, between trucks and piles of lumber, until I reached an industrial trailer at the building site.

"Wait here. I'll be right back."

I'd gone a dozen paces when several stern-faced men blocked my way. "Whadda we got here?" one asked, hooking a thumb in my direction.

"Looks like a church-going sissy-boy," said another.

The men laughed. Steam rising from their mouths made the cluster of men look like a multi-headed smoke-breathing dragon. That's if a dragon wore hard hats and tan, over-the-ankle work boots.

Ann stared at us, her nose practically pressed against glass.

"Who's in charge of this kindergarten?" I asked the men. "Doesn't anybody *work* around here?"

"None of your friggin' business. Take off, pansy," said a man who looked like Clint Eastwood on a bad morning.

I raised my voice to a shout. "I'm not going anywhere. Maybe I'll get a job here and outwork any three of you."

"Let's get him." The men charged.

Once Ann screamed, the men couldn't hold back their laughter any longer. They howled, doubling over with mirth. Some slapped me on the back and others punched me in the arms.

By that time, I was laughing and punching them back. "What a bunch of pushovers."

The foreman stepped down from the trailer, a foul-smelling panatela clamped between his teeth. "What the fuck's going on in my yard here?" He couldn't suppress a grin.

The men called Tommy Wallace "The Wall." He was as tall as I am and forty pounds heavier with a voice like a garbage truck rolling over a gravel road. "Hi Deac, need some work? We could use yah."

"Not right now Tommy. Thanks. But I do need some help." I looked over the group. "From all of you."

The men huddled closer, their faces rearranged into identical—almost comical—expressions of concern.

"Some very bad-ass scumbags are looking for this fine lady here. She needs your protection for the day. I've got to get over to the parish." I opened the car door, introduced Ann and handed over the boxes of doughnuts. Half of the men gathered around Ann; the other half went for the pastry.

"Nice to meet you all." Her smile charmed them instantly, and each called out his name in turn.

Wallace jerked his thumb in the direction of the trailer behind him. "She can stay in the rolling mansion." His voice gentled. "If it's okay with you, miss. I even got a little TV in there. It's kinda messy but clean and warm."

He turned back to the men. "Pass the word. Any new faces come within a hundred feet of my mansion and we swarm 'em like hornets. Got that, you gumballs?"

The men were too busy with doughnuts to respond with anything but nods and grunts.

Wallace looked at me. "She'll be safe with us. Me and one of these junk yard dogs will take turns hangin' around the rolling mansion."

The course looking crew nodded, thanked us for the doughnuts and assured us they'd be on guard. "Like my mother, she'll be safe," one of the workers said.

As I started the car, I looked at Ann, eyebrows raised in question.

"No problem," she said. "Nobody's going to get by these guys."

As we said our goodbyes I got another call. This time it was from a frenzied Mrs. Gonzales. "There's a bomb at the school, I mean a bomb threat. Can you come?"

"What about the police? The fire department?"

"They're here, but we'd feel better if you came. Everybody trusts you. Dear Jesus, I'm so scared."

"I'm on my way." I told Ann about the situation and peeled out of the construction yard. I drove back to Saint Sebastian's, hoping I wasn't too late.

CHAPTER FORTY-ONE

I heard the sirens first and then saw red and blue lights flashing from the emergency vehicles. Barriers had been set up in the streets and alleys around Saint Sebastian's. I parked on someone's lawn and ran toward the school. My heart was racing. If anyone hurt those children, I'd hunt them down without mercy.

School was out, but there were always kids around doing art projects, pumping iron or playing basketball in the gym. Many parents wouldn't be home from work for hours, so neighborhood kids hung around here even if they weren't enrolled.

I ran up to an officer who seemed to be in charge, figuring nobody would arrest me in this chaos. "Officer, I'm the deacon here. I'll check for kids in the—"

"Father, you can help by standing behind the yellow tape. Let us do our job."

Son-of-a-bitch. The man was a plank. He didn't even know the difference between a deacon and a priest. My fists were clenched tight, and I was on the verge of using them. Talking to this schmuck was futile. Nearby, a lieutenant with the fire department was giving orders. I tapped him on the shoulder.

He whirled around. "Deacon! Am I glad to see you. We've got to make sure all the kids are out—"

"What about your four?"

"Home with Mom."

"Glad you're on duty, Jack. We should check the gym basement. The kids play their rap music so loud down here, they don't hear anything … even sirens."

"Where exactly?"

"I have the keys. I'll show you."

The lieutenant beckoned to a few of his men, who ran alongside me. We rushed into the basement. I pointed the firefighters in different directions. Eight teenagers were in the weight room, music blasting as expected.

"There's a bomb threat," I shouted. The firefighters herded them toward an exit.

"This is bogus," one kid shouted.

"Yeah," said another, lunging for his boom box.

"What if our stuff gets blowed up?"

"The stuff can be replaced. *You* can't." No more mister nice guy. I got tough. "Grab your coats and get the hell out of here before I start kicking ass." The look on my face and the size of the three burly firefighters finally persuaded them.

I checked the gym and showers one last time as we ran out of the building. "What about the school?" I asked.

"It's empty except for the bomb squad and dogs,

A deafening explosion rang out, and we hit the ground. As I fell—ears ringing--I looked back fearing the worst. But the school and gym were intact. The blast had come from the church. Shards of colored glass rained down, along with a shower of red droplets. The huge stained-glass window over the entrance had been blown out.

I tossed a prayer heavenward and ran for the church.

CHAPTER FORTY-TWO

"Oh God, it's the choir loft."

I fumbled with my keys, hoping the locked doors meant no one was in the church.

I ran up the spiral passage to the loft followed by two firefighters and two police officers. Besides blowing out the window, the blast had damaged a few pews and exploded buckets of red paint. Scarlet paint dripped from the ceiling and down the walls, puddling on the floor. The church smelled like cordite and latex paint. But no one was inside.

I knelt in relief and folded my hands. "Thank you, God."

"Amen to that," one of the firefighters whispered. "What's with the red paint?"

A warning.

I had confirmation on that thought when a police officer held up a leg and talons of a large bird. "What the hell is this?"

The departments radioed their respective supervisors, and the bomb squad rushed in.

"Everybody out," yelled one man.

"Could be a second bomb!" shouted another.

"Glass crunched and paint oozed under my feet as I walked down the exterior stone steps. I looked up at the empty window; the stained glass window had been created for the glory of God more than a hundred and fifty years ago. What a damn shame to see it destroyed.

A long black limo pulled up in front of me, and the rear door opened. I was staring into the eyes of Archbishop Laine. "Jump in," he said, and I did.

CHAPTER FORTY-THREE

"Your Grace."

"I came as soon as I heard. Was anyone injured?"

"Not that I know of."

"I'm glad you're safe. What happened up there?"

I explained about the small explosion, the paint and the talon.

"What do you make of it, my son?"

"A message, I think. A warning that some very sick people can hurt innocent people and the church whenever they wish."

"Who would do such a thing?"

"I suspect it's the same men who tortured Sister Mary Margaret and took the Bible with the code." I leaned back into the comfortable leather seat. "That code was only the beginning. Now they want me to find a DVD. Incriminating evidence, I suppose."

"So, they threaten the church ... because of you? That's quite a complicated theory. Perhaps they're trying to pressure the cardinal. You know his life has been threatened—"

"Yes your grace. I mean, no, the bomb was not *about* me. I think it's about the DVD that belonged to ... the madam who was killed. They think I can find it."

"Can you?"

"God, I hope so. I'm working with the murdered woman's sister to find it."

The archbishop said nothing.

"I'm sorry I couldn't get a copy of the code for you. The police wouldn't give it up. I suspect someone in the police department may be involved."

The archbishop sighed. "There's trouble at the top, I dare say. I haven't mentioned it before, but I think the police commissioner... well, I don't have evidence to prove criminal acts, but I think he's a crook, certainly not fit for public office. And Clayton? He's a weak link for sure. The cardinal has been outspoken about their... misdeeds, and elections are looming." He paused, looking older and very worried. "I assumed the bomb was a warning to him. He's had death threats, you know. Now the DVD ... any idea what's on it."

"Not really, but these people will do anything to get it."

"Then we must have it. We've got to protect the cardinal, despite his feelings about the Gabrians. He looked off into the distance. Please continue your quest, despite the cardinal's objections."

"But why the objections... I mean, this isn't Gabrian—"

"No, but he thinks no good can come of our involving ourselves in his matter. The monsignor and I disagree with him."

I didn't know what to say. All of them were my superiors in the church. The archbishop was my mentor. "My I ask why the DVD is of interest ... to certain members of the hierarchy?"

"Me you mean. The DVD could contain incriminating evidence against members of our clergy. We must protect the church's already tarnished image."

"I see."

"Can you do this?"

"I'll do my best."

"You have my blessing and my prayers. If you need more people or any services, tell me or Monsignor Salvatore. We can call on your Gabrian brothers" .... He blew out a breath. "Despite the cardinal's misgivings all the way around."

"I appreciate your offer."

He rubbed his face with his palms. "I'm off to Saint Mary's hospital. Your pastor has suffered a heart attack, no doubt because of the bomb threat. But I suppose you knew that."

"No, I didn't. Please give him my regards." I didn't like Father Casey, but I didn't wish him ill, either.

"Go with God." He drove me to my car, passing paramedics and EMTs as they treated bystanders hit by falling glass and bits of debris. Hundreds of small red dots covered the vehicles nearby. As I turned to look out the back window, a large gray SUV passed, going in the opposite direction.

CHAPTER FORTY-FOUR

After two hours at Tommy Wallace's rolling mansion, Ann had taken action. When she was alone, she called the one person she knew who was important enough to help, someone she hadn't spoken to in years.

"Hello," the man's voice growled over the phone.

"A voice from your past."

The man's voice softened. "I'd recognize your dulcet tones anytime, anywhere. How've you been, Ann?"

"Not good. I called to ask for your help"

"Of course. You were special to me, you know. I've thought about you, or rather, *fantasized* about you a lot."

Ann grimaced and changed the subject. "Any leads in my sister's murder?"

"No, too many suspects. Dangerous business. You know that."

"Are you making progress?"

"Ann, we're doing all we can, but you know how it is."

"Yes, I know. Hookers aren't a high priority. Look, I don't know who, but I know why. I want to tell you something that might help you find her killer."

"Let's have it." He knew what was coming, but he'd play along. Contact with Ann could only help.

"I think she was blackmailing some of her high-end clients for one last fat paycheck to make a nest egg and leave the business."

"Blackmail is always risky. Do you suspect any particular clients? That would help."

"No, but they managed to get some incriminating evidence she had, with the exception of a DVD."

"I see. And do you have the DVD?" His voice lifted with hope.

"No, but I'm looking for it. I'm scared because they think I know where it is. Some men broke into my apartment, probably with police assistance. I barely got away... with help."

"I haven't heard anything, but I'll check. Must be some rogue cop operation. Is that deacon with you?"

"He'll be back soon."

"I see, and then what?"

"I'll help him look for the DVD. I have a few ideas."

"Like where?"

"I'm not sure."

"If you find it, what then?"

"We'll turn it over to the authorities."

"Good girl. Bring it to me. I'll see it gets to the DA with corroborating evidence for a good case."

"Okay, but first we have to find it. One other thing, have you heard anything about a young woman named Tamara?"

The man took a deep breath. "One of Amber's girls, right? She's been reported missing, but these girls move suddenly without notice."

The phone went silent for a while. "Yes, but not in this case. Something's wrong."

He switched gears. "Are you going to pick up Amber's business? Because if you are, I can help. I'd love to be your first client, babe. I've missed you."

Ann kept her voice even and calm. "It's been a long time. And no, I'm not going back to that life."

Another pause.

"One more thing, have you heard the names Bernie or Malachi?"

"I don't think so, why?" He frowned at this bit.

"They are definitely involved. They may be responsible for my sister's death."

"Last names? Descriptions?

"All I have is the first names."

"The more information you can give me the better. How about getting together? Perhaps we could discuss the matter over dinner … for old times' sake."

Ann held back screams of outrage. "No, I don't think that would be a good idea. But anything you can do to find my sister's killer…"

"Well, we could discuss it over dinner."

Ann fumed. He just wouldn't quit. "Sorry, no, but let me know about any developments in the case."

Halloran's voice registered disappointment, but there was always tomorrow. "Hey, it's my job. I get it. How can I reach you?" As if he didn't know *exactly* how to reach her any time he wanted.

"I'll call you."

"Fair enough."

"Thank you for listening. Goodbye."

"Goodbye Ann." He hung up the phone, a pleased expression on his face. Ann had told him everything she knew.

CHAPTER FORTY-FIVE

On the way back to the construction site, I picked up five king-sized pizzas from Leo's place, four for the workers and one to share with Ann. We were alone in Tommy Wallace's rolling mansion.

I filled her in on the bombing at Saint Sebastian's. Once again, I felt responsible for damage and injuries. The debts were piling up.

"I'm glad you're okay," she said.

"Thanks." I wanted to change the subject. "So, did the boys show you around?"

Ann was exhilarated as she told me of riding to the top of the building under construction. "I had to wear a hard hat. It was scary with no walls and the wind blowing. You know how I feel about heights. I don't know how they do it, working up there." She bit into a steaming slice of pepperoni pizza.

"It's a tough way to make a living."

"And you do it too?"

I held up my hand a moment until I could swallow. "Sometimes they send work my way. For me, it's usually carrying lath and wallboard wherever they need it. So they treated you right."

"Like visiting royalty." Ann adjusted an imaginary crown on her head. "One man introduced me as your girlfriend. They got a kick out of that."

I grinned. "I'll bet. They keep trying to fix me up. They're convinced I need a woman." Maybe they're right…. but I'm a deacon. God, my path was getting more confusing by the minute.

"I know why they treat you with such uh … manly affection." She took another bite of pizza. "You help them with their kids."

I shrugged and grabbed a paper towel off the roll. I was tempted to dab a bit of pizza sauce from Ann's chin, but I handed her the makeshift napkin instead.

Tommy Wallace came by to thank me for the pizzas. "We'll keep an eye on your lady friend anytime." He winked. "She gives the place a bit of class, you know what I mean?"

I knew. As we drove away Ann waved to the men on the site and some of them tipped their hard hats and bowed. *I'd never live this down.*

CHAPTER FORTY-SIX

"Allison had another office in a high rise off Wabash and Jackson. You know the area... next to downtown DePaul University. I don't have the exact address."

I nodded and headed downtown, checking the rear view mirror for that suspicious gray SUV. Traffic in the loop was miserable. We were under the "L" tracks on Wabash, and every time a train passed overhead, it dumped snow and ice on our roof. "I have an idea," I gave her the details. "Tell me when we pass Allison's building.

She scanned the cityscape and pointed. "That's it!"

I pulled into the closest parking garage. I jumped out and asked Ann to slip behind the wheel. "Take the underground level," I told her, "and stay in the car until I call you."

From the window of the college bookstore, I could see the traffic flow in both directions along Wabash Avenue. Within minutes, a gray Escalade slowly passed the garage and parked illegally on the street a block away.

I clicked in Ann's number on my cell. "We've got company. Meet me in the lobby."

"I'll be there."

We exited the lobby and crossed the street, me craning my neck every thirty seconds to see if we were followed. In the foyer of the high rise, we didn't see Allison's name on the directory board. Ann tapped her head and gazed upward. "What am I thinking? Allison sublet an office from a small insurance company, probably to keep her name *off* the directory."

"Good point." We narrowed the five companies down to two and hit it lucky on the sixteenth floor: "Chicago Life and Protection Insurance Company." Ann explained the situation to a suit that checked her ID and let us into a functional, no frills workspace.

We dug through paper work for a couple of hours, finding nothing. Then I picked up a file of rental transactions with the Belmont harbor yacht club. "Look at this." I handed her an invoice with "T & T, Belmont harbor, penciled on the side. "Do you know what 'T & T' means?"

"No."

"Someone told me Amber's girls entertained men at parties, dinners and cruises. Would that include cruises on the lake as well as ocean cruises?"

Ann avoided my eyes and looked down. "Yes. I knew of some of those venues." Her voice was stiff, artificial.

God, I hate it when something reminds Ann of her past.

She straightened her shoulders and took the file from me and flipped through the invoices. "The last unpaid invoice to the yacht club was the day before Allison was… murdered."

That made no sense to me. "All boats are in dry-dock by November."

Ann averted her eyes again. "Well, they don't have to actually take the boat out on the water to have a party. The club has some rooms available.

As we left, I asked Ann if I could borrow her credit card to rent another car. "The cops probably have mine earmarked by now."

At the elevator, two men leaped out of the stairwell, handguns drawn. I had no time to react. *Shit. How did they find us?*

"Let's take the stairs, shall we?" The man's voice dripped with mock courtesy. I took a good look at him: red beard, five foot ten, heavy.

"What do you want?" asked Ann. Her jaw was tight and her hands were clasped, as though trying to contain her fear.

"Turn around. I think you know," said the other man.

Bad tattoo on his neck. I memorized the barbed wire pattern. Probably got it in prison.

"Hand over the DVD and you two can walk outta here."

"We don't have it," I said.

His eyes were dead, no spark at all. This guy was seriously bad... dangerous. "Was I talkin' to you?"

Ann broke in, her voice steadier now. "We don't have it, and we don't know where it is."

"Now that's a real shame." The tattooed thug took charge. "Hank, I'll take the girl. You escort the deacon to his *appointment*."

I tried to postpone the inevitable. "Hey. We're trying to find the damned video."

"Start walking." Red beard used his gun barrel to point up the stairs. Ann gave me a woebegone look as she walked downstairs with the other man.

"Where are we going?"

"Not far." He poked the gun into my back—hard. Four flights up, I pushed open a heavy metal door and stepped onto the roof. The icy wind whipped into me and I let go of the door with a bang, hitting the man behind me. Things happened fast after that.

I smashed his gun hand into the metal doorframe and kicked him down the stairs. I followed him down—fast—before he could get up. But there was no hurry, after all. He lay at the landing, his neck twisted at an impossible angle. I leapt over him and kept running. Too many floors. An elevator would be faster... maybe. The car seemed to take forever to reach my floor. *Shit.* I had to get to Ann.

CHAPTER FORTY-SEVEN

The man with the tattoo left the stairwell at the fifteenth floor, pulling Ann by one arm. "I ain't about to walk when there's an elevator. Don't you scream and don't you run. I'll shoot you where it hurts, but you won't die." He squinted and turned his mouth down. ""Nah, I'll shoot the first kid I see and that'll be on you."

He came up close behind her. "Can you live with that?" He touched her ear with his lips. She shrank away, and he stroked her hair with the back of his hand. "Call me 'Jay', sweet bitch." Ann shrank away. "Feisty, huh."

The elevator door opened, and Jay's eyes moved from Ann to the people in the lobby. Bernie and Malachi were two blocks down on Wabash Avenue. Jay put his mouth near Ann's ear again. "See the little girl over there? The sweet little blonde? I have her in my gun sight. Do anything rash, and she'll be the first to go down." He jammed his gun into his coat pocket.

Ann glanced at the three-year-old, tightened her jaw and stood straight as she marched beside the man with the gun. Jay looked behind him and chortled. It'd be days before anybody found the deacon's frozen body on the roof.

CHAPTER FORTY-EIGHT

I charged through the lobby and scanned the street: The gray SUV was still parked at the curb. I saw Ann walking close beside the man with the tattoo. A cop was directing traffic at the intersection. I didn't have much time. I took the risk and ran up to him. "Officer, see that SUV? It's parked illegally in a loading zone. I gotta unload my truck before the store closes or it'll be my ass. I had to park my truck around the block. Can you help?"

"Yeah, I'll shag 'em along."

"Great. I'll get my truck. Thanks." I stepped back and let the cop take the lead. Then I drifted onto the sidewalk a few paces behind Ann and the tattooed man, who had a grip on her upper arm. When the cop tapped the Escalade window, the thug spun in the opposite direction, yanking Ann with him.

He was headed straight at me, but he didn't know it... yet. I was still hidden in the crowd. The creep had his left hand in his coat pocket. Judging from the bulge I'd say he had a gun. I rushed him from the side. Luckily I still had the knife I'd confiscated in Ann's alley. I thrust it through his coat pocket into his gun hand. He sucked air and, when he turned to face me, I bashed my forehead into his face. He fell to the ground, KO'd with a pocketful of blood.

"Man down!" I shouted to the milling crowd. "He needs a doctor."

Ann stared at me, her mouth hanging open. Thankfully, she didn't scream.

"Let's go." I grabbed her hand and ran for the garage. Over my shoulder, I saw the gray SUV pull out and the police officer head for the fallen man. "Let's get the hell out of here."

"The stairwell… what happened?" Ann asked.

"I stopped a man from killing me." I didn't mention the man was now dead. She looked at me in horror and began shaking.

By the time we were in the cruiser, Ann was sobbing silently.

She needed a few minutes to calm down, but we were out of time. I put my hands on her trembling shoulders. "Shhh now. Take a few deep breaths. You're safe. We've got to figure out how they found us. They're tracking us somehow."

Ann hiccoughed back her sobs. "I… I don't follow."

"Let's empty our pockets… and your purse. There's got to be a bug."

I took everything out… except the bloody knife. Ann reached deep into the bottom of her handbag and pulled out a small electronic gadget. She almost smiled. "Is this it?"

"Bingo. They're using a GPS tracker to find us."

"How did you know—?"

"I was an MP, remember?"

"How did they get it in my purse?" She peered around the car, looking for more bad guys, I guess. "They can do *anything*."

The incident on the sidewalk in front of the Pick-Congress flashed in my memory. That's probably when they slipped the bug into Ann's purse.

"No they can't do anything. We know about the device. We'll beat them at their own game."

She raised an eyebrow. "How?"

"You'll see." I motioned her back in the car and drove a couple of blocks to the Golden Dragon, one of Chicago's finest Chinese restaurants.

"This is your plan?'"

"We've got to eat sometimes."

"I'm too nervous. I mean, they have to know we're here."

I handed the keys to a valet. "I'm betting they'll leave us alone in a crowded restaurant. Besides, they want the DVD, and we haven't found it yet."

"It does smell good," Ann admitted. We decided on a couple of entrées to share, and I finished off an Asahi beer and ordered another before our meal arrived. We ate family style, not saying much.

Ann seemed calmer as she sipped a small glass of plum wine. Then her eyes brightened, and I could almost see a light bulb go on over her head. "Suppose Allison wasn't alone on her last assignment? Say she was at a party, maybe at the yacht club... with other women. If she was, we could find out who else was there. They might know something." She shook her head, suddenly looking fragile and afraid. "Who am I kidding?"

"No, that's a great idea. Really." I put my hand over hers and gave her my best reassuring smile. I wasn't just humoring her. It was a good idea. We'd follow up on that... together.

I paid the bill with more of William De La Croix's money and helped Ann into her coat. She turned quickly on her tiptoes and kissed me on the cheek. "Thanks for saving me... again."

I was still holding her hand and pressed it to my lips. "That's what deacon's are for."

CHAPTER FORTY-NINE

While Deacon and Ann dined in the Golden Dragon, Malachi and his companions ate Mexican take-out in the SUV. The burrito hadn't settled well on Malachi's stomach. In the SUV, Jay moaned intermittently, pressing his good hand to his forehead where deacon had butted him. The stab wound on his other hand was superficial. The bleeding had stopped.

"Serves you right. You fuckin' had her and let her get away." Malachi was royally pissed. "Where the fuck is Hank?" He didn't wait for an answer. The answer was obvious. Deacon was alive, so Hank probably wasn't.

"There they go." Jay said. Bernie was driving. "They're taking the 290 West out of town." He shot after them, staying about a mile behind. They all watched the blip on the green screen.

"Good. We're on them." Malachi gnawed his lower lip. "Wake me when they stop. I'm taking forty winks." One last fat paycheck then the Caribbean, he thought, closing his eyes. He could picture his secluded white frame house near the beach. Parrots and flamingos and dark-skinned girls. Maybe he'd take up painting in his retirement. Yeah, I'll paint birds. Fuck. *I'll paint birds on broads.* His lips curved into something that would never pass for a smile. *What kinda brushes and paint do you use on a human canvas?* He snorted. *Needles and ink—a possibility.* He could picture that, too.

Why the hell couldn't this last job be an easy one? When he'd contacted Halloran, all he got was a brusque, "Stay on their tail and nail the deacon."

The battle with the deacon had become personal. Malachi looked forward to defeating such a worthy adversary. Once he was eliminated and the DVD was in his possession, Malachi would give a copy to Halloran. He'd keep the original for his own insurance. Fuck their deal. Then there was Ann. She grew more tantalizing with every thought. He pictured her helpless, totally his… for a time. After that, she would be punished… slowly… like all women deserved to be.

CHAPTER FIFTY

Ann was quiet for a while and then asked the obvious question. "Where are we going?"

"Trucker's rest stop. Shouldn't be long." At the Itasca exit, I saw what I had been looking for: a flock of eighteen-wheelers surrounding a truck stop. I pulled to a stop and said, "Order us some coffee to go. I'll be along soon."

Fear returned to her face. "You're leaving me here… alone?"

"Just for a couple of minutes. I've got to talk to some drivers at the pumps. I don't think the creeps will go inside, but if they do, scream bloody murder. I know truckers. They'll protect you."

I struck up a few conversations with the drivers and asked about the weather west of Chicago. I did what I'd set out to do and collected Ann and our coffees inside the diner.

"So?" she asked.

"So, they won't be following us to the yacht club."

She smiled. "That's good news, Mister Mysterious."

I was mesmerized by her smile. "You have a beautiful smile. You have a beautiful everything." Corny, I thought. But she was gracious.

"Thanks. She took my arm on the way to the car. When she was inside, I leaned in to kiss her. She kissed me back, caressing my cheek.

I didn't know where this was going and, at the moment, I didn't care.

CHAPTER FIFTY-ONE

something was wrong. Malachi had left his fantasies behind to focus
on their task. Where was his prey headed? They'd been driving an
hour and were well into the bleak rolling hills of western Illinois. Is
the video out here someplace? It didn't make sense.

Finally, their target stopped moving. "Get closer," Malachi told
Bernie. They pulled into a large truck stop that smelled of diesel fuel
and cooking grease. The few passenger cars were dwarfed by big rigs.
Small groups of men stood around, mumbling trucker talk and smoking
over steaming cups of coffee.

The screen showed they were closing in on their quarry. Bernie drove
slowly between the trucks. "We should be right on top of them."

The men squinted through the windows in the dim light. The only
vehicle that was close was a dirty, stock-loaded eighteen-wheeler.

Malachi muttered out loud. "This can't be right. Don't tell me they
hitched a ride on that thing. I can't see anyone." He turned to the screen.
"Let me take a look at that."

A bright green dot flashed. Their prey was dead ahead.

"Where's the beeper? We can activate that to pinpoint the device."
He scanned the dials. "There it is." He flipped a switch and a repetitive
low steady bleep began.

"Let's take the damn thing outside."

As they walked toward the truck, the bleeps came at closer intervals.

Malachi pressed the back of a glove to his nose. "Goddamn, it stinks out here."

A bulky figure emerged out of the night. He had a salt and pepper beard and wore a Chicago Bears cap. "Can I hep y'all?"

"Is this your rig?" Malachi asked.

"Yep."

"You seen a couple, maybe give 'em a ride? Tall man. Good-looking girl."

"Nope. What's that there machine you got there?"

"Never mind."

With that, the driver dropped his civility. "Never mind yourself. Get away from my truck. I'm fixin' to head on outa here."

"You're not leavin' until I get some answers."

"I ain't got no fuckin' answers. I'm leavin'."

Bernie grabbed the truck driver from behind and pinned his arms. Malachi jabbed him in the stomach—hard—with his cane.

Malachi placed the tracking screen against the truck until the beeping became a steady hum. "It's got to be right here." He reached in and pulled the device from the corner of the truck bed. "Shit. *Hog* shit. They'll pay. Oh, they'll goddamn fucking pay." Malachi threw the glove away.

As he passed the driver, Malachi whacked him across the mouth. Blood spurted from the trucker's lips. "Throw the bastard in the back with his pigs."

Back in the van, Malachi called Halloran with the bad news. Malachi held the cell away from his ear while Halloran ranted. "Get your asses back here," Halloran said, finally. "I'll get back to you."

Furious at his failure, Malachi tried to blank out the voice in his head, the one that shrieked like his mother, *You fuckin freak. You can't do nothin right.* He cringed against the door.

Jay touched his shoulder. "You okay, man?"

Malachi bolted upright and shook him off. "Get your fuckin hands off me and shut the fuck up."

Jay nodded and disappeared behind the front seat.

Malachi closed his eyes again, determined to block out... everything but his fantasy. In his mind, he pictured Ann struggling against the straps he'd fastened oh so carefully around her naked torso.

CHAPTER FIFTY-TWO

By the time we reached the city, it was nearly midnight, too late for the yacht club. "I could use a shower and a good night's sleep, how about you?"

"God, I thought you'd never slow down. I'm bushed."

I parked behind the Knight's Inn on Sheridan Road on the chance that someone was still following us. We hustled down the alley up to our ankles in snow to the Holiday Inn. *Got to get a different car, and soon.*

We weren't alone. A young man with black greasy hair and a leather jacket over a black T-shirt was leaning against a shiny low rider. His baseball cap was turned sideways and he was cleaning his nails with a long thin knife. His gaze skidded across us. His eyes darted up and down the alley.

I sensed danger, but he appeared to be waiting for someone. *A drug score. Or he doesn't want to play right now.* Our eyes locked. The message was clear: We wouldn't mess with one another this night.

After we passed him, Ann spoke through chattering teeth. "I'm dead on my feet… and freezing." As we entered the hotel lobby, a blast of very warm air hit us. It felt great.

Ann had acquired a case of the shakes, so I left her on a plush couch in the lobby while I registered. Then I eased her into the elevator. An elderly couple with two suitcases stared at Ann, who *did* look disheveled and distressed.

"Just the flu," I told them.

The couple smiled sympathetically.

As soon as I helped her into our room, she started crying. I held her, trying to come up with the right words and sounding lame. "It'll be okay."

"Will I ever get to feel safe again?"

"Sure."

She put her face against my chest, and I felt her relax. "He said he'd shoot a little girl if I did anything. I felt ... helpless. And then you showed up."

"Anybody would've felt that way. Helpless? No. You're brave, Ann."

She looked up and smiled a little. "Not really, but when you're around, I feel a little more courage."

I relaxed too. I wiped stray tears from her cheeks and forehead.

She touched me back, running her finger along the diagonal scar that ran through my left eyebrow and then the cut on my chin.

"Looks like a faded red zipper," she said, and gave a little laugh. It was a wonderful sound. She kissed her finger and touched them again.

I smiled back. "Is that supposed to make me feel better?"

Our kissing was sudden, hungry and hard. Her body was against mine, and I let myself go.

She pulled away, stepping back. Was she having second thoughts?

No, I realized she simply needed room.

In a moment her coat, blouse, slacks and bra were on the floor, and I hadn't moved an inch. I was staring, mesmerized. She was so beautiful naked, and words failed me completely.

She helped me out.

"What do you have to say?" she asked.

"Beautiful."

"You're a man of very few words, Deacon."

"Sometimes a man doesn't need words."

She led me to the bed so I could show her what I meant.

I woke in the morning to the sound of the shower running.

I rose, stretched and started the coffee brewing. I didn't need to look at the bed to remember it. You don't forget a bed like that. When you finally give up, both of you, it's only because you're happy enough to fall asleep at last.

Opening the drapes, I gazed out at the whitecaps churning up Lake Michigan. Snow was still falling. The blue light of dawn silhouetted the skyscrapers. Whether joy or peace was the best thing a man could feel, I didn't know at that moment—and didn't need to.

I sensed her behind me. "Good morrow, O Captain my Captain. How's the horizon?"

I turned. Her hair was wet. She had a towel wrapped around her body.

She didn't take a step toward me. She didn't need to. I went to her. Her towel fell to the floor.

"Again," she whispered in my ear but I was already ahead of her.

CHAPTER FIFTY-THREE

Icy winds stabbed us as we stepped out of the car at the Belmont Harbor Yacht Club. Once inside the club, we headed for a table near one of the blazing fireplaces. Most of the patrons had done the same, turning toward heat and away from the spectacular but chilly view of the Lake. There was plenty to look at inside, given the seafaring accouterments on the walls and the fish swimming in large aquariums. The rectangular bar sparkled as the hanging glasses caught the firelight.

When the server brought our hot drinks, Ann asked her to tell the club manager we needed to see him. I watched her, wondering if she was one of Amber's girls. The skirt was short enough.

Ann took the lead. "When he comes, remember, you're Harry, my bodyguard. Just look intimidating. Let me do the talking."

The firelight put a glint in Ann's auburn hair and a glow in her eyes. She looked fabulous. But then, when didn't she? *Focus, Deacon.* I pulled my attention back to her words. "I'll give it my best shot."

We were halfway through our drinks by the time Charles Crawford appeared. He was a toothy shark of a man with a practiced welcome-to-the-club greeting.

The pleasantries stopped when Ann introduced herself as Amber's sister.

"Amber?" His smile faded fast.

She gave him a withering look. "No games, Charles. We both know my sister ran an escort service and regularly did business with you."

"Ah, yes... Amber."

"She was murdered a few days ago. I'm settling her accounts."

"My God, murdered. I'm so sorry." He bowed his head for a moment.

As if he didn't know. I kept my mouth shut, but it was tough. What an obsequious ass.

We followed him to a wood-paneled office with several decent seascapes on the walls. He motioned toward a pair of leather armchairs. "Please take a seat."

Ann went right to the point. "I found a bill for $683 that Amber owed you. It was dated this month. I'd like to clear that up."

Charles opened a computer screen and his fingers danced along the keys. "Your figures are correct."

Ann opened her checkbook and then paused. "No boats are in operation in the dead of winter. May I ask what the bill is for?"

"Certainly, the rental of a two-bedroom suite for one night and a dinner with wine for four. We keep a few rooms and suites ready for members. You know, small private parties or a sleep-over before they sail out.

"Fine. I also need the names of our two escorts, so I can pay them."

Charles said, "I know *nothing* about that."

The man was lying. I could see it in his eyes. I was done with strong and silent. I stood. "Think about this, Charles. Amber was found dead in the water the morning after her girls stayed here. Do you want to see the yacht club on the morning news?" I put both hands on his desk and leaned forward. "Do you really want the police poking around here?"

Charles cleared his throat. "No... no, I guess not."

I kept my voice low and threatening. "Well then, we need your cooperation. Look at your screen again and tell us the names of the girls *and* the men with them."

"The names are not on my screen. The women... I remember an Asian woman. She'd been here before... " He stopped and sat back in his chair. "I don't know... I think I should talk to the chairman of our board first. You can come back tomorrow—"

"Bullshit." I slammed a fist on his desk and Charles jumped like I'd slammed my fist into him.

"Okay... *okay*. But no one can know about this."

Ann nodded. "That's part of the deal."

Beads of sweat glistened on Charles's forehead. "Tiko, that was her name. The other was Tamara."

Got it. They were the T & T noted on the invoice.

"And the men with them?"

"I can't tell you who they were. They went directly to the suites. You must know that anonymity was paramount with Amber's... service."

I gave him my best glare. "Can't or *won't* tell us."

Ann intervened then, politely. "Can you tell us anything about them?"

"Only that one man was black and the other white."

"Thank you. Did you notice anything else... about this particular rental? Anything unusual?"

Charles squinted. "Well, there was one thing—"

Ann's eyes opened wider, but her voice stayed even. "Yes?"

"Amber and a gentleman with two black bags came in earlier in the day. She said they needed to 'check things out.' At the time, I wondered why. She'd seen the room before. Anyway, they stayed for about an hour... and when they left, their bags looked... well, they looked empty."

"I see. Anything different about the room?"

"Uh, no. Nothing was amiss, except for a crack in the glass coffee table."

Ann finished making out the check and handed it to him. "You've been most helpful, Charles. If someone should ask, we were never here. Isn't that so?"

"Ah, absolutely. I've never laid eyes on you."

I glared at Charles for another twenty seconds, then turned and left. "You were brilliant back there," I told Ann.

"And you can be very scary. I mean that. It makes me ... nervous."

CHAPTER FIFTY-FOUR

nn called the number embossed on her sister's business card and jotted it down. "Disconnected, but there's a new number." Within a few minutes she'd found out from Justine, Allison's replacement, that Tamara was gone—nobody knew where.

After some discussion Ann persuaded Justine to arrange a meeting with Tiko.

"Tiko wasn't thrilled about the meeting," Ann said.

An understatement. The door to room 1815 at the Marriott opened only as far as the chain allowed. Over Ann's shoulder, I could see green eye shadow and bright red lips. That's about it.

"Who is it?"

"I'm Ann, Amber's sister. I called a little while ago."

She looked past Ann to me. "And who is with you?"

"This is Deacon, my associate."

She said something in Japanese and opened the door. "I too, have an associate. He is Yoshi." Behind her was a man with the girth of a Sumo wrestler.

Sumo man and I glared at each other like two fighting cocks. He came toward me. "Please to raise your hands," he said with an unusually high-pitched voice. "You understand?" He patted me down, found the knife and took it. I let him. Why not? He might not know it, but we were on the same side.

"I am so sorry about your sister," Tiko began. "We were friends."

"Thank you."

Tiko's *associate* stood behind her, so I took a similar position behind Ann. The room smelled of incense.

"I have a couple of brief questions. I need to know about your evening with Tamara at the Belmont Yacht Club about ten days ago. Anything you tell me will be held in the strictest of confidence."

Tiko perched on a couch in front of Ann. She wore a jade green sheath dress with a long slit up one leg and several flashy rings on her fingers. She even had the enigmatic smile down pat. She tried to hide her trembling fingers with a dainty green handkerchief.

"What can you tell me about the evening?" Ann asked.

Tiko frowned. "The evening was usual except ... I heard the men speaking together in the middle of the night." Tiko seemed to shrink into herself. "The next morning, Tamara—and her client—were already gone. That was strange. Usually, the men leave together."

Ann nodded and extended a piece of paper. "Any idea what this could mean?"

Tiko inspected the graphic, which replicated the marks on Amber's key. "The arrows are familiar. Perhaps a sign or advertisement? The letters and numbers—no meaning for me.

Ann had saved the tie-breaker until last, the question that would probably give us the door. "Who were you with that night?"

"Two men."

"Their names ... descriptions?"

"No. Don't know their names. Better that way."

"Anything else, please."

"How do you say ... politi-shun." Tiko's eyes widened and her chin trembled.

Yoshi suddenly coughed loudly. Clearly a warning.

Suddenly, Tiko lost her enigmatic expression. She appeared shocked at what she had said. "I will not tell you any more. Do not say my name ever. Do not mention what I say ... said."

She looked down at her gold-flecked fingernails. "I do not want to answer more questions." Her gaze moved over our heads to the wall. "I am sorry for your loss, but cannot help."

Sumo man tossed my knife to me and signaled for us to leave.

Once in the hall I told Ann, "Tiko knows more than she's telling us. I'm sure of it."

"How do you know?"

"I've been lied to, far too often. I just know."

CHAPTER FIFTY-FIVE

Mitch Halloran picked up his private line on the first ring. It was V, who usually had something of interest to offer in exchange for a favor. Halloran hadn't tried too hard to discover his identity. He liked the interaction as it was. From listening to the voice over the past six years, he knew only that the man was older, educated, no discernible accent and concise in the words he used.

"What can I do for you?" Halloran asked.

"It's what we can do for each other," V reminded him. "I happen to know there is a missing DVD of great importance to you."

"What of it?" Halloran's heart rate started to climb.

"I don't know what's on it or where it is, but I will know before you do. I'm willing to let you know where to find it when the time comes."

Halloran kept his voice even, but he was thrilled by this news. "That's good of you."

"Knowing you're a generous man I have a few favors to ask in return."

"Naturally."

"I want you to extend your protection to a few people. The first is Sister Mary Margaret O'Sullivan."

"I don't know what you're talking about."

"I'm sure you do. Secondly, I don't want any harm to come to Deacon Adelius."

"I have no control over that."

He knew that V knew that he was lying, but V stayed congenial nonetheless. "If you want the DVD and you want our little chats to continue, work on that. V's voice slipped from light to dark—almost hushed. "What can you tell me about a prostitute named Tamara?"

Halloran considered the question and his answer. "Hmmm. I don't know, perhaps... um... a long deep water cruise?"

"I see."

"Now, I have something to ask of you. I'd like to know the whereabouts of Amber's sister."

"I suspect she is with Deacon Adelius. I'll get back to you on that.... Oh, one other thing. I'll be sending you a file on the transgressions of a certain priest. He works in the cardinal's office. You know what you need to do to nail the offender. I'm also faxing a monthly diocesan itinerary to you, up-to-date as of today. I think you'll find it helpful." The line went dead.

CHAPTER FIFTY-SIX

We had to find a safe house, somewhere, unknown to our pursuers. My mind snapped back to my church connections, and the answer came: Brother Chuck Williams, a fellow Gabrian. He ran a Carmelite Retreat House in Elmwood Park, northwest of Chicago.

I called him. "How the hell are you, Deac?" Except for a shaved head, Brother Chuck hadn't changed since our days of paying touch football in the streets. Still five-foot-ten, no neck, block of muscle.

I shook my head. "Not so good. I need some help, buddy."

"Whatever it takes."

We agreed to meet at a local coffee shop. Chuck sat at an angle and winced as he stretched out his left leg.

"Still having trouble with the knee?"

Chuck nodded. "Off and on, it's not so bad." He'd been a middle linebacker for the Chicago Bears until he popped a knee three years into his career. At least it didn't keep him out of the military—1st Airborne. As a Gabrian, he was tough and dedicated. He'd hinted at direct experience with pedophiles in the Chicago Projects where he'd grown up. Hinting was as far as he'd ever go. You didn't push Brother Williams. You trusted him. We both ordered coffee and garbage bagels.

"I need a safe haven for myself and a friend for a few days. She's picking up a few things at the mall." I gave Brother Chuck a condensed version of the past week, including the key.

Brother Chuck's response was a long low whistle. "Ruthless bastards. No wonder you need a hideout. And fast, I'd guess. I can arrange for two rooms, no questions asked. They're small cells for the retreatants—nothing but the basics."

"Great. We'll come in after dark."

Chuck told me to pick up our room keys in the office. "I'll leave the porch light on. Come see me in the main house after you're settled. "

"I can't thank you enough, but here's a start." I handed him an envelope with a packet of cash of De La Croix's money. "A donation to the Carmelites."

He flipped through the bills and raised his eyebrows. "Unnecessary, but every little bit helps." He raised his eyebrows and gave that contagious smile that usually warned of a joke to come.

"Or we could explore other payment ideas: You washing my underwear and my car—for a year—painting my room—"

"What a generous spirit." *God, it felt good to share a laugh with an old friend.*

"Godspeed. You'll be safe with us."

I put a call in to Monsignor Salvatore. He'd want to know I'd involved Brother Chuck and the retreat center in my quest. He gave me his blessing and asked if we had any leads.

"No, but we're working on it."

I helped Ann pack her purchases into the car, and we headed for the retreat house. "It's safe but Spartan," I warned her. The grounds were bare now but in the spring and summer, Brother Chuck made sure they were alive with colorful flowers. He didn't seem like the flower type, but you never can tell.

When she saw her tiny room, narrow bunk, pine desk and single window, she just smiled. "It'll do just fine."

That smile. I couldn't remember what I'd planned to say or do next. Go to my room I guess. I started to close the door and had a sudden thought. "We need a back-up plan in case… Well, someone should know about all of this, someone completely removed who could blow the whistle if it all goes south."

"Who?"

"An acquaintance. His family is in my parish." I told her about my backup plan.

"Great idea, but you probably shouldn't call. Your phone—"

"You're right. I'll find an outside phone. I'll ask Leo to deliver the message. That way we won't compromise anyone else."

"Sounds good."

"If you need anything call Brother Chuck. Get a good night's sleep. We're safe for now." I held both her hands in mine. On these grounds, in a woman's private room, even an embrace seemed out of place. "I'll miss you tonight."

"Me too."

After I'd made my call, I honored Brother Williams' request to see me before I retired for the night. "Hey Chuck, thanks again for putting us up." I tried to sound light-hearted, but I felt a lecture coming on.

"I'm glad to be of help. If you aren't too bushed, we need to talk." He waved me toward a wingback chair and poured me some Tennessee tea—three fingers of Jack Daniels—from a ceramic teakettle.

"Thanks."

The lights were low, the shadows emphasizing the barren room. A delicate carving of the risen Christ dominated one wall. There was a beat-up football on one of his sagging bookshelves. The atmosphere seemed oppressive somehow, adding to my growing dread of what Chuck wanted to say to me.

"So, your mission is to catch a murderer and find a DVD."

"Yeah, we're trying our best."

"And then?"

"And then get the information to the DA and take down whoever is behind two deaths, several assaults, kidnapping and who knows what else."

"So you're a police officer again. Does that suit you?"

"No, but the archbishop wants me to pursue this. I do owe him. Plus, I *am* worried about retributions—like the bombings at the school and church—if I don't find the DVD or if I do find it and give it to the authorities. And which authorities can I trust?"

I paused. I needed to talk about this. No guessing to it. I did need to unload all the drama of the past few days. Chuck was a good sounding board. "Someone's trying to kill me. The cops have been ordered to arrest me on sight. And I know someone in the police force is in on this. I've got to see it through."

There was a long silence as we sipped our *tea*. Oh, God. I knew what was coming next. I clenched my jaw, bracing myself.

"And the priesthood?"

I sat there for several minutes, leaning back in my chair, feet on a hassock. "It's over," I said finally. "I can't be part of this church." I didn't intend to do it, but the whiskey must have loosened my tongue. I talked on and on, releasing my feelings in a torrent of words. "My pastor's a drunk. The crimes of perverts and pedophiles are covered up. If they *are* exposed, people are paid off at outrageous expense. Unless we Guardians do the dirty work, the mission of the church suffers. I can't be part of it, not as a priest."

Chuck leaned back and looked at the ceiling. "'Nature alas, made only one being of you although there was material for a good man and a rogue.' Remember that one?"

"Yeah. Goethe."

"So it is for all of us. Tell me, inside you, is everything good and holy?"

"No of course not, but—"

"Do you think you are the only one disillusioned with the church? It's made up of sinners after all. I have seen horrors that would have plunged me into deep despair if not for God's grace." He breathed deeply and shut his eyes as if revisiting the darkness in his past. He probably was. "I don't have to tell you how many times Christ was betrayed."

"Yes, but—"

"But nothing…You think *I* haven't felt rejection and discrimination, even within our church? Chuck's shaved head gave off the radiant shine of a polished eight-ball. He leaned forward, muscles bunching under his T-shirt. "Yet here I am," he said. "And you, tough guy, you're in it with me."

I listened to Brother Chuck with my head bowed.

"We're God's hands and tools, Deac."

CHAPTER FIFTY-SEVEN

"Hey, Deac, how yah doin'," Leo shouted into the phone. His voice echoed like he was in a cave. I heard his boots pace the tile floor and pictured his arms waving. The man couldn't speak without moving.

Why had I called the pizzeria? I should have called his cell. "Leo! Turn off the blasted speakerphone."

I heard a click, and the echo disappeared. "So, what's up? You gotta payin' job for me, right? Should I bring my piece?"

"Yes, to the first. No, to the second. Leo, you've got to stop watching those old gangster movies."

"Hey, that's my *familia* you're talking about. Ain't you heard of the *Cosa Nostra*?" Leo roared with laughter. "Okay, whatcha got goin'?"

"I want you to go to the *Tribune* and talk to a reporter named Donald Stanichar. Tell him you have an informant in the parking garage with a big scoop for him. Shades of Deep Throat. I think he'll go for it."

"Hey, I saw that flick. What the hell are you talkin' about?"

"Jesus save us. No, not the porno movie. I'm talking about the Watergate break-in. You know, back in the '70s. The secret informant called himself Deep Throat... met reporters in a parking garage."

"Oh, yeah," said Leo, unconvincingly.

"Here's what I want you to do."

CHAPTER FIFTY-EIGHT

Donald Stanichar slouched before the piles of paper on his desk, rubbed his drooping eyebrows and pulled a long face. His ex-wife used to call it his "worried hound dog" look.

Today he had to come up with an A-1 story ASAP, and he wasn't inspired: a comparison of ACT performances of Illinois schools—yawn—or yet another piece on Asian carp in the Great Lakes.

His head was on his desk when the reception desk buzzed him, "You've got a visitor."

"Yeah? Who is it?"

"Leo's messenger service."

"Take a message." Stanichar hung up. Then he looked over at the front desk, where a short dark man was gesturing wildly. *Hmmm.* He looked determined, anyway. What the hell.

Stanichar stood up and waved the man toward him. They met midway through the maze of desks and cubicles. Nobody else looked up.

"So, you have a message for me?"

"Yeah, but I gotta be quiet about this." Leo looked around. "You ain't got a private room somewheres?"

"Right here."

Once the reporter closed the door behind them, Leo leaned close and shook his hand. "Leo Pazadelli—"

"Pazadelli Pizza?"

Leo ducked his head. "That's me. I'll make this quick. There's a guy waiting in the parking garage for you. He's got a big story… a scoop. You interested?"

"Maybe." Stanichar weighed his options. Walk-ins were usually duds, but Pazadelli seemed like the real deal. Good pizza, too. His gut said *give the guy a chance.* "So, what's the *scoop?*"

"I don't know exactly. He'll tell you, but he can't be seen up here with you."

Leo jumped up and looked through the glass partition like somebody was after him. "You comin' or what?"

"Okay, let's go." Stanichar signed out: 2 p.m. parking garage. Back approx. 3 p.m. His lips turned up slightly. At least they'd know where to find the body.

Leo punched an elevator button and then led the reporter through the cars in the crowded parking garage.

Finally, Leo stopped and opened the door to a dark PT Cruiser. "Here we are. This is how it works. Sit in the front seat and don't look behind you. I'll keep watch outside. Got that?"

"Got it." Stanichar got into the front seat. The rearview mirror had been turned down.

CHAPTER FIFTY-NINE

I stayed low in the rear seat. "Thanks for coming. Sorry for the melodrama, but it's for your safety *and* mine. Do you have a notebook?"

"Always. Tape recorder okay? I use both."

"No problem." I heard a click and then the sound of a notebook opening. I gave him some background and then got to the real point: "Murder is the bottom line. Some high-powered men in this city are involved in the death of a woman—Allison De La Croix—known on the street as Amber. She was a madam who ran a high-priced prostitution ring. She was murdered. She had a notebook that contained her client list. She was using it to blackmail some important people. Those people now have the notebook. But she also made an incriminating video. One that could send people to Joliet for a long time. One of her escorts named Tamara is also missing."

I paused to let Stanichar catch up. "Some of Chicago's finest are involved, at least in the cover-up. Somebody wants that video—bad. Perps have threatened Saint Sebastian's school and church if I don't recover the thing, wherever *it* is. Once I do it, they'll want me dead. Amber's murder and the church bombing a few days ago show what they can do."

"Who are these people?"

"That I don't know... yet. If anything happens to me, promise me I hope you'll pursue the story and take the intell to the DA—"

"Names. I need names, dates and facts," said Stanichar.

He was a reporter. Of course, I had to give him something tangible. "Sister Mary Margaret O'Sullivan, a nun at Saint Cathrine's, was helping me decipher the code in the notebook. These scumbags kidnapped and tortured her. You can check her records at Grand Hospital for the type and extent of her injuries."

"Is she still hospitalized?"

"No, she was threatened there. We got her to a safe house. Can't tell you where."

I could hear Stanichar tap his pen against the notebook. This wasn't enough.

"I'll give you two more names: Detective Ditmar who is involved somehow and an evil shit called Malachi. You'll get more information as I discover it. And I promise you'll get an exclusive when it comes together."

Stanichar blew out a long breath. "So, possible conspiracy, kidnapping and murder initiated by some power brokers—you don't know who—in Chicago. There are some big holes in this story."

"We'll plug'em." I snorted, almost a laugh. "If they don't plug us, first. Not a joke. Be careful. If they even suspect you know anything, that'll be the end of both of us."

"Who *are* you?"

"Just a man in the right place at the wrong time. I'm trying to take these people down before anyone else gets hurt, including me. That's enough for now."

The reporter paused for a moment and gave another big sigh. "Why me?"

"You've got a good family, you're a good investigative reporter and you have no connection to any of this."

The reporter didn't give up. "How do you know my family?"

I ignored that one. "You'd better get back to your office before you're missed."

Leo opened the door and Stanichar got out slowly, still scribbling in his notebook.

"Don't look back," Leo said, as he edged him toward the elevator.

CHAPTER SIXTY

"I got a call from an informant." Halloran paused for dramatic effect. He didn't get much satisfaction from Malachi, so he continued in a business-like tone. "Deacon and Ann are holed up in a Carmelite Retreat House in Elmwood Park."

"How'd your informant know?"

"Does it matter? I know it's good information. We've done business before."

"Everything matters." Malachi carefully enunciated his words in that breathy voice of his. "Such as, why did he tell you this? You're a cop. You *know* this could be a trap."

"Not a chance. That would sever our relationship, and he knows we need each other."

"So what does he get out of it?"

"Information, favors. You know how it works. We've had a good exchange over the years."

"Any ideas on extracting our hero and the girl?"

"That's what I'm paying you for. Now, get it done. Eliminate the deacon but don't hurt Ann beyond what's necessary. Without her, the DVD is lost."

Malachi grunted and punched the first number into his cell. "Pack your Bibles," he said into the phone. "We're going on a retreat."

CHAPTER SIXTY-ONE

I went to Leo's place to brief him, so he could help Stanichar if necessary. We sat down with a bottle of Chianti, an Italian drinking song playing in the background. Ahhh. Plácido Domingo... *La Traviata*. I could almost relax.

Then Leo went into his one-man comedy act: "A man rushes into a bar and orders a double shot. He drinks it down and asks the bartender, 'How tall are penguins'—"

"Ah, come on Leo," I said. "Don't you have anything but nun jokes?"

"Whatsamatta, *pisan*—you don't like nun jokes?"

"Okay, go ahead."

"Anyway, the bartender answers. 'Oh, I don't know, I'd guess about two and a half feet tall.'"

"The patron says, thank God, I thought I just ran over a nun." As usual he laughed heartily at his own joke.

We traded insults and stories. In a half hour, I received a call. "Deac, we've got company."

I didn't have to ask Brother Chuck who the "company" was. *Damn.* "Are you sure?"

"Deac, I walk this neighborhood every day. I know the faces. Three new bad asses showed up at Norm's coffee shop tonight. They had that look."

I knew what that meant. Hard-edged, tough. "Did one of them have a cane?"

"Couldn't tell. They were in a booth. I saw head and shoulders."

"How the hell did they—"

"Who knows? I didn't tell anyone."

"I told three people, total." Obviously one too many, but which one? "Get Ann the hell out of there."

"Done. I sent her out the back gate in our '78 Dodge pickup. She's pretty good with a floor stick shift, thank the Lord. I told her to get a motel and tell nobody—not even us—where she is until late tonight."

"What now?"

"Wait for their next move, I guess. The brothers and I will discourage them. How about you?"

Why had I thought Ann and I would be safe… anywhere. "Damn. I'm on my way."

CHAPTER SIXTY-TWO

Three men in long dark topcoats hiked the short hill to the administration building on the retreat grounds. Malachi followed, some distance away.

Brother Chuck saw them enter. He told the receptionist he'd be in the workshop, the furthest point from the staff and retreatants.

A few minutes later, the men approached the open door of the converted garage, Malachi behind in the shadows.

"Excuse me," said Bernie, "I'm looking for Brother Williams."

Chuck stood up to face Bernie. "I'm Brother Williams."

"I need to locate someone staying here.... There's been a death in the family."

"God console them in their grief." Chuck calculated his chances against the entourage. He was badly outmanned. "Who're you looking for?"

"Ann Drew."

"We have no one here by that name."

"I'm sure she's here," said Bernie. "She may be with a tall guy— Deacon Adelius."

"Our only retreatants are attending a *men's* AA retreat. I assure you I would know if a woman and a deacon were staying with us."

"I have it on the best authority," said Bernie.

"Perhaps your 'best authority' mistook a woman and a deacon at our noon Mass. No one of that description is on the premises now."

"Well," said Bernie, "we'll just take us a look-see and check on your rooms."

"I can't allow that. The Carmelite Retreat House is a holy place of prayer. The people you mentioned are not here. You have my word. And the anonymity of our guests must be respected. I must ask you to leave."

"Get out of our way." Bernie raised his hand, and the taller of the men pulled a 9mm Glock from his shoulder holster. "Now, stay put while we find her." Bernie backed out of the workshop, followed by the remaining thug. Again, Malachi stayed his distance.

The gunman stood in the doorway, the 9mm aimed at Brother Williams. "You'd better *hope* they find the woman." He shuddered as the frigid breeze blew in from the lake. "How d'ya close this fuckin' door?"

Before Brother Williams could answer, the man spotted the switch and lowered the garage door. Once inside he stuck the pistol in his waistband and began to light a cigarette.

"Mind if I sit?" Brother Williams asked.

"Yeah, sure, go ahead."

As he sat, Brother Williams yawned, stretched and hit the light switch behind him, plunging the room into total darkness.

"Okay, wise-ass. Turn the lights back on. You don't really want to piss me off so I start shooting."

Brother Chuck felt for a weapon on the workbench and came up with a large crescent wrench. He threw it, and when the gunman grunted in pain, Chuck charged him, body close to the ground, thighs pumping. He was back on the gridiron. He drove his shoulder into the man's midsection knocking him backwards onto the concrete floor. As the man tried to sit up, Chuck threw a muscled forearm into his face.

He was too late.

The man brought his gun down on Chuck's head.

When Brother Chuck regained consciousness, he was on the garage floor with three men standing over him.

Bernie kicked him in the ribs. "Where's the girl?"

"Only God knows," said Brother Chuck.

Malachi spoke from somewhere behind Brother Chuck. "You like to emulate your Christ, don't you? The truth will set you free and all that shit, right?"

"I swear to God I'm telling the truth."

Malachi surveyed the workshop. "Tie and blindfold this unholy monk.... I'm sure we can persuade him to tell us what we want to know."

CHAPTER SIXTY-THREE

I raced onto the retreat grounds. "Where's Brother Williams?" I asked of the first monk I saw.

The brother pointed, and I raced down the gravel path towards the workshop. The main garage door was closed, but I saw light underneath the side door. As I approached, I heard groaning inside. I tried to be optimistic but I had a bad feeling about this. I slipped Bat out from under my coat, ready for whatever was coming and pushed the door open a crack.

Oh my God.

Brother Chuck had been crucified. His arms were spread out, palms nailed to a 4-by-6 cross beam as he lay supine on the cement floor. Two pools of bright red blood were spreading beneath each hand. He was blindfolded, his mouth taped shut and his upper back and arms stretched out on a long piece of wood. They hadn't gotten to his feet. This was bad enough.

I rushed to him and pulled off the blindfold and tape.

He groaned. "Deac... for God's sake... get me out of this."

"I will, old friend, but I don't want to make things worse." I tucked my coat under his head. "I've got to get help."

This was my doing. Don't think about that. *Focus.*

"I'll get help."

"Get Brother... Birch," Chuck moaned.

The retreat corpsman was there in seconds. He started first aid, silently, but his lips were moving. He was praying.

I called 911 and knelt by Chuck's side, praying for my tough old friend. Tears streamed down his face as we pulled the nails from his hands. He didn't make a sound, but his muscles tensed into steel coils under what had to be excruciating pain.

Later, I stood in a stark emergency room at Saint Luke's Hospital waiting for word on Chuck's condition. The view of the bleak parking lot was depressing. Snow flurries drifted down on sparsely scattered cars that looked—to me—like grave mounds on asphalt. A big storm was coming.

Guilt swept over me like the cold waves of a following sea. So many friends had been hurt. Surely this wasn't part of God's plan… if He had a plan.

I might have doubts, but I hadn't stopped praying since I found Chuck and since Ann went into hiding… out there somewhere.

A doctor in green scrubs looked up at me, interrupting my thoughts and my prayers. "Deacon Adelius?"

"Yes."

"Your friend is fine. He's lost a lot of blood, and there is some concern about nerve damage in his right hand. We'll have to wait and see." The doctor shook his head. "I've never seen wounds like that. Hard to believe someone… " His voice drifted off. "Anyway, Brother Williams is medicated and not feeling much pain right now. What a character. He's already laughing and entertaining us with football stories." He took off his glasses and polished them carefully with lens cleaning tissue from a small packet. "Of course we have to file a report with the police."

"Of course. May I see him now?"

"Down the hall to your right. Follow the noise." The doctor walked away mumbling and flipping pages in a medical chart.

Brother Williams greeted me with a belly laugh. Incredibly, he was in high spirits or maybe just high. Two nurses and an orderly left the room as I entered.

"You on drugs?"

He laughed, "Yes, I am. Thanks be to God."

"I'm so sorry I got you—"

"You? You didn't get me into nothing. Did I tell you? I made another tackle. It was a thing of beauty.… And how else could I have gotten the stigmata? I'll be the envy of the brotherhood." He held up his bandaged hands. "Hah! I'll be delegating that blasted paperwork for a while."

"You always could see the pony beneath the pile of shit. And thanks for helping Ann get away."

"My pleasure. Tell her I'll pray for her."

"And we'll pray for you. Listen to the doctor and get better!"

Chuck smiled, so doped up he even looked contented.

A nurse's aide came to the door. "Someone's at the front desk asking for a Deacon Adelius."

In the lobby, a familiar tall white-haired man in a Chesterfield topcoat turned to greet me. William De La Croix said, "I don't mean to intrude, but Sister Mary Margaret contacted me. She received a call from… my daughter. She… the good sister, I mean, couldn't reach you, so I thought I'd better come by and tell you where Ann has concealed herself."

We exchanged hearty handshakes and left immediately for Ann's hideout. Clever. She had parked the truck in a busy shopping mall surrounded by three hotels.

Ann had given Sister her room number, so I called her from the lobby. Then De La Croix and I took the elevator to the third floor.

When she answered the door, she beamed until she saw her father behind me. "What's he doing here?"

"Sister called him. My cell phone is dead."

She turned away like a petulant child. I was in no mood for this bullshit. I followed her into her bedroom, and said, "Sister Mary Margaret is safe because of him. We had a rental car, hotel rooms and meals because of him. Do you think *I* had the money for all that?" I restrained myself once again from telling her De La Croix had bankrolled her spa on Michigan Avenue.

De La Croix stood framed in the doorway. "Ann, I wanted to help."

CHAPTER SIXTY-FOUR

We'd dodged another bullet. I felt rested but overburdened with so many thoughts and plans. We were stuck. The DVD was still out there and my friends continued to be hurt. Brother chuck's hand might be damaged for life. All my fault again. I went down to breakfast so early the next morning I expected to see only yawning waitresses, but William De La Croix was alone in a window booth. I slid onto a seat across from him.

"How'd it go last night?" I asked.

He shrugged. "It'll take time. She's got a lot to forgive."

I nodded, not sure what to say.

"She's a wonderful woman... despite the mistakes her parents made."

"That she is." And how I believed it. I took a sip of black coffee. "Someday she'll appreciate what you're doing. Soon, I hope."

He gave me a sad smile. "Well, here's to that day." He got up to leave. "I'll be going back to the Prudential. Good luck with the search."

"Sister Meg and I certainly appreciate your help."

Chuck called. He was so excited that he skipped his usual greeting and hurled his grand idea. "That key of yours. I think it means Hi-Lo."

"Come again?"

"The little arrows on your key. I knew I'd seen them somewhere. That's the logo for those convenience stores. You know the ones. They've got signs with the up arrow for 'high value' and the down arrow for 'low cost.' Everybody calls them Hi-Lo stores. Of course, it's just a guess."

I was stunned silent for a moment. "Chuck, you're brilliant. Why the hell didn't I think of that?"

"Because you're not flat on your back with nothing to do but think... and pray... that's why. And then again, maybe it's because you're not the sharpest knife in the drawer." He chuckled at his own joke as usual. "I *wanted* to help. Remember?"

"And you're doing okay?"

"Sure. I heal fast."

We began to speculate about the rest of the markings on Amber's key. Could BG 415 be an address? A designation of a particular store? A ranking of some sort? Our theories ran out of steam, but we were close. I could feel it. "I felt like rushing into the first Hi-Lo store I could find. I told Chuck. "This is a big clue. Thanks so much. Let me know if there's anything I can do."

"Well, there's the priesthood... then when you finish you could hear my confession. Whoa!"

Brother Chuck laughed, but we both knew he was serious.

I couldn't wait to give Ann the news over breakfast. She responded the way I hoped she would, those blue-green eyes widening in surprise. No sign of her irritation from the night before, possibly because her father had already gone. He'd left a note for her at the front desk.

She pushed aside her coffee and toast and whipped out her iPad. In seconds, she'd found and called the corporate number. "Yes, BG 415," she said to the umpteenth person. "Yes, please. Thank you very much."

She whispered to me. "BG 415 may be a postal box number. Some of the Hi-Lo's in the suburbs have them. They're e-mailing a list."

Ann's fingertip zipped across the iPad. Then she handed it to me. "Here they are. There are twenty-four in Illinois. I suggest we start calling."

"How about the greater Chicago area first. I can't see any reason your sister would have a box as far away as Carbondale or Springfield."

I pulled out my Illinois/Chicago map. "If you'll read the names aloud, I'll circle them." Soon we'd narrowed the search to the ten closest suburbs. "Now how would Allison identify the store location?" I mused aloud. "Please read them again."

I closed my eyes and Ann began to read, slowly this time: "Elmhurst, Evanston, Cicero, Joliet, Aurora, Mount Prospect, Buffalo Grove... "

We both jumped at the same time. "Buffalo Grove," she repeated.

"BG. That's gotta be it!" I grabbed Ann's hands in mine. She had thawed considerably since last night. I asked if she'd mind driving. I had a call to make.

As we proceeded north on the 295 Toll Road, I felt like we were rounding third and heading for home.

CHAPTER SIXTY-FIVE

I'd purchased one of those throwaway cell phones and called Saint Sebastian's. A Father Kowalski had taken over temporarily while Father Posjena convalesced. He told me that Detective Ditmar was looking for me.

I'll bet.

Maybe I was wrong, but I figured Ditmar was working the other side. If he knew my whereabouts, Malachi would, too. They were probably still pissed that I'd sent them on that wild goose chase... or should I say wild pig chase. I could picture their faces when they found their tracking device in the back of a stinking truck.

"Deacon?"

"Oh, yeah, sorry." My mind had drifted far from Saint Sebastian's and the good father.

"Monsignor Salvatore asks that you return his call, right away."

"Thanks."

We discussed minor parish matters, and then I called the monsignor. After a few pleasantries, he warned me that the police were looking for me with even more vehemence.

"I know. You warned me already. I need to stay lost for a while. I know I can't trust anybody, especially the police. Sister Mary Margaret is in a safe place. Ann is with me."

"Good. I wish I could say the same about the cardinal. If only he'd keep his political criticisms to himself." The monsignor made some worried *tsk tsk* sounds. "He's received another death threat and he pays no attention. I think we're all more concerned than he is. For some reason, he thinks the DVD you're after is related to the political corruption he fights so vigorously. Any progress on the DVD?"

Strange, I thought the official concern was that clergy might be compromised on the video. Now they were talking politics. Me? I just wanted to put down some real scumbags.

"We do have a promising lead."

"Oh?"

"It has to do with a key I retrieved from the dead girl."

"A key, you say? Do you know what it opens?

"Not yet, but we're close."

"Fine. Please keep me in the loop. How is Brother Williams?" After I told him I heard the same *tsk tsk* noises over the phone. "Terrible wounds. How is he doing?"

"He's tough. He'll be all right." I had a sudden thought. "Monsignor, did you hint to anyone that we might be at the Carmelite Retreat House?"

"Not a word." He dropped that topic and went back to his favorite: Gabrian business. "Oh, even in the midst of all this trouble, I'm sure you'd want to know that the police arrested Father Baksian in the diocese office right in front of everyone. I suppose someone provided evidence of his deviant behavior and turned him in to the Crimes Against Children Bureau. I wonder how the cardinal took *that* news? He thinks he can save everyone … even the perverts. The Gabrians know better."

Monsignor Salvatore sounded like he was gloating. The monsignor continued, his voice rising with zeal. "Even the cardinal can't stop our work, and he'd better not try. Baksian should have taken the Gabrian way out. He told the police that a church deacon threatened him with a baseball bat. Have you ever heard such nonsense?" Salvatore didn't laugh, but I guessed that about now he'd be smirking and raising his dark eyebrows.

"Unbelievable," I said.

"As a Gabrian, the archbishop is confident the right thing was done. Officially, of course, he can't condone the intimidation of priests. Violates their *civil rights*, you know. Never *mind* the rights of abused children." The monsignor's voice dripped with sarcasm.

"Thank God one more priestly pervert is off the streets." I agreed with him on that. "Pray for us Monsignor."

"Always, my son."

CHAPTER SIXTY SIX

It was Clayton who suggested a new perspective when he met Halloran.

"Mitch, as I see it, we have two problems. One is the DVD, and the other is Cardinal Schneider. He's killing us out there. Have you seen the latest polls?"

"Yeah, so?" Halloran lit a cigar and listened carefully, sharing nothing.

"By going after the video first and the cardinal second, we're giving him more air time. Malachi can't find the DVD. His skills lie elsewhere."

"So what are you suggesting?"

"I go talk to the cardinal. Maybe I can get him to back off. I tell him how much we regret our past and how we want to make amends and clean up the city."

"Why should he listen to you?"

"Maybe he won't but it's worth a try. I could tell him how much we would support Catholic Charities and other Catholic projects in the city." Clayton dropped his chin, frowning as he spoke. "Worse case scenario: If the DVD comes out, we tell the public it's a computer generated trick. *Our* experts will prove irrefutably that it's bogus. Tamara is the only witness, and she's not talking—unless through a medium." Clayton put a hand over his mouth, a second too late to block the incredibly bad joke. He blustered on. "Of course if we find the DVD we can destroy it and celebrate."

Clayton sat down, clutching his stomach. Mentioning Tamara had brought back the whole ghastly scene of her sinking below the water. He felt like he had a cement mixer for a belly.

"Well, as I see it, we have nothing to lose. Go ahead and give it a try." Halloran changed the subject slightly. "You got me to thinking. We can't shake this deacon, and Malachi isn't having much luck with him. I think we need a different approach."

"What?"

"Incapacitate him somehow. Throw suspicion on him. We'll make him *unworthy*." Halloran started pacing bringing all his practical knowledge of crime to work on the problem. "We'll reduce his credibility and isolate him."

"How are we going to do that?"

"Not sure yet. I need some time to work that out."

CHAPTER SIXTY-SEVEN

We charged into the Buffalo Grove Hi-Lo store, bypassed the coffee machines and headed for the mailboxes. Ann crossed her fingers while I tried the key in number 415. I opened the little glass door. Inside, was an unmarked DVD.

I wanted to jump and cheer, and I could tell from Ann's grand smile that she did, too. Instead, we did a high five and bought a couple of coffees and two 3-oz. liquor bottles.

Outside, the snow was coming down hard, so we fled to our car. I unscrewed the bottles and poured Bailey's Cream into Ann's coffee and Southern Comfort into mine.

I touched my cup to hers. "I knew we could do it."

"*You* did it."

"Not acceptable. *We* did it."

"Okay, you win, we did it." She kissed my cheek lightly. "Now what?"

"We've got to make copies of this DVD." I laid out my plan, hoping against hope that getting a copy to the right authorities would get Malachi off our backs... for good.

Ann looked worried. "What about the threats to the schools and the children. Maybe we should turn it in to the police."

"Wait a minute." I shook my head, with vigor. That was a really bad idea. "At least part of the police force is in on this... and they're looking for us. Who can we trust?"

"Maybe if we go high enough, say to the police commissioner."

I shook my head. "Nope. Not a good choice. He's running for mayor. Suppose he was one of your sister's clients? Suppose something on that video could damage his campaign."

Ann frowned, opened her mouth to speak... but didn't.

"Ann, what is it?"

She shrugged, her face a pale question mark.

I tried to be positive. "Let's watch the DVD first and then decide, okay?"

"I... I may not be able ... if Allison is on that... "

Hell, I'd done it again. Why couldn't I keep my mouth shut? "Of course, I see. I'm sorry. I'll view this myself. You don't have to watch it."

She made an abrupt turn, her courage rising. "I'll try to watch. We may need to testify later about what we both saw."

My excitement over the DVD faded, replaced by a feeling of dread. Anything that distressed Ann....

I jumped at the sound of someone tapping on my window. I wiped the moisture off the window and looked out at a tall gangly police officer. "License, registration and proof of insurance, please."

Reasonable request... unless crooked cops have an APB out on you. I'd try courtesy first. "Certainly, Officer. Is something wrong?"

"I need to check the car."

"It's a rental." I handed him the paperwork.

"I'll still need to see your driver's license."

My only hope—and a dim one—was that he wouldn't recognize my name. I handed him my license, and he returned to his car. Everything was electronic these days. He'd be back in less than a minute.

"Ann, we can't let the police get this DVD. I'll slow this cop down. Get away, any way you can. Go to your dad's, Leo's or to the monsignor at Sacred Heart. Look at the video, make copies and send them where I said: Stanichar, the DA and Archbishop Laine." So much for protecting Ann from the video... or anything else.

"What about you? How are you going to slow him down?"

"I'll improvise."

"Don't hurt him."

The police officer came back, gun drawn but hanging by his side, pointed at the ground. He looked very young and not very confident. I put the video in Ann's lap.

"Sir, get out of the car slowly and put your hands where I can see them. Miss, you stay in the car."

I got out of the car. "Officer, what's all this about?"

"You're wanted for questioning. Face down on the ground with your hands behind your back." He recited my rights in a dead monotone as I lay on the frozen pavement deciding on my next move.

The car door creaked open, and I heard the crunch of Ann's boots. I turned my head just enough to see her standing topless in the falling snow like some kind of a sexy angel, steam rising from her body.

"Officer," she said, "What's the fuss? We were just having a little party in the car, yah know?"

I'd seen diversions in my time, but none like this. The officer was in shock. Before he could speak, I kicked his legs out from under him, twisted the pistol out of his hand and knelt on his back. "Look, I know you won't believe this, but we are innocent. And we can't be delayed right now."

Ann had begun to shake with cold, so she jumped back in the car and got back into her clothes.

Our luck held. No one drove up to the store and, apparently, no one could see us through the falling snow.

"You've just made everything worse on yourself," said the officer.

"Let me be the judge of that." I walked the cop around to the back and waved to Ann to join us. "Buy some duct tape," I told her.

"A few minutes later I bound the police officer's mouth and eyes and loosely wrapped his hands and feet with the tape. Then I pushed him over, unloaded his weapon and threw it in the patrol car. Then I threw his car keys on the other side of the parking lot.

"That ought to hold him for a time."

"You didn't hurt him?"

"Absolutely not, maybe just his pride. Hey, terrific job. How did you even think of that?"

"I know how men think," Ann said. "Besides, I didn't want to be left alone with that DVD."

CHAPTER SIXTY-EIGHT

In a couple of hours, we had a new rental from the small Chicago executive airport—a nondescript gray Nissan—and made reservations at a downtown motel where we could watch the DVD. The falling snow muffled all sounds. Ann slept most of the way back to Chicago.

In a couple of hours, we settled into the Gold Coast Arms, a second-class motel that was warm and clean, but very basic. I moved a couple of chairs in front of the TV and put in the DVD.

"Here we go.... You ready?"

Ann was so tense I could see the veins outlined in her neck. "I guess."

The screen blinked on showing a well-appointed living room with the same nautical accents as the restaurant and bar of the yacht club. A woman's businesslike voice announced, "This is room 117 starboard at the Belmont Harbor Yacht—"

"Oh my God... it's Allison." Ann slumped forward, rocking slightly, her face in her hands.

I turned off the DVD and gently rubbed Ann's shoulders. The voices of the two sisters were almost identical. I didn't know what to say so I said nothing.

She rose, folded her arms and looked out the window for a few minutes. Then she took a few deep breaths. "Sorry. It was a shock. I'm better now." She sat in front of the screen, her face drawn tight again. "Let's continue."

"I can watch this by myself, you know."

She shook her head, and I handed her the remote. "Here. Now you can fast forward or stop it whenever you want.

Ann clicked the DVD on, and Allison's voice continued. "I have reserved this room and the adjoining bedrooms for use by Police Commissioner Mitch Halloran...Ann gasped and her face went white, but her sister's voice droned on. "And State Senator Frank Clayton. Accompanying them are two of my escorts, Tiko and Tamara."

"You okay?"

"Yes." She didn't make eye contact, just kept watching the screen. The camera's wide angle never changed, so the living room and both bedroom doors stayed fully visible, lighted only by two lamps in the shape of buoys with nautical shades. The audio was clear, even over the music, as the two couples had dinner and drinks.

Ann fast-forwarded the DVD in spurts. The couples laughed and began to talk provocatively. The men suggested that the women dance. "Sure, sweetie," said a young blonde, hips gyrating as she turned up the soft rock music.

Ann's voice was barely audible. "Tamara."

The only sound from the video was the music, a breathy female voice singing, "That something you said, the timing was right. The pleasure was mine ... " Tamara slowly unbuttoned her sheer blouse and slid out of her mini skirt in front of Frank Clayton, who sat watching from a comfortable chair.

I thought it looked like a cheap soft-core porn film.

In another chair, Mitch Halloran was getting a lap dance from a topless Asian woman we knew as Tiko.

"Hey babe," Clayton said to Tamara, "Time to adjourn to the boudoir." He looked over at Halloran and Tiko. "See you two later ... night, night."

Tamara had stripped down to a thong and was dancing toward another room.

Clayton kicked off his shoes and said in that smarmy voice of his, "If you're very, very good, I'll show you a genuine Illinois black snake."

"And if I'm bad?" Tamara said playfully over her shoulder.

"That snake is going to get yah."

Tamara laughed as she entered the bedroom. "I can hardly wait."

The door closed.

Back on the sofa, Halloran was kissing Tiko's breasts, and she was moaning in apparent excitement.

Ann's eyes were slits, her mouth a straight line. "Good acting."

I kept my mouth shut.

When Halloran stood, Tiko jumped up and wrapped herself around him. Halloran's breath came in fits and starts, but he managed to carry her into the other bedroom, teasing that he'd have to spank her for indecency and lewd behavior.

"Oh, don't hurt me, big policeman. I'll do anything you want."

He lowered his voice. "Anything?"

The second bedroom door clicked shut.

The DVD kept rolling, so Ann fast-forwarded until Clayton and Halloran reappeared in the darkened room alone. A microphone must have been hidden in the large coffee table, since we could hear their low voices as they pulled their chairs closer together.

Halloran was dressed—or rather undressed—in boxer shorts and a T-shirt. He had a whiskey glass in one hand and a panatela in the other. Clayton held a wine glass in his hand and wore nothing but trousers. "So," he began, "have you thought about what I said?"

"It makes sense. You *should* see the cardinal. Can't hurt."

"Really?"

"It would be great if he'd back off, though he still might have to be dealt with permanently… In that case, we'll have to have iron-clad alibis for the day."

Clayton nodded.

The first bedroom door opened, and Tamara bounced into the room wearing a short terrycloth robe. "Alibi? I'll give you an alibi."

Oh God. Was she that stupid? I thought.

The two men leaped out of their chairs. "What did you hear?" Clayton demanded, his voice rising.

Tamara froze in place, hands at her mouth. "Nothing. Just 'alibi,' that's all."

Halloran was across the room in a second. He pushed her onto the floor. "I want to know every single word you heard."

Tamara struggled to her feet. It was hard to tell, but she looked like she was shaking. "Just seeing the cardinal... and alibi."

"Stupid bitch." Clayton's fist shot out in an awkward right cross, like someone unaccustomed to fighting. The girl spun, lost her balance and hit her head on the corner of the heavy inlaid glass coffee table, twitched and stayed down.

"My God." Ann turned away,

Halloran knelt over the fallen girl, checking for breathing and a heartbeat. Then he lifted one of her eyelids and looked up at Clayton. "She's dead, you idiot."

Clayton twisted his hands together, his face contorted with panic. "It was an accident. She fell. I didn't mean—"

"And what will the police say to that?" Halloran snorted.

"What'll we do?"

"What are *you* going to do, asshole. Get a blanket to wrap her in." Clayton peered into the other bedroom and closed the door quietly. "Looks like Tiko's still asleep." Halloran poured some red wine on the carpet, no doubt to cover the small bloodstain.

Clayton returned with the blanket, but he still looked wild-eyed and stunned. "Now what," he stammered.

"Now you take her and dump her in the lake."

"But it was an accident. Shouldn't I... couldn't I just... explain?"

Halloran's mouth twisted in disgust. "Right. State senator arrested in death of prostitute. Police commissioner involved. News at eleven.... No, Frank. Spread the blanket out."

Clayton was shaking so hard, he could barely talk. "I can't."

Halloran gripped Clayton's arm and practically wrestled him to the floor. When they had Tamara encased in the blanket, Halloran said, "You're getting this body out of here... now."

"Where—"

"Across the state line so I won't have to deal with it. There are some derelict piers along the lake in Gary. Remove the blanket and robe, and then slide her into the water. Leave nothing behind."

Clayton nodded, dumbly.

"Okay, let's do it."

The men carried the body out of camera view.

As Ann fast-forwarded through footage of the empty room, I thought I saw a flicker of something … a reflection? No, I was probably imagining it.

We watched the men's return to the room and Clayton's retrieval of an overnight bag. Then the screen went blank.

I took the DVD out of the player. "No mystery why they're desperate to get the DVD. Now we know who Malachi is working for.… These guys are running for office in the fall, and they've got a dead girl on their hands. This DVD will take them down."

Ann was still staring at the blank screen. She didn't seem to be listening.

"Ann. Are you all right?"

She slowly turned her face toward mine, but she didn't meet my gaze. "I've really done it now."

"Done what?"

"How could I know that Mitch Halloran was…" Her voice trailed off.

"A shitty, no good lying cop?"

She finally looked at me, her mouth turned down like a tragedy mask. "I called him a couple of days ago and asked for his help."

"Who, Halloran?"

"I knew him from before. I thought he could help us. I never dreamed…"

Ann spaced out again. I tried gentle and then I tried firm. She had to focus if we were going to get anywhere. "Ann! When did you call?"

"When I was at the construction site."

"Why Halloran?"

"I knew he was a VIP in law enforcement. I thought he could help.... maybe even find my sister's killer. I knew him as a client, all right? Are you happy now?" Her face burned red with anger... maybe shame.

"God, I'm sorry. I didn't mean to go there." I paused, wondering what to say next. I wasn't going to remind her that I'd told her police and other officials were involved. "What did you tell him?" I said finally. "That's all I need to know."

She jumped up and began to pace, a healthy switch from her previous stunned silence. "Not much. I asked him questions about Tamara... about the police at my apartment. He knew nothing... I mean, he *said* he knew nothing. I told him I was searching for a DVD and that you were helping me."

"That's no secret. Go on."

"He didn't say it outright, but I could tell the police weren't aggressively looking for Allison's killer." Her face shifted from sad to furious. "Christ! I know how they think. What's one hooker more or less?" She gulped back tears. "He *claimed* he didn't know a Bernie or a Malachi. The bastard had the nerve to try to *see* me again... for old times sake." Hot volcanic tears streamed down her face. "Allison had blackmail in mind... and she got killed instead." Ann continued to weep. I wanted to hold her, to comfort her, but not after what we'd just seen and what she'd just said.

"I miss her so much." Ann had run out of tears, but her shoulders were still heaving.

"Shhh now. We'll tackle this tomorrow. It's late. First step: We take out Malachi before anyone else gets hurt."

Ann groaned, kicked off her shoes and slid under the covers fully clothed.

I knew better than to get in bed beside her now. I was too wound up to sleep anyway. I stroked her forehead ever so lightly. "I'm going out for a little while. I have the key. Don't open the door for anyone." I smoothed her hair. "Do you want anything?"

"No." Her voice was muffled in the pillow. She wanted to be alone, and so did I. A drink and some fresh air were in order.

I passed a couple of coffee shops and stepped into Mario's Bar and Grill. I ordered "Dewar's... a double" and sat at the back of the bar. I took a long swallow and felt the heat all the way down. I didn't want to think, so I ordered another.

Then I wanted fresh air again. "Gotta go." I paid for the drinks and left. I strode down Rush Street for a while. Snow was still falling and I imagined my breath had taken the shape of a trumpet in the cold air, a vision inspired by the whiskey or the jazz blaring up from basement clubs. I found myself in front of an old stone church, sandwiched between an art gallery and a nightclub.

Saint Michael's seemed like a good the right place to be right now, so I went in and knelt in a back pew behind a scattering of people, let out a long breath and relaxed into a familiar prayer. *Lord Jesus Christ, son of the living God, have mercy on me, a sinner...*

Praying was like casual conversation for me. When I was angry at God, I let Him know it. My feelings were still strong against the institutional church. In the fog of uncertainty, my anger was the dome under which I lived.

For days, I'd been running and fighting without pausing to think... or to pray. What happened to my dedication to the church? What about Ann, the cardinal, the innocents of our city who needed my help? Or was that my ego speaking? Could I really protect them? I tried to help, and people suffered. God's will? I doubt it.

My mood shifted when I thought of Malachi. That evil bastard had to be stopped. *Please, God, grant me the ability to do that.* I talked to Him a while longer and headed back to the motel feeling a little lighter. I guess I lightened my burden.

I would see this through to the end.

CHAPTER SIXTY-NINE

The DVD didn't show what had happened after Frank Clayton left the yacht club early that morning. There was no footage of the weeping and shouting of obscenities as he drove toward the Indiana border with an unspeakable burden in the trunk of his Jaguar. He kept to the speed limit. His heart nearly leapt from his body when a police car passed him.

Over and over, he'd replayed the scene: Tamara spinning… hitting her head… against the table, then falling to the floor.

Somehow, he'd found the derelict piers, but it took him an hour to get out of the car. When he'd finally forced himself to lift the bundle out of the trunk and roll it to the edge of the pier, he remembered Halloran's instructions. *Shit. I have to take off the blanket and the robe. I have to look at her again.* As he unwrapped her, he gagged at the stench and threw up.

The dead woman's face was ghostly pale, her eyes open and her tongue hanging out. That tongue had been in his mouth a few hours ago. He threw up again. The body was flaccid and hard to move. Clayton felt weak… unable to deal with any of this. But he did it. He rolled the naked body off the pier into the water and jumped back to avoid the icy splash. But he couldn't avoid Tamara's eyes, which seemed to stare at him as she sank below the black surface.

He sped away, almost skidding off the icy pier. The pier didn't enter his mind. Neither did the snow, the road or the passing car lights. All he could see in front of him was her face, a vision that would never fade from his mind.

CHAPTER SEVENTY

nn was still sleeping when I returned to the room, so I slept as best I could on the very short vinyl couch. She was asleep when I got up in the pre-dawn light, and stretched my aching back. *I'd check that DVD ... just in case.*

I slipped the disk into the player and turned the sound off. No sense Ann waking up to *this*. I fast-forwarded to the end and watched Clayton and Halloran drag the body out. I squinted at the empty room on the screen, backed up and slowed the speed, trying to see into the shadowy edges of the room. Something was different about the room... I looked at it again. There was a reflection in one of the mirrors. Maybe movements of the men, maybe a technical glitch. Nothing identifiable.

I put away the DVD and headed to the small lobby for coffee. Ann needed her sleep, so I sat awhile, paging through the *Chicago Tribune.* I nearly choked on my coffee when I saw a section A-3 photo of Police Commissioner Mitch Halloran and State Senator Frank Clayton holding their hands up in triumph. The headline read, "Frontrunners in early mayoral and gubernatorial polls." I ground my teeth. After what they'd done, the damned duo should be rattling the bars of a prison cell with those hands. And they will be, if I had anything to do with it.

On the Op-Ed page, Cardinal Schneider was pictured at a political rally, with a caption that mentioned threats against him. A headline read, "Separation of church and state?" Underneath were excerpts from Chicago citizens who had responded to that question: Half railed that a church leader had no right to espouse his political views in public. Half cheered the cardinal's attacks on the "immorality of corrupt politicians." What will those angry citizens think of our spiritual leader when he's proven absolutely right?

When I creaked open the motel room door, Ann was wide-awake, showered and ready to go.

"Better?" I asked carefully.

"Much. Sad to hear my sister's voice… horrible to see Tamara… but if we can stop this… "

"Yeah, that was rough. I'll call Monsignor Salvatore, and we'll start shutting down this miserable outfit."

"At seven in the morning?"

"Priests are early risers." I tossed the newspaper in her direction—pages folded back to show Halloran and Clayton.

Her face creased into a grimace. "How can they grin like that… "

"Because they're soul-less, greedy, power-hungry bastards, that's how."

I keyed in the monsignor's number to tell him about the DVD.

"God answers our prayers," he replied. His standard response.

"The archbishop, the cardinal and the citizens of Illinois, not to mention the DA, will be most interested. Is the evidence incriminating?"

"To the max. It's murder and cover-up."

"What now?" His voice was calm, matter-of-fact. I guess he'd heard worse in his vocation.

"The school has the equipment to make duplicates. I'll give a copy to Malachi and call it the original."

"You're a wonder."

"I doubt that. I'll get back to you with more details soon."

CHAPTER SEVENTY-ONE

t Saint Sebastian's Academy, Father Kowalski led Ann and me to the audio-visual room and asked a jovial assistant principal, Gregory Killeen, to make copies. "He's our tech wizard," Kowalski said.

"This could be hazardous duty," I told them. "Don't mention the DVD to *anyone*, including church officials or the police."

We stayed until the copies had been made. "I think the original and three copies are safest with you. I'll deliver one copy to our adversaries."

Killeen asked no questions. "I'll take good care of them for you."

We drove to Sacred Heart to see Monsignor Salvatore, who received us graciously. "Perhaps you'd like to escort Ann to breakfast," I suggested.

Ann frowned. "What about you?"

"I won't be long. I've got to set up a few meetings. I'll tell you about them later. Thanks for your help, monsignor."

Ann looked forlorn, like a little girl left after school. I couldn't help that. This was dangerous work, and I had to do this alone. First came Stanichar.

The reporter hit me with an excited barrage of info and questions. "I checked into Ditmar. Shady. Very shady. I've verified Sister Margaret's injuries... tracked a body in Lake Michigan, somewhere around Gary... a Jane Doe, but she matches the description you gave me on the missing prostitute. I need something solid now. Have you come up with the perpetrators? I need names. Evidence."

No question, I'd chosen well. The reporter would go to the moon to break this story. "Well done," I told him. "We have confirmation that Tamara was murdered. Keep this to yourself for now. What else?"

"Couldn't find the good sister, but I got hold of her medical records. Don't ask me how. Terrible injuries.... Do you know what sick fucks did this?"

"Malachi... He's Halloran and Clayton's hired gun."

Stanichar's mouth dropped open and he muttered, half to himself. "They're crooked as hell, but murderers? Oh my God, have we got a story. The people's right to know and all that. You *do* have proof, right?"

"We're going to bring this to a head very soon and you'll have your exclusive. First, we need a very private meeting with you, me and the DA. Tell him as much as you need to get him there. I have a proposal for him.

"You think he's clean?"

"As the new fallen snow, but it's tough to get through to him. Barry Pritchard won't take our calls unless *he's* calling the shots."

"I have every faith in you. He wants to be mayor, right? Tell him you've got the goods on Halloran. That you've got incriminating evidence that will put a lot of corrupt bastards where they belong. He'll be a shoe-in for Mayor."

"You *do* have incriminating evidence, right?"

"Sure do."

"Where do you want to meet?"

"You can work that out. I'll check back with you. I've got something to do first."

"Oh, yeah, about Ditmar. I'm sure he's dirty, but he seems well connected, especially to Halloran.

My next call was to Leo. "I have another job for you. Interested?"

"For sure."

"I'll give you the details when I see you. We've got to follow a guy and see who he's reporting to."

"Will this joker lead us to the guy that hurt Sister?"

"He might. Meet me at my apartment in the back of the church in a half hour."

"You got it. *Ciao.*"

CHAPTER SEVENTY-TWO

"Deacon and the girl found the DVD."

"Where is it now?"

"Deacon said he'd put it where he was told, but he's stowed the original and at least three copies at Saint Sebastian's School. You'd better hurry."

"Thanks, 'V', I'll get right on it. Not to change the subject, but we're doing an event on Sunday. And you can help."

"I can't be actively involved."

"It's very simple, minimal involvement. Make sure an ambulance is present outside the cathedral and directed to Northwestern Hospital."

"Why?"

"That's all you need to know."

"V" hung up.

CHAPTER SEVENTY-THREE

The youngster put a copy of Allison's DVD in the "Food for the Poor" box in the vestibule at Saint Sebastian's, just as I'd asked him to do. Then he took off happily with his newly earned dollar.

Malachi had been very specific about the delivery, so I hoped he'd pick it up himself or be nearby. He's too smart. He'd smell a trap and send a messenger. I yawned as I waited in the confessional. Give me a choice and I'll take action over stakeouts anytime. Waiting for something to happen is not my style.

Eventually, a youngish man with a scraggily beard, leather jacket and gray scarf rose from the side pew he'd been in, looked furtively around, took the DVD and stuffed it under his jacket.

The plan was for Leo and me to follow him in sequence on foot. So Leo picked up the courier up across the street and followed him at a leisurely pace for a few blocks. I kept the guy in my sights until he turned toward the lake. Leo had gone ahead and picked him up after he turned the next corner. The young man entered an old hotel that seen better days. I went in behind him and told Leo to wait two minutes, then follow us.

The young man and I entered the ornate lobby and got into a rickety old- fashioned elevator together, the kind with the wrought-iron doors. We rode alone to the top floor, six stories up. Leo would see the floor indicator and follow.

We got off. The man seemed oblivious to my following him. Never even looked at me. Not normal. Now I definitely smelled a trap. I slipped Bat out of my belt.

Instead of going into an apartment, the man abruptly disappeared into a laundry service room. I cracked the door just as he dropped something down the chute.

Hell. It was the DVD. I burst in, aware of movement to my right and my left.

"You looking for something, holy-roller?"

I ducked and held Bat over my head in time to block a knife thrust from the left. I spun Bat around and drove the handle into the man's neck. He crumpled, choking wildly. The other two came at me at once. Both had knives. I blocked a few thrusts but one of the men sprayed something in my face. Mace. I backed up, holding Bat in front of me for protection. But another knife came through the mist, sliced into my forearm and broke my grip. Bat was gone.

Then the cavalry arrived. I watched Leo through a chemical haze. He burst into the room and put his meaty fists into action. Blood began to fly, and the guy with the scruffy beard went down.

I grabbed the knife hand of the other man. We were so close I could smell his bad breath and see his bloodshot eyes. Leo jumped on his back and swung a forearm around his neck. I ducked his punch, but the guy slammed a fist into my shoulder wound. I saw flashing lights of pain, stepped away and picked up Bat.

No need. Leo pushed the man he was riding and threw several punches into his mid-section. The guy dropped his knife and crumpled with Leo on top of him. Leo jumped off and kicked the man in the ribs. Leo and I bent over breathing heavily.

Scruffy beard took off down the hall. Leaving a blood trail. *Good riddance.*

"Thanks, Leo."

"No problem," said Leo. "Where the hell is the DVD?"

"Bastard dropped it down the laundry chute. You can bet somebody was waiting for it. I've got copies, thank the Lord. Keep that to yourself." My eyes were killing me, and my sleeve was sticky with blood. Leo helped me to a slop sink, where I splashed water into my burning eyes. Then I peeled off my shirt and exposed a nasty cut halfway down my forearm. Leo looked the other way.

He never could stand the sight of blood. I washed the wound and bound it tight with strips of clean bed linen.

Once I'd bound my arm, Leo turned back to me. "So, what's all this about?"

"I hoped the head thug would be here, so we could settle this right now." I heaved a sigh, trying to rationalize the messy scene in my own mind. "Since we fought so hard for the DVD, maybe they'll think it's the only one." We left the unconscious bodies and went down to the street.

"So, *pisano*," said Leo, "That's done. Come on over for some pizza and primo olives just in from Sicily." He smiled broadly at me and spread his arms. "Bring your girl."

"She's not my girl." I looked away so he wouldn't see the painful truth in my eyes: I only wished she were my girl. *Maybe she was my girl.*

I had to laugh at Leo. Pizza, wine, olives and camaraderie—his answer to everything. "Great offer. We'll take a rain check. I got some videos to pick up and a meeting to make. Thanks again, *pisano*."

CHAPTER SEVENTY-FOUR

Malachi and Bernie rushed to Saint Sebastian's School, jumped out of the van and wove their way through groups of children playing in the schoolyard.

"All right, Bernie. We get in, get the DVDs and get out fast," Malachi told him for the third time, as they approached the old building.

The school secretary was at the copier, stacking the interminable paperwork that keeps a school running, when she heard footsteps. "May I help you?" She wore her usual smile but switched it off when she saw Bernie and a shadowy figure in the background.

"Yeah," said Bernie, "I gotta talk to the principal. It's important." Malachi hovered near the hall door, looking away.

"He's gone for the day, but I think I saw Mr. Killeen."

"Who's he?"

"Assistant principal."

"He'll do."

"I'll see if I can get him for you." She disappeared into a back office.

Shortly, the secretary returned, followed by a smiling Mr. Killeen. She eased her bulk onto her chair.

"How may I help you gentlemen today?" asked Killeen.

"We're here to pick up the DVDs that you duplicated for the Deacon."

The assistant principal tried lying. "What DVDs?"

Bernie pushed past the short swinging door and punched him in the face. The secretary was already screaming when Malachi pulled down his ski mask and stepped out of the shadows. "We haven't got time to fuck around. Where are they?"

Killeen tried again. "Deacon took them with him."

"Bullshit."

Bernie hit him again.

"Wait," Malachi said calmly, looking at the secretary's desk. "Mrs. Montero is it? What a nice Latin name. You will not scream again. Please ask Mr. Killeen to give us the DVDs so we can be on our way." He spun her chair around so she faced the assistant principal. Then he uncovered the talon head of his cane and laid the point of the silver tip just beneath Mrs. Montero's right eye. "I won't hesitate to put her eye out."

Mr. Killeen finally broke. "Please don't hurt Mrs. Montero. The DVDs are in the back."

"Lead the way," Bernie said.

He followed the assistant principal, and Malachi trailed them, pushing Mrs. Montero in front of him with the cane tip. Just then, a little girl came to the counter.

The little girl asked, "Mrs. Montero, I think I left my books here. Did you find them?"

"You don't want me to hurt her." Malachi whispered. "Get rid of her quickly. Understand?"

Mrs. Montero stuttered an answer to the child. "Yes, Susan, I'll get them for you." She rooted under her desk and set a small pink book bag on the counter. "There you are, dear. Run along now."

"Mrs. Montero, are you all right? Have you been crying?"

"No child, my eyes water when I'm tired."

"Okay, thanks. Bye."

Malachi took his position behind her again. "A good liar working at a Catholic school. Tut, tut."

They joined Bernie and Mr. Killeen in the next room.

"This asshole tol' me this is the original and he made three copies," Bernie said. "Deacon took one copy with him."

"Bullshit, there's more. Where are they?"

"I told you the truth," said Killeen. "Deacon brought this one." He held up the original. "And these are the copies he asked me to make." He held up two cases with labels different from the original.

"Did you watch the DVD?"

"No."

"Do you know what's on it?"

"No."

"I don't believe you." Malachi produced a roll of duct tape and ripped off one strip after another. In seconds, Mrs. Montero's mouth was covered and her wrists were bound. He pulled open her blouse and ran the tip of his cane between her pendulous breasts, creating a vertical red line.

"Tell me the truth," he said to Killeen, digging a horizontal furrow across the first cut to create a cross on the woman's chest.

Tears flooded Mrs. Montero's cheeks, but the tape muffled her screams.

Malachi held the cane tip near her eye again. "Save your screams, dear. I've only just begun."

"Stop," said Killeen. "She's innocent. I am telling you the truth I swear it. Please, in the name of God…" He fell to his knees. "I'm begging you."

Malachi pushed the woman to the floor beside Killeen. "Okay, we're leaving for now. But if you haven't been Catholic honest with me, we'll be back. I'll carve each of you into hamburger while the other watches."

CHAPTER SEVENTY FIVE

Malachi picked up the remaining DVD from one of his men who'd retrieved it from the laundry chute.

He watched it alone, twice. What a waste, he said to himself, as he watched Tamara fall. He knew politicians lived in a make-believe world, but this was beyond stupid. They were in deep shit, all right. He watched it one more time.

At the very end he saw the reflection. He zoomed in on the image in the mirror, continuing the spiral rotations until a face came into view.

He couldn't wait for Halloran to see that scene. Malachi pondered how this discovery could be used to his advantage. Certainly it would mean more money.

With the DVDs in hand, he had fulfilled his part of the bargain. Soon—very soon—he could move on, for good. But despite their deal, he'd keep the original DVD as insurance.

Plans had begun to gel for his last act—the assassination.

Malachi called his employer. "I got the DVDs—the original and two copies," he lied.

"Finally," Halloran said. "You certain that's all they had?"

Malachi snorted. "The church folk were very convincin'."

"When can you get them to me?"

"Meet me at six o'clock at Buckingham Fountain. I'll be expectin' the next installment of my fee."

"I'll be there."

"Alone. Are we agreed?"

"Yes. Is Sunday on?"

"Looks good for now. The prince will have a terrible accident. Develop your alibis. Once it's over... immediately... I'll need my final payment. I'm finished with this Chicago freezer."

"That'll work."

Malachi called Saint Sebastian's from a bank of public phones in the lobby of the Pick Congress Hotel. "Please have Deacon Adelius call me at this number right away," he told the receptionist. He read the number off the phone. "It's extremely important." He leaned back in a plush wingback chair to wait, a glass of Cabernet Sauvignon in one hand and the *Tribune* in the other.

CHAPTER SEVENTY-SIX

I called Stanichar. "Have you set up the meeting?"

"DA Pritchard finally agreed to meet in the top floor conference room at the Chicago Public Library—main branch on Michigan Avenue. Is 5 p.m. good for you?"

"Yeah, that'll work. You've got to persuade him not to take action against Halloran and Clayton until we get Malachi."

"I'll do my best."

"No, it's a must."

I returned to the school to pick up the DVDs. I'd leave the original in the school safe and distribute copies to Stanichar and the DA.

The scene at Saint Sebastian's was chaotic. An ambulance and three squad cars were parked in front of the building. Father Kowalski jogged down the steps through the gathering crowd to meet me. His face read, panic. "Two men came and took the DVDs," he said. "The ambulance is taking Mr. Killeen and Mrs. Montero to the hospital."

"Oh, no, for the love of Christ." Nobody knew about the videos. How could this happen?

I got to Mr. Killeen just as a med-tech brought him to the ambulance door. The assistant principal had been battered. His face was bruised and his left eye swollen shut. "Deacon, I'm so sorry. I had to give them the DVDs. They were torturing her."

Oh, God. The man was apologizing, and I was the one who had gotten him into this. "You did the right thing," I told him. "How is Mrs. Montero?"

"I don't know, medically." His voice dropped to a whisper. "The man cut a cross… in her chest." Before I could ask, Mr. Killeen told me everything he knew. "The man who did it was tall and wore a mask. His voice was odd, halting, and he used the head of his cane to cut Mrs. Montero. The other man was heavyset, and moved slowly, kind of average-looking with a dripping nose. I think he had a cold."

"Good observations. The police will thank you for that. I'll pray for you both."

I was bathed in guilt… again… and my stupidity was to blame. Why had I involved innocent people? Why had I allowed every single version of the incriminating DVDs to leave my hands? Now we had no proof. Could things get any worse? At this rate, they probably could. God help us.

As a police officer approached, I slid away into the crowd and headed for the rental car. Father Kowalski caught up with me. "I almost forgot. There was an urgent message for you. You're to call immediately." He handed me a slip of paper.

I didn't recognize the number, but I punched it into my cell phone. These were strange times. Who knew what would happen next?

"Hello, Deacon. It's over."

I knew that voice. "You caused a lot of pain and for what?"

The man chortled, breathlessly. "I could say the same … about you. Stay out of my way or there will be more. Forget evidence. Our experts will debunk anything and everything." He interrupted his own diatribe with more vile chortling. "Oh yes, and then there's Ann. … "

I wanted to say, *You son of a bitch, I'll rip your heart out.* "You worthless piece of garbage." I took a deep breath and forced my anger down a notch. "I believe you.… You have the original and all the copies."

"Good, then we understand each other."

CHAPTER SEVENTY-SEVEN

Malachi was two hours early for his meeting with Halloran. Despite the cold wind whipping off the lake, self-preservation and occupational paranoia had forced him to reconnoiter the meeting place. In winter, Buckingham Fountain looked like a dismal stone structure that belonged in the warm climes of sunny Italy. A few people scurried on their way to some place else. No one lingered at the fountain.

Malachi walked the area in an erratic pattern, not overly worried. He hadn't yet completed his contract, so he was still needed.

Once satisfied the area was safe, Malachi stood behind a statue to wait for Halloran. At least the concrete base provided a windbreak.

At five minutes to six, Halloran strode up to the fountain. Malachi waited another ten minutes, monitoring Halloran's movements and gaze. If others were around, he'd surely look their way. Malachi sensed no danger, so he approached the police commissioner.

"Finally," said Halloran. "Let's walk."

Halloran handed Malachi a briefcase. "This installment covers the retrieval of the DVD and copies."

Malachi handed a small bag to Halloran. "The original and two copies."

"One more payment is due after solving your biggest problems."

"How will I get it to you?" asked Halloran.

"I'll call you."

"Is Sunday still on?"

"That's the plan. What about the deacon and the woman?"

"What about them?"

"We can presume they watched the DVD before handing it over. They know too much."

"Not to worry. Without evidence in hand, it's all hearsay."

Malachi was enjoying the delayed gratification. "Look very closely at the exciting conclusion of the video, commissioner. Use the zoom. The deacon and the woman no doubt appreciated this ending as well. You *will* be calling me."

"What?" Halloran's face paled. "What did you see?"

"There was a witness, commissioner."

CHAPTER SEVENTY-EIGHT

Halloran and Clayton watched the DVD until the end and didn't catch it.

"What the hell is he talking about?" Halloran grumbled. "I don't see anything. Play it again. "Let's watch it again more carefully."

"What are we looking for?"

"We'll know it when we see it."

On the second viewing, Halloran stopped the tape just before it ended. "See right there." He zoomed in and pointed at the screen. Just barely visible in a decorative mirror was a blurred image of a face partially hidden behind a door.

Details were impossible to make out except that it appeared to be someone with long hair ... a woman. "Had to be Tiko. No one else was in the room. I knew who it was as soon as Malachi told me."

"But she was asleep."

"We were wrong about that." Halloran looked up with an expression of frustration and anger.

"I'll call Malachi. She's got to be silenced." He made the brief call to Malachi who was awaiting the call. After a heated negotiation, Halloran slammed down the cell phone. "This is going to cost us a bundle."

Clayton sat staring into space. "It already has."

CHAPTER SEVENTY-NINE

"Thank you for all of your help," I said to the monsignor. I exuded a sigh, melodramatic, I suppose. "Somehow Malachi knew the DVDs were at the school. He and his cohort beat up two employees and took the original and every copy."

Ann winced as though she'd taken a blow herself.

I felt foolish asking. If I couldn't trust Ann and Salvatore, who could I trust? But I had to question them. "Did *either* of you mention the DVDs to anyone... or where they were?"

"No," said the monsignor, shaking his head.

"Of course not," said Ann. "Who was hurt?"

"A secretary and assistant principal."

"Tsk, tsk," said the old man. "May God be with them. These evildoers must be stopped." He gripped my arm.

I bit my lip and inhaled sharply.

"What's wrong?" Salvatore asked.

"Just a scratch. We had some trouble when I handed over the DVD."

Before I could protest, Ann had taken my coat and asked the monsignor for antiseptic and bandages.

He ushered us into a washroom and supplied us with an antiseptic wash, an antibacterial ointment and an ACE bandage wrap. "Will this do?"

"Fine." Ann didn't ask if she could doctor my arm. She just did it. I wasn't sure how I felt about that at the moment. Afterwards I knew I didn't like it.

She finished wrapping my arm. "You'll need stitches soon."

"Right. Thanks."

She stayed to clean up, and the monsignor and I returned to his drawing room. He spoke in hushed tones, narrowing his eyes with intensity. "Our work must continue unabated no matter what happens."

"Yes, we must catch the villains who—"

"No, my son. I mean the work of the Gabrians!" His eyes seemed lit from within. "No matter what happens, we must go on!"

"Yes, Monsignor." What did the Gabrians have to do with all of this... or the cardinal? Wasn't the monsignor merely a go-between? This time I was glad to leave the old man and get some fresh air, cold as it was. What the hell is up with him?

The wind had increased in velocity; the snow was blowing in a diagonal direction. Thankfully, the car was still somewhat warm.

Ann rubbed her hands together rapidly in front of the heater fan. "Oh, that feels better."

I turned up the temperature.

Then she laid into me. "Where have you been? We've been worried sick."

"I delivered the DVD, but Malachi wasn't there. I just told you: I went back to the school to pick up copies and they were all gone, even the original."

She plunged back into her argument. "You left me there for a long time. The monsignor and I ran out of conversation an hour ago. Why didn't you take me... or at least tell me what was going on?"

I couldn't help scowling at the edge in her voice. I didn't like explaining myself. "If I'd told you, you would have wanted to go. And it was too dangerous. And I had Leo to help me."

"I could've helped, but you don't like that, do you? You don't need a *woman's* help." Her voice sliced like a dagger. "If I'm such a drag, why don't you just drop me off at the next corner and be done with it."

I recoiled at her ultimatum. "If you like." Okay, maybe I'd been abrupt, but I was steamed at losing the DVDs and wasn't in the mood for this. Yeah, I was crazy about the woman, but she was going too far. I'd call her bluff.

I pulled up to the curb and stopped the car.

Ann just sat there with her arms folded over her chest, looking straight ahead.

After a couple of minutes, I swallowed my irritation. "Do you still want to go along with me to meet with the DA and Stanichar?"

"I'm here, aren't I?"

I tried to change the subject. "You and Monsignor get along?"

"Famously." Her voice was cold. She knew she'd been parked there so she wouldn't get in my way, so she'd quit asking questions.

How quickly tension can develop between a man and a woman. We snaked along in silence through rush hour traffic on Michigan Avenue. I pounded the steering wheel in frustration. "No DVD. No evidence. I hate going in empty-handed. What am I going to say to the DA?"

"We tell him what we know and what we saw on the DVD. That should count for something."

"I guess." I felt like banging my head against the glass. Why hadn't I taken at least one of the blasted DVDs with me or left them all somewhere safe. I thought the school was secure. Who had betrayed us?

If I ruled out Ann, Kowalski and Killeen, the monsignor was the only one left. But why would he sic Malachi on us? Something was missing. It didn't make sense.

I parked off State Street in the underground garage adjacent to the Harold Washington Chicago Public Library. The foreboding neoclassical building contained the largest public library in the world.

When we entered the conference room, the DA and the reporter were waiting for us at an oak table that seated twelve. A tray with a water pitcher and glasses had been set on one of two sideboards. Obviously the presence of Barry Pritchard warranted special consideration. If the meeting had included merely a reporter, deacon and spa manager, we probably would have been stuffed into a library study room.

Stanichar introduced me, and I introduced Ann. We shook hands all around.

Niceties over, Pritchard glanced at his watch and appraised us with his pale blue eyes. "Well, you got me here. *Busy* comes nowhere near describing my life right now. So make it quick, and make it good."

Stanichar took out his micro-recorder. "May I tape—"

"Absolutely not!" Pritchard said. The reporter quickly stuffed the micro recorder in a back pocket and took out his notebook.

Ann began. "My sister—Allison De La Croix, street name Amber—was murdered. Police pulled her out of the river a few days ago."

"Yes, I remember." The DA gave the perfunctory line, "I'm sorry for your loss."

I took over, quickly outlining Allison's desperation at the church, the blackmail scheme, the coded Bible, Sister's Mary's kidnapping and the church bombing. "Detective Ditmar is handling the investigation, and we have our suspicions about him."

Pritchard made no effort to hide his impatience, pacing to and fro, hands clasped behind his back. We remained standing too, though the heavy oak chairs, with their old-fashioned leather padded seats, looked inviting.

"That's quite a tale," the DA said, "and you've brought the coded Bible?"

"Um, no. That gets complicated, but no, we don't have it."

The DA gave me a searching look. "So, without proof, you are asking me to believe that these seemingly disparate events are linked and that a veteran detective is involved?"

"There's more."

Pritchard raised an eyebrow. He wasn't buying it. I talked faster. I described the confrontation at Ann's apartment. "There was a police stakeout, for no legitimate reason. That's one reason we can't go to Ditmar."

I had saved the DVD for last, dreading the question I knew he'd ask. "A key in the Bible led us to a DVD that shows the death of a prostitute and subsequent cover-up."

"Images can be easily altered," Pritchard said. "Nonetheless, I'll take a look at the DVD." He extended his hand, expecting me to hand it over, I guess.

"We had it. Now we don't." I blew out a breath, embarrassed to confess how the original and all three copies had fallen into the wrong hands.

"Whose hands?" was all he asked.

"Police Commissioner Mitch Halloran and State Senator Frank Clayton are behind this."

Pritchard's head snapped to attention. "They have the most to lose. Clayton hit the woman, Tamara, which led to her death. That's on the DVD."

The DA's wiry body tensed with anticipation, but his words stayed in character. "That's quite an accusation.... Mere speculation at this point. Still... " He turned toward the window, muttering to himself. I thought I heard, "God-damned slimy bastards," but I couldn't be sure.

He turned toward us again, with an abrupt change of subject. "What do you know of Norman Balthazar?"

I shrugged, and Ann shook her head.

The DA answered his own question. "He was a crack code breaker, who worked directly under Halloran."

"Was?" I asked.

"He was found dead in an underground parking garage. Blunt force to the head. "

"The poor bastard was a code breaker," I repeated, thinking out loud. "Could he have deciphered the code in the Bible?"

"It makes sense," said Pritchard. "But you... we... have no proof."

"We will, when we recover the DVD. Until then, we *can* provide the names and addresses of witnesses to support what I told you." I reached in my pocket. At least I had something to show, paltry though it was. "This is the key that opened the mailbox where we found the video."

Pritchard turned it over in his hands. "Go on."

"A prostitute named Tiko can place Halloran and Clayton and Tamara at the Belmont Harbor Yacht Club on the night of Tamara's death. Also, Charles Crawford, a manager at the club, can verify that Tiko and Tamara were there on that night with a black man and a white man who resembled Halloran and Clayton."

Ann produced a business card that she must have picked up in Crawford's office. Bless her. She wrote something on the back and handed it to Pritchard, who nodded to her.

"Anything else?"

I almost said "if," but stayed with the definitive. "*When* you get the tape, you'll see what we saw: State Senator Frank Clayton and Commissioner Mitch Halloran with the prostitutes. Later they talk about eliminating the cardinal. Tamara hears them talking, and Clayton strikes her. "As she falls, she hits her head on the coffee table and appears to be dead. Halloran tells Clayton to dump the body off some pier in Gary."

"And Allison De La Croix videoed all that?"

"For a blackmail scheme," Ann explained. "We're fairly sure that was her intent. She couldn't have known what would happen to Tamara."

Stanichar had been silent, taking notes. "But we don't have the Bible, the code or the DVD... " he muttered. "How in hell...?"

I heaved a sigh and explained. "I turned the Bible over to Malachi in exchange for Sister Mary Margaret, who had been kidnapped. I gave Ditmar a copy of the code but could never get it back."

The DA shook his head, apparently confused. "Hold on. Why the nun? Who's Malachi?"

"Sister Mary Margaret began to decipher the Bible code. Malachi is Halloran's muscle, and he's vicious. They've threatened the Catholic schools and churches if anyone contacts the authorities."

Ann gave me a look, "Not to mention *us*," she said, under her breath.

Pritchard fell into a chair at the head of the table, holding his head. "Slow down. What are you doing, writing a thriller? Why is the cardinal their target?"

I said," I can only guess that he has been openly critical of Halloran and Clayton reducing their chances of being elected."

"For Christ's sake." Pritchard didn't raise his head, just kept muttering into the tabletop. "The pieces seem to fit… even without proof. I can't believe how this could this happen in *my* city under *my* nose?" He raised his gaze. "Okay, first things first. We put out an APB on Malachi. We'll need a description"

I sighed again. The DA wasn't going to like this. "He's tall, maybe six foot, dark hair slicked back. He carries a cane and has a distinctive voice pattern. I think I'd recognize it."

"You'd recognize his *voice?*" Pritchard's voice rose to a high pitch. "Nobody's *seen* him?"

"He stays in the shadows.., wears a mask," I said. "But he speaks oddly… and he always carries that cane. It's got a handle that looks like a talon."

Pritchard gave me another look, his mouth twisted in frustration. "I'm in the fact business and this is the worst accumulation of hearsay and nonsense since Bigfoot was supposedly seen in Lincoln Park." He paused and looked out the floor-to-ceiling view of his city. "But, I do have a feeling you're on the right track, but how are we supposed to—"

"It's not my place to give advice," I began, "but I do have some ideas, so here goes: You could pressure Ditmar. He'll want to save his sorry ass. Get him to give you the translated codes from the Bible. I'm betting he'll give up Halloran and Clayton, and more to the immediate point— Malachi."

"I'll take that under advisement," said Pritchard, "and I'll put out that sketchy description of our villain and see what we can uncover. If you hear anything else, contact me immediately. As the lady said, you're in danger, so I'd suggest you step back and leave the investigation to us."

I nodded, but Ann threw me a challenging look. She knew I wouldn't give up the chase.

Pritchard left first, shaking hands all around.

Stanichar waited and took the elevator down with us. "You'll keep me in the loop, right?"

"You've got it," I said. "Keep up your own investigation, but be careful."

Ann persuaded me to drop by the ER at Grant Hospital for some stitches in my arm. What the hell, I thought. A beautiful woman cared about my well-being. That was worth something. I'd already forgiven her for treading on my boundaries.

"Ann, you know I can't leave this case up to them. I'll get the miserable creep."

CHAPTER EIGHTY

Halloran called for a meeting with Ditmar. Halloran said, "I've got a few ideas to get this Deacon out of our hair."

"Any specific ideas?"

"Yeah, first tell me what you've got on him, from the beginning, even if it's supposition."

Ditmar retrieved a ragged notebook from his breast pocket. "Deacon came to our attention when a madam named 'Amber,' went to his church for help."

Halloran felt the color rising in his cheeks, but he held back any other sign of emotion at the mention of a woman he knew very well.

"Anyways," Ditmar continued, "Deacon says he tried to help her but didn't contact any authorities. His story is that some yahoos crashed in on them and shot her … and him. The next morning we fished her out of the river. Deacon was wounded, spent a few days in the hospital. I interviewed him there."

"Go on."

"Oh yeah, then there's the coded Bible. Deacon had a nun friend of his try to crack the code. Some men took her and beat her up. Deacon turned over the Bible to them to get her back. A guy who was with the nun got busted up the same night and ended up in the hospital. Deacon again. Let's see, you had your guy translate the code. Oh yeah, the firebombs in front of Ann's building that hit an unmarked squad car? No witnesses, but I'm betting the deacon was responsible for that too."

Ditmar gulped down a glass of water, turned a page in his notebook and began reading again. "Just a few days ago, a guy was found dead in a stairwell in same office building where Amber—Allison De La Croix—had an office."

An office manager told us Deacon and Ann were there at the same time. Again, no proof, no witnesses, but I'm betting the deacon pushed him down the stairs. The dead guy had a record as long as your arm, but it's still wrongful death, maybe murder. The deacon was an MP, so he knows how to handle—"

"Shhh, just a minute. I'm thinking." The commissioner rested his chin on his hands and closed his eyes. "There must be a way to get rid of the witness and the bull-headed deacon at the same time. He's violent, hangs around with prostitutes. She's vulnerable … "

"He was an MP, so he probably knows how to handle himself."

Halloran didn't answer, but he thought about Malachi's description of the fight in Deacon's small apartment when this mess began. A plan began to form in his mind. "I want you and your officers to be ready to move. I'll tell you when and where. It'll be in the next two nights. The timing will be critical."

CHAPTER EIGHTY-ONE

Because of my arm, Ann insisted on driving. I let her, even though I'd driven with worse injuries. No sense starting that tension between us again.

"We've got to get a better description of Malachi," I told her. "Pritchard's right. We didn't give him much to go on."

"I think he had a slight Southern accent."

"Hey. That's another piece."

She suggested asking Sister Mary Margaret, but I hated to do it. We'd bring up those horrendous memories again, as if they ever went away. "I guess it's got to be done." I punched in De La Croix's number.

He was cordial, as always, and relayed the good news that Meg was healing well, catching up on her reading and working on the computer. "A physical therapist—someone I trust implicitly—is helping with rehab. We have deli food and Chinese brought in."

"Sounds great. We have you to thank for keeping her safe."

"Believe me, it's no trouble. Just a minute. I'll give her the phone."

"Hey, Deac?" Sister said. "What's the news?"

I brought her up-to-date on everything, but she was most worried about the injuries to Mr. Kileen and Mrs. Montero.

"It was that awful man again, wasn't it. Are they all right?"

"They'll be okay. I took a deep breath before barreling in. "Can you remember anything else about … the man with the cane." I didn't tell her what we'd come up with, figuring it could color her memory.

She sighed and there was a long pause. "Well, I was blindfolded most of the time, so I don't know how much help I can be." Her voice faded, and I could tell she was mentally back in that warehouse.

"I'm sorry, Meg."

Her sobbing tore me up, but I just waited. In the silence, my body had a lot to say: My stomach constricted into a knot, and my arm ached. The stitches on my chin and shoulder itched. I could only imagine how Meg felt.

She'd calmed down a bit, I guess. At least she was only sniffling. "I'm sorry."

"Hey, we've been friends forever. You can let it out anytime you need to."

She took a big breath and began again. "When I first got there, he was standing behind bright lights so I couldn't see him clearly. But I know he was tall. Not as tall as you but at least six feet tall. His hair was pretty dark and combed straight back. After that, some other guy spun me around and put on the blindfold. Malachi's voice was soft, and his speech was a little different."

"How do you mean?"

"He dropped his 'ing sounds, like in singin' and readin'. Like country singers. You know what I mean?"

"Yes."

"Anything else?"

"He spoke very slowly, like it was difficult for him. Then there was that cane." She started crying again.

I was desperate for clues, but not this desperate. "Thanks, Meg. You've helped a lot. Just call if you remember anything else."

"I will. Can you put Ann on? Her father wants to speak with her."

Good timing. Ann had just pulled into a parking space at the hospital. I handed her the phone and got out of the car to give her some privacy. The conversation lasted about three minutes, an improvement. When I came back, Ann's face seemed softer, no longer hard-edged like it had been last time she'd spoken to her father.

I didn't ask about the call, just launched into my next idea. "Brother Chuck might have more on Malachi." I picked up my phone to call, but she laid a hand on mine. "Let's go inside where it's warm and you can get your stitches."

She was right. A frigid night was setting in. The waiting room was empty, so I was repaired in no time.

Then I called Chuck in Elmwood Park.

"How're you doing, you indestructible old curmudgeon?"

"Pretty well for an out-of-shape guy."

"What about your hands?"

"The doc says they're healing as well as can be expected. I can move my fingers a bit more. Apparently no nerve damage."

"Great news." I told him what was going on. "We need a better description of Malachi, though. Can you remember anything else about him?"

"The bastard was in the shadows but close enough for a glimpse before they blindfolded me. Let's see, tall, average build, clean shaven... weird eyes."

"How do you mean?"

"Crooked or one eye was different than the other... something."

"That'll help. Could you recognize him again?"

"Maybe."

"When we close in, I may call on you to join us. Are you up for that?"

"Am I? I owe that bastard.... Speaking of owing, you're buying me dinner at a nice steak house, not some glorified hamburger joint."

"It's a deal. Take care, you old reprobate—"

"I want the steak medium rare, slathered with onions, washed down with a Samuel Adams.... "

"So long, you con-man."

CHAPTER EIGHTY-TWO

"Now what are you going to do?" Ann asked as we returned to the car. I answered her, but I was talking to myself more than to her. "The only thing we can do is try to anticipate Malachi's moves and be waiting. We know he's after the cardinal." I kept my other thoughts to myself, Uppermost was what to do with Ann.

She must have read my mind. "I guess neither of us can go back to our apartments yet."

"Not until this thing is over."

"The motel is too depressing."

"How about joining Sister Mary Margaret?"

"And my father? I'm not ready for that." She looked down at her hands.

"Okay, I've got another idea—Leo."

She nodded, so I gave him a call. He said he had an apartment behind the pizza parlor that he rented out... for *special occasions*, as he called them.

I called Leo. "Sure she can stay here a while. And don't forget, I'll be close."

I knew he lived above the restaurant. "Sounds good, but don't you forget she's a lady."

"Hey, you trying to hurt Leo's feelings? You know I'm a gentleman."

"I know you're a lady's man."

"What else would I be?"

Ann gathered some belongings from her apartment and we met Leo in the rear parking lot. He opened the door under the stairs, took a deep bow and waved us into a furnished apartment with one bedroom, a full bath and a large all-purpose room for cooking, dining and watching a big screen TV.

"Smells good… like pizza," said Ann. "I'll be fine here for a day or so."

Leo took the hint and disappeared. "Tah duh!" he announced as he swept back in carrying a large sausage-and-pepperoni pizza in one hand and a bag in the other. He pulled out a six-pack of Schlitz, a two-liter bottle of Pepsi and two bottles of red wine. "I thought you might be hungry… and thirsty."

As he lit the candle stuck in the in an empty Chianti bottle, I saw that his knuckles were still bruised and inflamed from the fight in the laundry room.

"Thanks for everything," I said.

Leo shrugged. "It's nuthin'. Remember, *cara mia*, I'm right upstairs if you need me." He pointed a thumb at the ceiling.

She kissed him on the cheek. "Thank you, Leo. You're sweet."

We dug into the food. Between bites, we talked about the task before us… before me. I didn't want her anywhere near danger. That was a tough message to get across without insulting her. "Can you stay put for awhile?" I asked her. "It's safer."

"But I can help."

I detected a trace of resentment. "I know you can," I said quickly. "If I see a place where your expert assistance is needed, I promise I'll invite you to the party." By now, I knew Ann liked to be at the forefront, unless fire escapes were involved. "You've done some fine detective work. And you've been a big help. But I need to check everything out first. Since I'll be vulnerable, even on my own, I'd feel better if you hid out here for a while."

We embraced at the door and kissed, long and sweet, signaling the tension was gone. "Let me know what's going on. And be careful."

"I will." It took a supreme effort of will to leave her.

CHAPTER EIGHTY-THREE

I returned to my digs behind Saint Sebastian's. I felt comfortable in my own place again, and safe.

Nothing more could be done tonight, so I went to bed. Thoughts of Ann waltzed through my mind. I smiled to myself, remembering the warmth of her body next to me. We had more than chemistry, more than a shared goal to find her sister's killer. Maybe we could have a future together, something I wouldn't have considered a few months ago. I had an impulse to drive back to the apartment to spend another night with her... but it was late. I fell asleep, glad she was in my life.

The morning broke with the usual winter mantle of gray clouds and the howling wind off the lakefront. I pulled my muffler up to my ears for the trek to early Mass. I prayed, as always, to know and do His will. Father Kowalski and I caught up on parish news over a steak and eggs at the IHOP, next to O'Neill's pub.

It seemed like months not days since I'd talked with Glitter at the bar. ...

He told me none of the bystanders had been injured badly when the huge stained glass window in the church went down in the bomb blast. It had been boarded up, but the church had already received nearly enough donations to replace it. He said Mr. Killeen was better and back to work, but Mrs. Montero was still recuperating. I asked him to relay news about Sister Mary Margaret to Mother Superior at Saint Catherine's. I did not give him Meg's location.

Before my next appointment—this one at Holy Name Cathedral with the archbishop—I wanted to wander around a bit. I could use some inspiration. I was early and parked a few blocks away. Plunging my hands deep in my pockets, I turned my face away from the biting wind. My ears stung from the cold. Nevertheless, the sight of the gray stone structure always calmed me. The single spire rose to over 300 feet. Somehow, the architect had made the heavy stone seem light and elegant. Just behind the cathedral loomed the unique shape of the John Hancock building. Inside the church, the soaring arched ceiling brought a degree of grandeur. Surely nothing evil could touch such a magnificent and sacred place. *God help us.*

As I rounded the altar I found Archbishop Laine waiting for me, carrying his topcoat.

"Hello, Your Grace."

"Greetings, Deacon." He motioned me behind the altar where we could be alone. "Now, what's this all about?"

I closed the door of the vestment room and we sat in privacy. "I'm worried sick," I told him. "The church, our schools, the cardinal, Sister Mary Margaret, Ann De La Croix and God knows who else have been threatened. And we've got High Mass coming up on Sunday—everyone will be in one place. We'll have a cathedral full of sitting targets. We've got to do something."

The archbishop shook his head, wearily, as he listened.

"Malachi is the henchman, your Grace, but somebody hired him and his thugs. I can't prove it yet, but I think it's most likely Halloran and Clayton. The church hasn't exactly endorsed their political aspirations."

"In their political corruption, you mean," the archbishop said. "But they have their supporters. Some citizens don't like our—the cardinal's— criticism of the leading candidates. They point to the church's poison— the pedophile scandals. That broad net catches us all. Chicago citizens are up in arms."

"The Gabrians—"

"Yes, God bless the Gabrians."

"Maybe they could help at High Mass. I mean, the diocese provides some security, your grace, but—"

"Are the police any help at all?"

"I don't know who to trust but I believe Pritchard—the DA—is clean, but he could be a target too. I mean he's Halloran's opposition in the mayoral race."

"We *must* talk to the DA, Deacon. The diocese can't provide enough security. I know the cardinal doesn't take the personal threats very seriously, but I'll approach him."

"You're right." My ego had stopped me, and not for the first time. I was reluctant to go to Pritchard without proof, especially after the humiliation of losing every lick of evidence we'd had—Allison's Bible, the code, the DVDs.

I brought the archbishop up-to-date on everything else I knew. He gave me the cardinal's itinerary. We agreed to keep security tight and enlist the help of the Gabrians, even though it wasn't their primary mission.

"I think it's best we stay close on Sunday," I said. "Could you arrange to concelebrate the Mass and to have me assist on the altar?"

"Certainly." We parted in the usual way. "I'll pray for you, as always," he said. "Good-bye and Godspeed."

CHAPTER EIGHTY-FOUR

Frank Clayton was losing it. He couldn't sleep. Booze, pills, campaign work. Nothing helped. He had killed Tamara. Over and over, his mind replayed the blow he'd struck. He relived the moment when he realized she was dead. And he saw himself roll her body into the frigid waters of Lake Michigan, her eyes staring back at him.

He paced his office for the hundredth time, wearing a path into the Berber carpet. He swept all the papers off his cherry wood desktop and flopped into his plush imported armchair. Usually he felt important and secure behind his desk. The walls lined with framed photos of him shaking hands with politicians, arms around athletes and musicians—all the VIPs he'd met in his nineteen-year career.

Now he buried his head in his arms. All those smiling faces would turn against him—hate him—if they knew the truth. He hated himself. If only he could tell someone—someone safe—maybe he wouldn't go crazy.

Clayton thought of the gentle priest who had visited his childhood home, back when he was a practicing Catholic.

Yes, that priest was his only choice. He made a quick call then grabbed his coat and left by a side door.

Now he was pacing the sidewalk, trying to work up the nerve to enter. This was a bad idea. He shouldn't have called. He couldn't tell anyone. On the other hand, he couldn't break an appointment with a man of God. It wasn't done. He'd come this far, so he'd go through with it.

Clayton was ushered into a large room with windows overlooking the lake, but he avoided looking at the water. Instead, he examined the heavy wine-colored drapes, the paintings of various popes, a statue of Mary and a silver crucifix.

"Frank, how are you? It's been a long time." Cardinal Schneider entered the room and greeted Clayton.

Clayton didn't succeed at being his usual casual self and barely acknowledged inquiries about his parents. "Thank you for seeing me," he mumbled.

The cardinal motioned him toward a grouping of upholstered wingback chairs. As they walked over, Clayton noticed cameras and a tripod in the corner and mounted black-and-white photos taken of Chicago and its people. He remembered the cardinal's hobby and tried to frame a compliment, but his mind was blank. "Uh—"

"You noticed my cameras. A fine relaxing diversion. So we're both busy men. Why the rushed appointment?"

"I... uh... I've come to tell you that although I've made mistakes in the past, I wanted to reassure you that I have the welfare of the citizens of Illinois, and Chicago in particular, at heart. I believe that I can be a damn good governor."

"Oh, you do. And what have I to do with that?"

Clayton didn't mean to... in fact he was horrified when the words rolled out of his mouth: "Forgive me Father, for I have sinned.... "

At hearing the formal introduction to a confession, Cardinal Schneider was startled. "Um. Have you considered confessing to your parish priest?"

"I... um... You are my only hope. If you won't hear... my confession, I can't... I won't go anywhere else."

Cardinal Schneider gave him a long stare. Then he rose, went into an adjoining room and returned wearing a purple stole. "Pull your chair over to mine." He put his elbow on the armrest and covered the side of his face with his hand. He prayed and made the sign of the cross. ""Go ahead."

"O my God, I am heartily sorry for having offended Thee, and I detest all my sins… " Clayton began. The preamble words from his childhood confessions rushed from his mouth like a waterfall. "I recently lost my temper and hit a woman and accidently killed her." There, he had said it.

"The cardinal registered no shock or surprise. "What happened then?"

"I put her body into the lake to avoid detection."

"You are responsible for the death of another human being, accident or not. You have covered up the act and denied her a Christian burial. These are most grievous sins. You know what you must do."

"What?"

"Besides being sincerely remorseful, you must make amends and do penance."

"I am truly sorry. How do I make amends?"

"You must contact the authorities. It is the only way to free your soul. I can accompany you for support and we can consult an attorney."

"I can't… not right now. I'd go to prison."

"You said it was an accident."

"Yes but … Clayton spoke in a panicky voice. "This is a true confession and you are bound to never reveal anything I've said, right?"

"You are absolutely right. But let me help you."

"It's complicated. Someone helped me with the girl's body… and the incident was recorded on a DVD."

"Then you have a witness. My son, I'm only concerned with you and your immortal soul. You must confess as you have and make restitution."

The burden had been lifted, but only for a moment. Thoughts swirled through Clayton's mind. I confessed. Maybe that will banish the memories … time heals all wounds. … The cardinal was bound to secrecy. … Confessing to authorities was out of the question.

He rose abruptly, banging his leg against the chair. "Thank you for hearing my confession." Clayton practically ran from the office, trying not to look at pictures of Christ, Mary and several saints that seemed to stare down at him as he strode by. He left without receiving absolution.

He ducked into the nearest tavern for a brandy. He'd get through this.

CHAPTER EIGHTY-FIVE

I picked up my cell on the second ring.

A man's voice said softly, "You don't know me and I won't give my name, but my friend Tiko wants to meet with you."

"Why didn't she call herself?"

"I'm not sure, but she sounded scared and nervous. Her English is not always the best especially when she's emotional, y'know?"

Maybe she had a change of heart and wanted to tell me more about that night with Tamara. Sounded too good to be true. A trap was more likely.

I had to check it out. "When and where?"

"Midnight tomorrow, Hotel Claremont, room 1912." The phone went dead.

I'd be there but I needed backup, and my choices were limited.

CHAPTER EIGHTY-SIX

I called Leo and arranged to meet him at a coffee shop. I didn't want Ann to know anything about this plan. She'd either disapprove or she'd insist on coming with me. "So how's it going?"

"It goes fine, my friend, but that's not why you wanted to meet with me."

"You're right as usual." I told him about the invitation to meet with Tiko and how she fit into the investigation.

"So you think she didn't come clean on your first meeting?"

"No, I don't. It's possible she could tie Halloran and Clayton to Tamara's murder."

"So how can Leo help?"

"I know I'm a marked man. This could be a trap. I could use some backup."

"I'm in. Can I bring my gun?"

"If it makes you feel better, but let's talk first. You're agreeing too quickly. You will be in harm's way."

"Fuck this 'harm's way.' It'll be like the old days. You know, it can get a little dull around a pizza parlor. I can tell you I enjoyed the action in the laundry room with those *stronzos* the other day. I couldn't even sleep, y'know just relivin' what went down. That was some good shit. I been thinkin' about it ever since. So … yeah, I'm in. What do you want me to do?"

"Did anyone ever tell you that you're one brave, goofy character?"

"Yeah, all the time and that I'm good lookin' too."

Leo could always make me laugh. That was his holy gift to the world.

"Okay, first I want you to rent a room at the Hotel Claremont on the nineteenth floor. Try to get a room close to 1912. Give them some bull as to why."

"That where you're meeting Tiko?"

"Yes, at midnight. We'll be early. By the way, just so you know, she has a bodyguard who looks like a Sumo wrestler on steroids. This isn't like the DVD drop-off where I *knew* we were walking into danger. This should be nothing but a meeting with a hooker and her associate. With luck, I'll get what I need to put the right people behind bars."

He shrugged. "Okay, okay. I get it. I'll be there. Did I ever tell you the one about the social worker who wanted to give the nun a hug?"

"Yeah, Leo. You told me." Usually I got a kick out of Leo's jokes, but not now, not today.

I told him again that he was *back-up*. He was there just in case … He agreed to my warnings, but he had a suspicious glint in his eye. Leo would do his own thing, no matter what I told him. I felt more secure with Leo covering my back.

CHAPTER EIGHTY-SEVEN

Halloran easily discovered that Justine had taken over as madam of Amber's very high-end escort service. He relayed that news to Malachi, who called Justine and requested Tiko as his consort for the evening.

The fee was $1,200. Malachi wouldn't let the money and a girl like that to go to waste.

Tiko showed up at the Hotel Claremont, room 1912, fashionably late at 11:05 p.m.

"Welcome, please call me Malachi."

"Hello Malachi, I'm Tiko." She smiled and tilted her head sideways. As she entered she shed a fox fur revealing a short black cocktail dress with a jade pendant. Her luxuriant hair fell straight to her shoulders.

"Would you like a glass of wine?" asked Malachi.

"Chardonnay, if you have it," she murmured.

"I do." He poured two goblets.

She took hers to the French windows and pulled the filmy drapes aside. "You have a lovely view."

"When I travel, I like to stay on the uppermost floors just for that purpose."

"Shall we turn the lights down a little?" she suggested.

"Yes but only a little. I want to drink you in like this wine."

"Malachi, you are a romantic. Let me light a few candles."

After she had lit two aromatic candles, he asked. "Would you take off your clothes slowly for me?"

"I'd love to." She opened her clutch purse and placed it on the coffee table in front of him.

"He understood immediately. "Of course." He took out twelve one hundred dollar bills, folded them and slipped them into her purse.

"Perhaps a little music?"

"Sure."

Tiko began to disrobe to a mellow jazz tune. She was slow with just enough tease.

"Lovely," he said. "Bravo."

When she was completely naked, he beckoned her to kneel before him while he sat in a comfortable armchair. "Let's see how you can make me a happy man."

Under her expert and practiced ministrations, it didn't take long. When he had finished, he spoke in a voice loud enough to be heard in the next room. "Now."

Bernie and Jake charged through the bedroom door and grabbed her by her arms. She shrieked out in Japanese, *"Tasukete Kudasai!"*

Yoshi burst through the hotel door like it was balsa wood. *"Hashire!"* he shouted and threw a side *Shuto* blow so fast it was a blur, into Jake's neck. The man fell, and Bernie let go of Tiko to go after Yoshi.

Malachi shouted and when Yoshi turned in response, Malachi shot him in the chest with a silenced Sig Sauer. The giant kept coming and shouting to Tiko, *"Jikko, jikko,* ... run, run.

Tiko clutched her fur coat, screamed and ran towards the door.

Yoshi fell forward with the third shot, his meaty hands clamped around Malachi's neck. His dying grip weakened, and Malachi pushed him off, his face twisted in disgust at the blood spurting over him from the dying man.

"Get her, don't let her get away," Malachi shouted to Bernie.

Before she got to the door, Bernie grabbed Tiko, one hand around her waist, the other over her mouth.

"Let's get it done," said Malachi.

Tiko kicked and flailed her arms as Bernie half dragged her across the room, trying to muffle her screams at the same time. "Hold her still," Malachi said. He wrapped a length of duct tape over her mouth and around her head. Then he opened the French windows onto a small decorative balcony.

The two men lifted Tiko over the railing and dropped her off the balcony. She fell without a sound to a deserted and dark inner courtyard.

Malachi wiped the pistol clean. "We have to leave fast," he said. Bernie pulled Jake out the door, while Malachi set the shattered front door upright against the jamb. The trio took the service elevator to the second-floor parking garage reserved for extended-stay guests. They were out by 11:30 p.m.

CHAPTER EIGHTY-EIGHT

I was walking around the Claremont hotel, checking the underground parking garage and lobby. At 11:40 p.m. I went up to the nineteenth floor to scope out the corridor and meet up with Leo. As I passed room 1912, I noticed the door, although closed, was off its hinges. Bad sign.

I passed by and knocked twice at Leo's room. "Something's wrong," I said, describing the damaged door.

"What now?" Leo started pacing and biting his lower lip.

"I want *you* to stand in the hallway between the elevators and the stairs. We'll be linked by cell phone. If anyone is coming just say, 'Yes, dear,' and keep walking. If I want you, I'll say, 'come in,' and if I want you to get out I'll say, 'run.' You got that?"

"Yeah, sure."

"Leo, I mean it, if I say run–go."

Leo nodded.

"And buddy, hide the gun. We don't want to scare a hotel guest and have them call security."

"Right."

Let's go." I let Leo walk ahead of me to get into position, and then I called him on his cell. He put it to his ear and nodded. I took Bat out ready for action. I knocked on the door of 1912. No answer. I waited and knocked again. I pushed on the door and it opened easily and fell in at an angle.

I smelled it first. When you've smelled bloody death even a few times, it's unmistakable thereafter. I moved slowly through the lounge area and into the bedroom.

Yoshi was lying on his side in a pool of blood from a chest wound. Tiko was nowhere in sight.

Several men burst in from the door leading from the adjoining room. A uniformed police officer shouted. "Hands up. Kneel on the floor."

I shouted, "Run!" into the cell phone as I dropped it. I hoped to hell Leo could get away. He didn't need this.

"You're under arrest." Another cop read me my rights and asked me if I understood them.

"Yes." I was cuffed and asked to stand.

"I'm Detective Henry Stone," said a short man with graying temples and thick glasses. "Who are you?"

"Deacon Adelius."

"Before we go down to the station, I have a few questions. To start with, what are you doing here?"

"I had an appointment with a woman named Tiko."

"Do you know the deceased?"

"I believe his name is *Yoshi*. He is … was an associate of Tiko's."

The detective pulled out a spiral notebook. "Where's Tiko?"

"I have no idea."

Another detective interrupted to report he'd found a gun.

"Bag it." Stone told him. Then he turned back to me. "Is it yours?"

"No, it's not mine. I told you, I came here for an appointment, knocked and pushed the door open. It was broken. Found this guy lying here. Then you and your men busted in. That's it. How'd you get here so quickly?"

"I'll ask the questions," Stone retorted. He motioned to the other officers. "Take him to the station and call the lab and coroner."

I was escorted down through the lobby and outside. As I was placed into the backseat of a cruiser, I noticed Leo in the backseat of another. *Shit.* He didn't make it. It had been quite a set-up.

CHAPTER EIGHTY-NINE

I was left alone in an interrogation room, bare except for a metal table bolted to the floor and two chairs.

Recessed fluorescent lighting was strong enough to show stains on the greenish gray walls. One wall had a large one-way mirror where people could view the room without being seen. Standard issue. So, I wondered, who is observing me know?

I figured I'd be there awhile – standard operating procedure. I couldn't help worrying about Leo. He had a rap sheet. They might push him hard. I hoped he got rid of his gun.

The list of people whose lives got messed up because of me was growing longer. I felt guilty as hell about what had happened to them... but if they hadn't helped me, I'd probably be dead. Well, that hadn't happened. I was just in lockup answering questions about a murder... a well planned setup if I ever saw one.

The police knew exactly when to barge in. Halloran must think he's real clever getting rid of a witness and a pesky deacon in one blow, so to speak. Totally circumstantial evidence. They had nothing on me. But a night in lockup sure as hell slowed down my private investigations. With Tiko and the DVDs gone, I had nothing solid for the DA. And where the hell was Leo?

Periodically a detective would come in and ask me the same questions as the guy before him. One brought the news that Tiko's naked body had been found broken in the hotel courtyard nineteen floors down, and asked what I knew about that.

Over and over I told them why I was in the apartment, what Tiko had to do with Amber and how I was looking into her murder. More questions. More time alone. I was beginning to understand the term depression. *Dear God, the gloom of this place is getting to me. Let me know Thy will....* When I'm down, I pray, and I was definitely down.

When I opened my eyes again, Ann popped into my mind. What would happen to Ann if I didn't get out of here fast? I demanded my one phone call. A few hours later, an attorney from the archbishop came in to post my bail—$50,000. At least I had one friend left, and that friend was close to the mayor.

I wanted to post Leo's bail, too, but everybody told me he wasn't at the jail. There was no news of him whatsoever. I was sure I'd seen him in a police cruiser, so he didn't get away. I asked if he had been taken to another station but hit a blank wall. "No one knows nuthin," as they're fond of saying in Chicago.

At least I was getting out. I'd gotten Bat back, along with my other personal belongings. "This investigation is ongoing. Do *not* leave town," the last detective told me.

The guy was a moron. I had my own investigation. And I had to find Leo besides.

God, I could use a little help here.

CHAPTER NINETY

Malachi had dismissed Bernie earlier that day, paying him a generous fee for his services. "Go somewhere warm and far away. You will forget me *and* our business together. Isn't that right?"

"You know it." Bernie was happy to leave this employer. Malachi followed him down the stairs of the nondescript hotel.

"Bernie, my man, I have a surprise for you. Remember something was said about a bonus."

Bernie raised an eyebrow. "Oh yeah?"

When they reached the alley, Bernie saw a brand-new Mercedes convertible. "What's this?"

"A bonus for your efforts and a stylish way for you to leave this city for good."

"You gotta be kidding."

"It's all yours."

Bernie's eyebrows went up in surprise. As he stared at the car, Malachi slipped the leather cover from the head of his cane and high-stepped through the snow around the car. Bernie joined him, stroking the silver body of the sleek machine.

When they were behind the car, obscured from the street, Malachi held out the keys—"Here"—and dropped them in the snow.

Bernie bent to pick them up, and Malachi buried the talon-like grip of his cane between the folds of Bernie's exposed neck. The man collapsed onto the pavement, blood spurting onto the snow. Malachi looked quickly around, retrieved the money he'd just paid his enforcer and left him for dead. No loose ends.

CHAPTER NINETY-ONE

y first call was to Pritchard, not to complain about my night in jail; that was irrelevant, so far as the case was concerned. I wanted to give him the additional tips we'd collected on Malachi.

"I appreciate the data," the DA said, "but don't put yourself in any more situations. Last night was more than enough to damage your credibility. That and the lost evidence."

I groaned. Usually I don't give a flying hoot what anyone thinks of me, but with Ditmar and Halloran running the police department, the DA was my only hope. "It was a setup—"

"I'm sure it was, but step back from this case... unless we ask for your help. We've got it handled."

I wouldn't bet on that. It wasn't a matter of my ego or his know-how. I knew the DA was smart, but I was quite sure he underestimated Malachi. Plus, he wasn't as motivated as I was to stop the creep before he hurt someone else dear to me.

Pritchard wasn't through. "Matter of fact, I do have one favor to ask. Not sure if it's related, but a local hood was found murdered in an alley less than an hour ago, name of Bernie. You did mention a 'Bernie,' right?"

"I did."

Pritchard described the scene to me. "His blood is smeared in the snow in a strange way, almost like he was trying to leave some kind of message."

My eyebrows shot up. First the DA tells me to butt out of the case. Then he wants me to look at blood in the snow? *Make up your mind, Pritchard.* I shrugged. Maybe this was another lead. "And?"

"It wasn't much. I'm probably imagining things, but you've been following the case. Maybe you can make something out of it." He gave me directions to the crime scene downtown off Adams.

I had to call Ann, and my news was getting bloodier by the minute. First I told her about Tiko and Yoshi... and my night in jail.

She didn't say anything right away, but I could guess what she was thinking. More deaths. More violence. And Deacon's in the middle of it all. "That must have been dreadful for you," she said, finally. "Do you think we put them in danger? I mean our meeting with them?"

I could ease her mind on that score at least. "I can't see how. Tiko told us nothing. She didn't seem to know anything either, not about the blackmail scheme, not about the deaths. On the DVD, Halloran said Tiko was asleep when Tamara had her... accident."

"You're probably right."

I paused to gather strength to tell her the rest of it. "Leo's missing. Nobody's talking."

I heard a quick intake of breath. "Oh no, not Leo."

"I'll find him. That's not all. It's been a big night." I told her what the DA had said about Bernie. At least it sounded like Bernie from Pritchard's description.

"I want to see for myself," she said. "Maybe I can help."

"Maybe you can." There was a chance she'd recognize him, too.

I picked her up. Once we hit the downtown, it wasn't hard to find the right alley. Squad cars surrounded the scene, all of their lights flashing. When Pritchard saw us, he warned Ann away. "Miss, you might not want to see this."

He didn't know Ann. "I'll be all right," she said.

We walked around the yellow tape toward a small group of men. They were huddled over a body that lay face down in a large pool of blood.

"May I see his face?"

The officers turned his face toward me, and I recognized him as the burly man from Allison's funeral and from Grant Hospital when Sister Mary Margaret was there.

Pritchard flashed a light on the trail of blood in the snow. "Take a look. It looks like a long question mark to me."

I walked around to get another angle. Could be a question mark, even though there's no dot at the bottom. Could be Malachi's cane, though the drawing is more elongated and the top curve is crooked. But it couldn't just be the flailing of a dying man.

"So what do you think?" Pritchard asked.

"I'm not sure. That's a lot of blood. How did he die?"

"Sharp object, maybe a knife."

Or the sharp tip of the head of a cane. "You might want to compare the wounds of those suffered by Amber and Sister Mary Margaret.

The DA gave me a look. "You think the scumbag killed his own man?"

"Could be."

Pritchard ran hot and cold. Now he was asking my advice, ignoring his remark about my "situation" last night, as he called it. I didn't remind him. He could tell me to lay off the case, but he didn't know what I knew—that it would take both of us to put these bastards away.

CHAPTER NINETY-TWO

nn and I spoke over coffee. Despite her courage at the scene, she'd gone into shock after seeing Bernie lying in a pool of his own blood. Talking seemed to help. I sometimes forget that most people have never seen a dead body up close, let alone a bloody one.

After she talked it out, I held her for a long while, stroking her hair. "What are you going to do next?" she asked.

"Iv'e got to find Leo."

"Do you have some ideas?"

I told her about the confusion at the station. That I thought I'd seen him in the back of a police cruiser, but that the cops said he wasn't there. "Not good."

"Where would they take him?"

"I have no idea. They couldn't have any evidence against him. He wasn't even in the room." I stared into my coffee pondering. "I only hope he ditched the gun he was carrying. That could be a stiff charge against him, especially with his priors."

"Maybe he'll be okay." Ann touched my hand.

"Yeah, best not to pay in advance."

"Maybe he'll be at the palace when we go back there."

"Yeah, maybe." I tried to smile and look positive but I didn't believe it for a second and neither did she.

When we got there, no Leo. His head cook was holding down the fort but he hadn't heard from his boss. I hated to do it but I dropped Ann off at Leo's apartment again.

"I know where to get information about Leo," I told her.

"I won't ask. Be careful—call me."

"Right." We embraced and she kissed me goodbye.

No way would Pritchard be aggressive enough to suit me, especially with one of his own, so I put on my Gabrian persona. I knew I couldn't pray for help— this wasn't God's business—so I prayed for restraint. I knew the end didn't justify the means. I hoped I'd be judged by the outcome. I'd had enough of Ditmar.

I called The Swede.

Forty-five minutes later, Swen Eriksen buzzed me into his mad scientist's dream of an electronics shop. Bits of electronics gear, computer parts, DVD players and electronic whatchmacallits were strewn everywhere. He lived at the back of the shop, and I'm not sure he ever left.

The Swede was a hacker of legendary reputation. Sometimes he'd bend his broad shoulders over a computer and stroke the keyboard like an Andre Previn. Sometimes he'd bang it like Jerry Lee Lewis, his near-white blond hair flying.

I couldn't afford to buy new, but I was sure the Swede could build me what I needed. When I told him what I wanted, he fixed me with those ice blue eyes for a second.

"No problem."

He asked me no questions, just strode about the shop picking up a wire here and a plastic bit there from a shelf or a drawer. When he'd hooked everything together and tested it, he put it in a brown paper bag and asked for $187.

"Clergyman's discount," he said, but I doubted that. He was too shrewd a businessman by far. The set-up was basic, but he assured me it would do the job.

CHAPTER NINETY-THREE

My timing was lucky again.

I spotted my target leaving police headquarters and followed him to the Del Prado Hotel. I parked where I could see front and side entrances and slid low behind the steering wheel of the Nissan to wait.

Two hours later, he emerged from a side door with a woman on his arm. She kissed him briefly and slid behind the wheel. She was stunning, immediately recognizable from campaign photos where she gazed up at her husband, the commissioner. I looked at the man beside her now. She must like her lovers rugged, ugly… or both. And Ditmar, was he stupid or totally in thrall? I could only imagine what Halloran would do if he found out. Tempting, but I had no time for subplots. I needed answers, and I needed them now.

I'd failed in getting an address—from Google or any other search engine. I'm not good at that stuff—so I had to follow the cop home. I went on automatic, weaving through traffic and keeping Ditmar in sight. My mind focused on the man with a cane. I suspected men like him were spawned in some evil alien gene pool. When I pictured the brutality that my friends, and even Bernie, had endured, I was even more committed to finding the evil S.O.B. For now I had to get information out of this crook any way I could… in time to protect the city from whatever was coming. My adrenaline was rising like mercury in a thermometer. I was revved up, ready for whatever was to come. The vision of Leo's face in the police cruiser was ever present in my mind. I had to find him and soon.

Ditmar turned off Pershing Road and onto Racine Avenue, a quiet street of small apartment houses packed together. He pulled into an underground garage, and a security gate opened. How was I to pick the right door out of twelve choices? I parked a block away and slid Bat under my coat.

Surely he wouldn't put his name or initials on a nameplate, but there they were: an R.D. and an R.I.D. I couldn't be sure which was Ditmar. I was itching to barge in, but I stopped and took a deep breath. I didn't want to make a foolish mistake. I returned to my car and called the archbishop and Stanichar. Between the two of them, they had finally come up with the necessary information: Detective Richard Irvin Ditmar lived on Racine Avenue in Apt. 9.

I felt like a teenaged thief hiding in the shrubs outside the garage area, but I figured a tenant was sure to drive in if I waited. The night was cold—very cold—and as still as Bernie, lying in the snow. My eyes watered and my nose began to drip. Then I lost feeling in my ears and toes.

My thoughts drifted to Ann, as they often did. Can I love God and a woman, too? What was love anyway? Hate seemed easier. I could nail that one: Priests who abuse innocents... the man with a cane... politicians who cheated and lied. But love... that was more complicated.

It had been nearly a half hour—and I was half frozen—when a sedan finally headed down the ramp. The gate rose and the car pulled in. I slipped inside the garage just before the gate closed, crouched behind an SUV and waited for the driver to collect her belongings and key into the building. After she entered the elevator in the little vestibule, I slide Bat between the jamb and the door before it clicked shut. Then I pushed through and hit the elevator call button. A sign on the first floor read "Apts. 1-4," so I guessed Ditmar would be on the third floor.

Success.

I took a bulky newspaper from the hall table and wedged the thin side under his door. To hurry him into opening the door, I talked loudly, using two voices. And I flattened myself against the wall next to his door.

Ditmar opened the door and bent to pick up the newspaper. I pushed him back, slammed the door shut behind us and thrust Bat into his chest. Ditmar charged me, fists flying. He led with his left, feinted and aimed a kick at my crotch. I twisted, taking the kick on my left hip. It hurt like hell and pushed me backward into the wall. I bent over, swept Bat into his ankle and he flopped down on his back. He was red-faced and breathing heavily, his bulky muscles straining against his shirt.

"Stay down," I told him. "We need to talk."

"Fuck you." He staggered toward a chair with a jacket hung over the back. I knew there'd be a gun there so I hit his hand ... hard. He went down again and I got the gun out of his coat pocket, a 9 mm. I flicked off the safety and pointed it at his midsection.

"You want to play all night? It'll just mean more pain."

"I'll kill... you." Ditmar panted for breath. "Nah, I'll put you in lockup... with the worst perverts in Chicago... and leave you there."

I fingered the gun in my hand. "Idle threats. Crawl over to the couch, slide your hands and arms underneath and put your belly to the floor."

"Fuckin' hell I will." He rose awkwardly to attack, despite the gun pointed at him. I threw my left fist into his gut and slammed the gun into his jaw. He was down again.

"One way or another you're dead," he bellowed.

"Arms under the couch."

This time, he complied. Blood ran down his face and dripped from his mouth.

I took a seat on the couch out of his line of sight. "Let me fill you in on a few things. Your buddies Halloran and Clayton are finished." I tried a bluff. "The DA has evidence to put them away for a long time. Their complicity in the death and cover-up of a prostitute named Tamara is well substantiated. I also have proof they hired an enforcer to do their other dirty work, including the torture of a good friend of mine and the killing of Tiko and her bodyguard."

"I don't know what you're talking about."

"Point being, you are no longer protected."

"What the hell do you want from me?"

"Tell me the name of their hit man."

"What hit man?"

I tapped him on the top of his head with Bat. "No games. Who is he? Where is he?"

"I may have heard something about a black guy named Johnson."

"Liar." I hit him again, harder. My adrenaline was running fast, I looked around for something to help me make my point. I took the carved letter opener from his desk knelt on his back and stuck the tip inside his ear.

"Oh, shit!" He took a quick inhale.

"As disgusting as it is, I will shove this slowly into your ear until I get some answers. The pain will be excruciating. I pushed the point forward another few millimeters.

"No, stop! I'll tell you what I know." He voice tightened with panic.

"Good. The name of the hit man?"

"Malachi."

"What does he look like?"

"Tall, has black hair, slicked back, wears glasses.... *Jesus*, my hand's killing me."

Bad move, Ditmar. "Use the name of the Lord in vain again and I'll stick you." I wiggled the letter opener. "Your pain is nothing. Ask Sister Mary Margaret. Ask Brother Williams. Of course you can't question the rest of them. They're dead. Murdered."

"Don't know anything about that."

"You know about the Bible codes, right? What happened to them?"

"Halloran had them decoded."

"Who did it?"

"A tech... Balthazar."

"He was killed, wasn't he?"

"Yeah, I found out about it afterwards."

"In a murder, that's 'accessory after the fact,' isn't it?"

"I guess."

"And what did he find in the codes?"

"Clients of the dead hooker."

"And your protector was among them, am I correct?"

Ditmar had grown remarkably docile and helpful, just like the deviant priests I'd visited. Unfortunately, all he knew about the future was that "something big was going down soon." No dates, no names.

"One more thing. You know I was brought in for questioning in the deaths of a hooker named Tiko and her bodyguard."

"Yeah I knew about it. So what? You were there. It looked bad for you."

I ignored the digs and got to the point. "As I left I saw my friend Leo in a cruiser outside the station. What became of him?"

"I don't ... "

I pushed the opener another few millimeters into his ear.

"Okay, stop. Get that thing away from my ear. I'll tell you. My orders were to have a patrolman take him to another location for further questioning."

"Orders from whom?"

"Halloran, my boss."

"The million dollar question. Where was he taken?"

"Abram's Fish Wholesaler on Lower Wacker Drive.

Shit. Taken for further questioning ... at a fish market at this hour? Halloran must think he's a gangster from the forties.

I wished to hell Ditmar knew what his boss was up to. Thank God the detective at least knew where Leo was. Other than that, all he'd done was confirm what I already knew. Without knowing what was "going down," Brother Chuck, the archbishop and I would have to prepare for every eventuality... prepare, improvise and pray that would be enough.

I knew my next move no matter what. I had to get to Leo. I blew out a great sigh and asked Ditmar—for the record—if what he had said was true and that he had revealed the information voluntarily.

"What the hell are you talking about?"

I shrugged and shut off the digital mini voice recorder the Swede had provided. It was extraordinarily strong with digital clarity that no off-the-shelf recorder could match.

It was over.

The confession given under duress wouldn't hold up in a court of law but it would provide the DA with practical evidence—enough to convince the DA I was right about Halloran and Malachi.

I yanked the telephone wire out of the wall and tied Ditmar's hands and feet. "What are you going to do now?" he asked.

"Just shut up," I said. "If I were you, I'd pray for forgiveness and thank God you're still in one piece tonight." I held back on his tryst with Halloran's wife at the Del Prado hotel. The info could be useful later.

I called Pritchard on my cell and told him to pick up Ditmar and the digital recording I'd left on the kitchen table.

"But how—"

"Come now, and you'd better bring a paramedic." I hung up and watched for the DA. I'd duck out before he got into the apartment.

Hang in there, Leo, I'm coming.

CHAPTER NINETY-FOUR

Lower Wacker Drive wasn't far. When I was a teenager and worked for a printer, I routinely made deliveries to an address there. I prayed Leo was all right. Too many friends had been injured already because of me. *Please God, not Leo too.* We'd been friends since forever. And what would I tell his mother?

I thought nostalgically of our growing up years in the neighborhood. I could almost smell the red savory sauce bubbling on the stove in Mrs. Pazadelli's kitchen. She felt a sacred obligation to feed every kid who entered her house. I was a regular in that boisterous household. Leo and I had both been wild as kids, but Leo was wilder. Hard to figure with the great parents he had. I envied him his dad. Mr. Pazadelli was quick with a hug for his kids or with a backhand if they stepped out of line. But he was gone a lot, working long hours as a mechanic.

Leo's darker road started after I joined the Army. By the time I came back, he'd achieved minor status as a local criminal. Despite his illegal activities, we were still buddies. I prayed he'd stay out of prison. Leo wouldn't do well in the joint, given his small stature, big brown eyes and thick curly hair. I stepped on the gas pedal.

After one particular arrest and brutal questioning, Leo quit most of his illegal street activities. He still kept Glitter and a couple more hookers working, and he had a few small gambling enterprises. His love of Italian food–and probably his mother's cooking – had prompted him to open the pizza palace.

C'mon Leo, hang on. I'm almost there.

I slowed down and passed Abram's Fish market. In a couple of hours, the place would go from dark and deserted to a barracuda feeding frenzy. Before dawn, Chicago's best restaurateurs bought their fish here. I parked in back, stuck Bat in my belt and Ditmar's 9mm handgun in my pocket. I tried the back door. Locked. I couldn't see in, the windows were painted over. Leo might be here. He might not. They could've moved him elsewhere. I circled around to the open double doors out front.

Inside, a few dim overhead lights cast a dim glow over the open warehouse. Trays of crushed ice were ready to be laden with fish on display. The warehouse smelled just like what it was. My boots slipped on fish scales and guts on the wet concrete floor. This could put me off seafood for a while.

A tall thin man armed with a long thin curved knife for fish filleting came from the back of the warehouse. "Hey, you're early. We're not open yet."

"I'm looking for a friend–Leo Pazadelli–a short guy with curly black hair."

The man wiped the blade on his rubber apron. "Don't know no Leo. Come back later."

"I can't do that."

"Whadaya mean, you *can't?*" His hand tightened on the knife.

"I know he was brought here. Police Commissioner Halloran told me a half hour ago," I lied.

"Bullshit."

"If he's here, I'll find him."

"I can't let you do that. Now, hit the road." He started toward me. He and the knife looked bigger with every step.

"I don't want any trouble."

"Well, you're gonna get trouble if you don't leave."

I pointed Ditmar's gun at him. "Drop the knife."

The fishman's eyes went wide and blank as a dead Walleye pike.

He dropped the knife.

"Very good. Now we're going to tour of the entire place—offices, storerooms—the works. Understand?"

"No need for the gun." The man's head dropped. He looked guilty, like I'd caught him in a lie. "I don't know his name and I got nuthin' to do with nuthin', but there's a little guy in back … could be your friend."

As we walked deeper into the warehouse, I heard a door slam and another guy in a filthy apron turned up, coming out of the shadows,

"What we got here, Joel?"

"A tough guy looking for his friend."

"Come along," I said. "Joel here is taking me to my friend." Using the gun, I motioned the new man toward Joel. I walked behind them, the 9mm pointed at their backs.

Joel creaked open a storeroom door, and I blinked to adjust to the dim light. A bare foot protruded from behind some wooden pallets in the corner. "Stay still," I ordered the men.

A naked man lay crumpled against the wall. My God, it was Leo. Half of his face was bruised and bloody. He felt cold as death when I put my arms around him. "I'm here now, *pisan.*"

"Take off your sweaters and jackets," I told the fishmen. I motioned to the shorter one. "And you, take off your pants and boots."

They hesitated and looked at each other.

"Now." I pointed the gun above their heads and pulled the trigger. The blast was good incentive.

Leo opened one eye half-mast and mumbled, "Deac … thank God … I'm freezin' my balls off."

I motioned to the men. "Throw the clothes here and kneel facing the wall away from us." I carefully pulled the trousers, sweaters and boots onto Leo. Then I added my scarf and hat. He tried to cooperate, but every movement brought a moan. He was in bad shape.

"So fishmen, either of you lay a hand on my friend?"

"No!"

"Not me."

I couldn't help but think of Peter's denial of knowing Christ. "Raise your hands over your heads. Now put your palms against the wall."

The man who had joined us had bruises and swollen knuckles on his right hand. I didn't hesitate. I drove Bat into the back of his hand. His scream echoed throughout the warehouse and he clutched the mangled hand to his side, whimpering.

"Shut up, coward, and thank God you're still breathing."

I took a couple of steps back, and waited a few minutes for my breathing to return to normal and gave another command. "Now, brave boys, take off the rest of your clothes. See how you like the cold." I kicked their clothes out the door.

I lifted Leo to his feet, taking care to support his weight. The clothes didn't seem to help. He was still shivering uncontrollably. "You two will stay here for ten minutes. Open the door before that and I'll shoot you dead." I fired another shot just over their heads to make my point.

I half dragged, half carried Leo to the car and turned the heater to full hot with full fan.

"The bastard hit me ... while I was handcuffed ... wanted to know all about you and your plans. I told them jack shit."

"You are one tough wop."

"Hey, you be nice, you ... Greek church-lover. How'd you find me?"

"After a little persuasion, a Ditmar bird told me."

"Persuasion, huh ... like with your baseball bat."

"Well you know how it is."

Leo wasn't shivering quite so much, but he needed a hospital .... fast. I headed for Saint Mary's.

Leo made a scrunched up face. "Hey, I smell like fish, yuk."

"Yeah, you're stinking up my car."

"Deal with it, buddy." His eyes closed. "And thanks."

'Leo, I'm sorry I got you into this."

The poor guy tried to wink. "Hey, Leo's a big boy. Stories to tell ...."
He drifted off, just as I pulled into the emergency entrance.

Another friend down. Another hospital.

God let this end.

CHAPTER NINETY-FIVE

I called Ann to tell her my discoveries. I skipped the methods I'd used.
"I'm so glad you found Leo." She was silent then, but I could hear her breathing. I knew she suspected how I'd gotten the information out of Ditmar. She wasn't a coward, but she hated violence, especially when I was involved—on either side of it.

"Are you there?" I asked.

"Why don't you… I mean, I'd love for you to come over."

Her words were like a ray of July sunshine washing over me. "I'll be there as soon as I can."

"Okay."

Snow crunched under my feet as I walked from my car to the apartment where Ann was staying. The wind had died down but the forecast promised a big storm in the next few days. I stood for a moment, looking skyward. Should I be here?

I wanted to be.

Before I could knock, Ann flung open the door and leapt into my arms. She found my lips with hers, and I elbowed the door shut behind us. She was wearing a long white fisherman's knit sweater, long athletic socks and nothing else. She slipped off the sweater as we backed into the bedroom. Her skin was soft and warm. Two candles burned on the nightstands.

We fell into bed. She embraced me hard and wouldn't let go.

"I'm so frightened for you." Her words tumbled out. "I want you with me all the time. Can't the police handle the rest of this madness?"

"I—"

"No, don't answer. I take that back. I know you have to be involved. Just be very careful. The world can't afford to lose someone such as you."

"Ann, I love being with you. I could lose myself in you."

My words were dangerous, exhilarating.

I slipped out of my clothes and we held each other, words ceasing as our bodies melded together.

The next morning we shared bagels and strong coffee, a quick breakfast before High Mass. Ann seemed melancholy, her smiles forced... even false. I hoped it wasn't regret. As I dressed I caught a sadness in her eyes, so different from her passion the night before. "Is anything wrong?"

She held the edges of her robe in a short curtsy. "No, my liege."

"Will you be okay?"

"Sure, everything's fine." She kissed me lightly and stood in the doorway watching as I walked to the car.

Why didn't I believe her?

CHAPTER NINETY-SIX

The sun emerged from behind the morning clouds, making Chicago sparkle. *Are you running with me, Jesus?* I murmured to myself as I drove to the cathedral. Despite the brightness, it was bitter cold. I plunged my hands deep in my pockets and turned my face away from the biting wind.

As always, the gray stone structure seemed out of place in the center of bustling downtown Chicago. Like it belonged to another time. From every angle, one could see the skyscrapers of Chicago and thousands of windows.

Every time I walked through those bronze doors, I marveled at he delicate arches supported by pillars as they reached upwards. I supposed the architect had designed it so worshipers would feel drawn to God in heaven.

I had arrived very early, just for a quick look around. The bomb threats against churches and the threats against the cardinal had made me uneasy about any big church gathering. Holy Name Cathedral was expected to be filled—1,500 people—for High Mass today.

I went into MP mode, checking out several small rooms behind the sacristy where vestments, cups and other ritual items were stored. Some of the rooms were reserved for priests to don vestments or pray before Mass.

The most dangerous area seemed to be just outside the front doors where the priests or the cardinal would greet people after Mass.

I had no proof that the cathedral was the place where "something big was going down," but my story—and the Ditmar tape—had been convincing enough to bring out the DA and his troops. I'd do everything in my power to keep my city and my cathedral safe. At least there'd be several cops around.

Brother Chuck turned up next. I'd asked him to watch for Malachi, just in case. This was a big event in Chicago. Politicos and others would be in the congregation, so maybe some thugs would be among them. Chuck greeted me with the light touch of a glove. "No sense confusing the congregants," he said, flexing his hands. "You *know* what they'd think of these wounds... even bandaged. My left mitt is giving me some grief."

"I'm sorry to hear that. I appreciate you being here." I motioned him toward the front doors. "To start, you can focus your great powers of observation here. You could recognize Malachi better than anyone."

He gave me a look.

"Hey, sorry. It's a fact."

Once everyone is inside, the balcony and the altar are two good vantage points. You can figure out where to observe. Leave your cell on vibrate. Check in if you see anybody or anything even a little bit odd."

I headed for an altar exit, just to scout the area. The monsignor apparently had the same idea. We nodded to one another, and I stepped outside ... and saw an ambulance. That was a little unusual, but not unheard of for a large gathering like this one.

I frowned and looked back at the monsignor, who nodded again. "In the event of an emergency. Those threats, you know." He raised one bushy eyebrow.

He looked like a mafia don. Dark, Italian... suspicious. Why had I never noticed? *Was I profiling?*

He changed the subject before I could continue that thought. "My son, the archbishop and I had a long talk about you last night."

I looked at the ceiling, waiting for the inevitable speech. I could recite it from memory. It would begin, *We are concerned about your future in the Church... so much to be done... so few shepherds.... The church needs you.*

But Salvatore threw me a sucker punch. "I, too, was hopelessly in love once. Surprised? She was a social worker, and we parted because we were dedicated to our professions. It was the most painful experience of my life. You see, I know what I'm asking you to sacrifice. I know the power of sensual intimacy."

I bowed my head with a mixture of emotions, including anger. The man had gone too far. I didn't want to know his personal history, nor he to know mine. "I don't know what to say."

"I just wanted to get in a pitch for His side, my son." He bowed his head briefly and left. I donned a long wide-sleeved white tunic banded in gold for Mass, and Salvatore went to a small room off the sacristy.

Cardinal Schneider arrived shortly afterward with his usual entourage, including Archbishop Laine. "Why the ambulance?" the cardinal asked, as he entered the sanctuary. "I know, in cases of an emergency. Let's hope no one takes ill before my sermon. It's a humdinger."

"Let's hope not," I said, smiling at him. *No wonder the people loved this man.*

The organ began a Mendelssohn sonata and the congregation flowed down the aisles. I was glad to see Pritchard among them, standing in back flanked by a handful of men and a woman I took to be plainclothes officers. *So, he did take the threats seriously.*

Four young acolytes—one girl and three boys—waited in the sanctuary. They looked angelic in their white robes and gold braided belts. They'd preceded the rest of us carrying a long golden crucifix, and the thurible for the cardinal to incense the altar.

A few minutes later, the procession came down the center aisle to the choir's rendition of "Praise God from Whom All Blessings Come." The cardinal was last and looking resplendent in scarlet with a tall peaked mitre, carrying the crosier with a golden top.

I froze, staring at the cardinal like I'd never seen him before.

Oh my God … the crosier. The last time I'd seen that icon it was painted in blood in an alley.

CHAPTER NINETY-SEVEN

tanding with bowed head and hunched shoulders, Malachi easily lost himself in the crowd. Although he doubted anyone could identify him, he'd taken the precaution of changing his appearance. He had cut and bleached his hair and bought tinted glasses to camouflage his lazy eye. His suit, tie and topcoat were the color of tan motel upholstery, so nondescript no one would remember them. He took a seat about a third of the way from the altar, compelled to see how events played out and get ready for his next step. His great finale'.

The organ music was soothing as he looked up at the lofty symmetry of the grand cathedral. His only complaint was the abstract stained glass windows. He preferred realism, particularly of the crucifixion. He looked around with a critical eye. The floating crucifix was a nice touch, wooden and suspended from the ceiling.

Malachi had nothing personal against the Catholic Church. This was just a job–business—the best-paying one he'd ever had. He'd be retiring to those white beaches in a matter of days. And he'd had a bit of fun with the nun and good brother. He chortled to himself, wondering how Brother Williams liked his stigmata—a brilliant stroke.

As the choir began to sing, Malachi stood with the others and surveyed the congregation. My God, she was here. He hadn't expected that. When she turned a bit to the right, he could see her profile across the main aisle, a few rows in front of him. Like him, she was wearing dark glasses. Unholy thoughts surged through him. *Ann Drew, I'm coming*, he said to himself, her name sexy in his mouth. He had to remind himself that others would be watching for him. He didn't allow himself to stare.

Ahhh, there was the cardinal, impressive, representing the highest church authority next to the Pope. A prince of power who commanded respect.

Malachi thought of his employers, who craved rather than earned power, and the edges of his mouth turned down in scorn.

Malachi didn't regret his role in this drama, but he hoped the act would be done respectfully. He'd be meeting with the cardinal at Northwestern hospital. He was a pro. The prince's demise would appear to be from normal causes.

CHAPTER NINETY-EIGHT

With his life's blood, Bernie had painted a crosier. *God, help us.* I backed through the altar exit to alert Brother Chuck and Pritchard. I felt for Bat and slipped back inside the cathedral and stepped up onto the altar praying that we could protect the cardinal.

I saw no sign of disturbance, or a weapon… yet. Pritchard's group had spread out. If I knew the DA, more officers were already on the way. But if the weapon was a bomb…

Mass began and I moved my attention to the altar, where the cardinal was praying. In the meantime, his personal assistant took the mitre and crosier to one side and the tallest altar boy heaped incense onto the lighted charcoal in a golden thurible and shut the lid.

The cardinal circled the altar, swinging the thurible so scented smoke rose heavenward like prayers. I scanned the crowd again, alert to anything out of place. In a crowd of 1,500, my radar had honed in on Ann's glowing face and auburn hair. I was simultaneously happy to see her and sorry she had come. It wasn't safe… but she couldn't know that.

I refocused my attention on the altar. As the cardinal continued his circuit, Archbishop Laine and a priest moved to opposite sides.

Suddenly the cardinal bent over, his body jerking as he coughed and stumbled sideways. The archbishop caught the cardinal by the arm before he fell, but the thurible crashed to the floor spilling the glowing ashes and incense.

The music stopped, and the entire congregation seemed to hold its breath.

I took the cardinal's other arm as another spasm of coughing came over him. Then the archbishop began coughing. My own throat closed as I began to wheeze and cough. A chorus of coughs began from others on and near the altar.

I met the archbishop's eyes, and we mouthed the same words: The incense.

I held my right sleeve to my nose, still managing to half-carry the cardinal to the exit where the paramedics were ready with a stretcher. Brother Chuck's hulk was right behind them.

The archbishop was caught in a coughing spasm, unable to talk, so I took charge. "I think the cardinal inhaled something toxic," I told the EMTs. I turned to Chuck, "Get a sample of that incense in a wine cup and give it to the DA or one of the cops. I'll call you."

"Evidence, huh? You can trust me."

The monsignor was closing in, waving frantically, as the paramedics loaded the cardinal into the ambulance.

"You go with him. I'll finish Mass," the archbishop said to me, still gasping for breath.

"Will do."

After the EMTs prepped the cardinal and gave him oxygen, they assured me his condition was stable.

I suggested that they call for more ambulances. "Other people are stricken inside. If cardinal's in no immediate danger, I think he'd be more comfortable at Saint—"

"You have no authority," Monsignor Salvatore spouted. He shook his finger at me and leaned into the ambulance. "The cardinal *must* go to the closest hospital and that's Northwestern. We can't take any chances."

The EMT looked from the monsignor to me and back again. "I'm calling headquarters. Excuse me, Your Grace." He pulled the back doors shut.

Only a half hour before, Salvatore had talked to me like a friend. Now he was shrieking at me like I was the enemy. I'd never seen him so worked up except on Gabrian business, which this was *not*. Was he worried about the cardinal like the rest of us, or is he... what? His interference was odd. I didn't like it. And I could tell the archbishop had reservations about him. I saw the monsignor standing in the snow watching us pull into the street.

The EMT broke into my thoughts. "Headquarters okayed *patient choice*. We've got clearance. Where to?"

"Saint Mary's," the cardinal whispered. "Nuns... are good nurses."

The driver shouted over his shoulder, "Saint Mary's it is. Big fuss over a five-minute difference." He took off, sirens screaming.

The other EMT shrugged. "Interesting. Early this morning, our dispatcher got a caller asking where a patient would be taken if picked up at the cathedral. And here we are. Bizarre no?"

"What did you tell the caller?"

"I told him the closest hospital, which from here would be Northwestern."

"How did he sound?"

"I don't know, maybe a Southern accent. Not sure."

"Can I use my cell phone in here?"

"Sure."

I made two calls. No point in alarming the paramedics further. The first was to Chuck. "Going to Saint Mary's. The second was to Pritchard: "Assassin headed for Northwestern Hospital. Or already there. Monsignor Salvatore may be implicated."

Pritchard would know what to do to set a trap.

CHAPTER NINETY-NINE

Malachi watched the spectacle at the altar with childish glee. He had set it up well. The cardinal was on his way to Northwestern hospital, where he would be vulnerable to the rest of the plan. It would soon be over.

The archbishop tried to continue the Mass but settled for trying to restore order and calm the crowd. Half the congregation crowded the aisles struggling to get out of the church. Although the smoking thurible had been removed, several worshipers in the front rows were still coughing and a few had passed out. EMT's were administering oxygen and taking the worst cases to ambulances that had just arrived.

Malachi kept his eyes on Ann and pushed his way toward her. He managed to touch her coat, but the shifting crowd got in the way. All he needed was a moment to convince her to come with him to see the Deacon. Then he'd have her.

She melted into the rushing crowd getting further from him.

Malachi turned away. *Damn.* Another time my dear, and soon.

CHAPTER ONE HUNDRED

Malachi had been at Northwestern Hospital since 7 a.m. He spent his morning securing a set of greens and an I.D. badge for "Mike" with a photo that somewhat resembled him. As long as he was moving and had something in his hands, he looked like any other busy orderly. Carrying a clipboard helped. It didn't take him long to discover where the ambulances brought in patients and how they transferred the non-critical ones to the wards.

As he drove to Northwesten Hospital, Malachi was gloating. He'd played his role perfectly. The sacristan at the great Chicago cathedral had welcomed him as a visiting priest from a parish in Aurora Colorado. Not only that, the man had given him all the information he needed to set up toxic smoke in the thurible. Malachi could barely contain his mirth. The cleric was a dolt. He told him the type of incense they used at high liturgical services, showed him the small cardboard box stamped with "Floral Spring" and even told him where he could purchase some as a souvenir." What a joke. He laughed to himself. A deadly joke.

He stayed in his Roman collar and black suit when he bought the incense and stopped by the science building at DePaul University. He sauntered into the chemistry lab with no trouble. There was little or no security and the students were too absorbed with their experiments to ask a priest what he was doing there. He quickly found the potassium cyanide, filled his large paper coffee cup, put on the lid and strolled out. Mixing the chemical with the incense powder was easy.

He chuckled smugly, remembering how he evaded questions from a suspicious layperson at Holy Name. Just after he'd substituted his box of doctored incense for the regular one, the woman who had been working on the altar floral arrangements entered the sacristy to ask if he "needed help with something." He played the harried priest to the hilt. "I've lost my cell phone and I'm backtracking where I've been. I've got to return the archbishop's call right away."

The woman empathized and began helping him look. "Do you want to borrow mine?"

"Thanks so much," he'd told her, "but I'll check my car again."

If his luck held, she'd be elsewhere when he returned the original box of incense to its rightful place.

He enjoyed role-playing and smiled again as he checked his watch. He'd be visiting the cardinal later that evening.

Once the cardinal was in the hospital. A simple injection of air into the femoral artery would do it. His previous training as a lab technician was so helpful to him in his work.

CHAPTER ONE HUNDRED ONE

The DA knew it would be tough to find an interloper at busy Northwestern Hospital. Staff was coming and going, as were patients' families. The assassin could be masquerading as any of them, even a patient. So Pritchard baited the hook and hoped his trap would work.

A swarm of activity began in the ER when word came that an ambulance was bringing in Cardinal Schneider with a breathing problem. A gurney was ready at the entrance with police officers masquerading as attendants and two doctors.

Soon an ambulance with blaring sirens and flashing lights backed up to the ER door. The attendants carefully rolled their patient onto the gurney and rushed inside. They placed him in a curtained-off cubicle between two other patients. They pretended to take vitals, begin oxygen and issue routine orders and take the cardinal to his private room on the third floor.

An orderly with cap and mask came by. "Good evening," he said, to a male nurse outside the cardinal's room. "I'm Mike from the lab, and I need to get a blood sample. How's the cardinal doing?"

Instead of answering the nurse said, "Could I have a private word with you please?"

Malachi had no choice but to go along. "Sure, what's up?"

The nurse led him into a nearby supply room. "I've never seen you around here before."

"I work nights. We're swamped and short handed, so I'm doing a double."

The two men squinted at each other's badges. "You don't look much like your photo," the nurse observed.

"You got that right... um, Emit. Even my wife doesn't recognize me."

"Yeah, those I.D. photos. Your boss—Sam—doesn't seem to care much for his people.., works 'em hard."

"Yeah, well."

"But he cares about his Bulls. He always finds time to talk about them, no matter how busy you are."

Malachi merely nodded.

"I heard he used to play."

"Yeah, I heard something about that."

Emit Wilkins wrinkled his forehead and pulled out his cell phone. "'Sam' is short for Samantha, and she couldn't shoot a basketball to save her life. Who the hell are you?" He raised the phone, "Hello, security ... "

Malachi knocked the phone from Wilkins' hand and hit him with a right and a left to the jaw. The man fell unconscious to the floor.

He returned to the hospital in the evening. Malachi approached a uniformed guard. "Hi, I'm here to check on the cardinal's cardiac condition. Do you have to come in with me or what?"

The guard had his own clipboard. "No, but I need your name, time and purpose of your visit." He handed the clipboard to Malachi.

"Certainly." He wrote down a name he'd seen on a bulletin board.

He approached the bed. "Hi, I'm here to take care of you."

Suddenly *the patient* sat up and grabbed his arm. It was not the cardinal. "You're under arrest, asshole."

Malachi followed his primary instinct, twisted away. He struck the man in the throat and ran to the door. The police guard was standing in the doorway with a gun pointed at his chest. "Police! Stop where you are."

Malachi stopped and dropped his head in apparent resignation, then slung the clipboard sideways into the face of the police officer. A shot went off— deafening in the enclosed room—and Malachi felt searing pain as the bullet nicked his left ear. He clutched his ear with one hand

and kicked the guard aside. He ran down the hall and managed to duck into the stairwell just before three police officers flooded the area.

Malachi made it out of the basement door. A trap. A simple trap and he had almost been caught. He'd have to revisit the cardinal.

CHAPTER ONE HUNDRED TWO

ardinal Schneider drowsed in a drug-induced never-never land all the way to the hospital. He gave no indication of hearing as I explained all that had happened at the cathedral. "Thank the Lord you asked for Saint Mary's, your eminence. An assassin was probably waiting for you at Northwestern." Looking at his unconscious face, an idea flashed to mind.

"I know how we can keep you safe until he's caught."

The cardinal's mouth moved, as though he were trying to speak. I leaned in closer. "You ... "

"Yes, your eminence, I'm listening."

His eyes fluttered, trying to focus. "Your father ... proud." And he dozed off again.

My father? Surely, he hadn't meant ... "Cardinal Schneider, you mean 'our heavenly father,' right?"

The cardinal's eyes popped open. "No. Never had ... bad incense ... before. Stay close, Deacon."

"Count on it." The Cardinal must have heard part of what I said. He even attempted a joke. He was definitely going to be all right. "Your eminence, when you said 'my father' ... "

But he'd gone under again.

CHAPTER ONE HUNDRED THREE

The usual hubbub at St. Mary's ER intensified with the arrival of the cardinal on a gurney. Once inside, the staff took the cardinal's vitals and every test they could think of. They tried to get rid of me, but I refused. Fortunately, the cardinal backed me up, and he definitely had clout here.

Chuck roamed the ER area. When I heard the cardinal was going to a private room on the fifth level, I asked him to check out the entire floor.

I gave the cardinal a heads-up on our upcoming meeting and my plan. He agreed to the meeting in his room, and, grudgingly, to the plan. Soon, Stanichar and the hospital's CEO and the chief of staff appeared.

Before I could begin, Pritchard burst into the room looking miserable, "The assassin was there at Northwestern but we lost him."

"Damn. As long as Malachi's still out there, the cardinal is still in danger." I paused to let that sink in. The room went very quiet for a while. "I have an idea. To protect him, I propose that we put out word that the cardinal is dead or as good as."

"Dead?" repeated the chief of staff.

"We say he's had a heart attack… that he's brain dead. This should stop any attempt on the cardinal's life and give us a chance to nail Malachi.

The reporter frowned. "We lie to the public? I can't do that. What do we say later when he's found to be alive?"

"Mr. Stanichar, this is a matter of life or death. I'll leave it up to you to spin it. Say 'critical'… 'coma'… 'heart issues' instead of the 'D' word.

Later you can say you were misinformed or someone else died or he made a miraculous recovery, I don't know. I do know you're going to have one hell of an exclusive story to write."

"I don't like it any more than you do," Cardinal Schneider murmured. The words brought on a coughing jag. "Like the man said, we'll be lying to the public. And causing them pain."

"We need to keep you alive, Your Eminence," I said.

The cardinal's cough was part sigh, as he agreed. "Sad times. Not safe in the house of God ... or a house of healing." Then he shut his eyes again.

I lowered my voice. "How long do you think we need, Mr. DA?"

"I'd say two days max. Malachi's payoff should come very soon." He gave me a wry smile. "I received a very useful recording last night from detective Ditmar's home last night. I suspect a couple of politicians will give us the payoff details we need."

"And if we don't intercept Malachi at the payoff?" asked Stanichar.

We were all silent, probably sharing the same thought: *He won't get away. We won't let him.* Then there were the church and school bombings to worry about.

God help us.

So much could still go wrong.

Pritchard asked me to step into an adjoining room for a private discussion. "Look, I only half believed you at first, but the attempt on the cardinal's life convinced me. I believe Clayton is the weakest link. With the information supplied by Ditmar, I can convince Clayton that I've seen the DVD, He'll probably crack and want to cut a deal. I need to be convincing. Tell me exactly what you saw on the DVD and who said what."

I recited the details with as much specificity as I could.

"Great. I can add my own touches such as where Tamara was found and how the cover-up and location of the body had been suggested by Halloran. I'll tell him I can get him off the hook for murder if he cooperates. There will be several other charges, but, with a good lawyer, he'll get jail time and may not die an old man in prison."

"Sounds like a plan. Good luck."

We rejoined the rest of the group. The chief of staff's main concern was the placement of his patient and the safety of his hospital.

I reassured him that the cardinal would be secure. "I'd advise his release immediately, if he's well enough. The sooner he leaves the hospital, the safer he and your staff will be."

The doctors assented and left, probably grateful to get back to other hospital business.

"What did you have in mind?" asked Pritchard.

I called in Brother Chuck. "We've hidden Sister Mary Margaret O'Sullivan in a suite of rooms at the Prudential building owned by William De La Croix—"

"The businessman?" Pritchard asked.

"The same. He's Allison's and Ann Drew's father."

The DA had his cell phone ready. "I'll assign security."

I shook my head. "We can handle it. The fewer people who know the location the better."

"This is my call, Deacon. I'll put my most trusted officers on detail."

I bit my lip, thought about it, and decided to capitulate. The DA was right on this one. "Chuck, can you arrange transport for the cardinal?"

"Sure thing. I'm on it."

Pritchard assured me that the incense sample was in the lab and that he'd put a tail on the monsignor.

When everyone had left the room, I turned to the cardinal. His face was contorted in pain, his hands clasped over his chest, tears rolling down his cheek.

"Your eminence! I jumped up to get a nurse."

"No, my son. The pain is not physical."

I waited for him to explain.

"I've done something so terrible that it will separate me from the body of Christ. It goes against the most basic tenant of our faith."

Every man had secrets, but the cardinal? And why should he tell me? I was only a deacon. I couldn't hear confessions. "I'll call a priest."

"No, just hear me out. Please. What I am about to tell you relates directly to... to the acts of violence you are investigating."

"I would be honored, your eminence."

"One of the men you're after confessed to me that he was responsible for the death of a woman, a prostitute. For the sake of justice and for this city, I will reveal this ... if I must. God may not forgive me."

God forgives all. Why is he in such torment? I was slow to put it together, but then it came to me in a torrent: He couldn't reveal this information because it was gathered under the seal of confession. "My God, you can't do that," I burst out.

He didn't answer, but his eyes were like blue stones.

From what he'd said, I guessed he was talking about Tamara's death. "There is another way," I said. "You may not need to make that revelation if the man confesses to authorities."

"I hope that is so." Cardinal Schneider rolled away from me to face the wall.

I couldn't bear the thought of this holy man risking his soul. I'd find those DVDs for proof and Halloran and Clayton would confess.

In the meantime, my immediate concern was the cardinal's health and safety. I called De La Croix to arrange for the secret transfer.

CHAPTER ONE HUNDRED FOUR

D A Pritchard and two of his carefully selected detectives went to the offices of State Senator Frank Clayton.

"Good afternoon, I'm District Attorney Pritchard and we're here to see Senator Clayton."

"Do you have an appointment?" asked the receptionist.

"You kidding? Tell him we're here."

The woman's professional smile faded. She picked up the phone, announced their arrival and then rose to open the interior office door. "You may go in."

Clayton met them at the door with his usual beaming smile. "Good day, gentlemen. How can I help you today."

"We're here to ask you some questions, senator. Would you rather answer them here or at the county jail?"

"'County jail? What's this all about?"

"You are about to be charged with several crimes, the most serious being you're involvement in the death of a young prostitute—."

"I want to talk to my lawyer."

"Of course you have that right. Detective Girard will read you your Miranda warning in a moment, but before you lawyer up, consider this: I have in my possession a DVD showing you striking a woman named Tamara in a suite at the Belmont Harbor Yacht Club. She fell and hit her head on a coffee table and died. You and your buddy Mitch Halloran decided to dispose of the body by dumping it into the lake in Gary. That's where we found her. The night manager at the yacht club, Mr. Crawford will swear that he saw you there that night. You want me to tell you what the young woman was wearing? What *you* were wearing?"

Clayton sat back in his chair and picked up the phone. "I'm calling my lawyer."

"Detective Girard, will you read the senator the Miranda warning, please?"

"Yes, sir." The detective stood as straight as the flagpole behind the senator's desk. "Mr. Clayton, you have the right to remain silent and refuse to answer questions ... " While Girard droned on, Pritchard looked around the formal office, its walls decorated only with framed photographs, newspaper clippings and honorary certificates. Over Clayton's right shoulder, he saw a newspaper photo of the senator and the police commissioner, two grinning politicians with their hands clasped, arms overhead in triumph. Premature triumph.

At this moment, Clayton bore no resemblance to the photograph. Amazing the difference a couple of days could make. His easy smile was gone, and his face had turned the color of a rotting peach. He sat frozen and silent, his mouth slightly agape as the detective finished the Miranda with a question, "Knowing and understanding your rights as I have explained them to you, are you willing to answer my questions without an attorney present?"

Clayton cleared his throat. "I'll uh ... I'll listen."

Pritchard nodded to the detective. "That's good enough for now." He turned his attention back to the shrinking politician in the high-backed leather chair. "You conspired to get information from a high-priced madam named Amber who was blackmailing you both. We believe you hired an assassin named Malachi to get this information. Amber was subsequently murdered. We can also show that you and Halloran were responsible for the attempt on the cardinal's life. There are several other assaults and at least three other murders. Do you want me to go on?"

Clayton reached for the phone again. "My lawyer ... "

"We have a solid evidentiary case against you. Detective Ditmar will testify to what you knew and when you knew it. If you tell us everything you know, now, I promise I'll get you the lightest sentence possible. Once this discussion is over, all deals are off the table. You understand?"

Clayton nodded. Then he shut his eyes and balled his fists. His face went dark red and his cheeks puffed out like he was going to explode. And he did. When he started talking, he was like a steam engine plunging down a steep incline. "Tamara was an accident. I felt terrible about it and wanted to contact the authorities. That's on the DVD too, right?"

"Correct."

"It was Halloran who insisted we dump the body. Christ, he made me do it. I had nothing to do with Malachi and didn't know of his arrangements with Halloran. I also had nothing to do with the attempt on the cardinal's life." Clayton began breathing erratically, looking more than ever like an out-of-control locomotive.

Pritchard had a lot more questions but he decided to continue the interrogation at the county jail where there was a medic nearby. Now their suspect's breath came in huffs and he had turned yet another alarming color, this time approaching gray.

CHAPTER ONE HUNDRED FIVE

The transfer of the cardinal to the Prudential building went smoothly. For a brief time, De La Croix's suite was crowded. Then, Brother Chuck said his goodbyes and everyone left but Sister Meg, the cardinal and their guards.

I was just about to leave when Pritchard came in, so I waited for him to instruct the guards and pay his respects to Sister Meg and the cardinal.

Then the DA and I took the elevator down together. "So, how's it going with our perps?" I asked.

"The Ditmar recording won't hold up in court, of course, but it was enough to get a confession out of Clayton."

I nodded.

"Halloran and Ditmar lawyered up, but we did round up all four copies of the video of the prostitute's death."

Thank God. The cardinal was in the clear. But the original was still missing. "Four copies? What about the original?"

Pritchard shook his head and blew out a frustrated breath. "I'll show Halloran the video and let him assume it's the original. I hope he'll try to make a deal."

"What about the monsignor?"

"Suspicious. We suspect a link to Halloran."

The DA was forthcoming enough that I sensed some respect, maybe even some gratitude for my work on the case. So, as the elevator bumped to a stop on the ground floor, I pushed the envelope. "Where's the Malachi payoff."

"Clayton nailed it—tonight at a downtown Chicago hotel. We'll have Halloran with us."

I waited for more. "You're not telling me when or where?"

"Clayton didn't know the *when*, exactly. This is police business anyhow. You'd be in the way. We'll handle this one."

I broke this case and now I'll be in the way? I stifled a belligerent reply and kept on being my helpful self. I gave him Malachi's MO, including the laundry chute transfer. "When Malachi's involved, nothing goes down the way you think."

"We'll cover all the bases."

My mind was racing. "Since it's the last payment, Malachi may suspect Halloran of setting a trap so he won't have to pay up."

"We'll manage."

My money was on Malachi, not the DA's men, and I was determined to stop that evil S.O.B. "I'd still like to know where it's going down."

"Sorry. This is for the best. It could get ugly. Go back to church, Deacon, and leave crime to the professionals."

I slammed a fist into my other hand, trying to keep a lid on my fury. He tosses me a bone and then yanks it away. Pritchard turned and went down the steps towards his waiting car. I'd do my own thing.

After the DA was out of sight, I headed for the lobby to chat up the two plainclothes detectives left behind for added security. "I appreciate your doing this for the cardinal," I began.

After talking about the storm coming in, the driving conditions and the long hours, I sidled into my point: "That'll make driving hell.... How long you sticking around?"

One of the officers checked his cell. "Half an hour, we'll be relieved; then we head downtown."

"Well, see you later at the Hilton, then. That'll be the end of it, thank God."

"No, Father, it's the Sheraton."

CHAPTER ONE HUNDRED SIX

It was late afternoon and growing dark. I cranked up the heater and began to relax as I drove, despite the traffic. I counted our wins: We'd protected the cardinal; he was safe where he was. Pritchard and his crew were totally on board and setting up to apprehend Malachi.

My mind juggled half a dozen thoughts. I felt smug about getting the hotel info out of the cops. At the same time, it was so easy I had even less confidence in them. I wasn't convinced they could handle Malachi. I had to help.... could the monsignor really be involved in this dirty business?... Couldn't wait to tell Ann the latest.... Snow was falling fast. Glad she's snug in Leo's apartment. I'd be there in a couple minutes.

As I approached her door, I remembered the embrace the last time I knocked. This time, there was no response. I ran upstairs and knocked hard on Leo's door. He answered.

"Hiya Deac, come in."

"Have you seen Ann?"

He hadn't. I jogged down the stairs and knocked again. I couldn't stand it. I asked Leo to unlock the door.

Everything of Ann's was gone. She'd left a note for Leo. I read it aloud: "Leo, sweet man, thanks for all your help, the wonderful food and for the use of your apartment. I had to leave. Forgive me for not saying goodbye. Get well soon. Love, Ann."

I tried not to worry. She was probably at her own place. When I went to my car, I saw that hers was missing. I hadn't even noticed. Fine detective I was.

I called her apartment. No answer. Then I headed that way, squinting into the driving snow and trying to talk myself out of my growing apprehension.

I should have told her not to come to the Mass.

No, she's a grown woman, capable of her own decisions.

What if she's…

No, she's fine.

I'd stop thinking dire thoughts. I'd just go to her apartment. But why didn't she leave a note for me? I answered my own question. Because she didn't know I'd be there.

I ran into the lobby and rang her apartment.

"Hello," she said through the intercom. "Who is it?"

"Deacon."

Her voice sounded normal. Everything was okay. She just wanted to be in her own place. What a colossal relief I felt.

The buzzer sounded and I opened the door. She was waiting in the doorway and motioned me in. "How is the cardinal? The news on TV wasn't good."

I shook my head. "He's fine. We planted that story so Malachi would back off. The cardinal's fine. He's staying at your father's place."

Ann nodded. "That's good… really good. So, what's next?"

"The DA has a plan to catch Malachi."

Ann turned away and went quiet.

I spoke the obvious, "You left very suddenly."

"I had to."

"Why 'had to.'"

She patted the sofa. "Please sit down. I wanted to talk to you here in my own place. I knew you'd come, and I've been trying to figure out how to tell you."

"Tell me what?" *I knew. God, I knew.* My heart sank with the knowing.

"Let me talk and get it out." I could see her mouth moving, but I couldn't hear anything. My mind had put up a dam—a defense—against the flood of words I didn't want to hear.

"Deacon, are you okay?"

I heard that. "No, I'm not okay." I blinked my eyes, trying to focus. This beloved woman, the woman of my life, is trying to end our relationship. I have to hear her out. I forced myself to say, "Go on."

"When I saw you at Holy Name Cathedral this morning, I realized how much you are part of the church. The Church that needs you. The people need you. You're the most incredible man I ever met. I want you all to myself, but it's wrong. We'd both feel guilty later... resentful. We can't see each other, not like this."

"Dammit, Ann, Don't tell me how I feel." I tried to speak softer, tried not to make everything worse. "You're not giving us a chance." I reached out to touch her shoulder, but she edged away.

"Sometimes you scare me." She shivered as if this was one of those times. "Criminals, beatings, dead bodies... she rubbed her hands together as though to warm them. "Violence surrounds you—"

"Wait a minute! You asked for my help. We're solving your sister's murder."

Ann's head was in her hands, and when she spoke, her voice was muffled. "I know I did. I appreciate it. ... My head's in such a mess I'm not saying anything right. This is tearing me apart. But it's the right decision. It is. I know it is." She looked at me and gulped back her tears.

"Let's talk about this in a calmer moment. I can't think right now either. The cardinal ... Malachi... everything is too much." I reached out to hold her, to comfort us both, but she slipped away.

"You'd better go."

"For now."

I was nearly out the door when she threw her arms around me from behind. "I love you so much."

"I love you too." I turned to kiss her tears away, but she backed out of my reach. If she was breaking up with me, she was doing a strange job of it. I closed the door gently and walked down the hall, rows of doors like flat faces, silently mocking me. I ran down the stairs into the frozen street.

As I walked toward the lakefront, I barely noticed the icy wind whipping around buildings and the snow stinging my cheeks and eyes. She couldn't say, "I love you. Now go away." Who is she to decide for us both? Sure, I feel the pull of the church. Sure, she looks away when I pound a scumbag. So what? Nobody agrees on everything.

I felt like kicking the brick wall, kicking the trash can like a little kid. I even hoped a gang of thugs would show up itching for a fight. I threw myself onto a bus stop bench, images of Ann and me swirling in my head. I looked at the few people—couples—walking together and envied them… envied anyone who didn't feel my gut-wrenching pain.

The snow was piling up rapidly, and I picked up a couple of handfuls and buried my face in it. The icy pain was a relief… and it brought me back to consciousness. I did have a fight, waiting for me. Downtown.

Malachi and the original DVD.

I got in my car, avoiding Ann's street and her building.

This wasn't over. It couldn't be.

CHAPTER ONE HUNDRED SEVEN

As I drove to the Sheraton, I banished all personal thoughts and focused on Malachi's MO. My guess was he'd repeat himself: Drop the money down somewhere, like he had with the laundry chute, and have someone else pick it up for him.

I scanned the area around the hotel. North Water Street was too well lit and too busy. The service alley was better. Maybe Pritchard had it covered. If he did, I'd step aside. If he didn't... I was his backup, whether he knew it or not, whether he wanted me or not.

I grabbed Bat and took off down a one-way alley as dark as a tunnel. Now that I'd made my move, I could think of a half dozen other ways Malachi might plan the pickup.

I tried the handle on a set of huge sliding double doors of a building across the alley from the hotel.

They opened.

I followed the inner corridor until I reached a freight elevator. I got in. When it stopped on level two, I peeked out at a glass-enclosed passageway that reached over North Water Street to the NBC Tower.

Hell of an escape route. I crossed over, passing a rats' maze of offices and cubicles. Pritchard probably had the hotel covered, so I'd wait here. Maybe I could block the courier's escape route or even follow him to Malachi.

My cell phone vibrated in my pocket. Brother Birch was calling from the retreat house. "Brother Chuck's at Saint Luke's. He doesn't complain, but he was babying his left hand so I examined it. Swollen and inflamed, plus he's running a temp. I'm pretty sure it's infected so I think they'll keep him there a couple of days. Last thing he said was, 'Tell Deac I'm on the sidelines for a while.'"

"Thanks. I'll pray for him." My voice trailed off. "Tell him that and that his steak will be available soon."

I fell against a desk, feeling like I'd been pounded by a gorilla. My whole body ached with sorrow for my friends. That's three good people down. Their pictures flashed through my mind like scenes on the evening news: Brother Chuck's hands nailed to a demonic cross, Leo's pulpy swollen face, Meg's bruised body.

Enough, God. No more.

I grabbed my head and squeezed, trying to replace pain with pain. I'd never felt so alone. Ann had left me. It looked like Monsignor Salvatore had gone over to the other side. Pritchard and Stanichar were breathing down my neck.

Hell, here I was waiting again. Way too much time to be alone with my thoughts. Hate this. Images of Ann rushed into the empty spaces.... Maybe she was right. If I couldn't give her what she needed, there was no sense staying together. Still, things might change, in time,... mightn't they?

Enough! God help me, I had to focus and get that son-of-a-bitch. Malachi, when I'm done with you ...

I jumped to my feet and threw a left and then a right into the shadows, wishing I were slamming my fists into that ugly bastard's face. I swung Bat around in Kata-like exercises, trying to work off the guilt, the knowledge that it was all my fault... that if I hadn't gotten them involved in this mess, they'd be safe... unharmed.

Usually I could blast through those feelings with a few swings, a few kicks. But the waiting was getting to me. I couldn't stand this torment. My God...

In that moment, I stopped lunging, swinging, fighting and just stood still. A wave of calm rolled over me, my head dropped to my chest and I prayed.

God... let me know and do your will.

CHAPTER ONE HUNDRED EIGHT

"The cardinal is in a coma and not expected to live," the reporter continued. Malachi relaxed. No foul play was mentioned. The cardinal had been "overcome by smoke at Holy Name and collapsed later with a severe heart attack." A vigil service was underway in the hospital lobby. What a bit of luck. Malachi had narrowly missed the cardinal but the smoke inhalation had triggered a heart attack in the elderly prelate.

Just in case there was any suspicion, he knew he'd have to sneak back into the cathedral sacristy to substitute a fresh box of incense for the tainted one.

Malachi wished, not for the first time, that he had access to an overseas account. Halloran had too much power to be trustworthy. Malachi swirled the cane in the air like a fencing blade. But this was the last time. He'd be set for life.

He made the call to the messenger. "Are you ready?"

"Yeah. You got the rest of my money?"

"Yes, you'll get a flat $1,000 when you're done. Tell me the plan again. Every detail."

The young man repeated every step of the package recovery.

"Good. Get into position and wait for my call."

"You got it."

When Malachi called room 406 at the Sheraton, Halloran picked up on the first ring.

"Are you ready?"

"Yes." Halloran coughed a couple of times and cleared his throat. "Um... how do we proceed?"

Malachi's face tightened. He didn't like the nervous cough. Halloran usually sounded slick as an ice rink. But, then, usually the commissioner gave the orders. "Are you troubled by something, commissioner?"

"No. I'm fine."

"Relax, it's just about over." He gave Halloran the instructions.

"Yes, I've got it. Tying the scarf right now."

Malachi hung up and called his accomplice again. "Now."

The biker pulled down his visor, kicked his Harley to life and plowed through the ruts in the alley snow. Just as he'd been told, a package with a yellow streamer fell into the alley. He grabbed it and took off. He cleared the double doors, in the building across the alley. They closed behind him, just before squad car headlights appeared at both ends of the alley.

He rode down the hall and up the freight elevator to the second floor, as instructed. He raced across the glass breezeway into the NBC Tower building across the street.

Almost there.

CHAPTER ONE HUNDRED NINE

First, I heard the elevator chime, then a deafening roar. The growl of a motorcycle reverberated off the office walls. I caught a glimpse of chrome as a bike raced across the breezeway over North Water Street toward the office cubicles where I was hiding.

Bat over my shoulder, I stood ready for anything... except the biker's abrupt right turn. He skidded into another elevator on the far side of he room. I raced toward him, Bat extended, to prevent the doors from closing.

Damn. Three seconds too late.

I spun around. I'd get down the stairs before he hit the ground floor. *Shit!* The elevator numbers indicated he was going up. The roof?

"Pritchard," I said into my cell. "Your money's with a biker on an elevator in the NBC Tower. He may be headed for the roof."

"How the hell do you know that?"

"Never mind that. Get someone over here."

I'd never make it in time if I took the stairs. I pushed the call button and watched the light numbers descend.

The chime rang and the door opened. Nobody home, just the motorcycle on the floor, front end twisted to the side. I pushed the *up* button for the floor just before the roof. No sense standing in an open door, exposed to whatever action was going down. The elevator rose with a high-pitched keening noise.

CHAPTER ONE HUNDRED TEN

The young man in black leathers stumbled out of the elevator gripping the satchel. He took off his helmet and looked around warily.

Malachi double-timed toward him. "You made it. Any trouble?"

"No." The cyclist craned his neck. "What's that noise?"

"Chopper. You didn't try to open the satchel?"

"Nope."

Malachi reached for the satchel, but the young man pulled it back. "No offense, but my money?"

"Sure," said Malachi. "Here it is." He handed the biker an envelope. "You can count it while I check the bag." He bent over the satchel for a moment and then straightened. "Well, the contents seem to be in order. Is the money correct?"

"Yeah. I'm outa here."

"Remember, take the elevator to the basement, parking level two. It accesses the street."

"Got it."

As the biker turned toward the elevator, Malachi hit him on the back of the neck with the head of his cane.

The cyclist went down.

Malachi raked the silver talon of his cane across the biker's throat and grabbed the envelope before the dark pool of blood soiled it. Picking up the satchel, Malachi raced for the waiting helicopter, climbed in the back seat and buckled up.

The helicopter rose and glided over the cityscape like a malevolent dragonfly. Malachi emptied the money into his own leather bag, cut the satchel apart and found the bug he assumed would be planted inside. He took every stack of bills apart until he found a second tracking device. When he was satisfied the rest was clean, he tossed the bugs out the window.

The pilot's voice blasted through his headphones. "Hey, shut the window."

By the time they landed at O'Hare Airport and the rotor blades stopped, the pilot was calmer. "Need a ride to a main terminal or anywhere?"

Malachi squinted to read the pilot's nametag. "Nope, Spencer," he said. "Got a hot date."

"Lucky you. Well, I appreciate your business." The pilot fingered the cash in his pocket. "If I can ever be of service to you again—"

"Thanks anyway, but I'm leaving your air space, headed for warmer climes." Malachi went out front, hailed a taxi to Ditka's Restaurant and Bar not far from the airport. He took another taxi to within a few blocks of his rental house. Then he walked a zigzag route, staying in the light and among people.

He almost enjoyed the brisk walk on the snowy evening. After all, he was carrying a heavy bag, pleasantly full of cash. He was rich and felt on top of the world. The job had been completed. His professional career was complete, and he was in the clear. In a couple of days, he'd begin his new life in a beautiful place... a warm place.

He had only one piece of unfinished business.

CHAPTER ONE HUNDRED ELEVEN

A loud thrum rolled and I caught a glimpse of flashing lights as a helicopter lifted off. *I was too late, damn!*

The bastard got his money and flew away.

Looking up, I nearly tripped over the body. The cyclist lay in a spreading pool of blood, black as the night. His throat looked like an animal had gotten to him. Too late to check his pulse, so I breathed a prayer over him. *Donna nobis pacem.*

"You're too late, Pritchard," I said into my cell. "He took off in a chopper."

"Where are you now?"

"On the tower roof with the motorcycle courier who picked up the satchel. He won't be any help."

"We're nearly there."

In minutes, Pritchard and a couple of cops stepped out of the elevator. The DA stepped over the body. "So, what went down?"

I explained how the motorcycle courier had eluded the police, ridden between two buildings, taken the elevator to the roof and got his throat slashed for his trouble. "And now our bird has flown."

"But not far. We put tracking bugs in the lining of the bag and the cash. We'll get him yet."

"He'll check and double-check for bugs."

Pritchard shrugged as if he'd known that all along. "I'll call every likely helicopter pad to be on high alert."

"I'll leave you to it." As I turned to go, Pritchard tapped me on the shoulder.

"Thanks for the assist."

"No problem." As I headed down my thoughts whiplashed back to Ann.

Despite my sweat, I felt a sudden chill. Oh my God! Malachi had threatened Ann. He'd promised to hurt her if he didn't get the DVD. He got it, but that meant nothing to scum like him. Was Ann still in danger from this madman?

And Ann was home alone.

CHAPTER ONE HUNDRED TWELVE

Only two helicopters had landed in the last hour. The one at O'Hare had just come in from the NBC Tower. "Detain the pilot and passenger," the DA told airport security. "Use extreme caution. The passenger is armed and dangerous."

When Pritchard arrived at the heliport at O'Hare twenty minutes later, the passenger was long gone and the pilot was sitting in a little room with two officers.

"What the hell's going on?" he demanded. "I didn't do anything illegal."

"Your last passenger may have. I'm Barry Pritchard, Chicago DA, and I need a rundown on the client you picked up at the NBC Tower."

"What'd he do?"

"That's police business, but I can tell you this. You're lucky to be alive. So tell me about your client."

The pilot's eyes widened. "Sure thing. The guy called and asked me to pick him up from the helipad at the NBC Tower. He offered twice the going rate and sent half the money in advance."

"Did he give a name?"

"Mr. Cardinale.'"

Sick joke, Pritchard thought. "When did you first see him?"

"Less than an hour ago."

"Describe him in detail.... Wait a minute." Pritchard called in a detective to take notes.

"He was on the tall side, maybe six foot," said the pilot. "His hair was short and blond, looked bleached to me. He wore dark glasses which was weird because it was night." The pilot stopped.

"What else, there must have been more."

"I'm trying to think." He closed his eyes. "He had a cane, but he wasn't limping. He was clean-shaven. Wore black. That's about it. He didn't say much."

"Thanks. Now what happened before you took off?"

"He threw a briefcase into the chopper and told me to wait."

"Wait for what?"

"He didn't say, and I couldn't see where he went. I guess he met someone, because he came back with a small satchel, like a gym bag. Oh yeah, it had a yellow scarf attached."

"Then what?"

"He got in the back seat. While we were flying, he rummaged through the new bag, I think. He might have transferred something from one to the other. It's a short flight. I didn't pay much attention ... except to tell him to shut the window."

That's where the bugs went. Pritchard began to pace. "What happened after you landed?"

"He gave me the rest of the fee and a big tip. I asked if he needed a ride to one of the terminals, but he turned it down."

"Then what?"

"He left in a taxi."

"Can you replay the conversation you had with him?"

"I'll try." The pilot rubbed his forehead. "He said he was leaving soon for some place warm."

"Anything else?"

"No, that's all."

Pritchard sighed. "Good, we appreciate your help." He put a business card on the table. "If you think of anything else, call me at this number."

As Pritchard and his assistant were leaving, the pilot called out. "Oh yeah, one more thing. He said he had a date."

Pritchard raised his eyebrows. "What?"

"He said he had a 'hot date.'"

CHAPTER ONE HUNDRED THIRTEEN

Once back in his bungalow, Malachi moved fast. He'd be out of there soon... forever. Not that he disliked his small rental granny house behind the main house. It suited his purposes perfectly. Quiet, nearly invisible from the street.

First things first: He stowed the original DVD along with the day's payment and the rest of the cash for the contract in his usual hiding place in the exhaust tube above the stove.

A cool two million.

He opened a bottle of Cabernet Sauvignon to let it breathe. Then he set out red seedless grapes, brie, paté and crackers.

Time to celebrate, but not alone.

He showered, shaved and put on a black roll-neck sweater and the rest of his winterwear. He'd be tossing all this very soon. He laid a two-foot length of hemp rope on the seat beside him and drove off.

He'd bring Ann back to his place and take his time with her... without interruption. He conjured up her rooms with their soft colors, antiques and black-and-white art posters. Tasteful. Clean. He liked that. The promise of upcoming delights was like fire ants crawling across his belly.

The storm was worsening, and Malachi drove the Cadillac Escalade slowly. Nothing like a heavy car in the storm. When he arrived at Ann's apartment building, he used a small screwdriver to open the security door leading up to the apartments. When he got to her floor, he pressed his ear to her door and heard music.

Perfect. She was setting the mood.

Pulling the length of hemp from his pocket, he saturated it with lighter fluid and shoved it between her door and the hall carpet. He lighted it and fanned the smoke under her door. Thirty seconds later, he rapped on her door and called out, "Fire," loud enough for her to hear, but not her neighbors. The instant she opened the door, Malachi pushed her down, tossed the smoldering rope into the room and slammed the door.

She tried to rise and he slapped her in the face—hard. She stumbled backwards into the living room, blood seeping from a split lip. Malachi dragged her to the kitchen sink, threw in the smoldering rope and turned on the water. Seeing the blood, he soaked a dishcloth in cold water and bent to wipe her face. "There, there, my sweet thing. Let me help you."

Ann turned away, so he tossed the damp cloth in her lap.

"Listen. We're goin' to spend some time together, so you might as well cooperate." He paused a moment while she turned to face him. "And no screaming. It won't help and someone will get hurt, you or any good Samaritan who happens by. You don't want that on your conscience."

Fear radiated from the woman like the heat from a brush fire, giving Malachi a feeling of power. She'd be compliant, but only until she saw an opportunity to strike out or escape. Those two possibilities excited him even more.

He grabbed a handful of hair and yanked. "Now, promise me you won't do anythin' foolish."

"I promise," she whispered.

"Good, we understand each other." He loosened his hold on her hair.

She dabbed at her cut lip with the cloth. "What do you want with me?"

"Information."

"You killed my sister." It wasn't a question.

He raised an eyebrow, but didn't answer.

Malachi sensed her powerlessness. She *would* play along,

"I don't know anything useful. You might as well let me go." She eyed the door.

"Let me be the judge of that. I need your take on some of my plans. I have a fine red wine and appetizers waiting. Shall we go?"

Ann went to the hall closet for her boots. As she pulled them on, Malachi told her he'd seen her at the cathedral with the cardinal that morning. "Pity he's dead or as good as."

"You're misinformed." Malachi caught a flash of triumph in her eyes and turned away so she couldn't see the shock on his face. He'd set up the hit and received full payment. What could've gone wrong? Maybe she was lying.

Now he *did* need information but not here. If he had been duped, the contract wasn't complete. This wasn't over. He struggled to regain his composure. "My dear, now we must leave. We can talk of the cardinal later. Remember what I said, no foolish behavior." He waited while Ann put on her coat.

"Take my arm. I'm parked nearby."

He breathed in the sweet aroma of her hair, thrilled by her closeness, but watchful, too. Once in the street, she might try to escape. The snowstorm had chased away traffic and the street was deserted, so far. "Turn and face the car and put your hands behind your back." He bound her hands with plastic hand ties.

As he opened the door, a car approached and she rushed into the street, screaming for help. The car swerved and skidded on the snowpack. Malachi stepped in front of her, turning her away and covering her mouth. "Don't do this, Ann. I'll kill the driver. I swear I will." She stopped struggling.

"Sorry," he yelled, "the lady's a little tipsy. She's fine now." He waved, and the woman drove on.

"Now kneel on the floor on the passenger side. Keep your head down and don't look back at me during the ride." He put in a CD of Chopin's Concerto No. 2 to calm them both as he drove.

A police car passed him going in the opposite direction, and he waved and smiled. "Pleasant evening, officers."

CHAPTER ONE HUNDRED FOURTEEN

God, I hope I'm not too late. I hope my hunch is wrong. Maybe Malachi is already flying out of the city.

I was halfway to Ann's apartment when my cell phone vibrated. "Pritchard here. The chopper pilot's description of his client sounds like Malachi, but he's changed his appearance. He now has blonde hair. The client didn't say much except that he was moving to a warmer climate and had a 'hot date.'"

My hunch is right. "God, it's Ann, isn't it. I'm halfway there—"

"I've dispatched a squad car.... Hey, wait a minute. You're already on your way?"

I made the weakest of jokes. "Yeah, deacon's intuition."

"You were on the money with the tracking devices, too. Malachi tossed them, out of the chopper. One other thing: You didn't tell Ann Drew where the cardinal is, did you?"

"Yeah, I did."

"Damn. Let's hope my squad gets to Ann before Malachi does. We'll move in to protect the cardinal. Malachi won't slip away this time." He clicked off.

Pritchard was focused on the cardinal's safety. Sure, he's a prominent figure, but Ann... my Ann was in imminent danger. Why hadn't I insisted she stay at Leo's until Malachi had been caught? As if she'd have listened. I prayed God would protect that independent woman. I pushed the Nissan to its limits on the slippery streets. Visibility was nil. The apartment wasn't far but the drive felt like forever.

Ann's car was on the street.

A good sign.

A patrol car was double-parked in front of her building.

Another good sign.

I parked behind the cop car, shouldered my way through the outer door and ran up the stairs.

I practically ran into two police officers in the hall. "Pritchard sent me," I said. "Is Ann Drew here?"

"No sign of her. We knocked and listened at the door. Nothing but a faint smell of smoke."

So much for signs. "Break down the door."

"Can't do that without cause or a warrant. Who are you?"

"I'm Deacon Adelius. I've been involved in this case from the beginning. You need cause? Here." I kicked in the door, and the officers followed me inside.

I looked around frantically. Ann's desk phone and answering machine were on the floor. In the living room next to the coffee table were a few fresh drops of blood.

"Jesus, he's got her."

CHAPTER ONE HUNDRED FIFTEEN

Malachi half-dragged Ann through the snowdrifts. She managed to kick at a metal trashcan, but the dull thud was lost in the wind. They slipped on the icy steps and she scrambled out of his grasp. She made it to the alley before he yanked her backwards by the hair and then pushed her toward the house.

Inside, the table lamp cast long shadows onto the high walls as he cut her bonds and shoved her into an armchair.

Then, seeming to change personalities, he poured two glasses wine and nodded toward the hors d'oeuvres. "Did you see the cardinal yourself, my dear?"

She took a sip of wine, avoiding his eyes. "No, I didn't see him. I was told he had survived."

"Who told you this?"

"Deacon Adelius."

"Of course, your lover."

She reddened. "You're mistaken about that."

He shrugged. "And where is the cardinal now?"

She spoke slowly, as though begrudging every word. "He could still be in the hospital. Or they might have moved him."

Again, the disbelieving eyebrow.

"He said something about, 'need to know.'"

"That's right. I need to know." Malachi ignored the wine and stared at Ann. His plans had gone awry. This one wouldn't. He lunged toward her and ripped her blouse open, buttons popping. She tried to cover herself, but he slapped her hand away. She started an air splitting scream—a siren of a scream—and he hit her again. More blood spurted from her lip.

"Now take off your clothes and get in the shower and clean yourself."
She hesitated.

"I said *shower.*" He struck her buttocks with his cane.

She showered. He watched her.

Afterwards he dragged her into the bedroom and threw her onto the four-poster bed. She hunched against the headboard, wrapping her arms around her legs to cover as much of her body as possible.

Malachi was in a hurry, muttering to himself. He reached for her wrist, and she kicked at him to no avail.

He panted and swore but finally tied her wrists to the bedposts. Then he grabbed her flailing left leg, slipped a handcuff on her ankle and secured it to a bottom bedpost. He tied her other leg. She was spread-eagled on her back.

Malachi removed a syringe from a small leather case, and stuck her in the buttocks with the needle. She twitched and made an involuntary shriek. He stroked her thrashing body, muttering, "Later, you little bitch." Gradually the drug calmed her, and Malachi began: "Exactly where is the cardinal being held?"

She could no longer lie. Her words were nearly unintelligible. "My father's offices, Prudential Building, twenty-eighth floor."

"The name on the office?"

"De La Croix."

"Guarded?"

"I don't know." Her speech again became more muddled.

Malachi stroked her body once more before tossing a comforter over her. "Keep warm, my dear. See you later," he said. "After my *appointment at the Prudential.*"

CHAPTER ONE HUNDRED SIXTEEN

I watched the police drive the Cardinal, Sister Meg, Brother Chuck and William De Croix off to a safe house. Even their heavy SUV labored in the deepening snow.

I had a gut feeling that Malachi would come after the cardinal to finish the job. Ann would try not to tell Malachi anything, but what chance did she have? A shiver ran through me.

Pritchard agreed that Malachi would turn up. He stationed two of his men visible on the first floor with building security. "Inviting, but not obvious, so he'll think the cardinal is still here." Two heavily armed officers would hide in offices adjacent to De La Croix's. Pritchard and another officer would be inside De La Croix's office. Cameras monitored any movement in the hallways.

Pritchard insisted that I leave.

"We need Malachi alive to tell us where he's keeping Ann," I told him.

He narrowed his eyes and tightened his lips. "I'll handle it from here."

I had no choice. But where would the smart ass DA be without my help?

Nowhere.

I couldn't figure out anything else to do so I found a place in the parking lot where I could observe at least two sides of the building and settled down to wait. God, it was cold. Even with low visibility in the falling snow, I'd see the bastard when he comes.

CHAPTER ONE HUNDRED SEVENTEEN

Ann's temples throbbed. She blinked her eyes, trying to focus. She had no idea where she was.

Oh God.

Malachi.

She tried to move and finally grasped her situation. She was a prisoner, tied down. Tears seeped from her eyes.

But she was alone. He wasn't here. This is a good thing. She turned her head every which way.

She wasn't helpless. She worked to get one of her hands free. The knots looked impossible, but she pulled and twisted at the taut ropes. She could see the bedposts—teardrop shaped finials at the top. If only she could get enough slack. She stretched and strained, her arm muscles protesting as she tried to loop one of the knots over the finial. With a little slack, she could begin to loosen it.

Malachi's face twitched as he drove through the storm toward the Prudential Building. What if there was a trap? Why hadn't the cardinal stayed in the hospital? Why hadn't he gone to Northwestern hospital in the first place? Halloran had assured him the destination had been *handled*. Hadn't he bragged about getting help from an informer from the clergy??

He drove slowly and carefully, trying not to get stuck. Snow piled up everywhere; weird overhead streetlights cast odd shadows. Snow-covered cars lined the streets like cemetery headstones. *Fuck.* It would take over an hour to get to the Prudential Building. And they were probably waiting for him.

Ridiculous. There would be a trap and he had no Bernie to back him up. Why stay out in the cold when a lovely woman awaited him in his warm bungalow. This was crazy.

Let the assholes freeze their balls off waiting for him. He'd come back when there was no intense scrutiny. Or, he thought, maybe I'll skip the whole thing. I've been paid. Why complete the contract now?

Visualizing Ann on the four-poster bed, he turned the car around and headed back to his bungalow. The prince of the church could wait.

Ann had stretched to the breaking point without getting her wrist any closer to the top of the finial. Then in a burst of fury, she tugged first one arm and then the other in frenetic bursts. The old oak bed and headboard trembled with each movement, and her back ached with the strain.

With a loud crackle, the force of her right arm split the side of the headboard. The old board swung forward but held fast at the base. Her arm wasn't free, but it was much closer and she had some slack in the rope. She brought her wrist to her mouth and pulled at the knots with her teeth. Her neck went into a spasm and she relaxed for a few seconds.

She kept at it. The knot loosened.

CHAPTER ONE HUNDRED EIGHTEEN

Straining and twisting her back, she managed to untie her left hand and sit upright. Then she used her free hand to untie her right hand from the piece of headboard. A few more minutes to untie her feet and she'd be free. She threw back the covers and saw her left ankle handcuffed to the bedpost. *Shit!* Tears of frustration rolled down her cheeks.

One problem at a time, she thought. I'm better off now than I was a half hour ago. She untied her right ankle and stared at the handcuffs. Shifting her weight to the bottom of the bed, she pulled, tugged and kicked at the footboard until the sole of her foot was rubbed raw. The footboard didn't crack.

She looked around and spotted her coat. Her cell phone was still in her coat pocket… six feet away on a chair. She tried to pull the bed toward the coat but the heavy oak wouldn't budge.

When would he be back?

No, she wouldn't think about that. She wouldn't panic. She'd think.

She scanned the room again. The lamp! She hobbled to the bedside lamp and yanked the cord from the wall. She was able to tie the lamp and the corner of the bed sheet together. She spun the lamp clockwise and let loose. The lamp soared high, but fell six inches short of the chair. It took her three tries but she finally managed to sling the lamp carrying the bed sheet over the chair.

Gradually, she managed to tug the chair toward her. About halfway, the chair toppled over and the coat slipped off. She started over, tossing her makeshift hook until she snagged the coat and brought it to her.

She felt like Nancy Drew. A good feeling.

She put on her coat and dialed 911. The signal was weak, only one bar of power showing but she heard a welcome voice ask, "What is the nature of your emergency?"

Ann explained her predicament as quickly as she could.

"Where are you, ma'am?"

"Oh God, I don't know."

"I'm sorry, ma'am. We can only locate a cell phone within a six block radius."

Ann convinced the operator to patch her in to the DA.

"My phone's gonna die," she told Pritchard. "You've got to catch Malachi. He's on his way to the Prudential building. You've got to get him ... otherwise... " She choked back a sob.

"We're ready for him."

"If he hasn't gotten there yet... maybe he's given up for tonight and is coming back here." Her voice sagged, resigned, hopeless.

"Ann hang on, stay with me. We know you're in the loop area. What can you tell me that'll help us get to you?"

Now, she was sobbing between her words. "Nothing.... I don't know where I am."

"Ann, listen to me, I'm getting Deacon on the line. Maybe he can help. We'll search your area street by street. We'll be there very soon."

"Oh God, my cell phone's about out of juice."

CHAPTER ONE HUNDRED NINETEEN

P ritchard brought me up-to-date fast and patched me into Ann's call. "Ann. I'm on my way."

Her voice was high—nearly hysterical. "I don't know where I am." I heard choked sobs.

"Listen to me and focus, damn it. We know you're in the downtown district." Pritchard better be damned sure he's right about that. "We'll find you, but you've got to help. Close your eyes and think. What did you see when he brought you—"

"Oh Deac, he's coming back. I know it!"

I tried to calm her down. "Ann, focus, what did you see?

"He parked outside."

"Good, no garage. Go on."

"We had to walk around a couple of those trash bins."

So, they entered from the back, maybe an alley. "Did it seem like an alley?"

"Yes."

She seemed calmer, more oriented. "We had to go up some stairs, but we slipped and fell in the snow. I got away for a minute or two and ran to the alley." She sighed.

"Very brave. So, they were outside stairs. Concrete or wood?"

"Wooden, definitely wooden."

"Okay, how many steps?"

"Six or seven."

"Bannister?"

"Yes."

"Anything else about the outside?"

"Black SUV... a Lincoln I think, or maybe a Cadillac."

"Good. House or apartment?"

"House. It's old and small. Vintage. One bedroom." She gulped back a sob. "It's behind a bigger house, like they belong together. Deac, he made me shower... " More sobs. "He... uh... gave me a drug. I was out... I don't know how long."

My body tightened with rage, and I gripped Bat so hard my fingers ached. *Don't lose it, Ann. Not now.* "No more about him. We're coming."

In the time we'd been talking, I'd plowed about another mile through heavy snow, creeping closer. I wanted to get out of the car and run to Ann. Anything was faster than this. "Quick, before we lose the connection. What else?"

"High ceilings. Wait! I see some mail. I'll see if I can get to it and get an address." She grunted with effort and I could hear crashing. What the hell was she doing?

"I've got it!" she said. Then the phone went dead.

CHAPTER ONE HUNDRED TWENTY

The main streets were packed with slow-moving cars, so Malachi turned onto a side street he figured was north of his bungalow. The snow was now coming down heavy and wet. The navigation system in his car had gone out days ago, and he had no idea where he was. Even when he saw a street sign, ice and snow covered the letters. Chicago was not his city.

He gave up the side street for a more traveled one and pulled into an all-night gas station. The attendant was locked behind a glass wall. "Do you know the way to Harrison Street?" Malachi asked, trying for polite and pleasant.

"You want gas?"

"No. I'm full-up. But I'm a bit lost. Can you help?"

"I don't live around here. You're on your own." She scratched her bleached blond hair and shifted her considerable weight on the stool inside her cubicle. "I don't know how the hell I'm going to get home. It's piling up out there."

Tell me something I don't know, bitch. If he weren't in a hurry and she weren't locked in, he'd be tempted to strangle the woman. Instead, he forced a tight smile. "Do you have a city map?"

"No maps. For what it's worth, Harrison's probably south of here." She waved a flabby arm to her right.

He'd soaked his Oxfords up to the shoelaces in wet slush and for nothing. He turned away without a word and kicked his way back to the car. *What the hell.* He turned south on the busiest street he could find. At least he could drive in someone else's tracks.

Traffic was moving at ten miles per hour or less on LaSalle Street as he headed for the downtown loop. The Sears Tower on his right. That was familiar. But he hit a dead-end at the Chicago Board of Trade. He made a left and was making a right turn when a pickup slid through the red light and plowed into him.

As he stormed out of the car to examine the front end, a police officer headed his way. The traffic officer was so bundled he looked like a Michelin Man dressed in police blue. "Anyone hurt?"

Malachi decided to play out the drama. "I'm fine."

A short man in a parka got out of the truck. "You okay, man? I just couldn't stop."

The cop sighed. "You both know the routine. Exchange names, driver's license numbers and insurance companies." Having given the official line, he advised them to sort it out themselves. "You're not hurt, the cars are drivable and it'd take forever to get a squad car out here tonight for a fender bender."

They nodded, and the cop went back to directing traffic at his intersection.

Malachi felt like beating the man for slowing him down, but the cop was too close. "You know you slammed into me, right?"

"Well, yeah." The man stepped back as if expecting trouble.

Malachi tamped his rage down like smoldering tobacco in a pipe. "Look, I'm in a hurry," he said through gritted teeth. I'll pay for my damage. You pay for yours. What do you say?"

The short man looked skeptical but nodded. "If it's okay with you…" He jumped in his truck like he thought Malachi might change his mind.

When Malachi started his Cadillac, the front wheel wouldn't move. The fender had buckled into it. *Fuck.*

He got out to hail a taxi. After ten minutes of waiting, he trudged over to the officer. He asked where he could catch a cab.

"On a night like this, good luck."

"Well, can you direct me to Harrison Street?"

"Sure, go south for two—maybe three—blocks. You'll hit Harrison."

Not far, but walking was ponderous as snowdrifts continued to pile up. He cursed each step in the blocks of ice that were once shoes. The cop was wrong. Harrison Street was *five* freezing blocks away. He slipped and fell, wrenching his wrist in an attempt to break his fall. Snow crept up his pant legs, and he cursed the city and its winter. *Maybe I should've gone straight to the airport...* but no, Harrison Street finally appeared. And he followed the numbers, moving closer to what was waiting for him at 407 B.

CHAPTER ONE HUNDRED TWENTY-ONE

God give me a little help. I've got to get to her before he does. Got to.

I followed Pritchard's directions until I was in the six-block square where Ann's cell phone transmissions had emanated. The streets were difficult to drive, but the alleys were worse. I'd look for a bungalow behind another house. To avoid getting stuck, I'd parked at one end of an alley and walked three-quarters of the way, returned to my car and repeated the process in the next alley. It was painfully slow going, the snow a heavy wet blanket over everything. At least Malachi would be hampered, too.

Unless he was already there.

No, I won't dwell on that. I stomped through the snow in a pair of old rubber galoshes I found in the trunk, trying not to think about what the bastard had done to Sister Meg ... what he would do to ...

I kept calling Pritchard, who briefed me which streets and alleys his officers had already covered. We had so little to go on. They could've passed the damned house already. Hell, I might have passed it myself.

I trudged on, trying to banish all these dark thoughts.

Then I saw it, a small house set back from the street behind a larger one. Trash carts sat along the fence. Wooden steps led up to a storm door. The snow-covered steps looked undisturbed, but snow had been falling continuously...

I opened the gate and heard a fierce bark from inside. Ann hadn't mentioned a dog. The side door opened. A gray-haired man switched on the outdoor light and opened the storm door an inch. "What do you want?"

"Sorry to disturb you. I'm with the police. We're looking for a kidnapped woman in this area."

"Oh, dear," said a woman's voice. She pulled the door open another inch,

"She ain't here," said the man. "Close the door, Martha. People say stuff like that to get into your house."

The door closed, and the barking continued. "Good dog," I heard the man say.

I went to the next alley and the next. Over ten inches of snow had fallen and another foot was expected by dawn. I couldn't stand to think what might be happening while I was stumbling around outside… helpless. Christ, I hate that feeling. *Please help me, God. Come on.*

I tried yet another bungalow set back from yet another house. Snow was lighter in one parking space…. Two large trash carts were set near the fence…. Snow was disturbed on the wooden steps. It looked like only one light was on.

This had to be the right place.

Using the gas meter, I boosted myself up to look into the window, but the lower half was blocked by a window shade. Suddenly I was showered with glass. A lamp base crashed through the window. "Whoever you are, please help me!"

"Ann, it's me."

"Thank God. I'm handcuffed to the bed."

"Are you alone?"

"Yes, hurry."

I plowed through the snow, running as fast as I could in my galoshes. I kicked at the front door and the old jamb splintered easily.

I was in.

Laying Bat aside, I rushed into the bedroom. Ann was sitting on the bed, wearing only a coat. Her left ankle was cuffed to the bedpost. I held her tight for a second. "It's going to be okay."

Ann's breathing was ragged and shallow. "I saw your shadow at the window." She took a breath. "I was hoping… hurry. The bastard will be back any minute."

CHAPTER ONE HUNDRED TWENTY-TWO

Malachi trudged up the alley. Tea. He'd have a hot cup of tea… with her… and then, let the festivities begin.

He opened the rear gate. He saw fresh footsteps in the snow. Son of a bitch. He followed the footprints slowly, determining they were made by one person. The broken glass and lamp base lay on top of the snow.

When he heard Ann and a man talking, he pulled his handgun from its holster and stepped through the broken front door. Walking softly, he opened the bedroom door just as Deacon kicked in the footboard and freed Ann.

Malachi leveled his .38 at Deacon. "Such a home wrecker. Don't move, either one of you."

We were still as a tableau until Malachi spoke again. "Ann, you sit on the bed. Mr. Deacon, get on the floor. What a bonus to have the meddlesome deacon here with us tonight."

I didn't think he'd kill us outright. He was enjoying his cat and mouse game.

Malachi spoke again. "My dear, you look ravishing tonight. And you, Mr. Deacon, a colossal pain-in-the-ass to be sure. But still… a worthy adversary."

I followed his orders and crawled to the kitchen. Had to play for time.

Malachi ordered Ann sit at the kitchen table while he put a small pot on the stove to boil water. "My heart's set on a hot cup of tea. I'm chilled to the bone."

Even ordinary words sounded ominous coming from him. I had to make a move soon. If he tied us up, the night would become a horror show. I cursed myself for not calling Pritchard when I found the house.

My mind had been focused on freeing Ann as fast as I could. Now she sat half-naked, handcuffs dangling from her ankle. She was visibly trembling. She expected the worst. It wasn't going to happen. I wouldn't let it.

I tried reasoning with Malachi. I didn't think it would work. He wasn't a reasonable man. But maybe I could delay him, just enough. "Why not just let us go? You've won. You have your money. What would you gain by keeping us here?"

A small Phillips head screwdriver lay on the stove. Strange. The guy didn't look like someone who would make home repairs. If I could get to it I could use it as a weapon.

"A very rational approach, he said, I'll think it over." He continued to set out tea bags, sugar and milk. "In a few moments you'll serve the tea, my dear." Malachi sat at the small kitchen table pointing the gun at me. "Stand and remove that ridiculous coat."

Ann stood, trying to cover her body with her arms. She dropped her coat to the floor shivering even more. "That's better." He looked her up and down, as though appraising merchandise. "Ah, the split lip is healing nicely. My feet are freezin'. Bring a towel. Take off my wet shoes and socks."

Ann hesitated, standing with her shoulders hunched over,

Malachi frowned, aimed the gun at me and pulled the trigger. A deafening sound … and my left side burned with pain. The bullet had entered just above my left hipbone. A through and through. Lots of blood.

Ann threw me a towel so I could staunch the blood. Then she knelt in front of him pulled off his shoes and socks and toweled his feet dry. She stole a glance my way.

I tried to nod as if I were okay.

The pain in my heart was worse than the gunshot wound as I watched Malachi stroke Ann's silky hair.

His lips turned up in a facsimile of a smile. "Ahh, that's much better."

It hurt like hell but I pressed the towel against my wound with both hands. The pain was a shock to my system, and I was doubled over on the floor. But I didn't take my gaze off him.

Malachi looked at the stove—not at the burners or the pot—but higher. I followed his gaze up the exhaust cylinder above the stove vent. Something there drew his attention. It had to be important.

"I believe my tea is ready," he said in slow measured tones. I'll take it with a little milk and sugar. "Bring it to me."

Ann added boiling water to the mug and was about to set the mug on the table when he cupped her breast. She dumped the boiling water on the hand holding the gun. He howled, dropped the gun and yanked his hand away.

As the gun skittered along the floor, Malachi pushed Ann away, sending her sprawling. He and I scrambled for the gun. It had to be now. Ann had given us a chance.

He and I got to the gun at the same time and grappled for it, but he had his finger on the trigger and pulled. Shots went wild around the room until the gun clicked empty. Letting go of the gun, he lunged for the chair where his cane was hanging.

He got to his feet before I could and uncovered the handle, exposing the sharp silver talon. I expected him to swing it at me, but he released a catch mechanism and a long stiletto blade sprung out of the bottom of the cane. He stabbed forward, trying to impale me. I sidestepped the thrust but fell.

Then he tried the other end, grabbing the bottom of the cane above the protruding blade to swing the talon down on me. I saw it coming and blocked the blow with a kitchen chair. He grunted, his face grotesque.

I lunged forward on both knees, feeling as though my side would rip from my body. He was above me, poised to strike again. I punched his left kneecap with all the power I could muster. His leg collapsed and he landed on his back. He kicked at me with his other foot. I grabbed the bare ankle and twisted it to the outside until I heard bones brake with a grinding noise. He screamed.

He aimed the stiletto tip of his cane at my shoulder, but he was in pain and off balance. His stabbing thrust was weak. It stuck my shoulder with little penetration. I tore the cane from his grasp and put the tip of the blade against his neck. I leaned against the counter for support. "Now, you son-of-a-bitch, stand and put your hands on your head."

"I can't. My knee and ankle."

"Then pull yourself up on the chair. One wrong move and I'll—"

"You'll what? You're a *deacon*. You're not going to kill me."

"Don't count on it." I stuck him in the chest, barely breaking the skin, but he squealed like a piglet. I staggered toward Ann, who was holding the side of her face where he'd hit her.

"Thank God," she said.

I handed her my cell. "Hit redial. That's Pritchard's number. Tell him 407 B Harrison. Send paramedics. I'm bleeding like… " I was weakening, but *he* mustn't know this. We had to secure him somehow.

She made the call and put on her coat. "Help me tie this bastard up," I whispered to her. "I'm fading." We both looked around and settled on Ann's standby, a cord from the other lamp.

I threw a towel over Malachi's head. Before I could tie his hands behind his back, he threw an elbow backwards, catching me on the temple. I keeled over.

He pushed himself off the chair and hobbled toward Ann. Oh God, if he gets to her, he'll be in control. Ann rushed around him into the living room. None of us was in good shape. He limped after her as I struggled to get up. Ann found Bat and swung at him. He parried, knocking Bat from Ann's hands. It rolled toward me. Then he charged her, and she fought him off, scratching his face and screaming. "You filthy bastard!"

Bent over and staggering, I scooped up Bat. I caught up to Malachi in two stumbling strides and swung as hard as I could. I connected with the back of his head and he crumpled, fell and lay still. I collapsed beside him.

Ann knelt next to me, holding my head. I was losing consciousness. My voice was a croak. "Ann, tell them… hood above the stove. Something hidden… I think." All I remembered after that was Ann's soothing voice and Pritchard's shout when he saw us.

CHAPTER ONE HUNDRED TWENTY-THREE

I blinked, trying to focus on the blurry faces above my hospital bed. My head felt like it was stuffed with cotton balls.

"Welcome back to the land of the living," said a jovial voice.

"Um... uh... Archbishop?" My mouth wasn't cooperating, but my vision had cleared.

His head bobbed up and down. "How are you feeling, my boy?"

"Um... groggy. Uh. how long...?"

"Well, you lost most of Monday." The archbishop's smile was almost as broad as Brother Chuck's. "It takes a while to recuperate from the kind of repairs you needed. The surgeon said she'd never seen such a variety of wounds in one person at one time, but she assured us you'd be fine."

The archbishop looked at me with the tenderness I would expect from a father. "I don't want to overtire you, my son. I'll be back when you're stronger. Receive my blessing." After he left, I looked around the room. There were a couple of bouquets of flowers and some cards.

Doctor Dora Shepherd made a three-minute visit, the same time as my mother did. Handy, since she peppered her with questions about her one and only son. Then came good old nurse Wanda, who checked the fluids in my IV. She must have added more pain medication, because my eyes closed soon thereafter.

I woke looking up at Ann's face haloed by those incredible auburn curls.

"How you doing, Deacon?"

"Tip-top shape." I tried to smile, but my face wouldn't cooperate. I was lost in those blue-green eyes. Even with the purple-red swelling over her left cheekbone, she's perfect and lovely. Love... ly.

"Ice... your cheek," I murmured. "Anything... broken?"

"No, just bruises."

I thought back to the Malachi battle. How she'd worked herself loose from her bonds, doused him with boiling water, swung at him with Bat, fought him with every lick of strength. The woman had steel.

"Lean closer." She did, her lips hovering over mine. I kissed her gently. She kissed me back. *Love... you.* I hadn't said that out loud, had I? I wasn't sure. But I'd sure as hell thought it.

She straightened, suddenly businesslike. "I love you... " She stared at me for a moment, fingers over her lips. Then the words poured out, "I'll love you but now as a ... friend, no, much more. A much beloved friend. You saved my life. Now, get well and protect the people." She rushed out the door. I thought I heard a sob from her as she ran down the hallway.

She was leaving me again. If this is love, it was damned confusing.

I was still pondering our so-called relationship when the cardinal arrived. So far, my day was a dizzying array of people and news. No wonder they restrict visitors, but God, it was grand to see Cardinal Schneider safe.

"Your Eminence."

"Deacon, are you healing well?"

"That's what they tell me."

"Thank the Lord. I hope I'm not intruding. I wanted to see you privately, to thank you."

The cardinal was always a powerful spiritual presence, but I'd never seen him look so humble... or so holy. In my befuddled state, I couldn't form a reply. My mind was circling something else... something I *thought* he'd said... before.

The cardinal continued. "Barry Pritchard tells me that his officers found the original video exactly where you suspected it would be. You know what that means to me."

"Yes."

"In addition to saving my life… " He cleared his throat and crossed himself. "You have saved my soul. I need not break the seal of the confession."

"I'm glad."

He bent to kiss my forehead. "Bless you, my son. We'll talk soon."

"Your Eminence… "

The cardinal turned back. "Yes."

"You said something in the ambulance—"

"I scarcely remember that ride."

"Something about my father."

The cardinal raised his eyebrows. "He was a fine man. Your actions are a fine tribute to his memory." He crossed himself. "For now, heal and be strong. We *need* you."

A storm of emotions buffeted me as fiercely as Sunday night's wind and snow. The cardinal's words before—what I thought he'd said—had uncorked my deep longing for my father. Since boyhood, I'd tried to keep it buried, but here it was again. Unshed tears closed my throat. I admit it. I'd wanted to hear, "You're right, Deacon. You're father's alive and proud of you. Let me take you to him." But that was ridiculous. The cardinal… archbishop… my mother… they wouldn't hide my father from me.

I dozed then, slipping in and out of dreams. My father's face appeared, looking a lot like Christ. Would my father have wanted me to devote my life to the church? I know my mother did. Sometimes that tug toward the church feels like an echo of the longing for my earthly father.

I woke again to the savory aroma of pizzas sent over by Leo. I didn't know when I'd be allowed to eat pizza, but they were great for visitors and nurses.

A beam of sunlight streaming through the window seemed like part of my dream until it illuminated a spray of colorful flowers. *That has to be Chuck's doing.*

Beside it on my over-bed table was a box of Fannie Mae chocolates. I smiled to myself. *Sister Meg had been here while I slept.* My room was beginning to feel like a friendly bus terminal, what with all the traffic. At least my visitors arrived only in ones and twos.

Wouldn't you know it, the door opened yet again. This time Pritchard stepped up to my bedside. "So, you're looking tolerable for somebody who won another knock-down, drag-out."

I grunted a reply of some sort.

The city of Chicago has you to thank, *again,*" he said. "You must've been a helluva MP." He paused, squinting down at me. "Matter of fact, you'd make a helluva Chicago cop. For the record, you were never in the way."

Doesn't sound like Pritchard.... Maybe I was dreaming again. I squinted at him. "You're welcome."

"Everything's falling into place. Halloran, Clayton and Ditmar don't have a prayer. Too much evidence against them. Malachi's headed for a prison hospital. Blind, impaired... neurological damage. The doctors said he'd be living life on a much simpler level now."

A shiver ran through me. I was glad I hadn't killed him, but I *was* responsible for his pitiable state. I wasn't sorry. And I haven't forgiven him yet for everything he did and tried to do. *I'll have to pray for the gift of forgiveness.*

I pulled my attention back to Pritchard. "And the monsignor?"

A dark cloud passed over his face. "Vanished, I don't understand it. We know he was leaking information to Halloran. We searched his place but found no trace of him.

I willed myself silent, but, inside, I was relieved. *By now Salvatore was right where he belonged. In some remote place still being of some use to the Church. Bless the Gabrians for doing God's dirty work.*

Then there was the priesthood to consider. *Was that really my path?* My head ached, and I closed my eyes.

"Get well fast. The city needs you and your Church needs you too."
Pritchard said. "Oh, I think this belongs to you." He laid my aluminum
baseball bat beside me on the bed. "We retrieved it from at Malachi's
house. I'll be in touch."

I wrapped my fingers around the neck of my trusty Bat. My lips
curved into a smile as I drifted off to sleep. *There are so many ways to
serve you, Lord.*

FINIS

ACKNOWLEDGEMENTS

I doubt if any writer could be more grateful than me for the support and recommendations received by so many colleagues to bring my story to life. It is true, no one makes it alone. To the following people my abundant thanks.

Bruce McAllister, author and coach who was there at Deacon's birth and contributed so much to his development. His guidance for craft and style cannot be overstated. My thanks for never settling for anything less that my best.

Donna Kennedy, author and editor with a sharp eye for detail and keeping the story moving and making it a joy to read.

Marianne Stegemann who provided exceptional proofreading and positive feedback.

Debbie Larson, author and friend who edited the early drafts with artistry and no-nonsense feedback.

Maura Raffensperger who, as in the past, generously contributed her expertise in all things pharmaceutical.

Irv Burgraff and Jim Bisek my brothers, who kept me on track with details of Chicago that I had often misplaced in my memories.

Henry Stone, for his insightful comments as he read my early drafts.

Tom Wallace, supporter and editor, who saw things I could not see about the characters in my story and was unafraid to tell me the truth.

Dick Laine, who did yeoman's work reading several drafts and finding errors needing to be corrected.

Father Paul Johnson OP who advised me concerning some of the inner workings of the Catholic Church.

Barry Crawford, for his professionalism and commentary while providing precise editorial suggestions.

Roger and Aida Schneider for their willingness to read my drafts, give me feedback and support my efforts.

Steve Burgraff for his exceptional photography. Chris Burgraff and Marcus Burgraff for their continued assistance with computer issues. Dave Burgraff for his editorial commentary.

Marjorie Lewis, wife and cheerleader, always there urging me to persevere.

CPSIA information can be obtained at www.ICGtesting.com
Printed in the USA
BVOW03s2153300514

354970BV00002B/9/P